RIDE ON STRANGER

by the same author

Tiburon (1935)
Foveaux (1939)
The Battlers (1941)
Time Enough Later (1943)
Ride On Stranger (1943)
Lost Haven (1946)
The Honey Flow (1956)
Tell Morning This (1967)
Ma Jones and the Little White Cannibals (1967)
Tantavallon (1983)

RIDE ON STRANGER

by

KYLIE TENNANT

SANDNESS
MICHAEL WALMER
2025

PUBLISHER'S NOTE

There are displayed in this book attitudes to, and nomenclature for, race
that, though they were very common at the time of writing, are not
acceptable now, and are not shared by the publisher.

This book is republished because of its significance in literary history and
its humane excellence in all other respects.

For to one man it is consistent with reason to hold a chamber pot for
another, and to look to this only, that if he does not hold it, he will receive
stripes, and he will not receive his food: but if he shall hold the pot, he
will not suffer anything hard or disagreeable. But to another man not
only does the holding of a chamber pot appear intolerable for himself,
but intolerable also for him to allow another to do this office for him.

If then you ask me whether you should hold the chamber pot or not,
I shall say to you that the receiving of food is worth more than the not
receiving of it, and the being scourged is a greater indignity than not
being scourged; so that if you measure your interests by these things, go
and hold the chamber pot.

"But this," you say, "would not be worthy of me." Well then, it is you
who must introduce this consideration into the inquiry, not I; for it is
you who know yourself, how much you are worth to yourself, and at what
price you sell yourself: for men sell themselves at various prices.

—*Discourses of Epictetus,* Bk. 1, Chap. II.

One

I

To be born is to be lucky. Later, life may prove a failure or a success, depending on the outlook of whoever is living it; but that life is there should be a matter of congratulation daily renewed. So many find life a slender chance; and for the fourth daughter of Mr. and Mrs. Hicks the scales remained trembling a long time in the balance, weighed with a scruple and a doubt, hovering on a hair breadth of rage.

Three girl children did nothing to reconcile Ada Hicks to a fourth; and her husband, when he heard the ghastly news, stood mute and stricken, wondering why his wife always had to tell him things like that before tea when she knew that worry gave him indigestion. A man came in tired and hungry from a hard day at the butter factory, and there was his wife, a wife who had promised to love and honour him, waiting to upset his peace of mind, not to mention his stomach.

When Darcey Hicks recovered from the shock, he voiced his opinion of marriage; and his opinion was that it was a swindle. Here was a man going his own way, just a good-hearted, susceptible fellow likely to be encouraged by black eyes and white teeth and red lips. He acquires these pleasant perquisites and the female who goes with them; he settles down to whatever enjoyment they may bring, and in five years he has three small, squalling, damp babies, all female, all vocal and discordant interruptions of those home comforts a man has a right to expect. Was it fair, he asked, was it right? And his answer was: No, it is not right. There was something abominably unjust and disreputable about the whole transaction, and he was more than inclined to blame the owner of the dark eyes.

"One I didn't mind," he admitted. "Two's plenty. But to spring it on a man like this." His tone was one of outrage. "You got to admit a man's got a right to feel fed up. And that's the way I'm getting. I've never said anything before." He had forgotten his expressed disapproval at the arrival of his third daughter. "I been pretty patient. But things are going too far. You just can't go on having kids like this."

1

"Anyone would think it was my fault." His wife turned on him savagely. "Let me tell you something." She told him, omitting nothing that might cause him disquiet, reviewing their whole married life, harking back even to his behaviour in their courting days. "I might have known, oh yes, fool that I was, when a man doesn't even give a girl a box of chocolates before she's married, that he's going to grind her down and ill-treat her afterwards. My sister said as much. Edith distinctly warned me, and she was right. 'Mark my word,' she said, 'that man is going to be just a monster of selfishness. You could do better,' she said. 'You've been brought up a lady at least, and to go away to live in a little tin-pot place with a lot of cowhands; why, you don't know what you're letting yourself in for.' And she was right . . . oh! she was right, I'll say that for her. If . . ."

"Now then, Ada." The hysteria in his wife's voice warned Darcey that propitiation was necessary. The argument had gone on all over tea. Bedtime was approaching, and with it no promise of peace or that repose so necessary for a man who has a hard day's work before him on the morrow. "Now then, Ada, it's no use losing your temper about this. After all you're the one who told me children was sent from God. It's a privilege to have kids. Look at the fun of watching them grow up round you, taking care of you in your old age. Why, come to think of it, I can't see what *you're* moaning about. Think of all the people ain't got kids."

This solace came too late.

"That's all very well, but what I want to know is: Why don't you have the baby if it's so much fun?"

A discreet husband does not take up such a challenge. Darcey Hicks sat down on the side of the bed and began unlacing his boots.

"It's enough to make you believe there's more lives than one," Ada Hicks went on desperately. "And you're getting punished for what you did in the last. I must have done something pretty terrible to be born a woman. Look at what a good life men have. It doesn't matter whether they're married or single, they never have to worry, and a woman's life is just one long worry. If she isn't stricken down every month, she's worrying because she's not. She worries about having children, and she worries about not having any. She's just one big worry to herself that she can't get away from. We're a set of criminals." Mrs. Hicks began to cry. "That's what we are. And we get paid out just by being born women. Now this will be the fourth in six years, and how I'm going to stand it I don't know."

Her husband was rapidly losing patience. "I bet there's not a woman in Kerleuit like you," he complained. "Why, a man can't look at you without you go having kids. Other men get married without being loaded up with kids, kids, and then more kids."

"Why! how dare you say such things! You've got no more feeling than a snake!"

"I like that. Who was it said a minute ago . . ."

"Never mind what I said a minute ago. You're a cold-hearted reptile, and I'm through with you. I'm going home, to my mother and sister, d'you hear?"

"All right. Go then. But if you think it's fair having three children . . ."

"This 'ull be four," his wife mourned, forgetting she was through with him.

"When I'm only on wages at the butter factory, I'm blowed if I do. How can a man save or give any of them an education?"

"Well, if you don't like it," his wife flared, "you can do the other thing . . ."

"And girls, all girls. I'm damned if I don't believe this is going to be another girl."

"It'd just serve the poor little thing right. It's a fate I wouldn't wish on my worst enemy."

"There you go again," her husband pointed out censoriously, "complaining. I been trying to show you all along that it's just as hard on me. I've got to support the kids, haven't I? And on what? There ought to be something we could do." He was thinking aloud. "It stands to reason that if a man asked, he could find a way to help you out of this, Ada."

His wife stopped him indignantly. "I said you were a cold-blooded reptile, Darcey, but I take it back. You're a devil and that's devil's talk. What, for instance?"

Darcey scratched his head, looking at the ceiling as if he expected the solution to the problem to drop from it. "Damned if I know," he said thoughtfully as he climbed into bed.

For a long time after he was snoring his wife lay awake, tossing, brooding, considering. Her antagonism to her husband was a corrosive acid burning away all the gentler side of her nature. If only she could get away from him, go back to Headstown; but could she with three small children and the promise of another? There must be something, she thought, a woman could do. Her nerves were tying themselves into knots and even her body did not belong to her any more.

Here she was, she who had been the admired Miss Ada Shannon, so ladylike, so pretty and graceful when she played the piano in her mother's boarding-house in Headstown, buried alive in a crack in the hills where no one talked about anything but cows, and she had always been afraid of cows; no one to see except members of the tribe of Hicks, slow-spoken, cud-chewing, spiteful. What could you expect from people with a name like Hicks?

A sudden, bright, new idea minted itself out of her bubbling resentment. Ada prodded her husband in the ribs and he woke with a grunt.

"I've been thinking, Darcey," she spoke gently, and Darcey saw a ray of hope.

"What? Ada, you're not . . . You're not going to get rid of it?"

"How dare you suggest such a thing! But I was thinking, Darcey. Shannon would be a nice name, real uncommon for a girl. And it'ud do for a boy too, if it was a boy."

Darcey swore as he turned over to seek in sleep some solution to the perversity of females and fate and circumstance.

II

If Shannon was a dubious nuisance before she was born, her entry into the world spoilt a domestic triumph. It was a Monday and, of course, a washing day. No one in Kerleuit would dream of washing on any other day of the week; and there was keen rivalry as to the back-yard which should first nail its colours to the masthead of domestic efficiency. Mrs. Herbie Hicks had once gone so far as to break the Sabbath and wash all her clothes by night, hanging them out at four in the morning. But this had united the other women against her. Washing on a Sunday indeed!

Between getting Darcey's breakfast, seeing him off to the butter factory, attending to the wants of the children, feeding the fowls and cleaning the house, Mrs. Hicks hung out two coppers-full of washing. The back-yards of Kerleuit had no high fences to obscure the view of what went on next door; and after breakfast Mrs. Hicks stood to survey the neighbour clothes-lines, as the captain of an ocean-going craft might scan the signals on some foreign shore.

Jessie Ritchie had hung her husband's shirts all among the sheets and Mrs. Hicks clicked her tongue disdainfully. No such horror ever desecrated her own back-yard. There the sheets hung side by side, white as a bishop's shroud and as righteous. The pillow-slips were a choir of little voices chanting "Holy, holy, holy" to a mixed congregation of portly table-cloths, shabby work-shirts and pinafores, while the underwear effaced itself modestly behind a lattice. You would never find a white counterpane and a green blouse hanging cheek by jowl in Ada Hicks' back-yard.

She turned from the horrid sight of Jessie Ritchie's washing with the marks of the blue-bag still upon it like the brand of Cain, and contemplated the handiwork of her most dangerous rival, Mrs. Herbie Hicks, a sister-in-law and a foe. If Mrs. Herbie gave a cake for a raffle, Mrs. Darcey gave two. If Mrs. Darcey's hens won a prize at the show, Mrs. Herbie would fret for weeks. Now, surveying her sister-in-law's washing, Ada Hicks stiffened, then advanced to the fence stealthy as a hunting tiger.

Silently she counted the sheets, the towels, the shirts and pillow-slips. Judging by his wife's wash, Herbie had changed his shirt four times that week. Even the children's beds must have had both sheets changed. There were five table-cloths and a supper-cloth.

Rage shook Mrs. Hicks at such vanity and flaunting. She was not herself above mere earthly pride, and last week at the Church Tea she had mentioned to Mrs. Herbie that she believed in changing both sheets on the beds. Here was Mrs. Herbie calling her bluff. Mrs. Darcey had not changed both sheets. She had stripped off the bottom sheet and put the top sheet in its place, giving only one clean sheet per bed. Mrs. Herbie's wash showed two sheets per bed. She had twice as many husband's shirts and four times as many table-cloths. With a qualm Ada Hicks forebode their next meeting. She could just hear Elsie's sharp voice saying: "Seems to me, Ada, you're letting yourself *go*. I never believe in giving in to things. They say work does you good, but of course," with a significant pause, "if you'd like me to come in and give you a hand when you're feeling sickish . . ."

Never! Her lips set in a grim line, Mrs. Hicks went into the house and took from a press six perfectly clean sheets. She snatched up also four table-cloths and five of her husband's shirts. She collected some of the children's clean clothing and washed that too. Elsie was not going to say that Ada's children did not change every day. She was feeling very "sickish" indeed before she had finished hanging out, starching, ironing, scrubbing the floors, and cleaning the stove. If Mrs. Herbie dropped in, there must be no dust-marks, no smear at which she could point.

Mrs. Herbie did "drop in," but when she saw her sister-in-law, she turned quite pale.

"You let me get the doctor," she begged.

"Oh!" Mrs. Hicks moaned. "It was that big wash."

Of course the doctor said the wash had nothing to do with the gravity of Mrs. Hicks' condition; but as a loyal sister-in-law Elsie broadcast all over Kerleuit the story that "Ada had just worked herself into her grave when she should know better." Her demise was accepted as a foregone conclusion, and Mrs. Hicks would have gone down in glory and legend as a too conscientious housewife. Instead, Shannon arrived long before she was expected and rather blue. The doctor took great credit for saving Ada Hicks' life and warned her that she must have no more children.

As though determined to turn over a new leaf Ada Hicks presented her husband with George, Alfie and Johnnie, all in quick succession. And with each infant she became more and more resigned and grim and religious, until the kitchen clock could not fall off the mantel-piece without Mrs. Hicks pointing out that it must be God's will.

"I've never been the same since Shannon was born," she complained on one occasion.

"Neither have I," her husband surprisingly agreed.

"What difference could it make to you?"

"I got a shock," Darcey Hicks replied. "I got a real shock when the doctor said you was dead."

He wondered why his wife sniffed so scornfully.

Two

I

THE COUNTRY around Kerleuit was under command of the wind that broke over it in a surge of thunder-grey cloud racing over the open, rolling slopes from the sand dunes and the blue sea gap to south. The wind roared and sang across stretches of farm land, lush green and black, where the pig-wallow soil had been ploughed, perplexing it with cloud shadows and alternate gleams of bright light. Here and there, hedges of fir and pine, twice as high as the houses, hedges of dark trees around each field, put up a resistance to the wind. But the great knotted gum trees were bent sideways pointing north with every separate straining leaf.

The cows wandered on the cold slopes, each clad in a little grey-brown overcoat, nosing the wet grass. They climbed slowly along the sides of the old volcano cones that rose like green bubbles, round and squat from the plains; hundreds of green cones so smooth that they might have been moulded on a potter's wheel, and each holding within it a pool of blue water.

There was one big old volcano, its crater a mile across, and if you peered down the steep where nothing grew but bracken, down, down below was a stretch of lake with reeds rippling in it. In the middle of the lake a rise of ground showed a farm with sheep grazing there unconcernedly on the sunny bottom of the world, and cows in their overcoats munching beside the breeze-ruffled waters where grey cranes stalked. From the far-below farm rose the cry of a cock and the barking of a dog and the repeated crick-crick of frogs rejoicing in the reeds. The mad chorus of frogs bubbled up over the lip of the crater, quivering up towards the blue sky. The feet of rainbows rested often over this great pit, as though the rainbows knew that this was the end of the world where the crock of gold is hidden; but the farmer in the bottom said it was poor land and soggy, not much good for anything but grazing.

Across the Kerleuit country the boundaries were of loose stones. Every year the farmers took stones from the rich soil and every year more worked through. The gorse also they used for hedges and it made a rim of gold around every little field. What with the gold of the gorse and the misty yellow of the wattle and the rainbows lying over the blue of the crater lakes the bright country promised riches at every glance.

Shannon Hicks lay on the very lip of the crater gazing down while the frog chorus welled up about her ears. Far below the foot of a rainbow poised in a tantalizing way above the roof of a farm. At school they were reading a book about "a crock of gold at the rainbow's foot," and if the rainbow had only put its silly feet in some more accessible place, she would have pounced on that crock like a flash. Not that she knew what a crock might be, but it was probably some small sort of jug. Even a very little jug of gold would be welcome to the family outlaw at the moment. She sucked her hat elastic and peered over thinking what a beastly day it had been. The only ray that shone through her gloom was that she had caught her cousin Stanley a beautiful blow with a rock on the way to school that morning. Her aim was usually poor, and it had been just a brilliant accident hitting Stanley at all. He had been walking backward up the road chanting "Shannon will go to Hell" in a very taunting way. Tomorrow he might be waiting in ambush somewhere with his own supply of rocks, and his aim was much better than hers. On the other hand he had probably gone home and told his mother.

Anyway there would be trouble about her playing truant and over the soggy state of her button-up boots without Stanley adding his mite. If she could find a crock of gold, she would buy a little pony and ride away and never come back. That would serve them all right. And the Headmaster would be sorry he had driven her to it. At the very thought of Mr. Tracey with his fat fingers like bunches of bananas on a stalk, his stupid bumbling voice, his froggy bulging eyes, she picked up a big stone and flung it over the edge of the pit and watched it bounce down the slope. *That* to Mr. Tracey!

He had come into the classroom just before the mid-day bell rang when Miss Parker was giving Grammar, and the class resigned itself to hearing Mr. Tracey talk. He loved to hear his own voice, and he would tell them what a fine sort of man he was by a question and answer method. "Now you don't think I would do a thing like that? Or Miss Parker? We wouldn't do a thing like that, would we?"

"No-o, Mr. Tracey!"

"Of course Miss Parker might. I can't answer for Miss Parker, can I?" (Dutiful laughter and a subdued but baleful glare from Miss Parker.) "But Miss Parker is such a well-behaved lady that I am sure she would never do anything wrong. And as for *myself*. Well, boys and girls, your parents respect me, your teachers respect me, and I expect you to do the same."

They endured him, fidgeting and waiting for the bell.

"Now I want you boys to tell me what you will be when you grow up. Is there anyone here who has thought about that I wonder?" There was a forest of wildly waving hands. "I see one of the girls' over there," Mr. Tracey reproved. "Who is holding up her hand? Stand up, Shannon Hicks. Why were you holding up your hand?"

"Please, Mr. Tracey," Shannon beamed, "I want to be a lawyer."

If there was one child in the school Mr. Tracey really disliked it was this dark-eyed, wild-looking girl with the ridiculous name. He seized at once the chance of setting back an impertinent upstart.

"I was talking to the boys," he purred. "I wouldn't address a question like that to a *girl*, would I now? Why there is only one thing for girls to do, and that is to grow up to be good wives and mothers. Isn't that so?" He turned from the tittering class to Miss Parker. "Where did she get this funny idea, I wonder, Miss Parker? Why did you say you wanted to be a lawyer, Shannon?"

It was the robes of course, the beautiful red robes that Portia wore in "The Merchant of Venice." Shannon had been allowed to take a small part in the school concert.

"Well, what kind of lawyer were you going to be? There! You didn't even know there were difierent kinds of lawyers, did you? You see, it is much better for little girls like you to realize as soon as possible that they mustn't try to do things that are meant for boys. I hope you do realize that?"

"No!" she yelled at him furiously. "No!" Edging out of her seat she made rapidly for the door, trying to hide her tears. It was hard enough to be small, but to have one leg a little longer than the other because it had been badly set when she fell out of the pear tree, that was harder still. She was very conscious of that limp.

Mr. Tracey watched her go with an amused smile. "You see," he turned to the class, "what it is to give way to temper?" And to Miss Parker: "When she returns, send her to me."

But Shannon had no intention of returning. She did not even stop to snatch her school bag from its hook. She was off to the hills. If only there were bushrangers, she decided gloomily, she could have joined them and helped to steal cattle and stick up coaches. It didn't matter if it was wicked. Everyone knew she was wicked. She was the worst girl in Kerleuit, and if she went home, she would only get another thrashing.

From the hills the road led inland to Kerleuit cuddled down away from the wind. Kerleuit drowsed. It had an old dark church muffled in dark trees; and, across the bubbling creek, a sunny hotel where white ducks put forth from the kitchen garden and tilted up their pointed tails as they searched the water, quick-beaked. There were lilies in front of the hotel, marigolds, daffodils, and an old bee-beloved hawthorn tree. But no one except men could be seen going there as it was such a wicked place and sold beer.

In front of the council chambers there were two old cannons on which the children swung and shouted as they came home from school; but nothing else in Kerleuit was out of the ordinary; just a few shops and the butter factory that kept Kerleuit alive; the railway and post-office and a collection of houses sheltering from the roar of the wind and the empty spaces of the hills. There was nowhere to go, unless to the sea seven miles away, and the people of Kerleuit hardly ever stirred out. Nowhere to go except home, and it was growing darker, the tenderly lit afternoon fading to grey; and even brigands get hungry. Perhaps the best thing would be to sneak in the back door and hope, under the cover of darkness, for a chance to plunder the pantry. As for a beating, Shannon did not worry much about that. It would be painful of course, for her mother dispensed the middle, low and high justice with a grim impartiality. But Shannon could always turn her mother's corrections into a scene more destructive of the family credit than an unpaid grocer's bill. Her unearthly howls could be heard as far as the butter factory and suggested that a team of fiends had met with some unpleasantness while loosing the hounds of Hell on a damned soul.

Adjusting the hat elastic under her chin, the would-be robber chief set off for home, swaggering along so that the limp did not show. Striding there across the high country, she could forget that she was small and female, and became instead a piratical scoundrel, a prowling marauding rogue, fearing not even a mother with a strap. Not that her mother was waiting with the strap. Instead she was sitting tight-lipped, repeating to herself: "This settles it. I'm sending her to Edith."

II

Tea-time was always a crisis in the Hicks' homestead. When hungry, Darcey Hicks had a strong man's bad temper; when fed, he had indigestion. Strangely enough, this indigestion proved to be hereditary. The Hicks' girls, at the very height of a furious family row, would politely excuse themselves and go outside to be sick. They were quite proud of having inherited what their aunts maintained was "the Hicks' stomach."

As usual, the sight of his young shovelling food reminded Darcey, by force of contrast, that he had always wanted to own a herd of Jerseys.

"Bill Jennings bought that little bull from Hartley's place," he growled. It enraged him that his wife should refuse to let the girls milk. Why couldn't they make themselves useful? What was the use of girls anyway if they couldn't milk? With all the family milking, the money coming into the house would be just about double; and, starting with a few cows, they could gradually build up a real herd. Mrs. Hicks was adamant in her refusal.

"I've seen the families you say are getting rich milking. The children go to school and drop asleep over their desks. My girls aren't going to be like that, never getting their proper schooling. They'll milk over my dead body."

"Your girls!" Darcey would roar. "If they're your girls, you get out and work and keep them!"

But he was secretly afraid of his wife. In a battle of wills she always won, just by sitting grim and rigid, the picture of a respectable, God-fearing woman being an example to the community and getting her own way. He could bluster, but he never broke her.

Tonight, she refused to quarrel about Hartley's bull or anything else. When someone piped: "Where's Shannon?" and George shouted that Shannon had run out of the class, and Mr. Tracey said she was to be sent to him tomorrow, his mother dealt him a blow with a spoon and said to their father:

"I've asked Grannie and the others over after tea."

B*

An immediate hush imposed itself, as the children waited prick-eared for the reason of this family council. Something dreadful was about to happen. The last family council had taken place just before Mary was married in such a hurry that she had no time to collect a trousseau. The one before that was concerned with Uncle Harry who had been borrowing things from the back of Mr. Birtle's store and had to have someone go bail for him.

"You get on with your dinner," their mother ordered sharply; and to her husband: "I've had another letter from Edith."

So coldly did she say it that Darcey hesitated before he asked: "She still wants one of the girls?"

"Yes."

A subdued hush hung over the young Hickses as they set off to keep their cousins company. They whispered to each other fearfully that someone was to go and live with Aunt Edith.

At home, on either side of the dining-room table, Mr. and Mrs. Hicks sat in that uneasy silence which precedes the arrival of guests.

Grannie was the first to arrive, and this was only to be expected as the dear old lady exhibited an invariable greedy interest in the doings of her sons or daughters. In fact, she had become a kind of emotional tapeworm hanging cosily in the mid-gut of other people's affairs and digesting any entertainment to be derived therefrom. The good old soul was always ready to perform any little loving service, advising a mother on the care of children or the washing of flannels, putting a daughter-in-law in her proper place, anxious lest anything be "kept from her"; and whenever, which was seldom, peace brooded over the far-flung clan of Hickses, Grandma could be trusted to see that it did not brood long enough to stale its novelty.

Her voice was a begging whine, pious and gentle enough to delude the inexperienced into the belief that a tiger is no longer a tiger when it has artificial teeth like Grannie's. Her eyes were glazed with a milky yolk in which the pupils floated unpleasantly like corpses under water. This suggestion of corruption walking was translated into an odour of sanctity by the family saying that: "Probably Grannie won't be with us much longer."

As she came through the door, Grannie had already begun a long monologue on the lateness of her daughter Maisie. "Gallivanting to church

teas and them poor little hinnocents with hardly a rag to their back! I
says to little Jimmy: 'Where's your mother, love?' and he says: 'Gran'ma,
she's gone out.' Six o'clock and them poor little hinnocents without any
tea. Of course I took them in, poor little dears, but even if Maisie is me
own daughter, I made a point to say to Wally: 'Wally, I says . . .'"

"Will you sit on the sofa or in the big chair, Mother?" Mrs. Darcey said
in the tone of thin-lipped endurance most disliked by her mother-in-law.

"The big chair, thank you, Ada." Grannie appropriated her son's chair,
and was moved close enough to the fire to roast her. "I says to Wally:
'Thank God, Wally, I've got a good son-in-law in you, for that Maisie
she don't know how to treat children, and as for a good husband she don't
deserve one.'"

Darcey Hicks made a sharp, irritated movement that blamed his wife
with this visitation. Why couldn't Grannie be left to meddle elsewhere?
Why bring her into their affairs? Smelling about like some old blind,
malicious animal? Yet there his wife sat rigid on a hard-backed chair,
her hands folded in her lap, her whole attitude so much that of patience
on a monument that Darcey could have knocked her over with the greatest
pleasure. That again would only have put him in the wrong. He was
always in the wrong with Ada, whether he bullied her or, as now, sat
sullenly obedient to her will. They irritated each other to the point of
frenzy, yet there she sat, a model wife, entertaining her husband's relatives,
consulting them on what she had already decided. The red plush runner
on the table, the rose-bud pattern on the green wallpaper, were not more
set than Ada Hicks in her righteousness.

"So you've had word from your sister." Grannie made the statement
with a lugubrious shake of the head. "Poor Hedith. She keeps well? That's
the main thing, isn't it? And how are your own kidneys, Ada? No better?
Ah, dear, dear! You want to watch out for them, Ada. I always says the
kidneys are the first to go. Look at poor Mrs. Perry. First, it was her
kidneys, and then she had them fits, and after that they took her away to
the Home. Such a shocking thing for her fam'ly! It would have been a
mercy if the Lord had taken her before the Home did, I say."

Luckily Grannie was not required to keep up this flow of light chat any
longer as the rest of the family was heard scraping its boots on the front
verandah. The big working boots of Herbie and Wally, who had refused
to change, banged against the scraper and gritted down the hall; the tight

pointed toes of Elsie Hicks; the easy slippers in which Maisie had strolled up the road; all trod down the hall, leaving little deposits of mud on the spotless oil-cloth, and were tucked uneasily under the hard chairs.

Slowly Mrs. Darcey's best room became filled with a concentrated essence of Hicks, strong as a week-dead whale. The red plush runner on the table, the light of the kerosene lamp, the red roses on the green wall-paper, all were woven into the pattern of their antagonisms, and became charged with a potential violence that ridged the surface of the Hicks family as the weatherboard beneath the wallpaper ridged the surface of the green and red roses. The lack of air, the heat of the fire, the undiluted extract of Hicks, all were enough to render anyone unaccustomed to the family atmosphere as dazed as a crippled spider that a wasp was dragging underground.

"Don't tell me," Mrs. Herbie burst out with a girlish giggle, "you've had a letter from Edith about taking one of the girls. I *know* it. Don't tell me." In this way she had the satisfaction of snatching the important announcement from Mrs. Darcey's very lips.

"Edith has a lot of responsibility running that big house alone." Ada Hicks quickly snatched her sister back from Mrs. Herbie. "Not that Edith need keep a boarding-house." This was rather defiantly in reply to a malicious glint in Elsie's eye. "She has the money to stop whenever she wants to."

"Well, why don't she? Blowed if I'd keep on working if I didn't have to," Herbie Hicks threw in. "Sounds funny to me. Little enough Joe Wallis left her."

"Poor man," Grannie clutched at the conversation and managed to snatch a tail-feather. "Poor man, it was a blessing Hedith had his last hours! How many die away from home with none to watch the last of them. He lingered and lingered. Year after year he lay there with Hedith running that place on her own, and she can cook, if nothing else. Not that it was much good to him with dropsy. A strange woman!" Grannie made one last grab at their failing attention. " 'You know he's dead, Hedith dearie?' I says to her. 'Oh, of course, I know he's dead,' she says, 'but it isn't for me to pronounce. I've got to wait until the doctor comes and says life is extinct.' "

Mrs. Hicks rescued her sister from Grannie's octopus clutch. "Edith has been alone ever since. In her last letter she said something about her money and the way people tried to get it from her. . . ." (A curious noise as of Mrs. Herbie choking sceptically.) "And she suggested," Mrs. Hicks eyed Mrs. Herbie severely, "she suggested that perhaps we might like to let her have one of the girls with her."

"She must be lonely, poor woman," the kind-hearted Maisie sighed.

"It 'ull be a great relief to have Shannon gone," Mrs. Herbie murmured sweetly. "A great relief to you."

An angry flush spread over Ada Hicks' sallow thin face. "It will be a great relief to know one of the girls has *advantages*," she said in a level, deadly tone. "Advantages she couldn't get here." The contempt of that "here" reduced Kerleuit to a muddy cow-pock in a marsh.

"I don't see that being a slavey in a boarding-house," Mrs. Herbie hefted her battle-axe, "is such an advantage. I guess some of us'd think twice before we broke up our families and sent off a little girl to work for nothing. That's what it comes down to. Working for relatives is always working for nothing."

Mrs. Darcey finished her with one deadly thrust. "You ought to know, Elsie. Seeing you came to Kerleuit to work in the baker's shop. But you weren't working for relations, I must say that."

"Whoa!" Wally put in, as he might have stopped a team of horses. "Steady there!" For Mrs. Herbie had half-risen, her face pale with anger.

"My own sister," Mrs. Darcey dripped acid, "offers to take one of the girls. She's an educated woman, she's got money, she's got advantages. I'm not going to stand in my girl's light for all the tea in China." As no one offered her any tea, this inferred that any resistance from her husband's family was hereby declared useless and absurd.

"Eileen and Doris are older," Maisie offered timidly.

There was a silence while Eileen's love affair and Doris' bad health were considered.

"If it wasn't for prayer," Ada Hicks replied at length in her dry level voice, "I don't think we'd have Doris with us much longer. And Eileen would certainly be most upset at the thought of going." She turned to her husband. She felt that it would be correct for him to speak, if only to show that he was a party to the decision. "What do you say, Darcey?"

"Shannon," Darcey muttered, with a queer, half-ashamed air. "She's the one."

"If Edith does anything to improve Shannon," Mrs. Herbie had recovered her spirits and venom, "it will be a miracle. But you can't make a silk purse out of a sow's ear."

"Now, Elsie," Grannie reproved, "don't say that, dear. Don't condemn. Shannon may be strange, poor little thing, but she's your niece. Even if there's times I believe Shannon isn't all there, what can you expect when she had that fall and broke her leg? You can't tell what effects it'ull have later."

"And look at the way she goes round singing and shouting and wandering by herself." Mrs. Herbie was all virtuous disapproval. "None of the Hickses ever had *insanity*. If there was a strain on Darcey's side, I'd be the first to say it, but . . ."

"Let me tell you, Elsie." Shannon's mother was very formidable. She seemed to use up the light in her fury. The room was smaller and dimmer as she rose and leant over towards her enemy by marriage. "I won't have my girls insulted under this roof. Shannon has got more brains than the lot of you put together, and that's *why*, that's why she's going to Headstown to her Aunt Edith. And that's where I'd have stayed," she swung round passionately, her voice no longer dry and level, "if I'd had any sense." She fronted them all superbly angry. "Shannon's going to get a *chance*."

Aunt Elsie had risen and was walking indignantly towards the door. Poor Herbie followed her, mumbling something about it blowing over in a day or so.

"And let me tell you something, Ada." Elsie paused with her hand on the door-knob. "Before I enter this house again . . ."

She flung the door open and the speech she had framed died on her lips. Shannon, caught unawares, was standing in the passage.

"You'd better come in," her aunt said dryly. And then with a blaze of scorn: "Listening, were you?" She gave a short laugh. "Well, listeners never hear any good of themselves."

Shannon sidled into the room. "Mother," she said, with a hard self-possession, "before I go to my Aunt Edith in Headstown may I get my sewing from school?"

"Now, Shannon dearie," Grannie's light, wheezy voice asked reproachfully, "you don't want to leave your nice home and go away to strangers, do you, dearie?"

"Shannon," her mother spoke once more in the expressionless, con-

trolled voice which she used as a bridle on any tendencies towards unladylike behaviour, "you shouldn't listen at doors. It's not right. And we don't
want to get rid of you. We want the best for you." She was almost pleading. "You see that, don't you?"

"Yes."

"And you want to go to your Aunt's? You want to get on in the world?"

"Yes."

"Well, that settles it." Aunt Maisie hated anything uncomfortable. She
was all smiles. "You're a real lucky girl, Shannon. My word, I wish I had
such a nice aunt."

The girl turned to her father. "I always knew you didn't like me," she
said.

"Go on outside." His tone was rough. He was remembering how as a
baby she had trotted after him, doggedly, however little notice he took of
her. "Go on, out of here."

"I'll go." She made such an effort to suppress her feelings that she gasped
hard as though she had been running. "I hate you! I don't care how soon
I go . . . or how far . . ."

She turned savagely on her assembled relatives and, in a last satisfying
attempt to imprint her face on their memory, drew down the corners of
her mouth, protruded her lower lip, waggled her tongue, and pulled her
eyelids sideways, producing an effect far from pleasing. Then she wrenched
the door open and flung out.

"My gracious!" Grannie wheezed. "My gracious! But that's Shannon all
over. I don't know where she gets it. Really I don't."

No one paid any attention to her. They sat strangely awkward and
dispirited.

"Poor kid," Aunt Maisie said. "I don't see it's her fault."

Still no one said anything.

Three

The train reached Headstown early in the afternoon. It puffed past obscuring goods sheds, glaring advertisement hoardings; threaded a network of steel rails like a spider on a web, and pulled into a muddle of porters, luggage, swarming passengers, flights of grimy steps leading to a smoky, wooden bridge on which the ticket office roosted inside the clicking turnstiles, squat and watchful, guarding the approach to the Headstown main street. The winter sun shone down on wooden fences, asphalt paths, shops, gutters, grimy front gardens; all the dreariness of a second-rate town aping a city suburb, and almost attaining the necessary degree of ugliness.

The ingredients making up Headstown were, firstly, a good deal of smoke and soot from the railway goods yards—*this* distributed with a noble impartiality over everything visible—and, secondly, a fondness for iron railings wherever an iron railing was possible—and in many places where it would seem impossible—with a notable set of spikes atop each railing. The butcher's shop window, where otherwise a whitewashed stone ledge would have offered a comfortable seat, had a plantation of spikes running its length. The Mechanics' Institute, which was the colour of decayed cheese, had a memorable set of iron spikes to keep the weeds in a tangled patch by the entry from overflowing into the street.

There were a great many wooden fences shielding from the public gaze much that was not worth seeing, as for instance, washing, back gardens, hen houses, dumps of old tins in weedy paddocks where thin horses stumbled searching for something to eat. Headstown also suffered from a surfeit of monuments in little patches of park where no child ever dreamed of playing, no old people sunned themselves—these patches being merely interruptions in the ever-flowing dark road, uplifting the spirits by a glimpse of a grey granite obelisk with a mean dirty scurf of grass about it, a plaster fountain that would have tottered with the shock of water, two whitewashed children lifting coy skirts above leprous plaster knees, or a pair of concrete lions, each with its paws laid demurely together like mittens.

Shannon trudged along, panting and hot, in Aunt Maisie's cut-down coat, so heavy, so prickly, with a high collar that nudged her hat over her eyes unless she held her head down. She had two suitcases and a straw basket wrenching her arms. Almost suffocated, her heart beating loudly in her ears, she struggled through this surf of iron and wood and stone that threatened to engulf her, resting every now and then to rub her arms and pant her breath back, conning the little map which was to guide her to Clayton House.

Wild surmises leapt ahead of her and gambolled like wanton puppies in her way. Suppose Aunt Edith was not home? Suppose no one expected her? Suppose . . . Fronting another damnable little park, the Clayton House Residential announced itself by a brass plate, the professional plate usually reserved for doctors and dentists.

Clayton House belonged to the grim age of gentlemen's residences, and a dark screen of laurel and privet interposed to shield it from the vulgarities of the street, from the sunlight, the fresh air. It had a damp, gloomy verandah, floored with black and white tiles, overhung by an upper story whose row of windows were edged with coloured glass.

On tiptoe, Shannon crossed the black and white chessboard of a verandah, setting her luggage stealthily on the mat, straightening her hat, smoothing her black cotton gloves, before she summoned up courage to press the bell. No sound came from the house, so she tried the knocker. Again she waited. By applying her eye to one of the coloured panes in the front door, she could make out the dim bulk of a hall-stand, dark shut doors, the foot of a staircase.

A blue pane gave the same view as the red and amber pane; and again she tapped, her heart thumping louder than the iron knocker. Even while she stooped for another inspection of the hall, the panes were clouded by some black drapery and the door came open half a foot.

A thin, acid lady said sharply: "Nothing today."

"May I see Mrs. Wallis please?"

"You must go to the back door. All day long there's someone knocking at this door. I don't know why Beryl doesn't answer it, or even Mrs. Wallis. But not the front room! What *is* the use of being the Front Room," the lady asked bitterly, "if it means the front door as well?"

"Mrs. Wallis is . . ."

"I have no doubt if you go to the back door, you will see Mrs. Wallis. And, please remember in future, *not* the front door."

Abandoning her luggage, the newcomer jumped a bed of wet violets and fumbled for a gate in what seemed an impregnable green lattice. The snarls of an irate pomeranian dog on the other side did not make the gate any easier to open. These hostile barriers so bewildered her that she had begun to wonder if there were not also a wall of invisible glass, as in a nightmare, when an elderly man came stepping round the corner of the house, quieted the pomeranian, and opened the gate.

"You'd be the missus's niece," he said in a cracked voice. "Come along. He won't hurt you. Only guarding the place, weren't you, Jimmy?" He drew her safely past. "Ah! a great little dog he is! See that notice? 'Beware of the Dog.' That's him. That's Jimmy. A great one for hawkers. The missus don't like hawkers. Scared they'll murder her. They're a sight likelier to pinch my fowls. But not with Jimmy here, hey Jimmy?"

Jimmy, stepping high and haughty on his buff-coloured feet, trotted behind making a noise like a motor bike trying to start on a cold morning.

The back of the house was blinded by the glare of afternoon sunshine washed back from a yellow brick wall. Inside the kitchen, a thin sandy blonde in curl-pins was singing "Ain't We Got Fun," banging the pots down on the stove with a vicious emphasis as she did so. At the sight of Shannon, she ceased her singing for a moment and said: "Hello Tragedy!"

A certain lowering look bent upon her by the new arrival might have given some excuse for this greeting, a look that combined the pugnacious jowl of the bull dog with the eyes of a wounded doe.

"I wasn't met," Shannon burst out. "You're Beryl. You were to meet me. I wasn't met."

Beryl seemed to flicker like a candle in a draught. She had the restless flit-flitting common to a certain type of nervy blonde and very small birds.

"Meet you!" she yelled. "Meet you! I've been camped on that damn platform off and on since eight o'clock this morning. Oh, haven't I met you just, poor mug that I am! And my day off, but thinking I'll do a kindness to Ma, the only day that Ricky has the car and could drive me out home. And there I've *been*. Sending telegrams: 'Coming Tuesday.' Why the hell couldn't they say what train?"

"Well you didn't meet the train I came on," Shannon argued. "You didn't meet that."

The thin maid cast her eyes to Heaven as though pleading for guidance. "How could I with my hair up? You don't think I'm going to walk to the station in curl-pins, do you? There's a lot I'll do for Ma, but I'm damned if I'll be seen in curl-pins when I'm getting ready for the dance tonight." The outraged Beryl loosed all her exasperation. "And tonight I feel that mad I'm just going to let go. I'll get as tight as a fat lady's corsets."

"You said damn." The new arrival seized on this slip censoriously. "You should ask God to forgive you."

Instead Beryl dashed into the hall and howled up the stairs. "Ma!" The dim place quivered in every dust mote at the uproar. "Come on down, Ma. Come and see what Santa's brought you."

The outlaw of the Hicks family stood planted in the middle of the kitchen, somewhat in the attitude of Napoleon on his way to St. Helena. If her aunt was anything like this Beryl, she decided, she wouldn't stay a minute.

The old man shared her disapproval. He had seized a piece of cake in his left hand while he still retained his axe in his right.

"She didn't oughter do it," he announced, shaking his head as he chewed. "The missus has told her often enough."

The gingery blonde returned dusting her hands on her apron. She noted the missing cake.

"Gutsing again, Briscoe?" she reproved. "Go on, out of this! Get back to the wood-heap."

She accompanied this admonition with a sudden bright grin and a flick of the tea-towel, which sally Briscoe returned playfully by lifting his axe. They sparred round the kitchen stumbling over Shannon and dodging about her. The sudden vanishment of Briscoe and a lightning dart which set the gingery girl demurely at the sink indicated the arrival of Aunt Edith.

Aunt Edith was not like Beryl. She was tall and stout and wore a whitish-grey powder that made her rather puffy face look like bread rising. She had moles too, little bubbles of pale flesh that had risen here and there, one on her chin, one at the end of her left eyebrow, and the doyen and elder of all moles, with a little sprout of grey hair to it and a superior position of command near her right eyelid. When Aunt Edith gave an order, this elder mole leapt up, as if to say "At once," and the attendant moles looked meek and inconspicuous, as if they feared Aunt Edith might have them removed. Her hair was grey and elaborately coiled on top of her head, puffed out over little pads to make it look thicker as had been the fashion in Aunt Edith's youth. Her dress was grey silk, beautifully cut and girdled with a waistband of black and white beads that hung in front like some strange rosary and clicked as she walked.

A hard, dry kiss, a command to Briscoe to bring Miss Hicks' luggage upstairs, and Aunt Edith led the way majestically, going ahead through the gloom of the hall, the bright squares of red and blue and orange flung on the treads by the stair window, through the smell of linoleum polish and discouraged palm trees in a stand, past shut doors and hall furniture that looked as if it had been kicked by generations of revengeful horses, until she came to her own room facing out over the sunlit yard, a bright room with an open sewing machine under the window.

"Now, my dear," Aunt Edith drew her niece to her with white, square hands that smelt of eau-de-cologne, "let me look at you."

She took in the dogged figure, its black button-up boots; the hideous pink dress belonging to sister Doris and sacrificed in a fit of pious self-abnegation; Aunt Maisie's brown coat; the wiry, dark hair standing straight up and back from a tremendous forehead. Aunt Edith's natural kindness prevented her from giving any expression to her real opinion of her niece's looks. A resemblance to Ludwig van Beethoven, while creditable enough in a set of book-ends or a bronze bust, is out of place in a young girl, and Shannon's determined air, the complete lack of any lovable softness, might have alarmed a less decided woman.

"I hope I have done right," Aunt Edith spoke her thoughts aloud, "in asking you here, Shannon." She continued her scrutiny. "You have Ada's dark eyes and hair. Not at all like *him*." Her face moved in an expression of distaste. "I suppose he's still lording it over everyone, thinking she's no more than the dirt beneath his feet?"

"Daddy is very well, thank you." Shannon sat primly on the edge of a chair, her black cotton gloves folded in her lap.

"I suppose he is. Yes, he would be. That type is always the same. Well now," Aunt Edith roused herself from her dislike of her sister's husband, "we must take you along to your room and let you have a wash. Are you lame, child?"

"Not exactly lame, Aunt Edith," Shannon replied quickly. "I have one shorter leg and one taller leg. That was my short leg I was standing on."

"Why didn't you come to the front door?" Aunt Edith's conversation habitually went off at a tangent.

"I did, Aunt Edith, but an old lady said to come to the back door."

Aunt Edith's lips tightened. "I'll have to get rid of her. Intolerable. That woman does her best to blacken my name to everyone."

Shannon could not take her eyes from the collar around Aunt Edith's neck. It was lace, with little bone uprights stitched in it to keep it straight up to her ears, as though she followed the Headstown fashion of putting a little railing around herself. When she became angry, her whitey-grey face puffed over the collar as though it would escape out of the railing and cease to be the face of a stout, dignified landlady and become something very strange indeed.

"They're all the same. Whispering behind my back, blackening my name. I can't turn for them. Sniggering and spying. They ought to be wiped from the face of the earth. Even when I'm in bed at night, I can hear them whispering up and down the hall. All enemies. Ready to murder me because they think I have money. But I know it. I keep my door locked." Her face smoothed miraculously and became inanimate as baker's dough again. Shannon noticed that the powder had clogged in her grey eyebrows. "I want you to be a lady, my dear," Aunt Edith went on tranquilly. "No one could grow up a lady in company with that man." This, of course, was Shannon's father. "Common! Low!" She shook her head. "Unbelievably low! While you are with me, I want you to be always quiet, dignified, and self-controlled. Never anything rude or out of place. Always a proper distance between yourself and your inferiors. You will remember that, won't you?"

"Oh yes, Aunt Edith."

"Very well. I may, just for the time being, be forced to put you in with Beryl." By another of her quick changes Aunt Edith became all landlady. "But you need not associate with her. She is a good enough girl, rather low and common, but definitely not a fit friend for you." She led the way along the passage.

"Oh, that's all right, Aunt Edith. I won't mix with her." Shannon stuck out her jaw ominously.

Aunt Edith flung a door open. "A pig-sty as usual." Her voice was gloomy but resigned. "You could wade through the things on the floor." With surprising speed Aunt Edith was at the stair-head. "Beryl!" she screamed. "Why don't you put your things away. It's a disgrace."

"What-ho, Ma," came a howl from the kitchen. "Coming." Beryl appeared wiping her hands. This time they were wet from peeling vegetables. "*Now,* what is it?" she demanded amiably.

"Your room's an absolute pig-sty. You might have tidied it up a little knowing the child would have to share it."

"Not on your life!" Beryl replied indignantly, her face upturned so that the lozenges of coloured light from the stair window fell across it. "Like Hell anyone'll share my room!"

"That's no way to speak to me!"

"Well, shove her out on the balcony, Ma. She can dress in my room if you like." With this liberal concession, the gingery one returned to the kitchen whence she could be heard singing light-heartedly.

Shannon gazed after her with hostility. In her own aunt's house her life was to be ordered by a slavey.

"Why don't you sack her?" she demanded.

"Sometimes I think I will," Aunt Edith responded. She looked cautiously over the banister. "Just for now, perhaps, you had better sleep on the side balcony. Then you will only dress in Beryl's room, and it will avoid any unpleasantness."

Indignantly, Shannon followed her aunt back along the hall, and was shown the bathroom, the cubby-hole Beryl occupied, and the slip of verandah beyond.

Any time Aunt Edith found her boarders overflowing she partitioned the verandah into yet smaller sections or built an annex into the yard. Aunt Edith's favourite boarder could always look through his window into the kitchen; and Percy Bargo, who worked at the local billiard saloon, could put his head through into the dining-room. When he sprained his ankle, he used to have his dinner passed to him, and he would sit up in bed and talk to the others as they ate.

It was all very convenient, if a little cramped. Aunt Edith hated to turn money away. "I'll see if I can fit you in," was her invariable greeting to a new guest; and fit them in she would, if it was only with Briscoe in a kind of lean-to at the end of the yard.

"I am disappointed in Beryl," Aunt Edith remarked with stately disapproval, as she ushered Shannon into her quarters. "Not what I expected at all. Yes," she said to herself, "I could send her away, of course. She is a very common girl. I hate anything common. But she is a protection. All these people whispering and looking at me."

Shannon's dejection increased. It was no use pretending that there wasn't something wrong with Aunt Edith.

There was a sound of feet running up the hall and Beryl burst in after them, flung open the wardrobe and rummaged.

"Just the thing!" she cried. "She's got no right to wear pink. Here it is. And it'll fit her because it's too small for me." She was holding out a dress of soft yellow wool. "You know it makes me look sallow, Ma, and it's too short anyway. It'll fit her down to the ground."

"So it will." Aunt Edith was delighted. "Put it on, Shannon."

Beryl went on impulsively, "And shoes." She was tossing them out on the floor. "What size do you take, Shanno? Here, try these on."

Between girls, the exchange of clothes has gained the significance that the drinking of each other's blood had for their savage ancestors. Shannon went to her suitcase and rummaged in her turn. "Here," she said awkwardly, "you can have it." The offering was a small embroidered purse. "You can take it to the dance."

"Oh I couldn't take it!"

"Yes, you could."

"Certainly." Aunt Edith beamed over the love-feast. "And as soon as I have time, I shall run Shannon up some dresses of her own." Then she gave a heart-rending cry: "The dinner!" and swept out and down the stairs.

Beryl reluctantly took the purse. Otherwise, she knew, Shannon would not accept the dress. "If I'm a bit late tonight," she said carelessly, "don't worry about it. I'll try not to wake you."

The glow engendered by this newly cemented friendship lasted all over the babble of tea-time. Aunt Edith's cooking was of such a quality that the boarders were hanging on their door-handles and drooling impatiently long before the bell went. Then there would be such a scrambling and scurrying down the stairs, such a hurry to places, that the weaker or more dilatory were likely to find themselves prodding at a remnant left over from the bargain rush. The practice of getting in early before the bell went and waiting, although it was frowned upon, was often employed by those

Beryl nicknamed "the wolf pack," a contingent of gentlemen who had two helpings of everything including soup.

After dinner, Beryl vanished, leaving Shannon and Briscoe to a washing-up of such magnitude that it seemed to stretch away into sidereal years.

"This is a funny place, Mr. Briscoe," Shannon ventured.

"Funny!" Briscoe snorted. Then he considered. "If it wasn't for the way the missus cooks, I dunno if I'd be here. There's young Beryl gadding out at night; there's the boarders, and the furnace always needing attention. Then there's prejudice in the judging."

"The judging, Mr. Briscoe?"

"Me fowls," Briscoe explained proudly. "Ah, if it wasn't for prejudice, that Chinese Silky would have got a First at Warnham. That Golden Wyandotte would never have been put in the Any-Other-Variety class. As good a cockerel-breeding Wyandotte as you'd see on any show bench." He lapsed into a gloomy silence. "Then there's slugs and snails. I believe they throw 'em over the fence. And little Jimmy getting his foot crushed in the gate only this afternoon. There's always something."

Later that night Shannon was inclined to endorse this opinion. She had settled down to sleep on her verandah, not very successfully, for she was not used to sleeping alone, having always shared a bed with a sister or a clump of sisters; but after tossing restlessly, she finally drowsed off. It seemed only minutes before she was awakened by pebbles clattering on the window.

"Shanno," Beryl whispered from below, "come down and let me in."

It was not only a matter of letting Beryl in. She seemed to be uncertain of the stairs, and clutched occasionally at her guide, murmuring the while that it was a good thing "old Shanno" was there.

"Rotten," she murmured. "Bally blanky rotten dance. Quarrelled with Ricky. Beer no good. Upset me."

She scattered her clothes broadcast on the floor and flung into bed. Shannon tossed restlessly on her verandah.

"What's up, kid?" Beryl called through the darkness.

"I can't sleep. I'm not used to sleeping by myself."

"Come on then." Beryl was resigned. "You can hop in with me. It's been such a rotten day I guess I can stand it."

Shannon needed no second invitation. She snuggled warmly against her roommate; but presently prodded her awake.

"Now, what is it?"

"Turn over. You're breathing on me. Beer. I'd be afraid of going to Hell for drinking beer."

"Oh, all right, all right." Beryl turned wearily on her other side. "It's going to be lovely, just lovely, having you. I can see that."

They fell asleep rancorously, curled up like two kittens.

Four

I

John Terrill was a silent young man with tobacco-stained fingers, who kept an unsuccessful chemist's shop in Head Street. In all the time he had been at Clayton House he had never before found toffee marks on his books. It was not his habit to leave a book face upward in the sun; but someone had treated his copy of "Thus Spake Zarathustra" to a sun-baking that had buckled the cover. John Terrill's books were his treasure, the solace of an unhappy life, and he went hot-foot in search of Beryl.

"You've no idea who could have done it?" He was a favourite with Beryl, because he made no trouble; he had in fact that dread of giving trouble which afflicts quiet and retiring men.

"Nuh." Beryl turned her face away and studiously dusted the hall-stand.

Mr. Terrill was trembling with rage. You could have trodden on his ribs and he would have felt less anguish. He held out the disfigured copy as though he would call its scars to witness.

"You can tell Mrs. Wallis's niece that if it happens again, I shall complain to her aunt."

Books were a drug that Shannon consumed stealthily and with no moderation whatever. The vice grew with what it fed on. She would read anything from a dictionary to a treatise on turnips. Print fascinated her, dazed her, made her good for nothing.

"Now with me," Beryl pointed out indignantly, "I can take a book or leave it, just like that. I don't go prowling round pinching books."

But attempts to reform Shannon were hopeless. For a time she refrained from Mr. Terrill's bookcase and browsed through the Front Room's set of Dickens, taking more care with fingerprints. When excited, her habit of tearing off the corner of a page and eating it gave any book that passed through her hands the appearance of a mouse's last meal. No book-owner in the boarding-house was safe.

Shannon could be charming when she wanted anything. Several elderly

ladies who had library subscriptions pronounced her a "dear little thing."
Miss Savage, who worked at Head and Bodley's millinery department,
had a set of Mrs. Henry Wood's works.

"Poor child," she sighed. "One shouldn't be too hard on her. You know
she has some kind of impediment . . . her leg. She lay at the bottom of
a mine shaft for two days before she was rescued."

"She told me she was flung out of a sulky when the horse bolted,"
retorted acid Miss Crane.

"Dear me! But she wouldn't tell a deliberate lie!"

"Oh! wouldn't she?"

The night before, Miss Crane had been passing the sitting-room where
Shannon, all by herself, had been practising "expressions" in the mantel
mirror. She would raise her eyebrows and lower them again, experiment
in the production of dimples, sucking in the flesh of her cheek until a
dimple resulted. Deciding that her eyelashes did not curl, she spat on her
forefinger, liberally bedaubed the eyelashes and forced them back until
they did curl. Then she tried raising one eyebrow at a time, an interesting
thing to do, but demanding concentration.

"Just then she saw me," Miss Crane recounted, "and if looks could have
killed!"

Miss Crane had not Miss Savage's kind, believing nature which
prompted her to draw Shannon out about her family. It seemed that
Shannon had been adopted when a baby and brutally treated. It was
harrowing to hear her tell of it.

Shannon was merely settling down in Clayton House where, at first,
everything had seemed so strange. At home in Kerleuit, on Friday nights,
the mailman always brought through a load of saveloys which his wife
sold in the little shop she owned. Saveloys were the established Friday
night tea, but here it was fish. Here was no distant blue glimpse of the
sea. Although it was seldom that anyone from Kerleuit went down to
the sea, it was comforting to know it was there. Here the sea and open
country were very far away. There were fences of board or wire instead
of stone. Still she would grow used to it in time, and she did. Even when
her family proposed that she should come back for a holiday, to her aunt's
surprise, Shannon did not want to go. "But you must," her aunt told her,
secretly pleased. "It looks so bad not to want to go back."

"I'd sooner stay here." Not that she liked Headstown, but it was better than Kerleuit. Kerleuit meant church on Sundays, and her father grumbling all the week, and a queer sense of being a stranger cut off from the accepted worries and pleasures of her sisters and brothers. If she felt a stranger at Headstown, at least she had the excuse that she was one.

Then too, she would have missed Beryl. Although they quarrelled together, there was none of the venom in it that a quarrel at home could brew, no long-standing grudges and silences. She could always win Beryl round by an unwonted display of industry. For two such opposite natures they chimed well together; Beryl always loud and brisk, and Shannon small, dark and grim, with not infrequent bursts of self-pity and rebellion. "Moaning," Beryl called it. Beryl's own remedy for such moods was one which she advanced with a cheerful insistence. "Snap out of it, Shannon, it don't get you anywhere."

All in all Shannon was beginning to blossom and expand at Clayton House in a most surprising way. After her first warning from Mr. Terrill, she left his books alone, until almost every other source was exhausted. Then, indignantly, she made the discovery that Mr. Terrill had hidden away all the books he considered unsuitable for a young girl.

All would have been well, had not Mr. Terrill returned early one afternoon and found her happily curled up on his bed reading. His first impulse was to bash the girl's head against the wall, for he felt like all three bears rolled into one. Then realizing that this course might involve him in a certain amount of condemnation, he drew up a chair grimly and conducted an inquisition.

"How would you like anyone to come messing up your books?"

"I haven't any books." This was obviously a useless line of attack.

"It's sheer wanton destruction. You don't read the things. I'm going to tell your aunt that if you don't leave my books alone, I'll leave." He glanced sternly at his prey to see if there were any sign of repentance; but his own face flushed as he realized that she was still curled up on his bed.

"And this is *my* room," he added hotly.

His landlady's niece uncurled. "I'm sorry, Mr. Terrill," she said, with much greater timidity than she really felt. John Terrill was neither old nor forbidding; a rather big-boned, awkward fellow who looked slower than he was and older than his twenty-eight years. "You see, Mr. Terrill, you have all the books you want, but I have to think things out for myself, and it's a great waste of time, isn't it, when you could just read about them?"

"What kind of things?" For all his anger he could not repress a smile.

"Well, take the fact that the world goes round. Anything that goes round like a top or a wheel makes a noise, doesn't it? Suppose we were out in space, would we hear a kind of whistling hum as the earth went round? Well, why don't we hear it? Have we just got so used to hearing it that we don't hear it any longer?"

John Terrill considered this with interest. "It could lose itself in space."

"But suppose it doesn't?"

"That's nothing to do with my books." But his voice was milder. "Tell me," he asked, curious, "do you really *read* my books? To understand them, I mean?"

"Well, I didn't understand the long words in some of them," the prowler admitted. "But I liked 'The Revolt of the Angels' and 'Penguin Island.' How would you like it," Shannon's voice was appealing, "to have no books, not a single book of your own?"

"Look here," John Terrill said on a sympathetic impulse, "I'll tell you what I'll do. I'll pay a subscription for you to the library. That's if you promise not to come . . . borrowing."

"Would you *really*, Mr. Terrill?" Shannon brightened. "I'd like that." After all she had read most of his books from cover to cover. "Yes, Mr. Terrill, I'd like that."

"Shannon!" It was Aunt Edith's voice approaching down the hall. Shannon slipped out. She put her head in again to ask anxiously: "You won't forget, will you?"

I suppose she'll only take out the cheap fiction, Terrill thought scornfully, but it might keep her from interfering with my bookshelf. A few nights later, Shannon slid in again uninvited.

"Mr. Terrill, thank you for the library subscription."

"That's all right," he grunted, and turned back ostentatiously to his letter writing.

"Mr. Terrill, what's Erastianism?" She was holding Newman's *"Apologia Pro Vita Sua."*

"Why do you want to read that? Aren't there any light books in the library?"

"I like this sort of book," the infant philosopher explained. "Oh, Mr.

Terrill, isn't the library funny inside? Outside it's like old mouldy cheese, and inside," she bubbled, "it's all mouse dirts and a smell of tobacco smoke. And the librarian, do you know what he said to me? 'Have you ever read Homar Kam, Miss Hicks?' he said. 'Ah, that's a book, now that's a philosophy. I really try to live that, Miss Hicks.' And he's got five children and a wife who takes in washing! Don't you think, Mr. Terrill, that people are queer?"

She was evidently there to stay, and John Terrill abandoned the idea of finishing his letters which were, in any case, only long complaints of the dullness of Headstown. He leant back in his chair.

"Do you really want to know about Erastianism?"

"I want to know all about all sorts of religion. Beryl says it's bunk, but I don't see why there shouldn't be a God. Suppose instead of being a big thing spread out, God was the ultimate unit of smallness." She brought this out with great pride. "The ultimate unit. You can't have anything built up unless it's built up of something, and that must be built on something else, until you get down to the very last, so if you worked it out that way, we'd all be made up of the ultimate unit of smallness." She looked at him anxiously. "What do *you* think, Mr. Terrill?"

Mr. Terrill was interested. He had not expected to find in Headstown anyone so interested in abstract problems. He took out his pipe and lit it.

"Suppose there were no such thing as the ultimate unit of smallness and you went on to infinity?" he asked.

It was the first of a series of most enjoyable evenings. He lent her books with suitable cautions as to cleanliness and chewed corners. Sometimes they went for long walks and discussed books and metabolism and kinetic energy. When he launched into figures, he left her standing, but he would talk earnestly for hours on fixed stars and people with long names like Anaxagoras and Spinoza. "What does Kant say?" he would ask enthusiastically. "Here's what Kant says." It was some time before his companion discovered that Kant was a man.

Mr. Terrill was very severe with Einstein and he preferred Lamarck to Darwin. He would lie in the long grass and recite poetry in a thick mutter. Also he complained about his hard lot in being a chemist, when he wanted to be a farmer, an experimental farmer growing all kinds of new plants. Shannon here was on her own ground.

"All *I* want, Mr. Terrill, is just to find some place where I fit in. I don't really fit here, but there must be some place meant for me. Perhaps you don't know, Mr. Terrill," her voice was wistful, "what it is not to be really wanted. I mean the kind of person who can be done without."

John Terrill allowed her to talk, and in return he found that his meals had come to include all the choicest morsels, his dinner was kept hot for him, his linen was washed and his suits were brushed. Aunt Edith was highly indignant.

"I think it's positively disgusting," she declared, "the way you're always hanging about that man. He should know better than to encourage a young girl like you. I won't have it, Shannon, I won't have you always in and out of that man's room. Why can't you pick some nice companion of your own age? Or if you must be always hanging around the boarders, there are some pleasant, lady-like women who would like you to entertain them. There are some nice people here at the moment."

Aunt Edith had all the choice pests usually associated with boarding-houses, ranging from Percy Bargo, a hulking youth, who would pounce out and grab you in the hall, to a lady with a freckled child whose hair stood straight up from his head. He had a habit of greeting any new dish with a loud: "What's this muck?" And if asked if he wanted more dinner, would reply: "No, I'm full."

"Say 'No, I'm full, *thank you,*'" his mother would correct him sweetly.

"One of these days that kid will be found with his neck broken," Beryl would rage, and Shannon assisted her in planning many a fantastic scheme for ending the child.

"We could lure him down to the river," she suggested.

"You'd have to hold out some food in front of him all the way. I can't understand why Ma puts up with this mob. It'd take a million to make it worth while to stand their manners."

From early morning until dinner time there was cooking and cleaning and washing-up, varied by washing, polishing and scrubbing. Sometimes, in moments of despair, Shannon saw herself growing older and grimmer and more work-hardened, until she was quite grey, the drudgery of the Clayton Residential pushing her into an early grave.

"I've got to get out of this somehow," she mourned to Beryl. "If only I could run away."

"Where to?"

"Well, there must be places."

"Why don't you go home?"

"Why don't you?"

"Because," Beryl considered this, "you've got to have a job. Cheer up, kid. Tomorrow's Saturday."

"What's so good about that?"

"Well today's pay-day and tomorrow I blue it."

"I don't get any pay."

Aunt Edith, while she might pass over a few shillings for stockings or dress material, was what is known as "near." She never liked to see money seeking another home.

"You'd only spend it on books," she remarked unkindly on one occasion; and she was perfectly right in her dislike of Shannon's reading.

All that these conversations with John Terrill, all that reading did was to sour her taste for Headstown, so that it made her as sick as cold boiled cabbage. Somewhere, there must be people such as there were in books, people who were intelligent and good-humoured and great-hearted. Surely, to find them and live with them and be one of them would be the greatest aim of all. To be like John Terrill, who didn't care about what anybody thought of him, must be splendid. She worshipped John Terrill shyly at a great distance, and he accepted her, encouraged her, and liked her immensely.

"One of these days," he assured her, "if you keep up your reading, you'll do something with it. You see." And Shannon did keep up her reading, persistently, against all opposition.

Beryl did her best to cure her work-mate of this solitary vice. Her own idea of enjoyment was a medley of loud music, intoxicating noise, crowds of gay people, and a stalwart young man to cuddle her. She even lent Shannon one of her evening dresses and took her to dances, but without any real hope of reform. Her worst fears were realized when Shannon said she did not like the taste of beer; she found nothing but boredom in the mauling ways of young men, and had no ear for the music of the ukulele; and would sooner be home reading or out on the farm where Beryl's family, the McLaughlins, scratched a scanty livelihood. She could talk by the hour to Mr. McLaughlin about lucerne and pigs.

"You never really try," Beryl complained, "to be a good sport."

She was teaching Shannon to smoke cigarettes, and recognizing Beryl's real concern for her social welfare, Shannon did her best. She succeeded in acquiring sufficient of the social graces to subtract a young man from Beryl, before Beryl was tired of him, and then Beryl called her a "low-down, double-crossing, little louse." But Shannon would sooner have been discussing problems of religion and biology with her friend John Terrill.

She was intermittently sunk in dejection. This cold misery, this iron chain rusting in the heart, is the portion of all who taste the goblin fruit of literature, who have held out to them the glittering mirage of a life, where shining beings in the bright silk of immortality walk aloof from washing-up, the din of factories, and the private hells of those whose wistful faces have once looked through the windows of a printed page on paradise.

Aunt Edith was becoming difficult. One morning, she declared that the breakfast bacon had a funny taste and that chemist Terrill was deliberately trying to poison her.

"Well, give the bacon to Percy Bargo," Beryl advised. "Nothing would poison him." She exchanged commiserating glances with Shannon. Whenever Aunt Edith began to feel that one of the guests was plotting against her, that guest very soon left. She was so acidly polite to the object of her suspicions that they were glad to go.

"It's getting that way," Beryl summed up to Shannon, "that Ma'll drive them all out one after another. Not that I care. Not a bit of it. But this would be a good job, if you only did your share of the work."

Even when Aunt Edith did her best to make John Terrill's life unpleasant for him, Shannon did not really think he would leave. It was something quite other than Aunt Edith that sent him away, a letter from his father saying that if he was so set on farming, he had better try his hand at it. One evening, when Shannon knocked at his door with a book under her arm, she found him packing.

"Oh, Mr. Terrill, will you write to me?" she begged.

Mr. Terrill looked uneasy. He fumbled in his suitcase and brought out a little pile of books.

"Here," he said hurriedly, "you might as well have these, Shannon." With a book-owner's greed he turned them over before placing them in her arms. Not that he really wanted them himself. There was the second volume of Nansen's "Farthest North," a treatise on the bones of fishes, and a "Post-Biblical History of the Jewish People."

"Never you mind about reading books," he told her, "You just get

C

enough capital. If you've got enough capital, you can buy a property for yourself and do what you like." This was rather a brutal stroke, but Shannon took it unflinchingly.

"I don't believe you," she said. "I don't believe you'd do that anyway yourself. Just grab money."

"Wouldn't I just," her mentor said exultantly. "I'm going to have a place people'll come miles to look at."

For a long time after he had gone she remembered his kindly, thin face and was lonely. The house seemed duller, Beryl louder, her aunt's manner queerer. This last became so evident that Beryl took to commenting on it anxiously, particularly when Aunt Edith announced the grocer leered at her.

"If you tried to get her to a doctor," Beryl complained, "she'd bite your head off. She'll end in an asylum, poor old Ma."

Matters had stood at this pass for some time when Headstown broke out in a rash of red and white posters. Advertisements in the "Headstown Chronicle" lauded the powers of Mr. Vincent Sladder, Psycho-Ordinator, exponent of the new science of psychic healing, who would be giving a series of lectures and demonstrations of Scientific Healing in the Headstown Memorial Hall—this was a barn in a back street smelling of stale tobacco smoke and dust. It was the chosen camp of every travelling show, and Headstown prepared to enjoy Mr. Sladder in the spirit of those offered a free seat at the circus.

His first night was packed to the doors and people were turned away. Convincing cases arrived on stretchers and were deposited in the front row, until it came their turn to rise and testify that they were cured. On the platform, Mr. Sladder directed vibratory waves of healing thought over the audience, while his assistant clasped those parts of his anatomy where he felt the pain transferred to him by his would-be patients. Free consultation after the lectures ensured a rush of curious persons, all with vague pains which had hitherto withstood the doctors of Headstown who, with sour smiles that hid their inward fury, watched from a distance Mr. Sladder minting money.

Beryl returned from the first lecture in raptures. "He's marvellous!" she breathed. "Six feet tall and fair wavy hair. He ought to be on the screen. Oh, boy! watch me get my gun."

Shannon was puzzled. "I thought this Sladder was a measly, little, wizened sort of man."

"Not *him!*" Beryl scornfully brushed the faith-healer aside. "It's his assistant, Bleeby Peverill, and he's very English, with one of those haw-haw sort of accents and a cute bit of a lisp. Oh, he's ducky! He's really an artist, he says, and he thinks he can get me a job in Sydney with Mr. Sladder because I'm psychic." She did a war dance around the kitchen excitedly. "He held my hand and said I was as psychic as anything."

"How did you manage to talk to him?"

"I had a pain," Beryl said solemnly. "A god-damn awful pain. It came on half-way through the evening. He said it was because I was psychic and there were so many people there I caught it from them. Oh, he's a lad all right! And he knows it." Again Beryl performed an ecstatic jig. "We're going down there tonight, both of us."

"Not me."

"Now listen, Shanno." Beryl gripped her mate's arm. "Here's the one chance of getting Ma healed in a scientific psychic way. You mean to say you won't help?"

In the back row, Shannon shared none of Beryl's raptures, and the only effect Mr. Sladder's healing powers had on her was that she developed a dry sniff that might have been an incipient cold in the head.

After the lecture, Beryl towed her forward to meet Mr. Sladder's assistant, who had the face of an extremely elegant fish, and a narrow palate which jutted his upper front teeth forward. He had rushed down from the platform to sell booklets at the door as the audience surged out.

"Aw Bewyl," Shannon admitted that at least he was a fast worker, "I want you to meet the Chief. I've been talking to him about you."

"Well, we want to talk to him on business," Beryl confided. "At least, my friend here does."

Shannon was led up to Mr. Sladder, a small, foxy man with light green eyes in an ambush of courteous wrinkles. He held Shannon's hand far longer than she liked.

"Oh, yes. Did you say your aunt's name was Mrs. Wallis? Surely not Mrs. Wallis of Clayton House? Dear me. I remember I was called in just before poor Joe Wallis passed on. Old memories, old memories! Of course, I came too late to do him any good, poor fellow. And Mrs. Wallis—dear Edith? Not well? So. Hears voices? Poisoning plots? Dear me! Poor Edith!" He kept up a running fire of such comments while Beryl told her story. "How fortunate that as an old friend of the family . . . although . . . hah . . . certain developments made me somewhat uncertain of my welcome . . . how fortunate you should have consulted me." He put a fatherly arm around Shannon's shoulder from which she hastily drew away. "Now suppose you leave this entirely in my hands? No trouble, no, just an old friend of the family. Let us say I call on your good aunt tomorrow afternoon. Just an old friend making a call. And then perhaps we will see what can be done?"

They were no sooner outside the Head Memorial Hall than Shannon turned furiously on her friend. "Now you've done it. Oh, you poor simple mug!"

"What's up?"

"Bringing that awful brute right into the house. You've done it."

"Well, I like that! Gratitude! Oh, a fine lot of gratitude I get. She's your flaming aunt, isn't she? You never did anything but stand there like an attack of measles going somewhere to break out. You're a fat lot of help. You wait until I've got this job at the Psycho-Ordinator Centre . . ."

"The what?"

"You heard me. This centre in Sydney. Bleeby says I'd be a knock-out. They've got girls, diagnosticians they are—on the stage to help the patients. And Bleeby says . . ."

"Huh, you and Bleeby. That's sweet. Telling them about Aunt Edith to get in well with Bleeby."

They were still not on speaking terms next day. The animosity was so marked that Shannon sulked off down the yard to sit on a box and watch Briscoe wash his fowls. It was Saturday, and he was getting them ready to send away on Monday to yet another show. The fowls spent most of their time travelling in crates or dejectedly waiting to travel. Even at home they were never allowed more than a box two feet by three.

"Trains 'em," Briscoe explained, "for the show."

They were always standing in nice dry manure to make their feet yellow, or being waked at night to get them used to artificial light, or having a feather pulled here and there, or their combs docked so that they would breed better. Now they were being dipped spluttering into a big tub of soapy water and thence flung into another tub with a tablespoon of peroxide in it to whiten their feathers, after which they were finished off in blue water and choked again with a half-teaspoonful of brandy to keep them from getting a chill.

"Let me help, Briscoe," Shannon begged.

"You keep out of this, Shannon." Briscoe wrung another fowl out of the blue water and flapped it in the air to dry it.

"Shannon!" It was Beryl yelling, so Shannon turned her back and refused to answer. "Shannon! He's here! He's come!"

"Where?"

"Inside with Ma. And remember he's just Ma's old friend. You're to go in. She says so." Beryl was aquiver with excitement. "I tell you he's got her absolutely in his pocket. He's going to fix everything. I know it." Beryl became very solemn. "That's because I'm psychic."

II

Mr. Vincent Sladder, Psycho-Ordinator-in-Chief of the Psycho-Ordinating Clinic, Sydney (branches in Melbourne, Brisbane and all other capital cities), Thought-Power, Vibratory Force Exponent, author of "Your Bowels and You," "Forty Ways of Harnessing the Life Force," "Sex and the Soul," "Breathing for Beatitude," all in paper covers obtainable by post from Psycho-Ordinator Centre, Sydney, was really doing very well out of Headstown.

One of his most lucrative patients, Sir Pethwick Head, was outspoken in his view that there were no more untruthful charlatans than doctors, particularly doctors who told him he should avoid alcohol. They knew no more than the members of his own family who had been benighted enough to attribute Sir Pethwick's pains to incipient apoplexy. At three guineas a visit, Mr. Sladder was directing the life force into Sir Pethwick's liver, while Bleeby Peverill performed the more laborious chore of massaging some of the fat off him. Not only was Sir Pethwick good for at least four more "treatments," but here was Aunt Edith positively insisting that the healer remain at the Clayton House for the duration of his stay in Headstown.

Mr. Sladder, after a quick calculation of what this would save in hotel expenses for himself and Bleeby, and with happy memories of Aunt Edith's cooking, felt that this part of his tour was more than coming up to expectation. He sat back contentedly, allowed Aunt Edith to pour out her troubles, and was very much the old friend of the family.

Mr. Sladder was an unusual man, and he had an unusual style of dress. His white shoes, tight white trousers, and red and green striped blazer hardly suited his sandy moustache and sharp little green eyes. The Life

Force must have flared up through Mr. Sladder and burned all the sandy hair off the top of his head at some time, leaving a fuzz above each ear. He had trained a long wisp of hair across the forest clearing in his scalp, a long, sandy wisp, that for the most part stayed obediently flat, but in moments of excitement was likely to rise up and wave like an odd plume.

"Mr. Sladder, this is my niece, Shannon Hicks." Aunt Edith introduced her niece with an almost coy, simpering graciousness. "I knew Mr. Sladder many years ago, Shannon. By a strange coincidence he called this afternoon to ask after me."

"Ah! Shannon!" Mr. Sladder took her hand and held it between his palms, rubbing it in a way Shannon found unpleasant. Having massaged her hand and peered at it, he turned to Aunt Edith. "Shannon. How poetic! How Irish! Poesy and the Irish are never far apart. Look at the ferocity of the late terrible shootings in Ireland. The passion of poets." Mr. Sladder sighed. "It's a terrible thing, especially when they are supplied with modern rifles. Your family name, of course, Edith? I remember. Shannon—a beautiful name. 'The Shannon that never returned.' There was a ship, Edith," he noticed by the expression on Aunt Edith's face that she considered he was holding her niece's hand far too long, so he dropped the hand as though it had only just occurred to him that he still had it with him, "there was a ship left harbour. I saw her myself the day it happened. I remember it distinctly. The 'Shannon' was the name. And as she left the wharf with all sails set, the crowd began to sing, and they sang that very song, 'The Shannon that never returned.' I remember someone saying at the time: 'That is a very ominous thing, a very ill-omened thing indeed." And the 'Shannon' never did return. No. From that day to this the 'Shannon' was never heard of again."

"Run along, Shannon, and help Beryl," her aunt struck in abruptly.

As Shannon hastened away, ostentatiously wiping her hand on her skirt, Mr. Sladder could be heard loudly extolling her.

"What magnetism, my dear Edith, what eyes! She resembles you in that. Always so much magnetism."

"She's a great problem, Vincent. I'm sure I've done my best for her. I've tried to make her a lady. But when I'm gone, what will become of her?"

"Don't think of it," Mr. Sladder advised gallantly. "You're not a day older, Edith. Never were. When we had that unfortunate misunderstanding after poor Joe's death, I said then that you'd always be the same to me." He sighed luxuriously. "I remember the chicken we had at lunch that day. It was . . ."

"Yes, yes." Aunt Edith turned his mind to more immediate things. "But, as an old friend, what would you advise about Shannon now that you have seen her?"

"Humm. Yes, well I might," Mr. Sladder considered, "I just might be able to fit her into our organization at the Centre," then noticing Aunt Edith's hesitation, he hurried on reassuringly, "not yet, of course. She should learn a little physiology. It always impresses the Bone Diseases inparticular to be able to say: 'Ha, the femur. Yes, I can see it is the femur.' Nothing like a sound knowledge of where the bones and muscles are actually situated, although she could pick that up at the Centre in a matter of days—all she needs to know. I could do with some young lady," Mr. Sladder reflected, "who had been trained to be a *lady,* not, as so many of them are, only in the profession for what they can make. No real Soul-Force. One eye on the cash-box, and the other on the pocket where you keep your keys. No reverence for higher things. Now, taken young and *trained* . . ."

Aunt Edith was almost icy. "My plans for Shannon were not at all as you have suggested. I wish her to be a really womanly woman. She can cook, make clothes . . ."

"She's never learnt physiology?"

"Never. No lady has the faintest idea, I hope, of where her bones are situated. Much less," Aunt Edith hesitated, "anything more delicate."

Mr. Sladder was all deference and old world courtesy. "My dear Edith, you are perfectly right as usual. Perfectly right. And then she's to marry, eh? Settle down here in Headstown? Charming life."

"I think it is quite likely," there was still some starch in Aunt Edith's tone, "that Shannon will never marry. She has the ridiculous example of her mother before her. There is plenty to occupy her here with me. But I could wish she had a more affectionate nature."

"Yes, yes, just so." Mr. Sladder gave the ceiling a shrewd glance as though daring it to contradict.

Mollified, Aunt Edith abandoned the subject of Shannon's future for the more interesting one of her own health, the curious noises in her head, the way people talked about her behind her back, the attempts to poison her.

Mr. Sladder had a simple explanation and he put it forward with assurance.

"My dear Edith," he raised his hand in the middle of her recital of her suspicions of Terrill, the chemist, "my dear Edith, say no more. I know, none better, what you must have suffered. But you are mistaken, I say it with the greatest certainty, you are mistaken as to the cause of your sufferings." He drew his chair closer and dropped his voice. "I am going to ask you a question. I want you to answer it truthfully." He took Aunt Edith's hand. He was exceedingly fond of holding the hands of those he was addressing. "Tell me, my dear Edith, has it never occurred to you that this deplorable business was brought about with more than human cunning?"

"Oh, yes, yes!" Aunt Edith gasped in an excited, dry voice. "They're fiends. Fiends!"

"Exactly," Mr. Sladder nodded. "More than human in fact."

"What do you mean?" Aunt Edith glared at him suspiciously. "I tell you this chemist tried to poison me. Lately I've felt more and more sure of it."

"Ah, yes, but since? The noises are the same? The whisperings you hear? Just so. I tell you, Edith, I am one of the few men who can do anything for you. In fact," Mr. Sladder shook his head gravely, "with the prevailing lack of knowledge of stigmatic phenomena, I am the *only* man—I say it in all modesty—who would be capable of dealing with the situation."

A middle-aged lady is not the easiest person to detach from her own opinion. "I don't know what you mean about stigmatic phenomena. I tell you this man was trying to poison me. He was employed by my enemies."

"My dear Edith, what enemies could you have?" Mr. Sladder, for all that he peered at her keenly with his little green eyes, was still the dear old family friend.

It was Aunt Edith's turn to lower her voice. "There is my brother-in-law, Shannon's father. He has always hated me."

"Now, don't say that." Mr. Sladder raised his hand. "Of course, hatred is a very powerful phenomenon," he admitted. "Far more powerful than we know. The hatred of such a man could very terribly disturb the astral envelope which surrounds you. It could certainly cause these noises, these whisperings, these pains. Nay, such deadly hatred," again Mr. Sladder sunk his voice to a tomb-robber's whisper, "such hatred could kill."

"Don't say that!" Aunt Edith started back.

"I do say it. Your astral envelope is disturbed. The naked rays of hatred pour through the gap in your envelope tearing and burning as they go. But such power can be countered by a greater power." Mr. Sladder sprang up, so suddenly that Aunt Edith involuntarily put her hand to her throat and almost choked in her neckwear. "All it needs is someone to think against *him*. To oppose to his evil, good. And there is such a protection. There is such a power." Mr. Sladder patted himself on the pocket of his striped blazer. "Here. I can do it and I will."

Again he seized Aunt Edith's hands and gazed into her eyes. "You will feel better at once. The pains will vanish. The whisperings will cease. That is how you will know I am right, that I am protecting you as no one else could." He released her.

Aunt Edith felt very much shaken. She had to go and lie down. Mr. Sladder came and sat beside her and stroked her forehead. It was very soothing. Yes, she admitted, she did feel better when he was near her. He must not leave her.

For several days Mr. Sladder sat about concentrating. Sometimes he would stroll down in the direction of the Royal Hotel to concentrate better, and come back smelling of coffee berries. He spent long periods holding Aunt Edith's hand or stroking her forehead. He prescribed rest for her, and this meant that Beryl and Shannon had to do all the work, and were very bad-tempered about it. Shannon was indignant at the idea that her father would rend her aunt's astral envelope or project rays at her.

At the end of a week Aunt Edith was begging Mr. Sladder not to leave her now that she felt so much better. It was all his doing. And she rested so well with the sleeping draught he prescribed. She felt so peaceful. It was all as neat as a pattern. Aunt Edith had her hand held while she talked about the good old days before poor Joe passed on. Beryl, leaving Shannon to sleep by herself, would slip out to see Bleeby Peverill who had a room at the other end of the hall. Owing to her midnight excursions she usually went around all day yawning and only brightened up as evening came on.

The only person left out of this idyllic picture was Shannon. Mr. Sladder gave her gooseflesh; and as for Bleeby, he was Beryl's type, not hers. Time went on and Mr. Sladder and his assistant showed no sign of following its example. Certainly Aunt Edith was considerably better-tempered and more reasonable, but Mr. Sladder made up for this by becoming more and more obnoxious.

One evening when Shannon had made even less attempt than usual to hide her dislike, he waxed poetically unpleasant.

"There is nothing more beautiful than to watch the expanding of young souls, my dear Edith." He illustrated with his stumpy hands the expanding of a young soul. "We see the rose unfurling in the dew. Night after night we see the fair young soul expanding its petals to the night air. Is this right? In moderation, I would say, Yes. But in excess, what do we find?" He raised a warning finger. "The aphis settle. They settle slowly but certainly on the flower."

"What business is it of yours," Shannon flared, "if I go out at night?"

"Shannon!" Her aunt was shocked.

"One moment, my child," Mr. Sladder said grandly. "It is more my business than you may believe. I think the time has come to inform her, Edith."

"If you think so, Vincent."

"Your aunt, Shannon, has done me a great honour. Years ago when I asked her a certain question, recent bereavement was still heavy on her mind. But now she has reconsidered. Your aunt, Shannon, has promised to become my wife."

"I know perfectly well," Aunt Edith spoke with the defiance of those who feel they may be at any moment attacked, "I know perfectly well that you think, Shannon, I am fit only to slave for a lot of inconsiderate, whispering reptiles. But I have a right to please myself. And it's exceedingly kind of Mr. Sladder to agree that you may come to Sydney with us."

"To Sydney?" Shannon repeated.

"Yes, to Sydney," Aunt Edith swept on. "For a long time Mr. Sladder has planned to start a Rest Home to be run in conjunction with his healing centre. And I," Aunt Edith said it triumphantly, "I, with my experience, can look after the guests."

"Patients, my dear."

"The patients, Vincent. With Vincent's gift of healing and my experience, a Rest Home, once started, must be a wonderful success. All it needs is just sufficient capital . . ."

"We won't dwell on that side of it, Edith," Mr. Sladder cut in hastily. "It may never be necessary to call upon you."

"Well, I hope you're very happy," Shannon muttered, reluctant. "Excuse me."

She went off in search of Beryl, arranging in her mind certain scorching remarks on the subject of Beryl's psychic powers. But Beryl, when she heard, could only think of the joy of working with Bleeby.

"Good old Ma!" she exclaimed heartily. "She must have some money after all."

Five

Melbourne was buried in a fog that tasted like damp cotton wool, and looked as though some ghostly medium was holding a seance over the city, with a crowd of attendant shadows pressing their clammy hands on the flat tops of the buildings and oozing ectoplasm. The drifting, whitish mass poured and eddied around the spires, was exhaled along the streets, and hushed the noisy clatter of the late afternoon. Just as a hurrying crowd, surging along the footpaths, is now denser, now thinned to a mere handful of people, so the fog would lift a little, then fold again in a double thickness of clinging damp.

Under the sonorous arches of Spencer Street Station the platforms held the fog at bay and maintained their usual round by artificial light; with the dilatory rumbling of porters' trucks; footsteps of passengers tap-tapping, now fast, now slow, the message of their mission; the bell ringing; all the stir that goes before the departure of one of the hot-metalled monsters steaming gently in a separate fog of its own.

The leave-taking last minute crowd choking the windows of the carriages; the boys crying papers and pillows; the guard thumping heavy hot iron foot-warmers into each compartment as a rest for the frozen feet of the human cargo; all these regarded the fog as little as they regarded the steam from the engine.

Easter week was near and the holiday rush began. Each carriage was crammed with its load of carefully wedged, already miserable looking passengers, who stared with a dull hostility at the searching, forlorn wretches questing up and down the train for a place, where, if they might not lay down their head, they might at least assert a more humble portion of their anatomy.

"Any room in here?" They would stare past the bulk of the passenger blocking the window talking to the inevitable leave-takers.

"No. We're full up." Sometimes the speaker would turn to the carriage at large and ask: "Aren't we?" with an invariable chorus of affirmation from the other victims whose faces, under the mean light especially designed to prevent people reading in comfort, had already taken on the slack-jawed, staring pallor of so many corpses.

Thus they would sit all night, silent, envying those who slept, bolt upright, sharing the scant warmth of rugs and foot-warmers. When the lights were put out, they would sit in darkness, only the turn of a head against the dim window betraying to the watcher opposite that someone else endured. Meanwhile the train would race on and on; hooting its own strange note; boring and tunnelling through the fog until the fog thinned out; boring through the country like a grub through an apple; going north and east; thudding like some strong heart through the darkness; ravenously devouring the rails that spun and twisted in the flare from the train windows, and when all the lights were out, still spun unseen.

The train's departure was late, and impatiently the guards bundled in the last comers, impervious to the protests of those on whose toes they landed; hastily locking the door on them; leaving them to sort themselves out as best they could. The passengers made the best of it, grumbling, taking a child on their knee, moving up an inch or so, shifting parcels out of a carefully guarded space in which they had hoped to spread later.

The great bell was already clanging its challenge to the train as two girls flung themselves into a second-class carriage, and began frenziedly bundling their luggage on the racks, with the help of a gnarled old man who, to the relief of the other passengers, leapt out of the carriage at the last moment.

His companions leant from the window as the train moved and yelled together: "They're all right. They're in the van. Not a feather out of shape."

"Remember their feed, Beryl."

"Good-bye, Briscoe. Look after Jimmy."

"We'll see they win. Leave it to us."

Their shouts died away as the station dwindled behind them, and they turned to face the company into which they had been plunged; a dour-looking, unhelpful crew, consisting of one thin, weary woman and a fretful child; one stout, dull, red-faced man; one thick-browed, heavy-set man; a slender, pretty girl; a little boy; an elderly woman with a wicker basket; and a dark-faced foreigner.

This mixed bag began, not ill-naturedly, to re-arrange itself in the seating. A pall-like silence descended while the carriage assimilated the new elements. Then the child began to grizzle; and the thin, sandy intruder swooped on it, sat it on her lap, and fed it chocolate while the mother murmured a faint: "Oh, don't bother."

Beryl was always fond of children, and the tired child stopped whimpering to smile at her. The tension of the carriage was broken; and the mother, feeling it incumbent to start a conversation, suggested that "the fog might keep up all the way to Albury."

"It'll only be near the city," the red-faced man amended.

The fog, having wrapped a pall of respectability around the conversation, all agreed that there never was such a fog, that the fog of Nineteen-Eleven could not have been deeper; that there was no saying what caused it, perhaps the smoke; and the stout, red-faced man, a patriot and defender of the South, related a long story of a fog in Sydney which proved that the city for which they were bound could have worse and thicker fogs than Melbourne dreamt possible. All in the carriage were staunch Victorians, and his scathing references to the climate of Sydney were greeted with approval. You would have thought they had all been condemned to penal servitude at the South Pole from the tone in which they spoke. By degrees they passed to the demerits of Adelaide and Perth, and were presently completely at ease and regarded each other with beaming trust.

"Well, it's fine to know we've got a nice set of people to travel with," the red-faced man declared expansively. "I suppose you're all going up for the Show?" Without waiting a reply he went on: "That's where we're bound. I'm taking the Stephens' Murder." He noticed a slight ripple of recoil. "Only the figgers," he reassured them. "Sixpence a head admission. And blood! Well, I tell you there isn't another show that'd put a curl in your hair the way ours would. Isn't that so, Mamie?"

The tired woman was heard to murmur that John had a way of bringing out the details that was worth twice the money. "I've told him till I'm sick of telling him that he ought to raise the price." She appealed to the company. "The figure of Stephens's that nacheral, and the very axe he done it with. Of course, he says he wants the public to have the Best, but we got to get something out of it too."

She would have gone on to expound her view-point, if the two late-arrivals had not leant forward and clamoured eagerly:

"At the Show-ground how do you enter exhibits?"

"Is it too late for the fowl section? We've got two Gold-laced Wyandottes that a friend wants to enter."

"We can put you wise to all that," the red-faced man said good-humouredly. "Can't we, mother?" The elderly lady nodded her head sternly and clutched the wicker basket as if she expected someone was about to wrench it away from her. "Mother's been coming up for Easter since before I was born," the red-faced man declared. "She always takes the tickets for Billy Welcher's Ten Marvels."

He had hardly got the words out when the small boy rose and said rapidly: "Fair go, sports." With which he dived under the seat as they drew in at a station. The ranks drew together and out-stared the ticket-examiner.

"Train's pretty crowded," he remarked.

They murmured back at him, flapping their tickets that it was indeed crowded.

As soon as the train, huffing reproachfully at the delay, had cleared the station, the feet and short pants of the extra passenger emerged cautiously and the rest of him was helped out.

"You'll do it once too often, Tiny," the red-faced man warned. "If you'd take a child's ticket, it'ud save a lot of trouble."

The little figure dusted its knees and said in a high voice: "For Chrisake, George, have sense! What'd make me waste money on the railways?"

"Well, I wish I could duck under a seat," rumbled the big, black-jowled man. "A damn sight cheaper. But I ain't your size any more, son."

"Less of the son," the little figure snapped. "Tiny, that's me. Tiny the pocket tenor." To prove it he trilled: "Mi-mi-mi" with so comical an expression that they smiled in spite of themselves. "Looks like we're a lot of public characters, hey?"

The big, dark man confessed to being a heavyweight in strict training for a bout at the Stadium. The slender girl was "just Molly," but she frowned at the mention of strict training. So did the pocket tenor and the family taking the Stephens' Murder to the Easter Show. From the wicker basket "Mother" produced a couple of bottles of beer and an opener.

"Strict training or no strict training we all got to have one," the red-faced man announced. "Ain't there enough cups? You girls got anything to drink out of? Come on, Mother, don't be mean with it."

Only the foreigner with a shake of his head refused. At first they thought he was deaf, but he shook his head again firmly; and producing a knitted, woollen helmet, donned it, and sunk back in his corner, turning his dark, hawk-beaked face to the window. Now and then he muttered to himself, but could not be drawn into the general hilarity. "I am a poor man," he said with a shrug of his shoulders. "I am poor, and I mind my business." After this rebuff they left him to himself.

"Well, here's to us," the red-faced man proposed. "The more of us the better, and a good gate." With which genial sentiment he tilted a bottle to his mouth and, reaching into the basket, produced another.

The pocket tenor was finding a kindred soul in Beryl. Before they had gone far he knew all about Aunt Edith and Mr. Sladder. "Any time you want it," he assured her, "I could get you a job with Bert. He runs a roll-down show, and he's a pal of mine. You and your friend too. Couldn't find a better time to strike Sydney. Right at the top of a boom. Shouldn't have any trouble striking a job. You can always get in at the Show if you know someone like me who knows the ropes."

Beryl confided that they had a job waiting. "But what it'll be like with my mate always quarrelling with the boss," she admitted, "is nobody's business. He and Ma sent us on ahead while they sell up down there. If you ask me, he wanted *her*," with a nod at the silent Shannon, "out of the way."

After the second beer the pocket tenor raised his voice in song; and Beryl, the addict of a good time, shifted the sleeping baby in her lap and joined him.

Opposite the sullen foreigner Shannon stared out of the window. The train wheels beat monotonously, rhythmically below shaping in her mind a refrain that interested her more than the noisy carriage.

"Into what dark dream do the rails go that they should groan to lose it in the train's glow?" the wheels sang.

The carriage full of people seemed to have been there for centuries. They talked, laughed, drank, confided, getting noisier and hotter, until, she wondered, how with all the windows shut they could go on breathing. Opening the window, she let in a gust of wet air and a few cold drops of rain; but the intense disapproval of her companions caused her hastily to shut it again. The carriage was quieter now. They were settling down. The heavyweight and his girl twined up embarrassingly affectionate in their corner; and the red-faced proprietor of the Stephens' Murder, reiterating that "It was fine to have a nice set of people to travel with," got up and switched out the lights.

Six

To come by train to Sydney is to come in the back-door of the city. A flurry of frowsy suburbs, grey streets, brick-yards, old iron dumps—all these go by wearing the peevish expression of a housewife who, not having time to make the beds, grumbles: "You must take us as you find us." For the incoming ships are the shining towers lifted, the ripples spread on the blue carpet of the harbour, the hurrah of arrival. The trains find only a commonplace of advertisement hoardings, rumble, grime and confusion.

To the native the smell, the orientation of the place, is unique, unmistakeable; but to the stranger it is just city, any city, with ranked warehouses, clanging trams, cars shining and sliding, bustle of people, shops sucking in and pouring out their human food supply like so many water squirts on a reef. There is not even a swallowing movement, as the new supply of atoms pouring from the train is engulfed in the city's vast and nonchalant insentiency.

Far too soon Shannon and Beryl had started hauling down suitcases and exchanging addresses with their overnight friends, fidgetting and fretting, ready for an excited breakaway.

"No hurry until you see the mortuary station," their red-faced friend advised placidly.

As he spoke, the mortuary station appeared over to the left, tiny, brown and graceful under the angular city buildings. It looked like a little brown Hindu contemplating its navel between the river of railway lines and the jungle roar of the city; a gothic stone siding with pillars and arches, left over from the days when death was quiet and dignified. How many Sydney people had made that remark: "No hurry till you see the mortuary station," as they folded up their morning newspapers ready to leap off the train.

Beside the mortuary station waved a stumpy palm tree enforcing the idea that here was something fatalistic, eastern, as out of key with the great buildings as the grey stone tower of the church that had flashed by just before, a donjon keep on a rise. Here were people coming alive; but there was still a place for them if they came dead. Living or dead, the city would receive them, as it received everything, swallowing all the incongruous particles undisturbed.

Retrieving the Wyandottes from the tender mercies of the railway authorities was the first anxiety. The taxi driver was inclined to be sulky about this valuable cargo, regarding it as merely a couple of fowls in a crate. As for the Wyandottes, they had given up hope, and settled down into a dejected disregard of jolts and bumps.

It was Saturday morning; and the city swarm poured over the footpaths and across the taxi's front wheels, now and then necessitating a stop that almost bumped the passengers' noses on the driver's neck. They gazed anxiously at the changing streets, as if by so doing they could throw out a trail to guide them back, fasten the landmarks in mind, perhaps absorb some of the city, become part of it instead of just two alien particles whirling on the tide of traffic towards the Mrs. Lucy Rossingale to whom they were consigned.

"She's probably a good old stick," Beryl muttered hopefully, as they were speeding up the slope to King's Cross. "A good old stick, something like the Front Room; a bit selfish and maybe with little black mitts, but kind. Freddy says she's been more than an aunt to him. And after all if she's in charge of the office . . ." She must surely welcome them for their employer's sake.

In the train, in the taxi, they had been in a small world close-shut as the Wyandottes in their crate; but once set down on the pavement, the heartless preoccupation of everybody, the unapproachable indifference of the shop fronts and rich blocks of flats, even the vindictive way the sun showed up their travel-stains and tiredness, were so many blows in the face. All they wanted was to get under cover, away from the open pavements, the staring cold people, the staring light.

It was a very distinguished street with expensive slips of shops; some with only one article in the window, a hat, or an old chair, backed by rich hangings. A painted sign hung above a staircase leading down into the bowels of the earth, a sign that showed a curious-looking lizard, and, in explanation, the words "The Golden Griffin." Mysterious wafts of food came from below; and with one accord they moved to the menu card let into a little case in the wall. But the prices set them gasping.

The stairway of the Golden Griffin was flanked at street level by a flower shop blazing with iceland poppies, wall-flowers, violets, african marigolds and roses, whose sweet, earthy smell mingled with the savours of the Golden Griffin. On the other side was a pottery shop full of bowls and vases and jars of earthenware; blue, green, ivory, mauve and red. A notice in the window coaxed: "Why not a gift?" The whole street had a gay air of money, of luxurious, soft, costly trifles. It suggested spending and be hanged to the cost.

Between the flower shop and the pottery shop three steps led up to a glass door with a hallway beyond. Through this glass door they plunged, exploring for Mrs. Rossingale. A young lady at a desk in the hall directed them to the second floor; and, as there was no lift, they asked if they might leave their luggage. This young lady seemed no more impressed by the gold-laced Wyandottes than the taxi driver; but with a slight disdainful nod she allowed them to disfigure her hall.

"Blast Briscoe," Beryl grumbled. "A fine couple of mugs we look lumping that crate about."

The costly elegance of Mrs. Rossingale's flat-building made them feel dirtier and wearier than ever; the scornful glance of the young lady in the glass case branded the back of their travel-crumpled coats.

Outside the door of No. 5 they paused and inspected each other anxiously.

"You've got a smut on your nose, Shanno," Beryl whispered. They pulled up their stockings, straightened their hats, brushed at each other nervously; then knocked. The sound of an angry voice, a woman's voice, came from behind the closed door. They knocked again, and this time the voice ceased and the door was opened.

"Mrs. Rossingale, please?" Shannon asked.

"She can't see anyone." The door half-closed.

"Who is it?" a voice called. "Jenny, you tell me who it is this minute."

"Never you mind," the woman at the door said rudely. "You're not fit to see them." Then in a more patient tone, "It's two girls."

"Let them in at once."

"If you're well enough to see them, you can let them in yourself. Don't think you can treat *me* like a servant."

"You are making a scene, Jenny," the voice replied coldly. "Perhaps you had better take Sporty for his walk."

"Oh, very well." The door shut with a slam. Next minute it opened again, and a stout, angry woman shot out clutching the end of a lead to which was attached a slinking white mongrel. Blocking the door she turned for a parting shot: "You're driving me just too far, Lucy. You'll be damn sorry for this." With a twinkling of thick legs and white-heeled shoes she was gone.

"Come right through," the unseen Mrs. Rossingale encouraged. "I'm in bed with a really terrible cold."

To say she was in bed did not express the magnificence of her lying in state. Her white shoulders rose out of a black georgette nightdress embroidered with little flowers. There were flowers everywhere; on the little gilt-legged table by the bed, on the dressing table among the litter of scent sprays, jewel cases, framed photographs and other trifles of gilt and enamel; there was even a big bowl of red roses on the floor under the window. Their scent and colour on the air was like the pink brocade quilt on the bed, a muffling richness.

Beryl drew a hissing breath, as she stood in the doorway contemplating the lady who had been "more than an aunt" to Freddie, for Mrs. Rossingale ("stiffish with little black mitts") was a plump, delicious adventuress of the court of the Grand Monarch. She had gold-auburn hair and long green eyes with mischief in them; and, bitterest blow to Beryl, a square white dimpled chin. Everyone knows when she is out-classed, and Beryl, for agility of mind or lure of body, was to Mrs. Rossingale as a child's pop-gun to the latest thing in ordnance. Her first jealousy passed into avid curiosity. You could learn, Beryl decided, just by watching Mrs. Rossingale.

Shannon, on the other hand, had classed the lady as merely a costly trifle; and this beastly room cluttered with pink and gold knick-knacks filled her puritan soul with contempt. It was a stage setting; and Mrs. Rossingale had been expecting not two censorious fellow women but probably Bleeby or Mr. Sladder who would have been appreciative of her lying there all supple curves like a plate of white bait. But whatever her disappointment, she sat up briskly and dropped her swan's-death scene in favour of a rollicking gaiety guaranteed to dispel the bleakness that like a breath of cold air had entered with her visitors.

"Come in, darlings. I've been expecting you for ages. I'm sure you're Beryl and Shannon." She held out both her hands royally. "Take off your hats and sit down and tell me what on earth Vince Sladder's been up to."

Her tone admitted them to an equal friendship; it signed peace pacts; waved flags of rejoicing; embraced them. "My God! has he gone crazy or what? And here I've been lying in *agony* with that bad-tempered bitch putting the boot in. Oh, I must tell you all about it! And I know you're dying for a cup of tea. *I* am. If someone could put the kettle on?"

They had no sooner hurried to do her bidding than she remembered that there was a flask of "really good brandy" in the sideboard, and they had all better have some "just to take the taste of that Jenny out of their mouths." By the time Beryl had straightened the bed and got Mrs. Rossingale another hot-water bottle, and Shannon had run out to a shop and bought some cakes and another half-pound of butter and the luggage and the Wyandottes had been bumped up the stairs and stowed in a spare room, which bore traces of Jenny's occupancy, they were calling their hostess Lucy quite as a matter of course.

"She's been just poisonous." Every sentence Lucy uttered became dramatic, a streaming black headline heralding Further Revelations of a Startling Nature. "Jenny knows she's no good in the office, and that if anyone goes out, she will, so . . ." (That's why you're trying to win us over, Shannon thought.) "She's been minding that wretched centre—it's as cold as charity—and answering the phone, and looking after me, and all in all," Mrs. Rossingale admitted liberally, "she's had a pretty thin time. But nothing, nothing to justify the simply insane way she's been behaving. I ask you! You heard her? Absolutely insulting!"

"We don't want to take anyone's job," they protested.

Lucy looked from one to the other with the friendliest smile privately certain they were lying. "Have some more brandy," she suggested. "Vince Sladder can settle it when he gets back."

They had a good deal more brandy and Mrs. Rossingale insisted on reading Beryl's hand, relating anecdotes meanwhile of her uncanny ability in predicting disasters for her friends. Beryl was enthralled and began to feel a little jealous of Bleeby who was lucky enough to know this marvellous woman. Lucy appeared to have had such an interesting life; she told most improper stories about all the famous people she had met; but for all her acquaintance with celebrities, she was not overbearing or imposing. She was just a dear, rather pathetic baby, needing someone to care for her. At moments Beryl could have leant right forward and gathered her in her arms. It always worked that way. The number of people who had wanted to gather Lucy into their arms would have filled a small directory.

"Bleeby's been so-o horrid," Mrs. Rossingale pouted. "He's hardly written at all. He promised he'd write every day, and if it wasn't for him I wouldn't be getting my divorce. Although really I suppose that's a lie. It had to come sooner or later." She heaved a little sigh of self-pity. "I couldn't go on living with a man who's so mean. Jim's positively insane about money. He's got one of these delusions that he's being ruined. No, he's not here. I've left him."

Shannon had gone off to inspect the bookcase in the sitting room, but there was little in it besides brochures on palmistry. Lucy, finding that half her audience had deserted, raised her voice appealingly:

"Shannon, *would* you get me another cup of tea while you're out there? I've let this get cold talking." She turned confidingly to Beryl. "Your friend's a quiet little thing, isn't she?"

This remark reduced the less impressionable Shannon to the level of a half-idiot child, leaving Beryl and herself wise adults united in a smiling care of the helpless. "Of course you can see she's brainy. Likes books, doesn't she?" As Shannon brought in the tea her hostess proffered "a most interesting book by a friend of mine. You'll like it. It's got his autograph on the front and that makes it terribly valuable."

"Do you mind if I have a bath?" Shannon asked.

"Why, no." Her hostess was somewhat startled at the abruptness of the request. She was not accustomed to her audience tearing itself away, and had rather expected they would both sit at her feet for the rest of the afternoon in an adoring young-girlish way.

"Thanks." Shannon retired with the "Esoteric Aspects of Astral Life" by Mrs. Rossingale's friend, Southwell Vaughan-Quilter. Its red binding ran a little on the bath water, but Shannon had no scruples. After all it was a bribe, just Mrs. Rossingale's way of buying her over.

Mrs. Lucy Rossingale, Shannon thought, as she removed the traces of her night in the train, must really be very timid; trying to make people like her all the time. The guest felt a quiet, scornful pity for Mrs. Rossingale in her gold and pink frame working so hard, even on insignificant country bumpkins like Beryl and herself, always on the alert to be fascinating, never letting her face relax.

Shannon's selfish occupation of the bathroom missed for her the really epic row when Jenny returned. Sobbing heavily, the unfortunate Jenny was cast into outer darkness.

"Making such a show of me! How dare you!" Mrs. Rossingale raged.

"Before two people I've never seen before in my life. Why you low, crawling gutter-worm . . ."

Beryl apprehensively slipped into the bathroom. She lit a cigarette and sat down on the edge of the bath. Softly she closed the door to shut out the flow of home truths.

"Get out of there," she ordered. "You needn't think you're the only one who feels like a dried herring."

Shannon moved over. "You can have the other end," she proffered.

"Go on, hurry out," Beryl urged, as she accepted this half-measure. "She might be wanting something."

Shannon shut one eyelid drowsily. "Let her want." Nevertheless, as a heavy slam betokened the final retreat of Jenny, she reluctantly took up duty by the bedside.

"Oh, darling," their hostess moaned, "my temperature's going up and up. She's upset me so. Do you think you could just run down and buy some aspirin? And you don't mind using your own money, do you? I owed that beastly Jenny quite a lot and she wouldn't even take a cheque for it."

The aspirins duly administered, the invalid revived sufficiently to think of food.

"What are we going to have for tea? Poultry? I think it would be better if you borrowed the caretaker's axe. You could take them up on the roof and I wouldn't hear the flutterings and squawks."

Shannon, aghast at such blasphemy, explained that the Wyandottes were prize birds and belonged to a friend.

"Oh! I thought they were a present. I've been lying here *starving,* and the only thing I've wanted is chicken broth. Of course, if those wretched hens are *valuable,* I'll give you a cheque for them."

It was a contest of wills. Lucy was determined to eat those Wyandottes, not only because she would have the pleasure of asserting her powers of persuasion, but also because she suspected that Bleeby had been flirting, and she was symbolically getting her own back.

"Better keep in with her," Beryl advised, when consulted in the bath. "After all she's let us stay here."

"Like Hell I'll keep in with her." Shannon marched back to the bedroom. "Beryl thinks," she reported, "that I'd better go down and get you some chicken broth from the restaurant."

"Darling, it shuts tomorrow and we'll starve to death." Their glances locked. There was a brief struggle. "You're really very mean," Lucy wailed. "All right. Keep your rotten hens."

Shannon said carefully, "Perhaps it would be better if we found some other place to stay. We don't want to impose on you."

"Don't be a silly. I was only joking." Lucy curled down in the pink quilt and drawled, "You can't go na-ow." It was an exaggerated imitation of a coy heroine calling back her hero. "Maybe I ought to hold up a pair of baby's booties. They always do that in the pictures."

Shannon found herself liking their unscrupulous acquaintance.

"What is it?" Lucy said suddenly. "Come on. Tell me."

"Nothing."

"You're thinking something that amuses you. You get a sort of glint in your eye."

"I was thinking," Shannon brought it out reluctantly, "that you look like The Pride of the Harem."

Mrs. Rossingale went off into a fit of laughter. She almost choked. Shannon had expected her to be angry or perhaps raise her eyebrows.

"Oh!" she gurgled. "You're a devil. The Pride of the Harem! Oh, dear!" As Shannon trotted off to arrange for food with the restaurant, the joke was being shouted to Beryl in the bathroom. "The Pride of the Harem! That's what she said. I could slay her!"

It was harder to get away from the radiant personality of Mrs. Rossingale than to break gaol. She loved a listener; and, as Beryl who had consumed the greater portion of the brandy, was feeling rather sickish after the train journey, the two of them talked the week-end away, exchanging the most reckless confidences about their own and other people's intimate affairs. It was not much fun for Shannon; though of course it was educational; ripe stuff, not the kind of thing you find in books, unless they are medical textbooks, and usually beginning: "Well, take the case of a girl I know . . ."

It was not long before Beryl and Lucy had taken Mr. Sladder to pieces; then they moved to his marriage with Aunt Edith, reviewing it caustically.

"I don't believe in any of this old-romance stuff for a minute," Lucy contended. "He's just got a cheap housekeeper. And if ever he pays you two anything like a wage, I'll faint with surprise."

From this point they advanced to Bleeby Peverill; and on this subject

Beryl and Lucy were in agreement. They took his character apart and looked at the seams. By the time they had finished with Bleeby, it seemed impossible that the monster should still be at large. Laws should be passed to deal with him; the public aroused to its danger in harbouring him; any girl who was deceived by Bleeby should be taken into protective custody.

"You've got to admit he's good looking."

"In a sort of way. But when you think how he borrows *money!* And he's English." Lucy brought this skeleton out of Bleeby's closet with a nice show of reluctance. "That's the trouble with him."

Shannon was not interested in Bleeby Peverill, particularly when she could see from the window a stretch of housetops and treetops rolling down to the water, as though they would plunge in gaily when they reached the brim.

"I think I'll just go for a walk," she murmured.

"And while you're out," Lucy called after her, "do you think you could get me some cigarettes?" You couldn't even go for a walk, without Lucy wanting to turn it into an errand. When Shannon returned, they were still discussing Bleeby Peverill.

By Sunday night, Beryl had passed through all the stages of passionate friendship and come out the other side, gathering the history of Bleeby in the process.

"After all she got him this job when he was absolutely broke." Beryl moodily kicked at Shannon's suitcase, as they sat on the side of the bed. "I guess that means she's got some claim on him. Oh, it's going to be just marvellous! I can see that. With Bleeby and The Pride of the Harem acting like two doves on a bough. Damned if I wouldn't chuck this job if I knew where I could get another."

"Those show-people in the train seemed to think they could find you a job."

Beryl thought so long that her feet grew cold as ice and Shannon begged her to come to bed. "When we go out to dump those hens of Briscoe's," she said at last, "I'm going to rustle around looking for the Stephens' Murder. And then I'm going to meet Bleeby and wring his neck."

Mrs. Rossingale's plans for the reception of Bleeby had more of boiling oil in them. She wanted to watch his death agonies.

But, on Monday morning, when Bleeby appeared fresh and smiling, with a blithe: "Hello, all," the plans for his reception were temporarily shelved.

"Why hello, Bleeby," they chorused in tones of the friendliest fellowship.

"We heard you were off colour, Lucy." The lack of feeling in his tone brought Beryl's spirits up with a bound.

"If you knew what I've suffered. My God! I've been at death's door."

"Jenny didn't say that in her telegram."

"What telegram?"

"Father Sladder's coming up here with his war-paint on. I thought I'd scurry on ahead and give you the tip. You had a row with Jenny, didn't you?" He lifted one eyebrow reprovingly. "Silly of you."

"If he thinks," Lucy said incoherently, "that I can run that office and be in bed at one and the same time . . . That man has a hide! He doesn't mind dumping people on me as cool as a cucumber, turning Jenny out of her room, no wonder she's upset . . . and what kind of a mess that office is in, I'd better go straight down. You sit here while I dress, Bleeby, and Shannon and Beryl can clear away the breakfast . . ."

"We don't want to impose on you any longer, Lucy," Beryl broke in. "If you don't mind, I think I'll get my things and find some other place to stay."

"Well!" Lucy was apparently overcome by rage. "If you're not the limit. I suppose you think this is some kind of orphans' home or hotel, or, maybe, you're so used to boarding-houses, you think you can just walk in and out . . . like . . . like . . . How dare you!"

"You'll be so occupied now Bleeby's back," Beryl replied, with a sticky sweetness, "that I don't suppose you'll be wanting us making a nuisance of ourselves." She turned on the startled Peverill. "If you think you can come holding my hand and telling me I'm psychic and practically *lure* me up here, so that I can wait on your lady friend, you're mistaken."

"Now weally, my dear girl," Bleeby remonstrated. "Calm down."

"You can do what you like," Lucy flared at Beryl. "You can go to Hell or go back to your boarding-house for all I care. I simply haven't the time to waste on you. But I *am* responsible for you and I can't have you running loose all over the city getting into trouble. I suppose I'd be blamed for *that* as well as the mess Jenny's made of the office. So understand that if you leave this place, I simply wash my hands of you. And now I must get dressed." She drew Bleeby after her into the bedroom and closed the door on Beryl's glare.

"I'm with you," Shannon declared. "Let's get out of here."

The tears had started to Beryl's eyes. "The Stephens' Murder people will get me a job. I'm not, I'm not going to put up with that beast of a woman. I'm going out to see the man they said wanted a girl."

"Me too."

"Who the Hell asked you to butt in?"

"If you think you're going to clear out and leave me here," Shannon had moved towards the bookshelves and was thoughtfully abstracting a few volumes that had taken her fancy, "you're wrong. We'll drop Aunt Edith a note later." She trotted into the spare room and began flinging their clothes impartially into the open suitcases. "Come on. Lend a hand."

"But you can't . . ." Beryl wiped away her tears and turned from her own troubles. "*You* can't just clear out."

"Too right I can." Shannon gave her a pleased smile. "Why, it's just what I've been brewing over all the week-end. Give me those pyjamas." She straightened her back and stood holding the pyjamas by one leg. "I don't fit in here. Any old place Sladder is in, I wouldn't fit. What I aim to do is just go on and on until I find some place where I *do* fit. That's sense, isn't it?"

"It's sense, all right," Beryl admitted, sitting down desolately on the side of the bed. "But you're not leaving anyone you . . . you like."

From the direction of the other bedroom, the high, clear, bell-like voice of Lucy could be heard giving Peverill hell. "A servant in a boarding-house!" she was saying. "Oh don't talk to me! After all I've done for you! If ever I was *bitterly* ashamed, it's to think you would lower yourself to a common, cheap . . ."

"Bleeby's getting it hot," Beryl muttered.

"Why worry about him?" Shannon's attitude to Bleeby lacked even the toleration which she had extended to the Wyandottes. She considered it would do Beryl good to get away from him, and the sooner the better. Contentedly she packed in the books from the sitting room.

Bleeby and Lucy were still arguing behind shut doors, as the two guests crept away rather more like escaping convicts than girls who had asserted their rights to life, love and the pursuit of happiness. It took several trips to get the stuff to the pavement; and while they were nervously counting over their money and wondering how much a taxi would charge to take Briscoe's hens to the Show-Ground, Bleeby and Lucy appeared on the footpath. Bleeby crossed over at once, leaving Lucy to walk on scornfully.

"Come now, Bewyl," he began in his most cajoling manner, "my dear girl, I can clear this all up in a minute if you'll only give me a chance to explain. What's the use of wushing off? You're leaving me in a Hell of a fix. What am I to say when Father Sladder awives with his blooming bwide? Just tell him you've left? No, it's not good enough." He gave her a warm glance. "I've got to have a talk with you, Bewyl, so you see you'd better tell me where I can find you."

"I'll give you a ring," Beryl muttered sullenly. She would probably have stayed talking on the corner until Peverill won her round, had not Shannon tugged her forward to a taxi. Bleeby handed in their luggage gallantly.

"You won't forget to wing?" he reminded them.

"No," Beryl called back. As Bleeby turned to rejoin Lucy, Beryl noted with the keenest pleasure something that had not been apparent while Lucy occupied the pink brocade bed. Lucy, well-dressed, well-corseted, was still too plump, while, below the waist, she was built on the dachshund model. And she had thick ankles.

Seven

I

THE ROYAL SHOW is to Sydney the ninth wonder of the world; to every other city on the Continent a harmless little foible to be indulged or laughed out of mind. The inhabitants of the Midway Madhouse pour out of their suburbs every year to wander in herds through great open spaces of trodden grass and asphalt; through temples of industry; displays of pumpkins, lucerne and cotton, machinery, cattle-sheds and "all the glorious increase of the land." The backyard bucolics come pouring out of brown trams that, crawling in procession, look like grubs swarming with ants. They beat thin brown tracks across the green of the park from the slums of Redfern and Surry Hills in the direction of the high brick walls that surround the show-ground.

Outside the turnstiles, vendors vie for custom, waving gilded cupie dolls on canes, dolls with skirts of tinsel of teased bright wool; balloons, green, yellow, red, great aery bunches of grapes; or whistles that, uncurling a long paper serpent, tickle the ear, not only with a shrill noise but with a bunch of green and purple feathers.

Once plunged in the tangled acres of pavilions and booths, the citizens straggle to and fro, buying samples of toothpaste and jam and breakfast food. Small children are tugged screaming by maddened mothers through the throng, have their mouths smeared with fairy-floss and clamour for more bags of samples. Father goes off to look at the hogs or the harvesting machinery, leaving mother and the crying children to seek him through all the stretched-out confusion until, just as they are giving up hope, he is found quite by accident calmly smoking and contemplating a wool press.

These little separate panics of meeting and parting are all included in the gate-money together with the dangerous herd excitement which overcomes the visitors to the Show. They pay and pay, for the wandering in company with the bellies and rumps and shoulders of thousands of their own kind pressed into them in a moving, anonymous embrace, in a continuous serpentine clogged mass of humanity, open-mouthed, stupefied, fretting, laughing, as it goes. They pay to get their feet trodden on, to lose

64

their money, to tramp miles over dirty grey pavements, to fail to find a seat in an exorbitant booth selling muddy-looking water flavoured with tea leaves and a soggy imitation of the city's staple food, the meat-pie. They come back year after year. Their children come back when they are grown up to do the same thing, to suffer the same boredom, the mud, the grey rain, the biting wind or broiling heat, whichever happens in a particular year to accompany the smell of manure and hot fairy-floss, the human waftures of sweat, the blaring music, the screams of the sellers and the shift-shift-shift of thousands of feet.

The aberration this year was attended on Good Friday by a sousing deluge of rain. Humble followers of the Trots or the Sheaf-tossing sheltered under newspapers in the lee of the grand-stand. Faint and dejected were the cries of the urgers in the side-shows. The flea circus stood glum and deserted; the African Pigmy came out in his imitation leopard skin to borrow a match from the phrenologist; the Living Skeleton complained of the cold to two girls from the Jazz Follies. The only person not affected by the rain was a sad-looking, white-coated individual who paced up and down by the turnstiles, wearing on his back a placard which asked in large red letters: "Where will you spend Eternity?"

Not that the crowd cared. What did it matter where you spent Eternity if this was the only day you had to spend at the Show? The Show had stolen Easter from Eternity's indignant representatives, the Churches, and turned it to the worship of the rainbow, of Something-for-Nothing, of the bubble-tinted fairy-floss that melts in the mouth leaving only a hot metallic taste, sweet with no substance. Why should not Eternity also be one great heaven of herd and blare and holiday?

Down grey lanes, the wet ran in gutters and systems of lakes, brimming into each other as they rose from mere holes in the asphalt to compass the width of each alley. Dirty water, splashing and dripping from the tent shows, seeped under the canvas, carrying bits of sodden paper, cigarette butts, empty cartons, silver paper, all trodden into a mud that splashed at ankles and soaked the shoes. The country people were busy seeing Sydney and most of the city rustics had stayed at home, so the Show people grumbled and swore. The celluloid propellers hardly stirred on the end of the long sticks; the gilded cupie dolls sheltered from the damp; the toy aeroplanes no longer swooped and swung. Hardly a squealer unfurled its paper serpent in a stranger's ear.

But the Roll-Down Table was not doing too badly despite the rain. That may have been because it had a projecting top under which the players could shelter while they rolled the billiard balls down the green felt into shallow cups, each numbered to give the player his total score. At the back of the booth glittering boxes of chocolates, tier upon tier, awaited the victor. Fifteen scored a box of chocolates, a small box; eighteen a bigger box; and twenty-four a very large box indeed, although it was seldom that anyone scored twenty-four. Beryl could do it almost every time; she had an uncanny knack that was invaluable when Bert, the owner, wanted to show anyone, an inquisitive sergeant for instance, that Roll-Down was a game of skill not of chance. Beryl and Shannon worked hard behind the Roll-Down tables, pushing back the balls, keeping the scores, arranging pools, calling in hesitating players. Bert, jumping around like a more energetic species of performing flea, was here, there and everywhere, shouting as he rushed about:

"Come on now. One more to make up the pool. Only a shilling! (Looks as though we'll have to lower it to six-pence.) One more? Right you are! All ready? Gentleman on the end, Mike." This was his name for Shannon. "Gentleman on the end with the highest score. No—here you are—lady with seventeen. Only a shilling. Take your places for the great game of skill. Every score above fifteen gets a prize."

Bert was of such a stout and enterprising nature that, marooned on an island, he would have had all the inhabitants working for him inside a month. He was fond of relating his first brilliant success: how with a couple of trestles and a pail of milk he had improvised a milk bar one very hot thirsty day while a procession was passing, and so great was the rush on his stand that he was presently selling the milky water the glasses had been washed in. Flabby, genial, with three fleshy wrinkles for a forehead, he had one principle in life and that was never to do anything that was not "worth his while." If it was worth his while to pass a pound note to a policeman or give away a race tip or a bottle of beer, Bert would do it with an air of magnificent generosity. But money must boomerang back to his hand or it never left it in the first place.

"In this world you've got to sting or get stung," he pointed out to Beryl. "Why, all you ever earn on the square wouldn't make rations for a flea circus."

Bert had decided on sight that Beryl was the girl he had been looking for. Her rowdy vitality and shrewd humour endeared her to him; but it would not have been worth his while to let his affections be seen, if she had not also possessed the knack of scoring twenty-four almost every time she handled the Roll-Down balls. Bert was busy persuading her to do the northern run with him after the Show finished; and Beryl, by a pretence of hesitation, made life a lot easier for herself and Shannon.

Towards evening Bert sent the two of them off to get a cup of tea when a friend of his, a competitor in the wood-chopping, dropped in and good-naturedly volunteered to help take the money and roll back the balls.

"Wancha to come round to Tim's when you shut tonight," he invited Bert. "How about the girls? Bring them too, why don't you?"

"That's what I like about this life," Beryl observed, as they pushed their way along. "Always meeting somebody new." Beryl had been salving her broken heart very successfully. She stopped to exchange a word with the owner of the Stephens' Murder and asked after the old lady's bad leg. "He's a great chap, Bert. Took a hundred and fifty pounds at Brighton last year."

They turned into a refreshment pavilion decorated to resemble the interior of Aladdin's treasure cave with coloured lights studded in the papier-mâché walls. Large imitation stalactites dripped from the ceiling; but despite these indications of cold the Treasure Pavilion was so hot and stuffy that it made the customer feel as though he were soaked in melted butter. The noise which came from the rear of the pavilion was tremendous. It sounded as though all the china in the world was sent smashing at regular intervals over a rocky torrent bed. Even before the waitress brought them a meat-pie that might have been constructed of sawdust and a pot full of anaemic tea, their appetite had been removed.

"Let's get out of this," Shannon groaned. She felt as though every separate piece of crockery flung about behind the canvas partition was crashing against the side of her head. Beryl was staring at the proprietor of the place who, from a vantage point by the door, was savagely watching every half-penny that went into the cash register.

"Why, if it isn't the boy friend!" she exclaimed. It was indeed the dark-visaged foreigner who had shared their carriage in the train from Melbourne. Beryl gave Shannon a nudge. "Do you know who he is? That's Litchin. He's got three tea-shops."

As he scowled in their direction, Beryl gave Mr. Litchin a bright, bright

D

smile and nodded. Mr. Litchin, after a moment's hesitation, reluctantly deserted his post and came over to greet them. He seemed gloomy and abstracted, but no gloom could deter Beryl.

"I don't suppose you've got a job for a good waitress," she suggested. "Here's my pal, with plenty of experience, smart as they come. How about it, Mr. Litchin?"

Mr. Litchin (he pronounced it Lishen with a good deal of saliva in it) indicated by a vigorous shake of the head that he would as soon purchase a horse with glanders as the young lady's services. He drew out a chair, sat down at their table and said rapidly: "No, no, no, she is too young, too young, a little tiny gur-rr-l who should be with mumma." He had formidable black eyebrows, wild grey eyes and looked as though he were always about to do something desperate and unpredictable. "She should be with mumma," he repeated, expanding his red mouth in a close-shaven blue chin and glaring at Shannon. She returned his look sturdily.

"I cannot pay you." His voice was a whining sing-song. "I am a poor man, a ruined man, betrayed. Look!" He suddenly rolled up his trouser leg. "I have no socks. You see? Very poor. I have holes in my shoes. I am ruined." Beryl and Shannon exchanged smiles. Mr. Litchin tried to look like a mournful wolf; he turned up his big eyes until only the whites showed, as though appealing to Heaven in his agony. "They laugh," he groaned. "Look at the li-tt-el gurrl laughing." Then he too began to laugh. "I am a funny man," he chuckled appreciatively. "I am funny, eh? All ladies love me. Efen little gurrls, rude, laffin' little gurrls."

"Take a tumble to yourself, uncle." Beryl slapped him on the shoulder. "You don't need to wear holes in your socks."

"I love you," Mr. Litchin declared fervently. "I haf loved you since I saw you in the train. Why don't *you* work for me, eh? Not her. You are beautiful and very clever, and we get on together, eh?"

"No chance." Beryl jerked her head at Shannon. "There's the girl for the job."

"For you I do anything." Mr. Litchin was enjoying himself in his so suddenly assumed ardour. There had been no trace of this fatal passion while he was watching the till, nor when he first saw Beryl and Shannon had he made any sign. "You are not only beautiful but seductif. I would give you clothes and good food so you are not skinny any more . . ."

"Hey, hey!" Beryl said indignantly, conscious of the smiles of several customers at near-by tables. "Now, take a pull at yourself. Take a pull."

Mr. Litchin's mood changed suddenly from amorous longing to annoyance. "You are impudent. You abuse me. I will not have her," he shouted.

"Oh, well," Beryl briskly gathered up her coat and handbag. "No harm done. 'Bye, Mr. Litchin."

"Where you goin'?" Joseph Litchin shouted after them. "Why do you do this? Does she not work for me?"

Beryl sighed. "I wish I hadn't started it," she said plaintively. "You don't tell us what the hours are, where the job is, or what the wages will be . . ."

"Wait! Wait!" He beat her words down with his hand, smacking the air as though he would force them back down her throat. "Is it you who are to pay me? No. If you do not like it, I say I am not to be forced. I am the master. I can prevail."

Shannon groaned. Joseph Litchin, she was to learn, could always talk people into a coma, hypnotising them with his alternations of extravagant self-pity and rage, until they were willing to agree to anything from sheer exhaustion.

"I will give you a pound a week and you can eat as much as you like at mid-day. Look! when I come to this country I am glad, glad if I can eat as much as I like. You are so lucky to work for me." He chuckled unpleasantly. "All ladies love me. Efen li-tt-el gur-rr-lls. Rude, laffin' li-tt-el gurrls."

"The least she can live on is thirty-five shillings," Beryl declared.

"You are mad," Mr. Litchin muttered scornfully. "Go from my sight. No, wait! You are alone, you and your friend. I am a kind man, a good man. I give you twenty-three and six-pence."

Beryl was annoyed. "Why didn't you say in the first place you didn't want anyone?" she snapped. "Come along, Shannon."

Part of the way back to the Roll-Down tent Shannon was busy telling Beryl what she thought of her for making them look a pair of fools. Then she began rehearsing a sketch of Mr. Litchin engaging a waitress.

"You are mad! you are mad!" she exclaimed rapidly. "I can prevail," and waggled her hands like Mr. Litchin. The two burst out laughing and on their return nearly sent Bert wild by flapping their hands at each other and giggling.

They were beginning to tire of the joke by the time darkness fell. The rain was now drumming down, slopping over the gutters, beating against the corrugated iron roofs of the pavilions with a steady roar.

Bert was disgusted. "Might as well shut up," he declared, "and go over to Tim's." He glanced out into the rain. "Who's your friend?"

Mr. Litchin was standing under the shelter of the Palace of Industry opposite and making frantic signs to Beryl who fronted him much in the manner of a ruffled kitten, as he advanced to the Roll-Down pitch.

"You clear out of here, see?" she commanded. "Trying to get people cheap as though they were some kind of cabbage."

"Plis!" Mr. Litchin raised his hand with a frozen dignity. "Not one word. I am not come to be insultit." He pushed a piece of dirty paper across to Shannon. "You will go there on Tuesday morning at half-past seven. Thirty shillings I pay. I am ruined but I have a kind heart." And he hurried away.

"He's balmy," Beryl said despairingly.

Shannon studied the address reflectively. "I don't mind mad people." If Mr. Litchin was mad, it was a form of lunacy profitable to himself.

They put up the shutters along the front of their booth and bolted them, turned off the lights, and made for Tim Brewster's.

II

Mr. Timothy Brewster, the junior partner of Littlewood, Brewster & Son, had been coming to the Show so long that the four-square bungalow where the firm displayed its wool-presses and harvesting machinery had become a combined parcels-office, lost-child deposit, news-exchange and club-room.

Tim Brewster had a little cubicle partitioned off in one corner between the harvesting machinery, and here his friends, when they felt the world was too much with them, would retire to rest their feet, brew cups of tea on Tim's gas-ring, and exchange the latest scandals. Tim never seemed eager to go home. He was a tired-looking little man whose hair had worn thin on top, and he had three horizontal worry wrinkles above his eyes. His wife was a member of many societies and she also produced pageants. Tim saw her between rehearsals, and his house was always cluttered up with people he did not know, so he preferred the office, or, in this case, his display room at the Show.

He had worried himself thin in the service of Littlewood, Brewster & Son, and was always secretly depressed that the firm might end in bankruptcy. For twenty years, during which he had done the work of three men, he had allowed himself to be patronised by his father, for what old Brewster called "lack of dash and guts," and by his wife for his fussing.

But at Show time, he had other things to worry about besides the office. At least six people came in free on his exhibitor's ticket, and he disapproved of anything dishonest, while he was far too kind-hearted to hurt his friends' feelings by hinting that this was so. Then there were all the other manufacturers' representatives dropping in to tell him their troubles, and tired wives of friends sitting about his office, while the children played about among the exhibits and kept Tim Brewster in a constant fret for fear they hurt themselves.

He had to wangle free samples of tea and cake and biscuits for his visitors; and to feed the people who called on Tim in a week would have taxed the resources of a zoo superintendent. He kept a stock of sweets for lost children, and the last words of any number of mothers, when plunging into a dense crowd, were always: "Now if we get separated, you go straight to Mr. Brewster's place."

Tim knew everyone from the President of the Royal Agricultural Society to Len Parsons who swept up the litter in the alleys and the old fellow who hawked cupie dolls at the gates. It was a wonder he ever found time to distribute the booklets on the care of reapers and binders which were his special pride, but he was always running out of supplies and sending frantic calls to the office for more. In his spare time he was to be found by the horticultural exhibits. Azaleas were his special passion, and one of his most dreadful crimes was that on several occasions he had gone down with a trowel to the Botanic Gardens, and with the help of a fellow azalea-lover, a priest with a big umbrella, he had pinned down several azalea shoots with hairpins until they rooted; and again, with the help of his ally and the big umbrella, had dug these furtive treasures from the ground and carried them away under his coat.

On the particular wet evening, when Bert, despairing of custom, had decided to drop in on him, he was deep in conference with the son of a seed merchant in a wholesale business, a young man who was not particularly interested in azaleas, but who wanted an advertisement for a magazine he was starting. He was a literary young man called Eddie

Quinlan, and he was quite willing to supply samples of his parent's azaleas in return for one advertisement.

With this unscrupulous couple was closeted old Brewster, the parent of Tim, who had come to the Show because it was his nature to be gregarious and social. At seventy, old Brewster, with his handsome, crumpled, old face and snow-white moustache, was so much more gay and debonair than his son, that the relationship seemed merely a clever joke at the expense of the public. If a gold mine was found, old Brewster would accept a seat as a director, without really troubling to enquire about the gold. Old Brewster was the first man an oil syndicate thought of when putting down a bore. He loved a gamble, was always shamelessly insolvent, and had just borrowed ten pounds from his son.

"You'll get it back, my boy, you'll certainly get it back," he assured him untruthfully, as he pocketed the money. "We certainly have a nice little place here." He turned and button-holed the young man with whom Tim was so anxious to talk azaleas. "I don't think I ever told you, Mr. Quinlan . . . it is Quinlan, isn't it? . . . about the time I was in France with the engineers. The tourists they used to call us . . ."

His son was able to excuse himself the hearing of this oft-told anecdote, for Bert was calling thunderously: "What-ho, Tim! Anyone home?"

Tim opened the door so that a stream of light fell among the harvesters, throwing their shadows like those of so many praying mantises along the wall. "Come on in," he welcomed. "Pleased to see you, Bert. And you brought the young ladies. Let me introduce Mr. Eddie Quinlan."

Mr. Quinlan was still in the grip of Tim's sire. Once he had started on a story, old Brewster's hold on it was as tenacious as that of his son on an azalea plant.

"Well, we were in this dump behind the lines and the blowflies were pretty bad, so I went up to H.Q. . . . How do, Bert, take a seat . . . I went up to H.Q. to see about some timber and wire netting for a meat-safe. When I found the chit they gave me could be altered, I . . . er . . . naturally altered it. Let the girls have the two boxes, Timmy, I'll sit on the sink. Well, we took two five-ton trucks to collect the stuff for that meat-safe and built a neat three-room bungalow with it. Old Bull Spence, who gave me the chit, happened to be inspecting a month later, and we did him rather well. After dinner, he lay back in his canvas chair and said: 'Of course, it's all very nice, boys, but where did it come from?' and I said

'Just some iron and timber we had over from building that meat-safe, sir.'" His eyes danced from one to the other mischievously. He might be seventy, but he was still as resourceful as ever, still appreciative of a pretty girl. "If that box isn't comfortable, Miss Hicks, you can always sit on my knee."

Shannon had plunged without waiting for the conclusion of the anecdote into a description of Beryl's new and ardent suitor. She gave them Mr. Litchin with his funny lisp and his waggling hands. Shannon's own special charm was not so much a matter of features, of figure, but of the extraordinary rapidity with which she could change her voice, her expression, her whole character. It was the charm of clear moving water, rippling and chuckling and twisting. When she was dull, her face grew as thunderous as the sea under a cliff; then it would suddenly light up and sparkle. Mr. Litchin had annoyed her; now, for revenge, she would turn Mr. Litchin into something grotesquely funny.

"You let Litchin alone," Beryl said, pretending to be cross at the laughter, and delighted by Bert's unfavourable reception of the story. "Uncle Litchin and me get on very nicely together."

"You heard what happened to Phil Saunders's wine bar?" Tim Brewster struck in. He was afraid his father might start on another anecdote and if it was the one about the Maori War, Bert's girls might not think it nice.

"Apropos of Miss Hicks looking for a job," old Colonel Brewster began simultaneously, "did I ever tell you about the time I'd come over flat-broke on a timber boat from New Zealand, and the doorman of a big engineering firm, when I tipped him my last half-crown, said to me: 'Well, I don't know who to see, but I'll tell you who to avoid'?"

"This wine-bar of Phil's," Tim went on, talking against his father. "I told him he'd made a mistake taking a pitch between a merry-go-round and the electric wax-works. They want to popularize their wine, Wilton's Wines, you know, free drinks and all that sort of thing. Phil, I said, you'll strike trouble . . ."

The young man who had come to argue Tim Brewster into an advertisement for his magazine found himself crouched on the floor between Miss Hicks and Miss McLaughlin, both of whom talked across him as though he were not there. He preferred Miss Hicks, because she was little and merry, not quite so overpowering as the blonde. He offered her a cigarette.

"Have you ever read Buckarin?" he asked earnestly. "You should."

"Phil Saunders had spent no end of money, but I was right. I saw him the other day and he was ready to throw up the sponge. 'It isn't the noise,' he said, 'Tim, it's the women.' Now don't think I mean this personally, Miss Hicks, Miss McLaughlin. 'You know, Tim,' he said, 'what women are. They get a few drinks in and turn nasty. You can't throw them out without a row and getting a bad name, and then they're sick, and you have to call the ambulance and shut the place . . . Oh a fine time, I've had . . .'"

"Business is bloody awful," Bert agreed.

Beryl leapt up, as the kettle boiled over with a hiss, and the tea was handed around with some difficulty in paper mugs that bore the stamp 'Setter's Biscuits, The Best.' In the process, Shannon spilt a good deal of it on Mr. Quinlan's beautiful grey suit and sponged it off with a grubby handkerchief and many apologies. She could see that the accident rather upset his good opinion of her.

It was snug in Tim Brewster's little office with the rain roaring on the iron roof and the cold wet seeping in in a clammy gust whenever they opened the door. They sipped their tea and gave old Brewster his head. He was in the middle of a long anecdote of his success in detecting the tricks of an Indian conjuror, when there was a muffled crash outside the door and the sound of someone falling.

Tim opened the door and called into the darkness: "Anyone there?"

A voice recognizable as the voice of Mr. Sladder called back: "Would you ask Miss Hicks if she would come out for a minute, please?"

Shannon and Beryl exchanged glances of alarm.

"Come right on in," Tim Brewster fussed. He was wondering where they were going to put this new visitor, for the little office was already as crowded as a sardine tin. "Any friend of Miss Hicks is welcome. Have a cup of tea?"

Neither his niece nor his wife's maid seemed ready to introduce him, so Mr. Sladder mentioned courteously, as he took Tim's box: "Sladder is the name, my dear sir, Vincent Sladder."

There was an awkward silence. Even Brewster Senior realized that there was something wrong.

"How did you know where to find us?" Beryl asked sharply.

"The superintendent of the poultry section was very helpful, and then

I have . . . ah . . . ways . . ." He accepted the paper mug Tim Brewster handed him. "This is very hospitable of you, sir, very," he said warmly. "Your health. I think I know a friend of yours, a Mr. Quinlan. I was happy to be able to rid him of a rheumatic complaint of the left hip."

"This is Eddie Quinan, his son."

The atmosphere seemed to warm a little and there was quite a round of introductions.

"Doctors, doctors," old Brewster grumbled. "Now, take me. Never had any good from a doctor in me life."

While Mr. Sladder was explaining that he was not a doctor, Mr. Quinlan created a diversion by taking out a series of snapshots and handing them round.

"Her name's Lolita," he said proudly. "Silly sort of a name, isn't it? But her grandmother would insist on it. Myself, I wanted to call her Lenina after Lenin, but there seemed to be no real enthusiasm for it."

"I should think not," Beryl exclaimed. "Saddling a baby with a name like that."

"This is her getting up the front steps." The photograph showed a large expanse of napkin and two fat legs.

"What a magnificent child!" Mr. Sladder said warmly.

"The pater spoils her," the child's father told them proudly. "Her grandmother spoils her. Now, the pater never took any notice of us, but he hangs round Lolita and shows her off. Of course," the young father admitted judicially, "she is a nice kid, but there's no sense in spoiling her. He takes her out in her little blue dress . . ."

"Talking about blue dresses," old Brewster had been shuffling the snapshots, like a desperate gambler looking for an extra ace, "did I ever tell you about Maori campaign, not the Maori War, when we marched from Openake to Parihaka?"

"My dear sir," Mr. Sladder cried enthusiastically, "you don't mean to say you were present on that historic occasion?"

Beryl and Shannon exchanged glances. Pop Sladder was out to be the life and soul of the party. What was his game anyway? He had fastened on the gathering like a leech.

"There was the Alexandra cavalry, fully forty of them, all armed with old curved swords and pistols. The artillery had old muzzle-loaders that must have come out of the Tower of London. And there was Colonel

Whitmore riding ahead through the mountains on a white horse like Napoleon, and the drum-and-fife band tootling through the defiles. We should have been massacred by all the rules. We ran out of food; it rained all the time, for three whole weeks, and the blue dye ran out of our uniforms and down into our boots . . . We were blue from head to foot . . ."

"Marvellous!" Mr. Sladder laughed heartily. "Marvellous."

"And as for surgical supplies," Old Bob Brewster smacked his lips reminiscently over the flavor of his anecdote, " 'The Auckland Herald' wrote a leader on them: 'The memorable expedition,' those were the exact words, 'the memorable expedition carried no surgical equipment other than two hundred-weight of Epsom salts, a supply more calculated to send men to the rear than to the front.' Oh, we ought to have been massacred, And," his voice rose triumphantly, "we got back with the prisoners and without firing a shot."

"That's a good one," Bert put in. "Medical supplies, huh!" He winked at Mr. Sladder. "These damn doctors take you down for all you've got."

"Talking of doctors," Mr. Quinlan interposed. "Fifty quid it cost for Lolita. Not that she isn't worth it, but under a decent system we'd all have doctors free."

"They have this Hippocratic oath," Mr. Sladder explained smoothly.

"Aesculapian," from Colonel Brewster.

"This oath, my dear sir, about never allowing anyone else to make any money. What happens," Mr. Sladder's voice took on the deep, noble tone he used for lecturing, "what happens to any forward-looking pioneer with vision such as myself? A man who uses new methods and scientific principles? What happens to you when you try to do a little good? The B.M.A. interferes. That's what they're there for. It's criminal that these medical sharks should be waiting about sneering down their noses like the mummied cats the Egyptians worshipped."

Shannon stood up. "I think we must be going," she said abruptly.

There was a little stir at their departure. Mr. Sladder, it was plain, was reluctant to leave this congenial gathering. Mr. Quinlan also looked dejected; he was beginning to like Shannon who had displayed a proper appreciation of the snapshots of Lolita.

"Don't you come, Bert," Beryl commanded.

Beryl, Shannon and Mr. Sladder found themselves outside under a sky from which the clouds had rolled off in ragged grey patches revealing the stars.

"A most changeable climate," Mr. Sladder observed. "Summer vestments in the morning and two overcoats in the afternoon." He hummed to himself under his breath in what seemed the best of humours. "Your aunt has been very distressed," he observed presently, as though he were pointing out that tomorrow might be fine. "She says you are to come home with me." There was no answer. "On the other hand, if I gave you your fare to Kerleuit, I could put you on the train, or I could," he reflectively eyed a lamp around which two moths were flitting, as though he wondered where they came from in this wet weather, "I could ask the police to take you in charge as uncontrollable."

"You don't seem too keen on the police yourself," Beryl observed.

"What was that?" Mr. Sladder asked sharply. Then he resumed his geniality. "You're mistaken, Beryl. I have the greatest respect for our force."

"Not from what Lucy said."

"Lucy is no longer in my employ." Mr. Sladder resumed his humming, but there was a note of aggravation in it. Presently he stopped and addressed himself to Beryl. "Have some common-sense," he said plaintively. "People come to you and practically force you to take the money. We'll admit there's a law against what they want you to do. But when they come to you and beg you to take the money . . ." He was silent, shaking his head as though he were arguing with himself. "Lucy had no right to say anything about that side of the business. It would not concern you." He sighed. "It would be quite all right too if it wasn't for the ten per cent who die on you. The trouble is to avoid that ten per cent. You find these cases," he flung out his hands, as though to appeal to the two silent listeners, "you find these cases. Either half-starved or something wrong somewhere, and they deliberately deceive you by looking healthy. Why a colleague of mine had a woman die on him in exactly nine minutes, and he got five years. Five years for trying to do a kindness, and not even the sense to get his fee in advance."

"Well, look, pop," Beryl said shrewdly, "we'll do a deal with you. You let us alone, and we'll let you alone. Can't say fairer than that?"

"But dear me, Beryl," Mr. Sladder sounded shocked, "what would my wife say? You must remember," he shook his head severely, "you and Shannon are only young, inexperienced girls. You mustn't expect people to let you go about unprotected, falling into bad company. You might get into serious trouble." Again he shook his head. "Why where would we be, if everyone expected to do just what he liked, go where he liked, and as he liked? We are living in a civilized age," he glanced at them disapprovingly, "and you can't go running round like savages. Besides, look at the splendid opportunities that you would have as members of my staff . . ."

"You've just told us, pop," Beryl reminded him, "that if the cops catch up on you, you'll be lining a cell."

Mr. Sladder hummed to himself, as he considered this for a minute. "Well, well," he said genially, "all this is rather sudden. I don't like to remind you that I paid your fare up here on the understanding that you were my employees. However . . ." A beaming smile overspread his face. "I see I can do no good, and you are set on going your own way. You don't mind if I don't come with you any farther? I think that's my tram. Shannon," he called over his shoulder, "be sure and write to your dear aunt, and if you would ever like . . ." His voice lapsed into an unintelligible mumble, as he began to run towards the tram stop.

Beryl and Shannon stood for a minute looking after him.

"Why, the louse!" Beryl exclaimed. "He's glad to get rid of us. What do you know about that?"

Shannon did a little dance of relief and excitement. "I'm so glad," she exclaimed exultantly. "I like this city. You can go off with Bert if you want to, but me," she took a long breath, "I'm going to lift the lid off this town."

"You'll see," Beryl said gloomily. "You'll soon change your tune."

Eight

I

Mr. Litchin found an emotional luxury in having so many women working for him. Whenever he descended on the Pompadour Cafe, the manageress had hysterics and usually one or other of the girls as well. He was always sacking someone and taking her back with a great waving of arms and shouting. Every time Mr. Litchin appeared, the girls hated him worse, and Mr. Litchin, quite obviously relishing his power, sacked people left and right, took them on again, and rolled in his own emotions like a dog who has found a particularly odorous and enjoyable patch in the road.

Days at the Pompadour were spent in a rush of orders, carrying loaded trays in a crowded space full of the stir and departure of customers, the ting of the till, the babble of voices. The air was heavy with the smell of coffee, hot toast, meat pies and other of the cheaper forms of edibles. The Pompadour was a pitcher-plant to entrap the suburban flies who liked to combine a cheap afternoon tea or lunch with an atmosphere of what they believed to be luxury. Hence the mirrors lining the walls and giving a spurious air of spaciousness, the soft upholstery of the chairs into which fat women with tight shoes sank with a sigh of relief. Although there were many panels of mirror, the lights were not bright. No need to let the customers see how they really looked. Better to flatter them with a "cosy" atmosphere and save overhead on the electric light bill. The afternoon tea trade was a good business proposition. Women on shopping expeditions would pay a shilling for a "dainty" afternoon tea: two microscopic scones and a pot guaranteed to contain exactly one and a half cups of liquid. They were paying, not for the tea, but for the mirrors, the vases of flowers, the chairs upholstered in tapestry, the hum of chattering strangers around them, for release from their natural state, shut away in their little separate houses, in their own petty worries.

Behind the swing doors in the kitchen, grey, cement-floored and infested with black beetles, the staff led a life of exasperating bickering. Over-

79

worked, underpaid, their most constant grouch was the boss and all his ways; but there were other disadvantages: the heavy, unmanageable swing door which must be pushed open with a loaded tray, three troublesome steps, the inconvenience of the kitchen where everyone trod on everyone else, the complaints about the service, the scarcity of forks and china which kept the kitchen staff frantically washing up all the time. There was raised blood-pressure and high voices over the roster. They worked a broken time arranged by Mr. Litchin. No one understood the roster, least of all Mr. Litchin, but he stood by it as his brain child and fought for it with outrageous insistence. Shannon, although she lived close by to save fares, often had only time between shifts to hurry to her lodgings, wash her spare uniform, starch it, and rush back to the Pompadour. Mr. Litchin's other serfs were in the same plight.

"He says to me," one waitress would complain to another, " 'Well you're off from half-past eleven till four.' That's no good to me, I says. Why it takes me over half an hour to get home and another to get back."

"He ought to be taken to court."

"But you can't get him there, Dulcie, that's the whole trouble."

Such exchanges formed half the conversational stock of the Pompadour. Little wonder that the waitresses adopted to the customers an attitude of savage politeness, a grim, reluctant attention. They hated the customers because Mr. Litchin liked them. And, indeed, the type of bargain-hunting womanhood most given to frequenting the Pompadour was not endearing, particularly on a hot, stuffy Friday afternoon, when they swarmed in from the suburbs to gape and spend, gape and spend, like goldfish finning between the great plate glass windows of the big stores. Hell, for these, was an eternity of looking in windows with no money. Heaven, a bargain counter where you could buy and buy for the joy of buying. They had been beaten on the head by advertisers until they were crazy to buy. They came into the Pompadour shedding brown paper parcels and complaining how exhausted they were. Little wonder that a waitress with aching feet should adopt a somewhat aloof air when she asked: "Has your order been taken, Madam?"

"No it hasn't, and I've been waiting here for ten minutes. I've a good mind to complain."

The centre, the core of the city, was built up around these women and their conviction that social status was judged by "nice things"; their will-less, avid snapping at every baiting, their spending of money as a pleasure in itself. Layer on layer the great buildings towered up. Floor above floor. "See our ground-floor bargain counter: Sports' suggestions. Second floor: Ladies' millinery, corsets, hosiery, beauty salon. Third floor: Underwear, shoes, handbags, perfume, manicure sets, confectionery, cut glass, china." Everything from guitars to tinned soup, from radio sets to pot plants, waiting for somebody to buy. To be in a city roaring like a great beast, with the hunger to buy is a soul-searing experience for those who have no money.

Shannon worked twice as hard as the others, grateful to Mr. Litchin for giving her work and desperately afraid she might lose it. Occasionally Mr. Litchin cast a scowl in her direction or discussed her in an undertone with the manageress who, while she might find fault enough while Mr. Litchin was not there, always grudgingly told him that the girl was "not bad." The haunting fear of being out of work preyed on Shannon's mind. It was impossible to save any money, even to buy clothes. The other girls seemed to manage it, but they had families to fall back on and could afford to be independent. Her greatest fear was that she should fall sick. Sometimes she felt very weak, but that might be due to a breakfast of tea and a slice of toast. Lunch for her at the cafe was often coffee and another slice of toast. She hardly ever felt like eating there. The manageress kept a sharp eye on the food; and left-over curry or stale scones and meat pies were good enough for the staff.

II

Ginevra House was a tall, dim set of lodgings, four stories high, approached from the street through a tiny patch of what had been front garden before Mr. Knowles took charge. He left the running of the house to his wife and daughter-in-law; but his own exuberant fancy had run riot in front of the house, so that strangers often stopped to stare at such a display in a busy city street. The path had been chastely decorated with beer-bottle tops set neck downwards on each side of the gravel. Instead of flower beds, patterns made of chips of coloured glass showed, on one side a Union Jack, and on the other a rising sun flanked by a kangaroo and emu. Near the gate was a showcase containing specimens of Mr. Knowles' work as a maker of vases and ornaments. This he did by encasing bottles in a coat of plaster, gilding the same and sticking pieces of broken glass in the resultant horror. He also displayed boxes, gilded and incrusted with imitation roses, and a modest notice: "J. Knowles, Artistic Gilding. Orders Executed."

Few orders came his way, so that he had plenty of time to potter about in the underground flat which served as home for his wife, his daughter-in-law and his son, a dim place where the electric light burned on even the brightest days; or tend the ferns in a dirty little fernhouse in the back courtyard, which served as a club and gathering place for all the mosquitoes in the city. Whenever they heard human meat approaching, they would fling themselves on it with humming enjoyment, rising from the green whiskers of fern as from an ambush.

"Nice little place," Mr. Knowles hinted, showing the new lodger his fernery. "Come and sit here sometimes if you like."

His voice was husky, his eye very watery, and his nose red, for Mr. Knowles, needing empty bottles for the exercise of his art, always procured them full and emptied them himself. He wheezed about the cobbled courtyard to the rear of Ginevra House, making a feeble pretence of usefulness by sweeping at the husks which dropped from a clump of bamboo by the back entrance, a bamboo that had manners as untidy as those of a feeding draught horse. It blew and clattered when there was no noticeable wind and strewed its litter even in the street.

"Nice to have a bit of tree," Mr. Knowles declared.

Mrs. Knowles, a stout, white-haired, old lady, was very proud of her husband and his artistic temperament.

"Not that I haven't had trouble with him, Miss Hicks. There was once when he'd had a few and he lay down in the road and refused to get up. His was always a very obstinate family. When I tried to lift him, he took a swing at me with his stick. A policeman come up and he said: 'You'd better take him home, Madam. I'll get him into a taxi.' But do you know he wouldn't get into that taxi." Mrs. Knowles' voice was full of pride. "The only way the policeman could make him was by saying he'd take him to Newcastle in it. He'd always wanted to go to Newcastle. 'Now you promise,' he says solemn to the policeman, 'if I get into the taxi, you'll take me to Newcastle.' But, of course, he didn't, he brought him right home, and, oh! wasn't I grateful to him! And didn't Dad kick up a fuss about it! 'I'd never have got up out of the road,' he said, 'if I'd known I was dealing with a liar. If there's one thing I can't stand, it's a liar, and I'm through with him and the whole police force.' That's the kind of man he is, very stubborn."

Old Mrs. Knowles, who left the work of the house to her daughter-in-law, whom she despised, for a poor frightened creature with no spirit to her, could always find time for a little chat on the stairs with her lodgers. She was as persistent as a mosquito, and her talk was inevitably of Mr. Knowles, her son, the Reverend Dr. Maurice Knowles, or her husband's family, and particularly of their aristocratic, stubborn spirit.

"Mr. Knowles' sister was the same." The old lady attached herself to her hearer by clutching the arm leechlike. "She was out at Gladesville Asylum, and many the time I've said to her: 'Oh, Annie—Annie was her name— if you'd only do what I say, darling, you could come home right away.' I remember she came out to our place for the day once, and I says to her: 'Annie, if you'll only pick up that dish-cloth, you need never go back to that awful place. Now, *do* dear,' I'd say, 'just pick up the dish-cloth.' No, she wouldn't. While she was there, they'd never get a word out of her. She just wouldn't speak to them. She wouldn't speak to anybody, not if you dragged her by the hair."

There were times when the lodgers fervently wished that the same pride restrained Mrs. Knowles.

"Then there was Ella, my daughter, and it was that man drove her to it. If ever there was a man that Hell gaped for it was him! And she was always so fashionable! She reads an article in the papers about people jumping over the Gap, and sure enough, Oh Lord! to think of it! She goes right out to the Gap and jumps over, she did. She jumped over. It catches my breath when I remember the poor girl."

It was a pleasure to get out into the street away from Mrs. Knowles; to hear the trams roaring past; and the rain dripping down on the pavements, turning them to a shining blackish grey; and the lawyers scurrying along to the Law Courts in their rusty gowns, with newspapers or umbrellas held over the rats' nests of horsehair perched atop their heads like some forgotten Christmas favour.

Ginevra House had been repudiated by these gentry as too ramshackle for offices, and it was only waiting for certain trustees, certain of those dusty-looking lawyers with papers, to make up their minds when it should be pulled down. Behind it, in Macquarie Street, lurked the doctors; all around the lawyers and the roar of trucks and presses from the newspaper offices; while ahead lay Mr. Knowles' favourite hotel; with only the little, green spire of St. James around the corner to point Ginevra House to a better world.

The Knowles family had been sorry for their little lodger and quite decided to make her one of the family. "But she slips in and out," Mrs. Knowles would complain, "and I can't be always up and down stairs. She ought to know some nice man to take her about." This motherly interest was sometimes hard to avoid.

The lodgers showed no such friendliness. They were wrapped in their own troubles as in a blanket of thorns. An elderly woman on the back landing had a cancer which she tried to convince herself would respond to patent medicines. She grew every month more shrivelled and gruesome. A young couple who had come to the city looking for work had an ailing baby and never enough to eat, which made them bad-tempered and quarrelsome with each other.

There was one lodger who quickened Shannon's interest. His name was Mervyn Leggatt and he worked as a clerk in the post office, always dressed neatly, with a stiff, white collar, glossy boots and pince-nez glasses. But this outward neatness and stiffness was contradicted by a gloomy, rather savage air, and a harsh, resonant voice.

"He's real clever," Mrs. Knowles told Shannon. "He's doing an economics course at night and he thinks very hard. Takes it all out of you this thinking does. But he's clever all right, nearly as clever as my Morry." Mrs. Knowles' son, Morry, was away being "cared for," but Shannon had heard all about him.

The forbidding austerity of Mervyn Leggatt froze any attempt at conversation. It is impossible to stop a man on the landing and ask him to talk to you, when he is quietly and seriously going about important business. If Mervyn Leggatt was only washing a pair of socks in the hand-basin in the bathroom, he did it with the savage desperation due to the last pair of socks in the world.

"I'd like to talk to him," Shannon thought wistfully. She had no one to talk to except Mrs. Knowles for, at the Pompadour Cafe, when not discussing the boss, the staff talked horses and exchanged racing tips. The months went past, and the crowds on Saturday afternoon went to football matches instead of cricket, but she had still found no opportunity of breaking through her fellow lodger's stern preoccupation with his mysterious and momentous affairs.

However, three young men called Jackson had taken the first floor front and were only too willing to relieve her loneliness. They showed her all the accomplishments of practised lodgers: how to coax the most out of the gas-ring for the least money, and where she should go for fish and chips. ("It's dirtier than the other shops, but you get more chips.")

Of the Jacksons, Doug, the eldest, was a waiter; Ashton was temporarily resting from his labours in the chorus of "The Frilly Follies"; while Bart, the youngest, rested, it seemed eternally, a dead weight on the shoulders of his brothers. They were trying to get him into the police force, but Bart was six-foot-two, clumsy, good-natured and timorous. His chest was an inch under the regulation measurement, but his brothers daily hounded him through the exercises to acquire the extra inch and the place in the Force.

"If you think I'm going to support a lazy, big bastard like you forever," Doug snarled at him over the fish and chips they shared with Shannon, "you're mistaken."

"I want to be an artist," Bart whined.

"Well get to Hell out of this and be an artist, but if I have any say," he waved a piece of fish menacingly, "you'll be a cop."

Bart appealed to Shannon. "I'm scared of the traffic."

"You'll get used to it," Shannon consoled him. She took a firm tone with Bart because his brothers did.

Bart lapsed into a large, unhappy silence which was his only retreat when his two brothers yapped round him like fox-terriers tormenting a blood-hound. One morning, on hearing a tremendous crash, Shannon had run to the window to see Douglas lying in the courtyard more surprised than hurt. A few minutes before he had been out on a little balcony urging his brother to practise with the boxing gloves. "Go on, hit me," he implored. "At least try to hit me." And with one clumsy swipe Bart had knocked him backwards over the balcony rail. On seeing what he had done and hearing Douglas pounding upstairs for vengeance, Bart had fled and was away all day.

Ashton gave Shannon racing tips, which caused her an immediate return to favour with the staff of the Pompadour, where she had been regarded, from her hard-working habits, as a "boss's pet," or possibly a spy on them. But even with the Jacksons she was still dreadfully lonely.

She would take solitary walks, strolling unmolested through places where well-brought-up young ladies would have thought twice before going with an escort. She was particularly fond of the Domain by night. Here were great avenues of Moreton Bay figs; great bulks cold as stone with loose-wrinkled grey skin for bark and roots that went powerfully twisting down into the earth like an elephant's trunk. At night they were full of birds fighting and screaming harshly over the red-brown fruit that strollers trod underfoot into a pulpy mess on the footpath. When the Southerly blew, the stiff leaves of the great trees twisted rim-on to the blast and roared all together, straining away from it, while, on a sunny afternoon, their undersides glanced like a shoal of silver fish against the blue sky and racing clouds. By Rushcutter's Bay the footsteps of the water went faltering, drunkenly, up and down a stone wall, and the little boats at anchor made a sipping noise, as if they were all drinking like cattle, gulping the night tide, dipping their noses into the black sea as into a great gulf of black wine and belching and sucking it under their bows.

Shannon came to know as friends the spires of the stone churches going up above the green trees, the parks with bird-bespattered bronzes; the skyline jagged with roof tops; the terrace houses in folds like a concertina; sharp steep streets; little steps leading down shabbily. All these became as familiar as the figure of Mr. Knowles going out to collect the morning paper and bring in the milk.

With no friends, the city became her friend; the water that had always light in it; and the starry city glowing through the night; hills above green-leafed streets; houses with their curtains folded like tired feathers drowsing one against the other; the strange, lonely city that was itself and no other, a place unique and unmistakeable, a hive of lights and noises, seemed to lull its noises as she passed and know her.

It was a half-unwelcome interruption of her narrow life when Mrs. Knowles appeared wheezing at the door one Sunday evening and invited her to tea, a special tea to celebrate the homecoming of Morry. Shannon had seen the Reverend Dr. Knowles, that was how he styled himself, and she had not been impressed. He wore clerical garb, had thick blubber lips, thick glasses, and a grating laugh. From some strange source he had acquired a Scotch accent so thick that it made his speech even more unintelligible than it might otherwise have been. His gutturals squelched like big boots in the mud, and to hear him sing "Annie Laurie," as she had been compelled to do once before, was to plumb the depths of noise.

But it was a miserable afternoon, the gutters running and the bamboo dripping, the broken water spout grizzling to itself beside her window.

"I might later, perhaps," she hesitated, "but I can't stay long."

"Now, you come along, love." Her landlady laid a clammy hand on her own. "Tonight's something special. I've invited Mr. Poate specially to meet you, and he'll be disappointed if you're not there. Oh Lord! won't he be disappointed!"

Shannon was about to ask who Mr. Poate might be, but Mrs. Knowles flowed on without giving her the opportunity. "There's a bit of cold pork and some stout, because Morry likes it, and it'ull fatten you up. That's what I say to Essie." Essie was the unfortunate daughter-in-law. "You want a bit of fattening up, I says, with Morry coming home. They like them fat, men do. And when you meet Mr. Poate, I want you to be nice to him, see?" She winked knowingly. "Put on the pretty dress with the blue spots, and let's see you brisk up a bit. Times I think, to look at you, that you might go out and go over the Gap like Ella. So you come on down and have a good time. You want to while you're young."

"I don't think I can come, Mrs. Knowles." Shannon began to feel uncomfortable about this very special invitation. "Really, I have to go out."

"Now you come along," her landlady commanded. "This Mr. Poate is a man that might do Morry a bit of good, and work him in on a good thing. No reason why he shouldn't do you a bit of good too, is there?" With another series of winks and nudges and smiles, Mrs. Knowles turned away to negotiate the stairs. "Mind," she warned in a scream from half-way down, "we're expecting you now."

Shannon waited until a few minutes to six o'clock before she descended to the basement and was welcomed into the tiny dining-room where the table was already laid with the stout and pork, a dish of tomatoes sliced in vinegar, another dish of onions sliced in vinegar, a dish of lettuce, and a great deal of bread and cake.

"Ah! the bloom of the brae," Dr. Maurice Knowles bleated at her, giving her a salutation at once patronizing and pontifical. "Ah, ye're a bonny wee thing," he boomed playfully. And turning to his wife he patted her hand. "Is she no a bonny wee thing, ma luv?" he asked. "Is she no' a bonny wee thing?" His wife gave a timid nod and seemed to shrink away from him. He was not a prepossessing creature, with his huge thick-soled boots and awkwardly-cut coat, from the sleeves of which splay hands hung like the paws of a gorilla. One of these hands he now employed in twisting a strand of his wife's hair, while the other he placed amorously around her waist.

"That's it, Morry," his mother encouraged. "You be happy while you're young." She led her lodger to Mr. Poate with the air of one who has brought on a tasty dish for tea. "Now you two get to know each other." She nudged Shannon into a chair so narrow that she was squeezed against Mr. Poate in a way she found very little to her liking.

Mr. Poate was dressed in a manner far too sprightly for his years. His false teeth were like a nosegay in his face, festive, but hardly belonging between those wrinkled jaws. They seemed to be loose, for he worked them about in a perpetual smile. He cackled at Shannon that Sydney was a big place, wasn't it? Came from Melbourne, did she? See much of the city? Couldn't he take her out somewhere? Go and have a bit of lunch? See a few of the sights, eh?

After each enquiry Mr. Poate would give a little cackle and squeeze her arm. Shannon, under the eye of the watchful Mrs. Knowles, was hysterically gay and charming, but she was pleased when a shifting of chairs to the tea-table allowed her to slip away from him. She was instantly replaced by Mrs. Knowles who insisted that "the young people sit together."

The tea-table conversation was fortunately dominated by old Mr. Knowles who was carrying on a theological dispute with his son. The argument had reached the stage when the solar system had been dragged in to support the argument of Mr. Knowles senior.

"They'd only stir it one way," Mr. Knowles said gravely. "Now, if you was stirring a pudding or a cake, you'd only stir it one way, wouldn't you, mother? Well, a law like that holds good for everything, don't it? That shows that however far you went, it would only be stirred one way."

"But suppose it wasn't?" Shannon asked for something to say, and to keep the conversation going, for Knowles junior was absorbed in his eating. He ate ravenously, with an active slobbering, tearing apart with his hands and conveying to his mouth such morsels as he found unmanageable by fork, while he sideways watched his wife with a wistful greed and cunning as if to say: "Yes, I know, I know it makes you sick to see me. But that doesn't affect the food. I must get as much of that as I can."

"Suppose it wasn't stirred one way?" Shannon contended.

"It would explode," Mr. Knowles said severely, "or curdle or come to a bad end some way. No, you got to admit that she's *only stirred one way*."

"But there might be bubbles spinning around?"

"There might," Mr. Knowles admitted, with scientific impartiality. "But we don't know, see? And that being so, so we can't say."

His son gulped down the last of the tomato with a strangling sound and began untucking the serviette which he wore round his clerical collar like a bib.

"Above all yeer speculation, feyther," he pronounced sententiously, "there is the Wurrd." His was the simple reproof of the Minister, the majestic pronouncement of the Man of God.

"That's so, my boy, that's so," his father agreed humbly. He waited to hear more from his gifted son, but the Reverend Dr. Knowles had reached for the cake. He had reverted from the Minister of the kail-yard school, the thick-booted sturdy Scot with his feet on the earth and his head in the heavens, and had become all kail-yard.

It was his mother who adopted the languished conversation and nourished it with some strong observations on a long-vanished lodger.

"I went to see her in hospital and she says: 'My! what nice firm arms you've got.' She kept on saying it, and one day I see her arm, poor woman. It quite turned me over. Without a word of a lie, it was a stick with a claw at the end of it. She'd lie there and cry by the hour and tell me about her home and the curtains on the window. 'But I won't be going back there,' she'd say. 'I won't ever leave here.' 'Why, of course, you will,' I'd say to cheer her up. 'Do you think so?' she'd say, and be brighter for a while. Poor woman! And her husband coming night and day to give her anything. 'I don't want to die,' she'd say. 'Oh! I don't want to die.' "

The bells of the churches began to ring very appositely in the gloom which descended on the table during Mrs. Knowles' long-drawn description of the young woman's last hours. A sharp nudge from old Mr. Knowles, who had marked the sudden loss of appetite on Mr. Poate's part, recalled to their hostess that she might be spoiling their son's prospects and she fell silent. Shannon insisted that she should wash up, when Mrs. Knowles proposed that, despite the rain, Mr. Poate and their lodger take a little walk, but Mr. Poate cackled out that he was, as churchwarden, expected at divine service. Perhaps next Sunday afternoon he might take Miss Hicks to see some **of** the sights? The Knowles family turned such a concentrated gaze on Miss Hicks that she stammered out her pleasure and thanks. As soon as Mr. Poate was gone, they drew in to the table and, almost disregarding her, began a family post mortem of the party.

"If ye'd only shut yeer gob, feyther," his son complained. "Yammering there as ye weer." He turned on his mother. "And ye'd no more sense than to go maundering on about dying and he with the rheumatism. Didna I tell ye that he's got the money and it'd be a g-rr-an-d opportunity for me? He's the guardian of the boy, and he needna get him a tutor, but send him to school."

"I think, if you'll excuse me," Shannon broke in desperately, "I'll run along now."

"Noo, dinna hurry," Knowles junior became the Dominie addressing the Flower of the Brae. "Before ye gang along there's a wee little bit paper I'd give ye." He fished clumsily in his pocket and with much labour extracted some pasteboard slips wrapped in tissue paper. "I always carry ma carrd," he explained simply, "so that if I should be taken wi' one of my fits, they'll know where to send me."

"Maurice!" his wife burst out desperately. "Really!"

The card read: Rev. Dr. Maurice Knowles, M.A., D.D., LL.D., F.E.B., Ginevra House, Sydney.

"What does the F.E.B. stand for, Dr. Knowles?" Shannon asked.

"Fellow of the Education Board," Dr. Knowles told her, rubbing his hands complacently. Shannon was too polite to point out that, as far as she knew, there was no such board.

"So if ye heer o' anyone wanting a tutor, ma bonny wee flower, or a mon to take charge o' theer affairs, ye'll just tell them of Dr. Knowles and his letters and show them that wee bit cardboard." He reverted to the Minister. "But 'tis no the letters. That's but wardly. In the kirk, shud I get ma pulpit—and 'tis the warrk of the deil I ha' no got one—'tis no the letters that count." He drew himself up. " 'Tis the Warrd."

"Lord! Morry, it's a treat to hear you," his mother cried, as she conducted her lodger to the door. "All he needs is the chance." She clutched her visitor imploringly. "You won't go being nasty to Mr. Poate, will you, love? Just be a bit nice to him for my sake."

The girl felt a strange spasm of pity for the old woman beseeching help for her monster.

"I'll try," she said, but as she climbed the stairs, she felt herself shaking with revulsion, so that she paused and pressed against the wall. "Oh!" she said softly to herself. "I wonder if there's anywhere where people are clean?" She started forward again as she heard Mervyn Leggatt open his door. He passed her with his usual nod and she felt by his mere passing that she herself was somehow too low for notice.

III

However, when she came to retail her encounter with Mr. Poate to the Jacksons, she was feeling in a very different mood, flippant and grim and gay. She gave them a magnificent imitation of Mr. Poate amorously working his false teeth around his mouth.

"Did he say he was going to take you to lunch?" Bart asked hungrily.

"You know that Knowles woman is nothing better than a procuress," Ashton observed, arranging his feet on the table and settling down with his sporting news. "That looney son with all those fake degrees never saw the inside of a university."

"What's a procuress?"

Ashton clicked his teeth regretfully at her ignorance. "She finds girls for men," he answered shortly. "Has the cove got any money?"

"He had very nice clothes."

"What you need," Ashton sat up again, struck by an inspiration, "is brothers. A set of brothers."

"If he was taking you to lunch," Bart chimed in wolfishly, "you might work us in somewhere."

"String him along, kid," Douglas encouraged, illumined by the vision of unlimited free feeding. "We're with you."

Mr. Poate's temper, not to mention his pocket, was sorely tried by this influx of relatives. Shannon's brothers met her accidentally every time she and Mr. Poate went out together. There was always one or other brother cruising about with the eye of a hungry gull and an appetite to match. Occasionally Mr. Poate might manage to snatch a chaste kiss, if his little companion was not quick enough to dodge it, but after three week-ends of expensive sight-seeing, that was absolutely all he had snatched. He had paid fares for harbour trips, tram fares, admission money to surf pavilions, money for ice-creams and lunch and lemonade and chocolates. He was beginning to work his false teeth with an annoyed clicking noise.

When Douglas during their last little outing together had suggested that they separate for a few minutes, Mr. Poate had ostentatiously fished out a supply of pennies and distributed them all round. Shannon, her sense of humour budding, admitted to herself that for once Mr. Poate had scored. There were times when she felt almost sorry for his being such a devil and getting nowhere. But he would insist on treating her as a sweet little thing with the dew on her, and playing up to the part of a sweet little thing was a trial.

"What is little Fuzzy thinking of in that curly little head, eh?" Mr. Poate asked coyly, as they sat looking at the harbour. It was a beautiful sunny afternoon with the white sails of sixteen- and eighteen-footers sliding across a smacking green expanse of waves.

"I was thinking how pretty," little Fuzzy simpered. She really had been wondering when he would try to put his arm round her waist again. Sure enough, Mr. Poate, like an aged, meditative boa-constrictor, was cautiously sliding out his arm. "Why here comes Ashton!" she cried with gay surprise, and jumped up quickly.

"You'll have to kid him a bit, sis," Douglas advised that night. "He's getting fed up."

"Not as fed up as I am," Shannon pointed out. It was all very well for the Jacksons. They didn't wake up in the night and lie hardly daring to breathe because they thought Mr. Poate was outside their door.

Mr. Poate ambushed Shannon outside the Pompadour one evening and doddered along beside her, finally cackling out a proposition that they should have a little party, just the two of them, eh? That night in her room? No need to bring in any brothers. Shannon's sweet innocence was so thick and sticky that she could hardly be made to understand what he meant. How about him bringing up some champagne, eh?

"Tell him to leave the champagne in the hallstand," Douglas advised. "No sense wasting it."

But Shannon, sick and tired of the whole affair, entreated them to get rid of Mr. Poate.

"Well, he doesn't seem to be good for any more harbour trips," Ashton summed up. "He's just trying to get his money back."

So Doug and Bart interviewed Mr. Poate when he came round that evening, Doug to do the talking and Bart to expand his chest which had now gained the inch necessary to admit him to the Police Force. After Douglas had told Mr. Poate what Bart would do to him, if he ever bothered their little sister again, Mr. Poate faded away and the Jacksons returned to a diet of fish and chips.

"I don't suppose old Knowlsie could dig you up another boy friend?" Ashton asked gloomily one evening when the fish and chips were particularly dry.

Shannon was only too afraid that Mrs. Knowles might try. Her son, it seemed, had become the tutor of Mr. Poate's unfortunate ward; but Mrs. Knowles did not on that account show any signs of tending her when Shannon developed a bad cough. She couldn't be running up and down the stairs, she complained, if that little thing was taken sick.

Bart had reluctantly departed for the police barracks; Douglas had gone to a new job in a mountain hotel; and this left only Ashton of her friends. Ashton, it is true, when she was forced to stay in bed, would stroll in companionably with a paper parcel of fish and chips. He tried to dose her with rum and lemon; but she did not take kindly to the remedy, and pleaded that the rum hurt her throat. He became quite alarmed, when she was delirious and insisted that Mr. Poate was trying to knock his way through the walls. He almost thought of calling a doctor, but he had no money and certainly Shannon had none. She was always worrying about the Cafe and her job, restlessly beseeching him to tell Mr. Litchin that it was not her fault. In her dreams, Mr. Litchin changed faces with Mr. Poate or Mr. Sladder and pursued her down grey streets, so that she must go on and on without rest, looking for some refuge.

When she woke with her brain clear and a feeling of immense weakness, the red of sunset was on the wall and it was very cold. She did not know what day it was, but from below in the yard came Mrs. Knowles' voice shrilly enquiring what Dad thought he was doing watering those ferns till they were all mucky. The sound seemed very far away, farther than the big ships loading at the wharf, or the leaf-shadowed Gardens where the birds would be twittering and fighting before settling down for the night; the swans waddling ashore, poking their snaky beaks in search of bread crusts. Ferries would be crammed with business people going home, reading their papers with all the windows of the ferry boats shut and a smell of engine oil and cigarette smoke to give them an appetite for dinner. The dark green-furred headlands would be sliding past, the red roofs of the houses like poinsettias, poinsettias in a garden with a white picket fence. Under the red roofs of the contented little suburbs housewives had their hot meals cooking and the kettles boiling. Up the rich North Shore line, the trains hot and stuffy would be rattling and clacking and stopping, the dim reflections of the passengers in the window like ghosts sitting among the crowd. At Lindfield there were port-wine magnolias and Methodists. St. Ives had dark, glossy, green leaves with oranges on the trees and fallen to the ground, all satisfied, all comfortable. None of the port-wine Methodists had influenza. No, there was something wrong with that. She had overheard a woman at the Pompadour say that Lindfield was famous for port-wine magnolias and Methodists.

Her brain was still not quite clear. She shut her eyes wearily. Now, if she turned over in bed with her face to the door—but it was too much trouble to turn over—she would be facing the long, ragged strip of land that enclosed half Sydney Harbour from the pounding ocean. On one side of the strip the little quiet beaches, all overgrown with ugly houses; on the other, the blown froth of the surf. She would turn over and shut her eyes and pretend she was looking along the busy tramlines rattling people home.

She did turn over and gave a shriek of fright. Mr. Litchin was silently peering in at the doorway. Ashton, who had been coming up the stairs, arrived at the same moment, and angrily asked Mr. Litchin what the Hell he was doing.

"Plis!" Mr. Litchin raised his hand in that hierarchic gesture he always employed when he was about to be haughty and magnanimous. "Not a word. She is ill, she is dying, she suffers. She cannot but be ill here. I am taking her away." He shouted down Ashton's mumble. "Yes, I am taking her away where she will have fresh air, to my own sister I take her. I am a kind, good man. If my sister does not take her in, I throw my sister into the gutter. I abandon her. Come, you can walk to the bus and a taxi is too much money. I am a good man, but I will not be robbed. I am poor, I myself was friendless in this country. Come with me." He was still talking as he led the dumbfounded Ashton off to help him cheat Mrs. Knowles out of her last week's rent.

As for Shannon, she lay stiff with astonishment and weakness, then she began huddling on her clothes, shivering half with cold, half with apprehension. The voice of Mr. Litchin was approaching up the stair still announcing to a chorus composed of Mrs. Knowles and Ashton and three ground floor lodgers that he was a good, kind man who had saved many lives, had earned much gratitude, but that he would not be robbed, never, never.

Nine

I

By the time they had reached the bus terminus Shannon was sure she was dying; and when it appeared that they had still a mile to walk along a dark, uneven road, she could have lain down then and there from sheer weakness. Mr. Litchin drove her on relentlessly. He had had a fine time in the bus explaining to several uneasy fellow-passengers that he was a good fellow who was saving Shannon's life. Now, however, her feebleness annoyed him and he went bounding ahead energetically, leaving her to follow as best she could. Sometimes he sang to himself or shouted back to her. As the darkness of the scrub closed round them, his companion called to mind the newspaper accounts of several grisly murders. Maybe Mr. Litchin was going to push her over a cliff. She did not care. She was too tired. Even when Mr. Litchin vanished inexplicably from the pathway, as though the earth had swallowed him up, she only sighed and sat down on a rock. Presently he could be heard roaring in the darkness:

"Up! Up! I am here! Sasha! Clive! Joseph has come!"

A drowsy voice, a man's voice, exclaimed: "My God! it's Joseph, Sasha. The first night we've gone to bed early for months!"

"Send him away," a deep, ringing contralto responded. "After the cow I will not have him. Send him away."

"Yes, Joseph, what the devil do you mean by it? I always said the cow was nothing but sheer imposition . . ."

"Silence! Silence! I command it!"

"Did you or did you not tell Mrs. Brewster she could have the cow? Did you or did you not say we never milked it?"

Joseph was babbling out the story of his rescue. "Where are we going to put her?" the man's voice complained; and Shannon could not be sure whether this referred to herself or the cow. A dim lamplight showed the bulk of a weatherboard bungalow and towards this she made her way.

"I won't have you bringing your mistresses here, Joseph," Sasha was saying.

96

Joseph roared: "No, no! You speak of the gutter. I am a good man, pure of soul. I save the life of a poor, half-witted thing."

True enough, Shannon thought. I must have been half-witted to let him bully me into coming here.

"I refuse to be burdened with any more of Joseph's strays. I have suffered enough."

"You live upon me. You suck my blood!" Joseph screamed. "You a sister? Never!"

At this point Shannon said weakly from the doorway: "May I come in?"

The room was lit by a kerosene lamp, and had much the same wild, dishevelled look as Mr. Litchin. Beside her benefactor stood two people evidently his sister and her husband. Sasha had certainly not been expecting visitors. She was clad in a man's flannel shirt and woollen underpants which came to her ankles. They looked like Mr. Litchin's underpants, but they did nothing to disguise the overwhelming magnificence of the lady's figure. Her husband, a thin, bony youth, was wrapped in a pink dressing gown with yellow flounces which he clutched modestly about him, as he turned reproachfully on Joseph.

"It's chicken-stealing," he exclaimed. "Chicken-stealing absolutely."

But his wife swept down on Joseph's victim and embraced her. "So little!" she cried. "But of course! At once! Fry some onions, Clive. Poor little one! She shall sleep on the sofa. We will all have a cup of coffee."

"Onions!" Clive was all eagerness. "The very thing for a cold."

Still modestly clutching his pink dressing gown, he set about lighting an old stove, seemingly crammed with rubbish which he raked out impatiently, filling it with chips and brushwood which presently poured out a cloud of choking smoke. Meanwhile his wife made much of the guest, and Mr. Litchin stood in the middle of the room and delivered himself of a little, triumphant recitative about his goodness of heart and promptitude in saving lives. When the onions and coffee were ready, they all had some. Two tousle-headed children pattered in demanding drinks of water and were given some onions. All was peace and welcome, Joseph at intervals jumping up to kiss them all round, assuring Shannon that he did not mind her germs as he bore a charmed life.

An unlucky reference to the mysterious cow started a violent quarrel, and they all appealed to Shannon passionately. She had to hear all about how Joseph had appeared with this cow one evening, bestowed it on them, and had been giving it away to other people ever since. The three were still quarrelling about the cow when Shannon dropped to sleep on the sofa, and the quarrel went on overhead mingling vaguely with her dreams.

Next morning she could not remember where she was. Several hens were pecking about the floor and a cat was sleeping on her pillow.

"I say," Clive burst out, as soon as he saw she had opened her eyes, "I didn't like to wake you, but Sasha's had a splendid idea. You can be the Spirit of Eureka." At her bewildered look, he explained more fully. "In Mrs. Brewster's pageant. Nobody wants to be the Spirit of Eureka, and there's only about five lines. It's the most awful thing, really I don't know how she ever came to think of it. But we'll all have a swim and I'll go over and borrow a mattress for you to sleep on, and then we'll tell Emmie Brewster that we've got somebody at last."

"And the best part of it is," Sasha put her head around the door of the bedroom, "you'll be staying with us, so you'll be handy for rehearsals."

Their guest struggled into a sitting position, dislodging the cat as she did so. "What time do the buses leave?" she asked, coughing weakly.

"Why you can't go. Joseph would just about murder us. And you'll like sleeping in the shed on our spare bed. It hasn't a mattress but I'm going straight over to borrow one now."

"After breakfast," Sasha advised. "First you must milk the cow."

"No, I'll go now and get it over. I suppose I'll have to flirt with the hags. They think we're infamous as it is. 'Ow, Mr. Peake,'" he imitated a cockney whine. "'What a thing to say.'"

"My husband is a great favourite with our neighbours," Sasha declared proudly. "He flirts with them all. As soon as you are well, he will flirt with you. I like him to have all the experiences." She gave the object of this solicitude a fond, wifely smile to which he returned a wink which was evidently meant to indicate unspeakable depths of licentiousness.

"And now while he is away, we will make you better."

Sasha pounced down on her guest, and, talking all the time, chivvied her into a tiny, chilly bathroom, where she proceeded to strip her and scrub her under the cold shower, as though she had been one of the children who, in the kitchen, were munching black bread and radishes, before straggling off to school. As soon as they had gone, the guest was dumped naked on a blanket in the back yard and massaged vigorously with olive oil, while the kindly Sasha deplored the patient's white skin.

"And so thin, so dreadfully thin! It is the unhealthy life in Joseph's dreadful, clattery place with no air. And living in a back room with no sun. Look, Clive, how her bones show!"

At the sound of her host's returning footsteps Shannon effaced herself behind the shed.

"Don't upset the poor girl, Sasha." Clive dumped the mattress on a rusty iron bedstead which stood beside a copper and two tubs. "Showing her off like a corpse! You're nothing but a savage. Just savages, you and Joseph both."

"I refuse to have you say that I am like Joseph. I refuse to have you say it." And then to Shannon. "You can come out. He is gone inside. I am sorr-ee you are ashamed, but you have no need. You have a good body, but your breasts are very flat."

Her husband put his head out the kitchen window. "Stop embarrassing the girl. How often must I tell you to leave her alone? She'll burst into tears or something. Joseph will kill us with a carving knife and there'll be no Spirit of Eureka."

"She is nothing to Joseph. She says so." Sasha began to prepare breakfast, talking all the time. "After breakfast we will go and have a swim. It will be muddy if the tide is out, but when the tide is in there may be sharks. And then we'll go to Emmie's and rehearse."

The threatened swim, the thought of which had sent a shiver all over the invalid, proved less of a trial than she expected. True, the trail down to the water descended from rock to rock to a crazy jetty leaning over a stretch of black weed and mud in which migrant limpets had left little tracks. Across this quagmire scuttled crabs with red nippers from the mangrove swamps, crabs that popped down into their holes with the panic of a nervous old lady nestling under the bedclothes. They made a rustling, scurrying noise as they sidled to and fro through the trickles. There were also armies of blue crabs with cream claws deploying in battalions and turning gravely from right and left as danger threatened, retreating in a masterly manner with pincers aloft but harmless; occasionally some general who had been left behind, scrambling over the backs of the rank and file until he attained his rightful place leading the retreat.

Shannon almost snivelled from weakness and distress at the thought of joining them in their weedy home. If she had any money, she would not have stayed a minute to be bullied by the beautiful savages who now wallowed in a rum-coloured creeklet far out in the mud. However, making the best of a bad job, she waded out and, lying in the warm salty water, found it surprisingly good, bracing her. Back again in the untidy kitchen, after a meal of garlic, olive oil and rye bread, she felt that perhaps she might survive. She was far more cheerful than Clive who had gashed his foot on an oyster shell.

She was so much better that she could even face the prospect of sleeping in the shed with an escort of cats, midnight visits from the cow, and some fleas. She slept soundly with the moonlight shining in her eyes. Tomorrow she would write to Aunt Edith in a humble spirit and to Beryl in a spirit of desperation, but in the meantime, if the free life was filling her with garlic and homesickness, it was also making her stronger.

II

Mrs. Emma Brewster had faced determined opposition when she decided to live at Fort Bukloh. It had been built by her father-in-law after he returned from a sojourn in India where he had been occupied on frontier defence works. A windfall from a rich relative decided him to build a home as a surprise for his wife. At first he had thought of calling it Khyber, but poetry prevailed, and the completed structure was christened Fort Bukloh amid the united maledictions of all the builders who had had to handle the great lumps of sandstone and reinforced concrete. The Colonel had quarried his own building material on the spot and designed the house himself.

"There is going to be one house in this gim-crack city really well built," he declared. All the bedrooms were semi-circular like gun emplacements and hung out over the side of the cliff, giving a magnificent view which made qualmish people so nervous they could hardly sleep a wink. The living room, as big as a church, had its roof upheld by squat pillars of concrete. "No potty damn gardens," the Colonel decided. It would have been impossible in any case to make a garden in solid rock. A drive curved from the summit of the cliff to the level of the roof as a concession to civilized living; but the Fort squatted between the ragged, rocky knees of the hills and looked so like a large rock itself that, at a short distance, it merged by natural camouflage with its background.

Far inland the water ran bitter and salt. The grey rocks, like old bones, the shaggy beggarly trees and parched bush, stood uneasily embraced by tentacles of water that twisted and shone between the mangrove swamps. Into this Eden descended the Colonel's wife to view the promised surprise. A bush fire, for which the Colonel apologised, as though he were personally responsible, had swept the height, cracked all the Fort's windows, and sooted the walls; but this slight blemish did not influence Mrs. Brewster's opinion. It would have been the same in any case.

She was not, she said, an Afghan, nor was she a lizard. Apart from the criminal waste of money and the bitter impropriety and selfishness of building a house in which no sane person could possibly live, he had insulted her personally, robbed their children, and disgraced their name. After Mrs. Brewster had concluded her views on Fort Bukloh, the Colonel moved into a city flat and cowered whenever Fort Bukloh was mentioned.

Mrs. Emmie Brewster, his son's wife, not only took pleasure in disagreeing with Mrs. Brewster Senior, but she had ambitions. She wanted Fort Bukloh and she was going to have it. "I see it as a Centre," she replied to her husband's protests that it was seven miles from the nearest golf course, "a Centre of protest against the falsity of city life." The heat-crazy scrub, the broken grey rocks sloping down to mud flats, swamps and oyster leases would form a background for the week-end residences of those who pined for release from the crowd and clamour. Here they might joy in open spaces, developing their bodies and their minds.

Her husband shrewdly agreed that perhaps some of her looney friends might buy up patches of otherwise unsaleable scrub if it were subdivided. No harm in trying. Sure enough, between Mrs. Brewster's enthusiasm and Mr. Brewster's business efficiency, the peninsula commanded by Fort Bukloh was presently dotted with little bungalows and ramshackle dwellings comprising the Balm Point Colony, in which artists in smocks, nudists well-guarded by mosquito net, writers and would-be-writers of The Great Australian Novel, mingled together in all stages of sunburn and sand-fly bites. They discussed one another's work in tones of savagery, gravitated to the hospitable shelter of Emmie's Fort where they ate her food, sneered at her imported celebrities, and thanked Heaven they could get back to their city flats on Monday. Some of them lived in the colony all the year round, but these were for the most part poor outsiders who had bought land, because it was cheap and they hoped to start a poultry farm where there were no building regulations or health inspectors.

One of the great attractions of Balm Point was Emmie's open air theatre, which had formerly been the quarry. Overseas visitors were brought to see it. Sometimes performances were given of Mrs. Brewster's own dramatic works.

"Australianism is the keynote," Mrs. Brewster proclaimed. "Our remote European heritage must be transmuted; there must be a synthesis of cultures in this country, cultural reorientation." She invariably paused at this point for murmurs of agreement. "We must follow," Emmie declared, "in the naked footprints of our own aboriginals. Alcheringa, you know, the Spirit of the Place. That is what we seek to realise here."

Sometimes when there was no performance of Mrs. Brewster's dramatic pageants showing the growth of Australianism, there would be lectures by Mrs. Brewster herself on National Culture and What It Means.

"A Great Work, dear lady," Bleeby Peverill said gracefully when he was first introduced and had kissed her hand. Bleeby Peverill had been taken as a visiting lion to the Fort, and, on his return to Sydney, had settled down as a resident or permanent lion. He was now painting pictures of women with three or four heads symbolizing the changeable feminine mind. If asked what his pictures were "about" (and some people actually had the temerity to ask him such a question), he would pass his hand wearily across his brow and say: "Just a mood, my fwiend. Weally nothing more than a mood."

Bleeby worked hard for his keep rehearsing Mrs. Brewster's pageant. "The Growth of Australianism," which Mrs. Brewster hoped to present on a series of motor lorries next Eight Hour Day, was her most ambitious effort to date. It included a tableau of the Native Culture, decorated with boomerangs and spears and primitive works of art; and since certain aboriginal half-castes who had been approached had held out firmly for trade-union hours and pay, the male members of the colony were forced protestingly into the part of aboriginals defending their culture in a coat of blacking and loin cloth. No one wanted to be the Spirit of Eureka Stockade, because Mrs. Brewster had planned her pageant so that the Spirit of Eureka, clad in a flag of the Southern Cross, was held aloft in the brawny arms of several gentlemen who always complained about the weight.

Shannon, being small and light, was much more suitable, for instance, than Sasha who was the Spirit of the Future in several yards of white gauze with a gold fillet around her hair. Mrs. Brewster found it difficult to hold her cast together. Even Bleeby Peverill was but a reluctant performer in the part of the Spirit of England. He had to wear a top hat and his patriotism was stirred by this insult.

He recognized Shannon immediately. "Don't say anything," he whispered hurriedly, "about the . . . the other job I had. I lost it." He brooded for a minute over past unpleasantness, then asked: "How's Bewyl?"

"I don't know. I haven't seen her." They found themselves exchanging confidences. There had been, Bleeby told her, a most dreadful explosion which cast himself and Lucy into outer darkness, and as they were not speaking to each other anyway, he had made a new start.

"You don't know anyone who wants to buy half a milk-wun?" he asked Shannon wistfully during a rehearsal. When he heard that Shannon did not know anyone who wanted half a milk-run, he sighed wistfully. "I met a chap, fwightfully decent chap, who wants to sell out, a model daiwy. If I could find someone to go halves, I needn't . . ." He gestured towards the assembled spirits. "All this," he finished plaintively, "is dweadful dwivel. I only need a bit of capital and I'd be out of it like a shot. Don't tell Emmie."

Shannon fervently agreed with his traitorous dislike of Australianism in the spirit and the flesh. Beryl had not answered her letter; Aunt Edith had replied with a note which stated that Uncle Vincent was opposed to sending any money. Shannon must return to her aunt who was brokenhearted to think that any niece should be so ungrateful and unladylike. In a fierce whisper Shannon confided in Mr. Peverill that she was stranded like himself. Mr. Litchin had blandly taken on another waitress in her place, and she had no money for fares to the city so that she could look for a job.

"Weally," Mr. Peverill exclaimed. "Orphans of the storm." He drew her farther away from their fellow performers. "I can borrow Emmie's car, let you and I go and have dinner some place. I was going in to town to see if I could borrow some money. If I don't get away for a few hours," Mr. Peverill indicated the Spirits, "I'll get a club or a boomewang or something and bust out."

They had a splendid time dining and dancing. It was two in the morning before they returned, but Sasha was waiting up excitedly for Shannon. "Didn't I tell you," she demanded, "that I would find you someone to marry?"

"Don't be a mug." With returning health Shannon was better able to withstand Sasha's headlong flights of fancy.

"But I tell you it is so. I know instinctively." Sasha almost hugged her. "You, all so cold and grave, thinking with your head. But I, I think with my loins."

"Oh, don't!" her guest moaned. She was in no mood to have her evening spoilt by Sasha's physiological mysticism.

"Tell me, Shannon," Sasha asked seriously, "I believe you have a frigid nature. Do you ever have orgasms?"

"You go to Hell!" Shannon said indignantly. Some girls might endure the restrictions of a nice home with worried parents who were anxious to preserve them as marriageably sound, but it was far worse living with people who regarded a pleasant evening out as inevitably erotic. She was beginning to look upon the frankness with which Clive and Sasha discussed themselves and other people as a vice. Honesty, like anything else, could be carried too far; and their honesty was merely a lack of reticence. Why should anyone be interested in whether Sasha's liver or kidneys were working? But conversation at breakfast always turned on their functioning. Shannon was tired of having her own liver and kidneys discussed, and she certainly resented her glands becoming public property.

That was the trouble with these free-lifers. They were so wrapped up in their bodies that they were never really free. They never forgot themselves for a minute. Reverting to the wild, healthy life of the aboriginal was just sinking back into your body. There wasn't anything uplifting about eating and sleeping and getting food. No, she decided, as she retired to her shed in the yard, civilization may have its bad points, but better be cooped up in a city flat than in a patch of scrub with Sasha and her kindly interest.

Bleeby Peverill did not get off so lightly. Exhausted by his night's dancing, and torpid from a few too many drinks, he fell asleep in the car by the Fort's entrance; and was found next morning, still sleeping, with his feet on the steering wheel.

Emmie Brewster was disgusted. "It is not in the Spirit of the Place," she said sternly. "That wicked little wretch of a girl is a False Note. She has no right here. Has she ever done anything Creative? Imagination has a hard enough fight against Commercialism and Alienism as it is. Look around you." She gestured beyond the weedy lawn to the ti-tree scrub, the bleary daylight pitilessly revealing the stretch of grey rock, and below, the mangrove swamps and mud flats. "It is not in the Spirit of the Place. Alcheringa, you know."

"I see your point," Mr. Peverill agreed penitently. After all, you can't quarrel with free shelter, even if the bread is too lavishly buttered with National Culture.

Shannon spent most of her time racking her brains for some shift which would remove her from Balm Point and the tyranny of Australian National Culture. She could not help liking Sasha and Clive, but she did not like sleeping in a shed with the wash tubs, a broody hen nesting under her bed, and the cow. She did not like being dependent on their kindness when they had no more money than herself. Clive was nominally attached as sub-editor to a magazine devoted to the doctrine of fresh air and vegetable foods which came out in a chaste green cover under the title of "Foliage." It was full of airy poems and green buds of prose by unknown but aspiring vegetarians and was always on the point of withering away completely. It struggled into print whenever the editors scraped up enough money to pay the printer something off his account, and like everything else at Balm Point it was a Protest, this time a protest against the poisoning of the human system with animal foods. Its editors and contributors always had a very lean and hungry look.

"One time," Sasha told Shannon, "dear Joseph sent out a huge bundle of broken scraps for the chooks, and do you know," she laughed happily, "Clive and I sat down with the children and ate them all ourselves."

With enforced rest and returning health, Shannon grew restive under the missionary spirit of her hosts. In the very middle of an eager discussion on the uplift of the Proletariat (for all the Balm Point residents were full of admiration for the Proletariat and were advanced revolutionaries) she mistakenly burst out: "But isn't it reactionary of you to cling to old outworn ways of living, fresh air and vegetable foods that people have been absorbing for thousands of years? Why can't you learn to live in cities, you're always talking about the Proletariat?"

"Yes, but we want them to have fresh air, good food like us."

"How do you know they will want to live like you?"

"Oh, naturally everyone wants what makes them strong and healthy."

"Why?"

"Because it will do them good," Sasha snapped back irritably.

"But how do you know they will want it?"

"I know it instinctively."

"But, suppose," Shannon pursued her point stubbornly, "suppose they've already adapted themselves to something that doesn't do them good. Suppose they've got used to it. Just because *you* say so, they aren't going to change back. Because *you* don't like living in a back room or a flat in a slum, it doesn't say that someone more adaptable isn't quite enjoying it."

Sasha and Clive always became furiously angry when opposed. They shouted at her together so that it was quite impossible to argue with them. "I still don't see," their ungrateful guest contended. "You talk about losing touch with nature. But how about losing touch with other people, ordinary people? If you don't live under the same conditions as they do, how can you tell what they want?"

"You! You to talk! When you come here with influenza, dying almost. Yes, sick as can be."

"But maybe," Shannon argued, "it's good to have influenza and build up a resistance to it. Maybe a set of diseased ancestors is what people need, so their children will only have influenza a little bit. Look at the people of the South Seas. They lived on fresh fruits in the open air, and when influenza hit them, they just died off because they hadn't been toughened to it."

After a conversation such as this, it would be hours before Sasha and Clive could bring themselves to speak to her. "You have the mind of the middle class," Sasha would say insultingly, "the policeman mind."

The third time she said this, Shannon was struck by a brilliant idea. Bart! Dear Bart, who had been made a policeman but who always wanted to be an artist! "I say," she said eagerly, "do you think I could have a friend come on the night Mrs. Brewster is having this weird Abbot to talk?"

"Why, certainly." Sasha scented romance. "Is he physically attractive? Does he appeal to you?"

"Not a bit. I want to see if he'll lend me some money."

So Bart Jackson was duly invited to meet the artists of Balm Point at the reception Mrs. Brewster was giving to the Abbot of the Order of Human Brotherhood. Bart wrote back delightedly accepting the invitation. Shannon would have invited Ashton too, but Ashton never had any time for artists.

The Abbot was to address a gathering of Balm Point colonists in Mrs. Brewster's open air theatre, but on the Sunday night appointed for the great event it rained.

"It looks as though the Spirit of the Place," Shannon whispered to Bleeby Peverill, "doesn't want to hear this bloke."

She was feeling gay and exultant because Bart had lent her a pound and promised to lend her another. Mr. Peverill shook his head gloomily. The gathering was transferred to Mrs. Brewster's drawing-room which was large enough to hold twice the number. The rain had kept away people who had no cars and all who knew from bitter experience what it was like to stumble from the bus terminus down the unlighted, stony track which wound artistically across Balm Point. But there was a fair number considering the weather, for the Abbot was a colourful figure and had recently been interviewed in two of the daily papers with a handsome photograph inset.

"Even if he lacks the National outlook on culture," Mrs. Brewster was busily telling her visitors, "he has a Movement, a powerful Movement behind him and we must hear his Message."

Thank Heaven, Shannon thought, I can get out of this place. Why, I might get out tomorrow.

The guest of the evening was late, very late. Mrs. Brewster, after a good deal of whispering and consulting, stepped forward and announced that until Abbot Quilter arrived, Mr. Bleeby Peverill, the celebrated English artist, would recite from the works of a fellow intellectual, Mr. Aldous Huxley. The guests composed themselves on chairs, on cushions on the floor. The stop-gap took his place self-consciously by the long French windows at the end of the room, and newcomers like Bart Jackson assumed a look of strained attention. Mr. Peverill began on Mr. Huxley's poetical works like a small boy obediently reciting his home lesson. Presently he began to enjoy himself. By the time he had worked his way through seven poems he was obviously congratulating himself that the guest of the evening had not arrived. He went on and on, while the audience became increasingly restive, his cultured Oxford accent sounding to the less educated as though Mr. Peverill had a mouthful of toffee.

"There is no past," chanted Mr. Peverill, "no woots, no fwuits,
  But momentawy flowers,
  Lie still, only lie still, and night will last

Silent and dark not for a space of hours
But everlastingly."

This was just what the audience was afraid might happen. There were rebellious murmurings, particularly from those who had no cushions between them and the floor, and from the more advanced intellectuals of the colony who considered Mr. Huxley a reactionary.

Just as the restiveness engendered by the twelfth poem was becoming almost murderous, the lights failed. The failure of the lights was no unusual occurrence at the Fort. Sometimes the water supply failed too.

"Keep your seats, my fwiends," Mr. Peverill called. "I will pwoceed."

The lights were off for a quarter of an hour, and Mr. Peverill's voice went bravely on, gobbling out poems. When the lights came on again, the room was empty, save for Mrs. Brewster who was dozing on the sofa, Shannon who had stayed from a sense of loyalty, and Bart Jackson, fatigued, but still heroically ready to learn about artists.

Mrs. Brewster was ready to bite her nails with annoyance, for the scurrying of gravel on the drive, a sweep of headlights, announced the coming of the great man.

"They've all sneaked away," Shannon whispered to Bart. "She'll have to go and round them up." Sure enough, Mrs. Brewster could be heard making excuses at the rate of three a half-minute.

"I was detained," the Abbot replied in a deep voice with no hint of apology to it.

He entered the room with Mrs. Brewster and a few of the fugitives trailing behind him. His dull purple robes would have been striking enough, but Southwell Vaughan-Quilter inside them was not only a big bulk of a man, he was handsome. He did not pose, but he had a natural insolence that took it for granted that he should stand squarely where he showed to best advantage by a large bowl of rock lilies.

"Nice bit of colour," Bleeby Peverill hissed to Shannon under his breath, as he drew her forward to meet the speaker of the evening. Shannon found the visitor overpowering. For a few minutes the Abbot was left with just the faithful few, while Mrs. Brewster went off to the rear of the house to rouse the truants where they were brewing cocoa.

"Miss Hicks is the Spirit of Yeweka," the irrepressible Bleeby announced to the Abbot, "but she wouldn't be if she could get a job. Dweadful being held up in a flag like an auction."

"I can quite imagine it would be." The deep tone in which Southwell Vaughan-Quilter pronounced the words made them sound like some reprieve from a great personage. His glance swept over the shrinking figure of the Spirit of Eureka as though he did not notice the shyness which had come over her. "Perhaps we could persuade Mrs. Brewster to abandon that part of the pageant?"

"Oh, don't!" Shannon burst out. "She'd like to sell me down the river as it is, cheap." No sooner were the words out than she blushed hotly. She was not given to blushing, but her remark sounded so unpleasant. Mrs. Brewster in the doorway had probably heard the Abbot and would know they had been talking about the pageant.

As he turned to his hostess, there was a glint of amusement in Vaughan-Quilter's face. He was quite unperturbed by the flippancy of his audience, and he had not been speaking long before it was evident that here was a man who could hold an audience. His subject was "Astrological Influences and What they mean to Us"; and as few of his hearers were in any way believers in astrology, he had a task before him.

Shannon, cramped into a hard corner of stone with her back against a pillar, was far more interested in watching Southwell Vaughan-Quilter, Abbot of the Order of Human Brotherhood, and analysing the overpowering impression he had made on her. It was like being struck by lightning, she decided. He was not only tall, he was rather broad with the amplitude of a great armchair. His face was dignified and gracious, as though he knew he was conferring an honour by regarding any object on the physical plane, when his thoughts should be exclusively on spiritual things. His face was handsome, stern and rather square, with a massive brow and deep-set brown eyes, a curved red, rather feminine mouth, and dimples. He had wavy brown hair parted in the middle. The only thing that was missing was the halo, but if he had extended one of his white, square looking hands to the shabby little object in the corner, she would have kissed it, awe-stricken. She had never seen such a man in her life; he loomed up like a mountain when he rose from his chair and surveyed her with a detached yet friendly gaze, perfectly self-possessed and gracious, just as he would have been self-possessed and gracious in the middle of a jungle. Shannon could imagine that any tribe of natives meeting such a creature would worship it on sight. When he spoke, his voice came up to his appearance. It was curiously deep and mellow, as though more at home in a church chant. His voice was English, a rather pleasant lazy drawl.

Had they studied, he asked them, the curious tides in history, the rise and fall of civilizations, and enquired if there might not be some cause external to our own world at work behind immediate causes which brought these tides to their height? Take the mysterious outbreak of the Black Death in Europe, the fire and plague of London, predicted by most negligible and obscure astrologers. If we thought of ourselves as results rather than causes of life, we would see we are but a film on a tiny floating bubble poised in a sea of light, its surface splashed by waves from worlds themselves mere pulsating organisms, mere plankton enfurled in gulfs of brilliance that rose and changed and fluctuated with time.

"For three centuries the world has seen a spawning of the human race, a swarming from one part of our globe to another, the occupation of waste land by those driven out by the pressure of numbers. Now that the planetary conjunction which produced this phenomenal breeding is passing, we hear statesmen shrieking of race-suicide and under-population. They do not look to the external cause but run like frantic ants on an ant heap where excess fecundity has left in its train the problems of race antagonism, the overpopulation of the globe, the accentuation of greed and stupidity with the red star of chaos rising over us all. We have before us an age which would make the cities of Sodom and Gomorrah look like quiet country villages."

Outside the windows, the ragged clouds were rimmed with moonlight and a faint sound came through the silence, the creaking of swans, like the oars in the rollicks of some aery boat. Southwell Vaughan-Quilter stood with his hands clasped behind him, his bulk filling the window, as though he warmed his hands behind him on the moonlight, on the grey ashes of the hills, in the same position that a ruddy householder might stand warming his hands at a hearthfire. As he stood thus, with the dim light of the room half-revealing him, Shannon thought how grand he was, how really grand, a man big enough to take the whole world for his hearth-rug.

Of course what he was talking about was tripe, but if she couldn't work in a couple of questions to show that she had read his book, she would die in the attempt. There was nothing small about the Abbot's plans. He had decided that what was needed was more abbeys like his own, where occultists might study and plan for the ending of the age of chaos. When it came to prophecy, he dived deep.

"Now we know not where to go or what to seek. All is made strange around us, bitterness and the ache of despisal are all we hold. There is starvation and rage and conflict. But the wise will sit in peace and resist the stir and swirl because they know why it has come about. It may be that civilizations may fall about us, cities roar in our ears, and the land shrivel in fire like a feather. But, my good people, to those who know all, this is nothing. It is for us to preserve the secrets in the waste of death."

He went on happily treading down the convictions of his hearers as he might have walked on grass. As he concluded his discourse, a grim silence fell, in which the Marxist section of the audience could be seen panting with eagerness to rend him. In this silence, the voice of Miss Hicks, the Spirit of Eureka, enquired blandly:

"Mr. Vaughan-Quilter, do you believe that the doctrine of the Third Cause, as set out in the fifth book of Rama, is the true esoteric explanation?"

"I do, very largely." The Abbot's face lightened with interest. Here, he seemed to say, was someone who was not stony ground for his words.

"And you would take the Third Cause to mean what Heppel says it means?" Miss Hicks continued sweetly.

"Yes, certainly. I will tell you why I think he is right." The Abbot launched eagerly into an involved explanation of the Third Cause which took up a quarter of an hour, was utterly unintelligible to the audience, and led Mrs. Brewster to declare that there was no more time for questions.

After supper, she took charge of the Abbot and turned the conversation to her own pageant.

"You have no idea what a trial it is," Mrs. Brewster confessed, "to try to make people *see* that the Spirit of Australianism must be paramount."

"You have one very interesting little girl here," the Abbot hinted.

Mrs. Brewster's dislike burst out in a splash of venom. "She is really a very difficult case. Poor child, of course, one doesn't quite know what to do with her. Quite alone in the world, I understand, and penniless, but such a trial. You can see how I am placed, Mr. Quilter. This little thing is living with some crazy young people near by, and naturally . . ."

"Naturally," the Abbot agreed, "you have done your best for her."

"But she quite spoils the *spirit* of her part. No Australianism." Mrs. Brewster did not mention the painful episode of Bleeby Peverill found sleeping in the Brewster car on the Brewster front drive. "If you should hear of anything that would suit the poor little thing, it would really be a work of mercy to find her an opening."

"I might," the Abbot said reflectively. He was watching a rowdy party of pageant actors at the other end of the room. In their midst Miss Hicks was giving a lively imitation of Bleeby Peverill trying to buy a milk-run from a deaf old dairyman. "I'll see what I can do," he promised.

There was a tone in his voice which made Mrs. Brewster feel that perhaps she had aroused too much interest.

Ten

THE ABBEY of the Order of Human Brotherhood occupied a point of land jutting out into the blue of the harbour. It was a pleasant, rambling edifice combining grey sandstone with green window shutters, wide verandahs and dormer windows. To these had been added a rampart, crenellations, gargoyles and other architectural features, which formed a tasty combination about 1850, but only escaped being an eyesore eighty years later by the mellowing influence of time. Besides, no structure can be quite an eyesore when it is set in sloping gardens, green trees and water. The Abbey was peaceful, and, from certain angles, majestic; where it was not majestic, it was just a trifle ridiculous.

The members of the Brotherhood paid their board and their initiation fees, assembled for devotions at set hours, and lectures at others, but most of them went in to the city to work, catching the ferry boat and sitting cheek by jowl with suburban business men who were all convinced that anyone who lived in an Abbey and believed in human brotherhood must be mad. This impression was confirmed by the two bishops and the abbot wearing purple robes instead of serge suiting. Why should a man go about like a pansy when he could wear civilized clothes?

But it was known that the Abbey had "money behind it," and anything connected with money cannot be altogether mad. The Order of Human Brotherhood went its mystic way in the knowledge that there is safety in numbers, particularly when the numbers are in a bank book. The Order owned a city church, small, rich and dim, where the bishops and their flock assembled on Sundays; a hall and a network of lecture centres, a share in a printery, the rent of three city buildings and other miscellaneous property.

So that when Abbot Southwell Vaughan-Quilter approached Bishop Steele with a request for a typist's services, his request was not unreasonable. No one knew better than Bishop Steele that the flourishing condition of the Brotherhood's finances were due in no small measure to the Abbot.

Southwell Vaughan-Quilter had arrived in Sydney with a distinguished manner and a brazenly, offensively handsome person as almost his only assets. Perhaps to these might be added a mind stuffed with odd knowledge, crammed with weird convictions which his blazing earnestness made almost tenable. He was the supersalesman of the Unseen, and once he had jammed one foot in the crack of his listener's mind, there was no shutting it on him. He believed in his own product so firmly that he made a vendor of merely material goods look like a little boy from the local school selling raffle tickets for the Red Cross. Vaughan-Quilter had big, sweeping ideas, and he swept down on the Brotherhood unfurling the most extraordinary credentials from overseas brotherhoods. He was made welcome in the dim but amiable hospitality of the Abbey for the space of time it would take him to give his series of lectures on "Noumena and Phenomena of the Fifth Cycle," which series was under the auspices of an international body for the propagation of speculation on the utterly unknown.

Bishop Steele, who was then only Abbot Steele, had conducted the visitor round the grounds and lamented that funds were too low to employ a gardener. There was really so much to be done and so little money to do it with.

"I will see to that," Southwell Vaughan-Quilter had declared calmly. "This place is what I have been looking for all my life. I know myself. I know my mission and," he gripped the bishop by the shoulder, while a singularly pleasant and wicked smile curved his well-shaved mouth, "inside six months you won't know the place."

He was as good as his word. The insolence with which he fleeced wealthy old ladies was only measured by their adoration of him. In a blaze of candles and a jewelled cope, the new Abbot was worth paying to see, much less hear. His sermons on "The Coming Redeemer: Man or Superman" filled the church with hot, packed, expectant worshippers, until the air seemed heavy, soaked with human emotions, like cotton wool dipped in petrol and as ready to explode. It was quivering with a dangerous excitement; the congregation full of half-mystic, half-erotic exultation; the sanctuary blazing like a Christmas tree with candles and brass, amid which the servers-in scarlet and rose and plum colour moved like so many bright birds through a forest of fire; while in the vestry Bishop Bulfram called Bishop Steele a damned old fool, and Bishop Steele retorted that in his next incarnation his confrere might regret that remark. The new Abbot had quite overshadowed Bishop Bulfram who, when he lifted his big white gloves to give a blessing, put enough force into it to knock out an average prize fighter. Bishop Bulfram was accustomed to tower over the congregation, red, fat and stern-faced, as over a vanquished opponent. The truculence of Bishop Bulfram would have served him well in the days when a bishop's duties included leading his people forth to repel the heathen or the retainers of some neighbouring lord. He had, from motives of policy, done nothing against Vaughan-Quilter except hint that he was a charlatan, a sensualist, and had only been born once, which, as members of the Brotherhood would tell you, quite accounted for any other failings.

They were all very definite about how many times they had been born, some of them having such distinct memories of previous incarnations that they became an embarrassment to less pretentious believers. "Only a young soul," was the most disparaging remark, and the highest praise was "pure white, like Bishop Steele."

Bishop Steele was the least formidable of human beings, his loving-kindness having long ago reduced his frail person to a mere husk from which the exotic orchid of his unworldliness threw fantastic sprays of blossom over everything it touched. It was to Bishop Steele then that Vaughan-Quilter announced his need of a secretary-typist. He seldom approached Bishop Bulfram if he could avoid doing so.

"Why, yes, yes," Bishop Steele hastened to agree. "I will speak to Herbert at once." This kind intervention irritated Vaughan-Quilter like a nettle.

"I don't see," he observed majestically, "that it is such an immoderate request. The girl I have in mind will be very inexpensive. Quite a bargain," he added sarcastically.

"Yes, my dear fellow, certainly," Bishop Steele agreed. "I'm sure that Herbert will sanction anything you think fit."

Bishop Bulfram intimated that the proposed secretary-typist should be of irreproachable morals and willing to accept instruction with the novices. She would then be allowed to offer her services in a voluntary capacity. An exchange of cold notes on the subject finally brought the good bishop to concede free board and lodging in return for the secretary's services. If she should prove satisfactory, perhaps some slight wage might later be arranged.

"This is only being done to annoy me," Vaughan-Quilter declared, pacing up and down Bishop Steele's room so fast that his purple robe swished against the furniture. "I shall hire a typist from a city office and there'll be none of this haggling."

"Herbert feels," Bishop Steele attempted to put in a word, "that there are so many of the novices who would do it for nothing."

The Abbot's face set firm. "I will not be treated by Bulfram' like this. I told this Miss Hicks that I would get her a job and I shall see that she gets first chance at this one. She is a good little thing, a bright intelligent girl." He broke off. "I hope you don't think," he intercepted a fleeting interest in the saintly Bishop's eye, "that I have any personal regard for the girl?"

"Why no, Southwell," Bishop Steele protested. "Certainly not, certainly not."

The manner in which the Abbot had so far escaped entanglement argued either a very lofty spirit or a finished technique. The Abbot was so careful to let everyone know that he was vowed to celibacy that he might just as well have put up a sign. With so much competition in the way of lady novices, elderly deaconesses and female worshippers, one small secretary should make little difference.

Miss Hicks was installed in an attic smelling of mice and for several days she crept around timidly and spoke only in a whisper. Her typing had done well enough for Mrs. Brewster's programmes and she had put in a little spare time on an old machine at the office of "Foliage," but for the letters of the Abbot she was hopeless. The typing fell into a system whereby Miss Hicks took down letters in a weird shorthand she had invented for herself and typed copy after copy until she had one perfect. When she was reported for stealing out of a class on Cyclic Processes to practise her typing, the Abbot did not know whether to be displeased or not. She was so anxious to be of use that he did not have the heart to tell her how bad she was. She felt it nevertheless. She was in awe of the two Bishops; Vaughan-Quilter she addressed in a reverent hush that made him fidgetty. The Abbey to her harassed nerves was a heaven of peace and order.

The peach trees had finished flowering and were glowing with tender green leaves; and in the sunlight she could see from the study window the elder brothers pacing the walks, white-bearded men in dove-grey robes, and stately-seeming, all peaceful. The long, cool lawns sloped down to the tangle of lantana that hedged off the rocks and the sea. Even a giggling group of novices flirting with a telegraph messenger over the wall were blessed damozels. If only she could stay here, away from the hard asphalt and the harder faces scurrying along the streets.

But, in this earthly paradise, the lady initiates snubbed her at first, the elders ignored her, and her only real friend was the cook. The cook was no vegetarian and she was interested to hear all about Aunt Edith's boarding-house and the convalescent home.

"Why you'd sooner stay here I can't imagine," she assured Shannon. "Half of them living on melon seeds and mush, and the other half eating fruit with the skin on it. Myself, I can't work on an empty stomach, and I told Mr. Bulfram that straight. 'Have what you like,' he says, but of course I don't, the way he's always watching the bills. But seeing you've been used to good cooking, Miss Hicks, if you was to come down quiet-like . . ."

"Oh, I wouldn't dare," Shannon breathed. "Why the other day one of those girls said she could see my aura and it was red. She said a red aura meant you were carnal."

"I'd give them a red smacked bottom," the cook declared stoutly.

"Besides, Mr. Vaughan-Quilter might find out."

"Him!" the cook said derisively. "Why, one day I seen him in the city in a restaurant, and he was eating meat. A good big fat steak it was with onions. Take it from me," the cook added, "he ain't as holy as he looks, and what a waste if he was."

Shannon was so heartened by the discovery that her idol had his little failings that the same afternoon she helped herself to a few of his expensive cigarettes, and her attic began to lose the depressing smell of mice.

February came, and the crocuses were flakes of radiant white, foam caps on the green waves of grass. The Abbot launched the appeal for the Bishop's Rose Garden. "Sacred to the Memory of those who have passed on. For the privilege of scattering the ashes of a relative on a rose bush, a payment for the upkeep of the garden would be expected, with an extra sum for the engraved verse (with name of relative) in the Grotto of Remembrance."

"Not only have we the rose garden in hand," the Abbot dictated slowly. "There is also the Bishops' Walk, if some good soul would come forward to pay for it."

"Too bald," his secretary interrupted.

Vaughan-Quilter could not have been more startled if the table had bitten him. He stared at her with raised eyebrows and a freezing expression.

"Too bald," she repeated, in a rush of nervous energy. "How about this? 'When the crimson flames of the roses are burning lamps lit by the memory of love, will you think a little of the quiet walk we are planning for our Bishops? In the grey evening, while they pace meditating, above the murmur of the sea, what soul-force, what uplifting vibrations, may we not help them to radiate over a waiting world?'"

"Somewhat florid, Miss Hicks." His tone was noncommittal. "We might use it."

He did use it. Nor did he ignore further suggestions, and before the letter was finished, Miss Hicks found she had contributed almost all the wording. She gloated secretly. When it came to appealing for money, the Abbot admitted, her touch was particularly deft.

Southwell Vaughan-Quilter hated these constant appeals for things that did not really interest him. Besides, there was something very materialistic about it. It was all very well to talk about: "Supply being a well-spring for the adept in tune with cosmic harmony." Miss Warburton, of the wealthy squatter family, hadn't given that new organ because she was a source of supply, but because she was personally devoted to him.

Once, gazing at a piece of glowing Indian embroidery, he had suddenly seen a hideous god improperly consorting with seven or eight goddesses or milkmaids. The pattern just rose out of the richness until he wondered how it had escaped notice before. In much the same way this problem of money was always sneering out at him. Anyway, there was no need to waste his time on the details of money-getting now that bright little Miss Hicks was doing so well.

"I think," he said casually one day, "that I might as well leave you to draft out that appeal for the new hall furnishings. Just bring it to me when you're finished, and I'll run it over."

To Shannon this was an immensely important job. She was useful, really useful! As she gathered more and more of the business, running errands to the printer, arranging programmes, ringing up speakers and influential patrons, her tone took on something of the dignity of the Abbey.

"This is the Abbey of Human Brotherhood," she would announce to the transmitter. "The Abbot's secretary speaking. Oh, yes, Mrs. Brewster, I will see if he is engaged." And she would cock an enquiring eyebrow at the Abbot on the other side of the table. The Abbot usually shook his head. He hated telephones. After a silence, Miss Hicks would lie apologetically and deferentially.

"I think he is in the Bishop's study, Mrs. Brewster, discussing the Sunday service. Is there any message I could take?" It pained her to see how readily the Abbot accepted such small deceptions; but he never allowed her to presume upon the more and more trusted position she had come to occupy.

One morning, in a gay mood, she pointed out that the two hands carved over the Abbey gate, which represented the two planetary causes drawing life from opposite directions, could just as easily represent the Sign of the Itching Palm.

"Shannon," Vaughan-Quilter replied sternly, "that sign is one of the most solemn emblems of our faith. And don't steal any more of my cigarettes. I'll see you have some sort of an allowance in the future."

Fully an hour passed before it dawned through her humiliation that he had called her Shannon and had promised her a wage.

II

If the Abbot now gave Miss Hicks a salary of a pound a week, he saw that she earned it. Within the first week of the new regime, he carelessly informed her that she would be taking the Tuesday afternoon class on Personal Magnetism.

"But could I do it?" Shannon glowed delightedly.

"If you can't," the Abbot drawled, "I don't know anyone who could."

For a compliment so dazzling she would have dared much worse than a class mainly composed of elderly, rather stringy ladies who were at first a little discontented when they found that the Abbot's secretary was all they were to receive for the guinea. There were some protests from members of the Brotherhood, Bishop Bulfram, in particular, asserting that so serious a duty should have been entrusted to a more responsible person.

"Well, you take the class yourself," Vaughan-Quilter responded. "A set of stringy old fowls. What do they want personal magnetism for? Shannon can give them all they'll ever need and still have some left over."

Shannon, once launched as a public speaker on personal magnetism, surprised herself. She had come to terms with several of the younger and more impressionable lady novices who were now her dearest friends, ready and willing to lend her small sums, silk stockings, or their second-best dresses on lecture days. Besides being a triumph for personal magnetism, this was a very advantageous arrangement, because the lady novices knew everything that went on in the Abbey and invented a great deal more. They had one particularly good story to the effect that the Abbot was wildly in love with one of the choir boys. This they vowed must be true because if it were not, why should the Abbot be so impervious to the slenderest of ankles, the neatest of lady novices? They employed Shannon's descriptions of the Personal Magnetism classes, and they gathered in her attic and made dreadful jokes about the class members and their need for personal magnetism. Shannon's wider experience of the city they found enthralling. She told them all the bluest stories she had collected in the cafe or at the Showground, and not one of the circle asserted that her aura was red. They wanted more. Life at the Abbey, they maintained, was very dull and the parents who had placed them there under the care of a couple of shrivelled deaconesses, misguided to the point of insanity. The ribald, not to say heartless, remarks of the young lady novices were illuminating to Shannon.

As for the classes on personal magnetism, she kept carefully to the Abbot's published pamphlet, and taking it chapter by chapter, from "Breathing In Vitality" to "The Expanded Vehicle," she found herself gaining more confidence at every lesson. One afternoon, she slipped unconsciously into Mr. Sladder's manner, his very words, and that afternoon she did better than ever before. Scientifically she blended in a little of Vincent Sladder with the more cultured aphorisms of Southwell Vaughan-Quilter, and was startled at the resemblance between the two, a resemblance that bred an uneasy doubt. Of course Southwell Vaughan-Quilter was one of the greatest men on earth, one of the most honest and spiritual, but, just occasionally, very occasionally, wasn't there a slight resemblance to Uncle Vincent and Uncle Vincent's filthy little authoritative pamphlets, "Your Bowels and You," "Fifty Ways of Harnessing the Life-Force"?

The ladies of the Personal Magnetism class had a line of conversation which seemed to be most fashionable among those seeking the Middle

Way of Brotherhood. They talked about their insides; they told each other with unction of the amounts of warm water their insides could absorb. They were particularly interested in Miss Hicks' remarks on the poisoning caused by animal foods. "You have it all at your finger tips, my dear," one lady gushed.

"It is most important that I should," Shannon replied gravely, with a touch of the Abbot's sententiousness. Some of it was Sasha's arguments, other scraps had come from a brief glance at "Foliage." In her attic that evening Shannon was attacked by an unwonted gloom. She had been so pleased at her success with the class, but suddenly that success sickened her. Cant, she thought, and this brought to light a recollection of John Terrill declaiming: "And what would Kant say?" John Terrill's gloomy warning: "Don't worry about anything but money. Just follow the money, Shannon." I won't, she thought, not for all the brotherhoods in the world. But for Southwell Vaughan-Quilter? That was a different matter.

The Abbot, pleasantly surprised that none of the Personal Magnetism class had demanded her money back, was preparing more work for little Hicks.

"I don't see why she shouldn't fill in half an hour on Thursday night's discussion. We need another speaker." He mentioned the matter carelessly to Bishop Steele.

"But, Southwell," Bishop Steele was pained, "we have a duty to our people. Miss Hicks . . ."

"She'll do to fill in." The Abbot was in a cantankerous mood and impatient. He had been quarrelling in a chilly way with Bishop Bulfram and had begun to fear that Bishop Bulfram was building up a very formidable faction against him. After all little Hicks was his own particular devotee, and she was capable. Why not push her along? "She can't do any harm in half an hour," he argued. "She can talk about predicting the future. She's good at that. She'd predict anything."

Bishop Steele shook his head. Southwell was becoming more and more difficult. He did not seem to pay attention lately. His first blaze of enthusiasm had died out.

"I'll tell you what it is." Vaughan-Quilter seemed to divine his Bishop's thoughts. "I'm not used to this kind of easy life. If it weren't for Bulfram trying to knife me, I think I'd get out. My mission here," he reverted to his clerical manner, "is, I feel, almost ended."

"Don't say that, Southwell." Bishop Steele was secretly relieved. "Why, we wouldn't know what to do without you." But how peaceful to have only Bishop Bulfram and none of this disharmony! Again, the Abbot seemed to read his superior's thoughts. He growled something inarticulate and prowled off to his own study where he proceeded to put Miss Hicks in her place.

"I've been making enquiries," Shannon began in tones of friendly equality, as he came in, "about broadcasting possibilities. You remember Clive Peake who runs "Foliage"? Well, I met him yesterday and he told me Bleeby Peverill is doing well at it. If Bleeby can get a radio session, it ought to be worth the Brotherhood's while to look into it. So I went round the studios and collected some prices and figures, and I thought . . ."

Vaughan-Quilter's manner was biting. "I'll let you know when I want anything of that nature." Above the Thrones, Dominions, Intelligences, his manner indicated, there was One Supreme. He seated himself at his table as though he were the One. "Will you take a letter, please?"

Miss Hicks said nothing; she looked as if he had hit her. Her pencil travelled quite speedily after his words.

"And don't go changing or improving it," he admonished in a more human tone. Then, seeing how white and stricken she looked, he repented. "By the way," he added, "I've put you on the programme for Thursday night. You can have something ready, can't you?" She nodded. "And don't look as if I was going to bite you." His tone became irritable. "You'd better get that stuff to the printer today."

It comforted her a little that, if he was worse tempered, he had lost his early courteous forbearance of her as a helpless object of charity.

Thursday night, despite her previous experiences in conducting the class on Personal Magnetism in this hall from this same platform, found Shannon blue, her teeth chattering with terror. There was such a big audience. Instead of a couple of rows of front seats, as in her little class, the whole hall was filled. The cold dread of failure gripped her again. It was lucky the Abbot was not there, she thought bitterly, to see her downfall. But once on the platform, her preliminary quaver of nervousness served her well. She was a good speaker and an excellent mimic.

Her opening was that of a timid, pathetic little girl fighting, Oh so bravely! to speak clearly, and the audience sympathized; but as soon as she had them secure, she launched out in full force in an imitation of Mr.

Sladder. It was a modified version, but it had the force behind it, as she told them what the discovery of the Brotherhood way had done for her, how it had lifted her from poverty, ignorance, despair to a secure belief in the Oneness of Being, the impermanence of the material body, and the illusion which we call the world. It was the picturesque detail, the description of her lodging-house days, that went over best. Earnestness, girlish simplicity, conviction, and, best of all, they could hear her in the back seats. The round of applause, when she sat down, was equal to that received by the lecturer for the evening.

She could see Southwell Vaughan-Quilter in the back row. He was surrounded by a girlish flutter of novices, but he was there, and he had heard her! A second glance, for she was still on the platform and could not stare openly, showed her someone sitting next to the Abbot, someone vaguely familiar. Racking her brains while the lecturer worked up to his climax, she brought back the memory of Lucy Rossingale. Of course it must be Lucy who knew Southwell Vaughan-Quilter, had known him a long time. The sight of Mrs. Rossingale chilled her triumph.

As soon as it was politely possible, Shannon hurried down the hall towards the Abbot who was talking to Lucy in a way he never talked to his secretary. Lucy gave her a beaming smile.

"Well, well, well!" she cried. "So this is where you've been all the time. And your aunt and uncle combing the city for you." She would say that, Shannon thought. "Here's dear old South telling me you're practically his right hand. Isn't that too marvellous! And you were priceless tonight."

"I don't think you need have been quite so materialistic." Vaughan-Quilter coated the bitter pill with sugar. "But it was exceptionally good." He turned to Lucy. "You were saying something about coffee?"

"I think we ought to take your secretary as chaperon," Lucy said playfully. "You must come and see me, darling." She gave Shannon's hand a little squeeze. "I'm in radio now, you know. Did you ever think of writing copy?"

Vaughan-Quilter did not give Shannon time for reply. "Mrs. Rossingale has been talking to me about radio, Miss Hicks. She seems to think there are possibilities that it might be a vehicle for our message." His tone was speculative.

"Yes." Shannon smiled very pleasantly while she tried not to show her feelings.

"Give me a ring, darling," Lucy broke in. "I've moved but I'm in the phone book. Sure you won't come and have a cup of coffee with us now?" For some reason Lucy seemed anxious to include her.

The Abbot glanced uneasily around him. Shannon could see him mentally hurrying Lucy out of the hall. "Well, be good, Shannon, and be sure you *do* come and see me." Lucy gaily waved her good-bye.

Left alone with the lady novices and their "Darling, you were marvellous," Shannon felt her face stiffening until the bright, polite smile was something infinitely weary and sad.

"Let's get along," she urged. "Or we'll have Meggy hounding us." Meggy was the fussier of the deaconesses. It would not be safe to think until she was back in her attic. Besides it hurt.

The night had confirmed her in an impulse that had been growing underground in her mind. She must get away from the Abbey before she became too glib. That night she had been downright dishonest; but worst of all she had a new view of Southwell Vaughan-Quilter. She couldn't stay on, seeing him every day when it was so hopeless to love him. She loved him, not as a saintly Abbot, but as a very human sinner, mentally dishonest as herself.

He doesn't believe all this, she thought. He really doesn't believe it— half the time. But, anyway, I'm going away. I've got to go on, somewhere else, quickly. I've got to get out. Her thoughts beat around and around. Where to go? Back to Aunt Edith, to Joseph Litchin and the Pompadour, to Balm Point?

She would not let her imagination dwell with Vaughan-Quilter in Lucy's flat. It made her aura too red.

III

Southwell Vaughan-Quilter had always liked Lucy Rossingale because she was humorous, good-natured and astute. You could talk to her. He found himself pouring out all his irritation, telling her of the serious rift that was developing between himself and Bishop Bulfram. The Bishop insisted that more and more money be placed in building investments. Vaughan-Quilter wanted to found a university of students of the Middle Way, a university that should teach out of doors in magnificent gardens, where peripatetic philosophers against a background of marble columns and blue sea should lead the seekers to new truths that had nothing to do with the material plane. But when he tried to remodel the Abbey into his own university, the Bishop blocked him. Southwell Vaughan-Quilter might bring in the money, but the Bishop controlled it.

"I tell you I'm getting very tired of it, Lucy. People being fleeced for thousands of pounds and it's all being stowed away to keep the Abbey in comfort."

Lucy, who had long ago discovered that the art of charming was to listen intelligently, curled up more cosily on her rose-coloured cushions. She casually glanced at her watch and found it was long after midnight.

"Why, I could start a movement on my own which would leave them all high and dry. I've only got to leave the Brotherhood and three-quarters of their people would go with me. And they're so narrow. No vision! No real inspiration. Just muddled priest-craft and a lot of half-mystic, half-erotic maniacs swallowing it."

"How did you come across Shannon, Southy?"

The Abbot was not pleased to be interrupted in his recital, but he gave her a brief outline of his visit to Fort Bukloh. "You know I never neglect an intuition, Lucy."

"She's a bit of a find, isn't she?"

"Quite useful." The Abbot reverted to his more pressing worries. "Now, this is the kind of thing I mean. Just listen to this. Can you imagine that Bulfram should put away twenty thousand pounds, twenty thousand pounds, during the last year in building investments, and not a penny for a practical idea like mine."

Lucy expressed her amazement. "Have another drink, South," she offered. "Just to take the taste of it out of your mouth."

By two in the morning Southwell Vaughan-Quilter was holding her hand and telling her about his vow of celibacy. He always reached that stage about two in the morning. When he left her flat, he had still said no word about radio, and when next morning Miss Hicks brought up the matter, he brushed it aside vaguely with a promise that "they would go into it sometime."

He was so busy that he failed to notice any strain in his secretary's manner. All day he was off in the city seeing influential patrons and enlisting their support for a move to separate the finances of the lecture centres from the Abbey. Everything that came from the lectures should henceforward go to a fund for establishing his university, and the Abbey and church could live or starve on their own finances. He kept his secretary hard at work arranging appointments and for the next few days he was in the city, while she attended to messages, programmes and proof-reading of the latest booklet entitled "Star Watchers, Our Unseen Guides."

When Lucy rang up, she was told that the Abbot was out, but Lucy in her most alluring voice explained that she wanted Shannon to come to lunch with her. Cautiously Shannon agreed. If Lucy had any little schemes, the lunch would bring them out. Lucy suggested the Pompadour, but Shannon refused and gave no reasons for her refusal, so the meeting was settled for a similar restaurant where Lucy arrived breathlessly and dramatic a quarter of an hour late.

"But if you only knew what a vile morning I've had, you'd realise I couldn't be here a minute sooner. I tried to ring the Abbey but they said you'd gone. I thought of sending a messenger here to wait for you and tell I'd be later. Really I did."

"It doesn't matter," Shannon muttered, drawing well back into her shell as Lucy's charm flowed over her.

"But I know how you rush off and I was worried to death you'd rush off again. What on earth did really happen to make you and Beryl Whats-her-name disappear as though you'd been wiped off the face of the earth? You can't imagine the row there was about it, your aunt blaming me, and Vince Sladder sizzling at the seams, because, I *must* admit," Lucy admitted it handsomely, "the office had got a bit out of hand with no one there to see to things. And then Bleeby rounding on me and accusing me, *me*, mind you, of turning Whatsisname against him. Why I hadn't the slightest idea," Lucy's tone was outraged, "that there was anything at all between them. Now how could I have any idea? You remember the way Beryl Whoever-she-was talked about him as though he was the baker or someone? Well, I wasn't to know till she flared up that she was having some kind of underhand affair with him. And as for Bleeby Peverill," Lucy's tone was stern, "when I think of that rat, it makes me just *ropeable!* He leaves me to face all the music about you two."

A waitress who had stationed herself by their table was beginning to show signs of impatience. "No, our order hasn't been taken. Wait till I look at the menu. I think I'll start with an oyster cocktail. Leaving *me*, as I was saying, to face the music, and the next thing I know he's crawling into 2RQ as though butter wouldn't melt in his mouth, and getting himself a job there. I should think he'd have more self-respect than to ever come near me again. Of course I always speak to him in the corridors, but he can see I'm still mad about it. The low worm! Imagine!" Lucy's voice rose. "Suppose *I'd* practically accused him of kidnapping two strange girls he'd never seen before? What are we going to have after those oyster cocktails, if they ever come?"

The meal proceeded to an accompaniment of Lucy's views on Bleeby Peverill and his perfidy in working on what she regarded as *her* radio station, Beryl's deep treachery, Shannon's incredible gullibility in getting herself mixed up in the affair.

"I *do* think you ought to make it up with your aunt," Lucy insisted. "If you'd seen how cut up the poor old thing was! She kept on worrying and making Vince's life hell. I'm sure she wasn't satisfied until she'd blackened *me* very thoroughly, so thoroughly that I really quit before Vince was persuaded into throwing me out. The same with Bleeby. There's no doubt who's running the joint now your aunt is around." She reverted to her neglected meal. "Look, why don't you see her and clear it all up?"

"I wrote her a letter."

"Now, you *know* you can't say anything in a letter. Suppose I were to invite your aunt and Vince up to my place and have you there too? Then you could all talk it over."

Lucy as a bringer of peace puzzled Shannon. She could not imagine what Lucy thought she would be making out of it, and she felt too jaded and depressed to bother asking her. "I don't know," she said moodily. "I'm thinking of leaving the Abbey. They're a frightful set of fakes."

"No!" Lucy was genuinely surprised. "Why I thought you and Southy were clicking very nicely." Her eyes twinkled naughtily. "He's got very good taste, that lad. But not really, you are not really going to leave?"

"I don't know," Shannon said again listlessly. "The place makes me sick."

Lucy was silent for a moment, thinking. "I don't know if I could do it," she reflected aloud, "but I absolutely *must* have someone to look after my mail." She calculated for a minute. "I don't suppose they'd pay you more than the junior typists, say thirty shillings, and just at the moment I'm all alone in the flat, so you could come and live with me, if you liked, then your aunt would know you were safe and well looked after."

Shannon eyed her suspiciously. "What's it got to do with Aunt Edith?"

"But, my dear, aren't I telling you?" Lucy's tone was frenzied. "You've simply got to see reason. You can't possibly go prowling about like a lone wolf. After all, Shannon, you're only a young girl, and I know, I tell you, I *know* what trouble you could get into. You're so very innocent, dear, but men are, after all, only men." Her tone was sweetly maternal. "You're going to promise me that, if you leave the Abbey, you won't go bolting off into the blue again, but you'll just try my idea first. Really, Shannon, you're so downright positively exasperating! And you could be so useful at 2RQ." The more she thought of it, the more the idea appealed to her. There was no need to tell Shannon why she wanted to be on good terms with Vince Sladder again. All in good time.

"You've known Mr. Vaughan-Quilter a long time?" Shannon asked.

"Dear old Southy? I knew him in London when I was there years ago. He was Classics Master at Harrow one time."

"Do you think he's the kind of man who ever marries?" Shannon asked gravely.

"Well, I should say so!" Lucy gurgled with joy at the naïve question. "Seeing he has a wife and two children in England."

"Oh!" Shannon swallowed hard. "But his vow of celibacy?"

"The type of wife South has," Lucy assured her, "would make any man take a vow of celibacy. This is stone cold, I wonder if I can get that girl to get me some more coffee." She averted her eyes from her stricken companion and allowed her time to recover.

The core of kindness in Lucy was touched by the girl's bleak expression. Most young women would have offered confidences or wept or shown some emotion, but Shannon went on steadily eating her lunch with a set face.

"I'll tell you why I want to make it up with Vince Sladder," Lucy burst out. "Don't think I'm hanging any strings onto the job at the studio even if the idea doesn't come off, I mean, that's all right. I do need someone to look after my mail, and it's a huge mail. I get more mail than anyone on the station. But," she went on impulsively, "I've got a Hell of a contract.

I didn't read the damn thing when I signed it, and now I find I've got to find the advertisers to sponsor my session. You've no idea what it takes. Selling radio advertising in this city is like selling some rare kind of Iceland moss. Now, don't stop me for a minute." She patted Shannon's hand. "I want to get it all off my chest while I'm feeling honest. I do want you to make it up with your aunt, because it's sad for her, poor old thing, but Vince these days is making pots of money. He's not only got this home for psychopathic cases who can't be certified, but he's in a company for making a vibro-massage machine, and here's where I come into it. I want the advertising contract for that machine. I *know* I'd be able to put it over. And if it wasn't that Vince is scared of your aunt, he'd hand it to me like a shot." She sighed, appreciative of her own frankness. "Now you can't ever say that I didn't tell you straight out just why I wanted you to patch it up with auntie."

Shannon had recovered, thanks to Lucy's kindness in giving her a breathing space. "She wouldn't take any notice of me, neither of them would."

"Well, if you were working with me and going home at week-ends like a good little girl, it would be a sort of bond, wouldn't it now?" Lucy smiled. "Trust me to show auntie I'm not a bad sort, poor old auntie." She smiled at Shannon, and the likeableness of Lucy was something that even the hardest could not resist. "We'll have a lot of fun," she promised. "It's awfully interesting at the studio. And you're doing *good* all the time, that's what I like about it. Anyway, you think it over."

"Let me pay." Shannon reached for the bill.

"But I invited you," Lucy protested.

"That doesn't matter." Shannon recklessly dipped into the Rose Garden money. Lucy never paid for her own lunches, and she would feel so sorry for herself if she had to do it now; she would feel she was losing her charm. It made her feel good to be paid for, and Shannon didn't care a curse in her present mood; why not pay for Lucy's lunch anyway? She felt kindly towards Lucy, almost she wished to apologise for what she had thought about her and Southwell Vaughan-Quilter. She knew without Lucy telling her that one of the schemes behind today's invitation, for Lucy always had two or more schemes warming up at one time, was to see if there were any way of linking the Abbey up with the 2RQ Women's

Session in some financially remunerative manner. Good old Lucy! Never a quiet moment for her brain. Always on the move, unresting, untiring, and ceaseless as light.

All the way back to the Abbey, Shannon found herself working up to a mood of bitter hilarity. For no apparent reason small things took on a significance: the child leaning over the side of the ferry boat earnestly asking: "Does this boat make soapy water, mummy?"; the shops on the Quay, the smell of beer and prawns in a chilly nook at the bottom of George Street; the floating scurf lapping against the stone of the wall, a scurf composed of a sodden cigarette carton, several pieces of coke and weed, a splinter of wood, a soaked newspaper and a half-eaten orange, all these had an air of abysmal dejection that amounted to a comedy, which had gone so far down through the depths of bitterness that they had come out the other side into whirlpools of wild laughter.

So she had been worshipping a saint, a celibate saint, who was nothing more than a talented opportunist with an incompatible wife and a couple of children. "Well, well!" she murmured impersonally to herself. "Shannon Hicks, the fool of the family!" As she strode off the ferry, she felt positively light and airy, as though a burden had fallen from her. Southwell Vaughan-Quilter she still loved, but with a tolerant derision that did not hurt unless she let herself think seriously. Nothing hurt much if you laughed.

The only begetter of all these changes of mood was talking on the telephone as his secretary walked in. He motioned to her to wait while he finished his conversation.

"Where have you been?" he asked, as he put down the receiver. "The printers have been ringing up all the morning about 'Star-Watchers.'"

"I took Lucy Rossingale out to lunch and embezzled some of the funds for the Rose Garden," she replied deliberately.

"Oh, well, it doesn't matter." He was bored. "What did you do with those press-prints?" But a little later he asked: "What did Lucy have to say?"

"She's offered me a job." Shannon's voice was still hard and light. "I'm almost thinking of taking it."

"Shannon!" Vaughan-Quilter almost shouted with amazement. "Why, my dear girl, I've been practically flinging opportunities in your lap. What on earth can there be to make you discontented? I haven't been nagging you, have I?" He smiled genially. "Of course I know you're not getting enough to keep you, but I'll see about that right away. Yes, come to think of it, you're right to think of leaving. I'll see you get a fair allowance, but," he paused disarmingly, "I've been paying you myself sooner than have any trouble with Bishop Bulfram about it."

Shannon swallowed hard. Her airy flippancy was leaving her. "It isn't the money," she almost whispered. "Don't think I'm not grateful, grateful, grateful for all you've done."

"Then what is it makes you think of leaving?"

Shannon took a deep breath. "I don't fit in here. It's better that I go on and find some place I do fit in. Look, South," her voice was Lucy's voice, winning and charming, "just don't ask me why I'm going. Truely, it isn't anything I could tell you, and I know it's mean of me, but there it is. I just choke when I think of going on."

The Abbot was not only wounded; he was a mingling of a number of very complicated states of mind. He had a trained secretary saying she was leaving, which hurt his business sense and vanity; he had bright little Hicks wanting to walk out as quietly and as little known as she had come; a girl to whom he was more attached than he would like her to know, so little attached to him that she could calmly consider going away from him with only good-bye and thank-you.

Shannon was talking at random: "All those awful women at the classes talking about purifying their souls with hot water and purges. Why one of them asked me if she recognized a loved being she had met in a previous life, and the loved being was a different sex from last time, did it make any difference."

"But, my dear girl, you don't take any notice of a sprinkling of fools among fine spiritual people."

"Don't I? Don't I just? Why I see myself getting worse every day. What's the use of clearing off from Uncle Sladder if I get more and more like him? All this deception, and you have no idea the way the novices talk. It would chill your spine. *What* an earthly paradise!"

"I have a very fair idea of the way novices talk." He smiled at her vehemence. "You do take things seriously, don't you, Shannon? After all, you must have a sense of humour to get through life." He laughed genially. "Suppose you think it over for a month and then see how you feel before you go dashing off?"

F

He strolled over to the window and looked with a faint frown at the garden which was to have framed his strolling philosophers. From a passing ferry boat a faint strain of music drifted over the water, and with it the murmur of the sea, inarticulate but heavy with sardonic meaning. A wave of the incoming tide lipped around a ripple of weed and said sharply, "That's it," and flung itself aground with emphasis, as a speaker might bring his fist down on a table top. Another wave which had slopped over a pock-holed rock and sent a sea-gull mincing away on red feet, drawled, "Sure," as it came crawling up the sand.

All the blue-changing eddies, the bright sun-broidered, flickering water, shone below the window, and shivered and slapped itself; wave quarrelling with wave, heedless of the noise it was making, a noise that took no account of human sounds, of voices speaking half-truths, of the dim uproar of the city, the hopes and aches and foolishness of human cross purposes.

Eleven

I

RADIO STATION 2RQ occupied the two top floors of the Majestic Theatre, and a stranger, intending to go there, searched up and down a block of city shops until he located a narrow swing door which led through a malodorous corridor, past the stage doorkeeper's coop, to a lift which had more temperament than any imported prima donna. This lift would sail past the office where some infuriated and important executive was banging the bell, and stop with a lurch for a diminutive office boy on the top floor. Before the lad could open the door, it would be off again to the ground floor, and rest there for five minutes, while a group of jazz-band artists exchanged compliments with George, the cleaner. As soon as they had crammed themselves and their instruments into its tiny space, the lift would refuse to go at all, and when they got out, it would sail away gaily and stick between two floors.

More language and fury had been wasted on the lift than on the Copyrights and Performers' Association, but there was no more hope of persuading the lift to reasonable ways than there was the Association which waited to extract its pound of flesh from the body of 2RQ like a vulture; and did so every time a record was played, a song sung, or any music broadcast on which it had a claim.

If, despairing of the lift, you ventured up the stairs, you were just as likely to land in the chorus dressing room as in the manager's office of 2RQ. By climbing firmly up stone steps for a long time, the clicking of a battery of typewriters and the crash of the lift stopping for once in the right place, would lead you to 2RQ. If it was Thursday, you would know the studio by a hungry-looking crew waiting in a line outside the cashier's window. These were the artists and artistes, ventured down from the sound-proofed top floor to be paid. Some of these would be asking for letters at the switch-girl's desk, others wandering into the programme department to discuss bookings, still others gathering into groups for a little mutual back-patting.

133

Around them and past them hurried the heads of departments, their secretaries, their under-secretaries, their typists, filing clerks, messenger boys and under-messenger boys, on whom the artists cast the wistful eye of those who saw others in a settled job and envied them.

The organization was expanding like a huge mushroom, and more tables, more typewriters and filing systems moved in every month, paper folders and envelopes accompanying them in stacks the size of an elephant's daily meal. 2RQ was only one station of the Forsyth Network, but it was the biggest and most popular. This meant that everyone from the log girls logging the programme to the least of the accountant's department was overworked. The publicity staff exchanged hot words with the office boy over the duplicating, the programme's department complained about the switch-girl's inattention. The manager sent memos typewritten on little slips of pink, yellow and blue paper. The heads of other departments followed suit. Anyone who had not three separate jobs to attend to was considered to be lying down in the road.

As the personnel of 2RQ swelled and swelled, the responsibility of providing everyone with morning and afternoon tea assumed gigantic proportions. H. P. Holburry, manager of 2RQ by the grace of God and a board of fractious controllers, sent around memos urging the utmost economy in lead pencils and another set of memos pointing out the necessity for curtailing the time spent on morning tea. It took—and he had records and graphs to prove it—three girls an hour each to make tea. And it took the staff an unlimited time to drink it.

"That's all very well for him," one of the tea-makers grumbled. "He had three big-bugs in to see him the other morning and sent out to have fresh tea made. I had to pinch some of Clarrie's biscuits to send in to them. How does he think I buy those biscuits on fourpence a week? He won't eat any other kind. You type me out a memo, Joan, and tell him from me that, if he wants those special biscuits, he'll have to throw in more than fourpence a week for them."

Above the jealousy and back-biting inseparable from the working of a broadcasting station, Lucy Rossingale with her Women's Session shone like a star, the blood-red star of war. Woe be to the announcer who carelessly crumpled up an envelope and threw it in the waste-paper basket while Lucy was on the air. He would be hauled before the chief and charged with conspiring to ruin her, conspiring with the head of the programme department, the anonymous letter writer and the switch-girl.

"Who has the biggest mail on this station? Why during the Spring Sale bargain offer I had two hundred letters in one day! You've only to look at my mail, Mr. Holburry . . ."

The storm might rage for hours or days and the switch-girl reduced to tears, the manager to a limp, exhausted ghost of himself, but Lucy would emerge from it all brisk and refreshed. "You've got to show them you won't stand too much," she advised fellow announcers who had not her spirit.

For the sake of peace, the manager instantly granted her request for a personal secretary to attend to her mail. "You won't mind, Miss Rossingale, if the girl in her spare time should attend to Bleeby Peverill's mail or the Children's Session mail?"

"If she has any spare time," Lucy agreed, all sweetness and light, now that her end was gained. Shannon was to live with her as companion-secretary, so Lucy would certainly have priority, and she would be able to make sure there was no spare time.

Bleeby Peverill was doing a series of recorded music programmes. His rather bored voice announcing: "This is Bach's B Minor Suite, a singularly beautiful and satisfying example of The Master's work" was sponsored by Leak's Liver Pills, The Best for All Ages. Naturally he disliked Leak's Liver Pills and swore fluently between sessions, but he swore even more fluently when the manufacturers of the stuff told him his session was too highbrow and made him insert their advertisements into the Roses Are Blooming Session.

This session, which brought Bleeby Peverill's mail almost to the peak reached by Lucy's, was made up of gentle lyrics and little scraps of senti-ment, ditties about life's eventide and the dear eyes of a girl with golden hair. It made Bleeby Peverill so sick that he was considering retiring to a monastery. In the meantime he framed emotional monologues to a background of music.

"We are once more in the beautiful rose-grown arbour by the sea. The gentle sunset is dying and the light fades, old memories of days gone by come crowding around us. Now the gate clicks, and there is a figure walk-ing in the twilight down in the garden path. Ah, we can catch the wustle of her dwess . . . it is the girl of our dweams. (Swell that damn thing up a bit, Jimmy.) Yes, it is she. By Jove, that won't do. The gang who are

listening to this will be old maids and stout women with their bunions
up on a sofa cushion. Change to the love of our dweams. No, that's not
good enough. It is he, the man of all men, for whom we have waited."

Bleeby took immense trouble to get all the lush records of dying love and
fit them in, and his hard work was rewarded by an ever swelling daily
tribute from ladies who "loved his voice." So much so that Lucy began
to grow jealous and complain that the publicity department was sending
out photographs of Bleeby Peverill far more often than her own.

"It really isn't much to ask, just to be given some kind of fair play. A
Mrs. Simpson wrote in to say that she had written twice for my photograph. Shannon, where are the letters from Mrs. Simpson? Why hasn't
she been sent a photograph?" Shannon would conscientiously search for
some non-existent letters.

"Of course, Lucy is a darling," Bleeby Peverill confided in the darling's
maid-of-all-work, "but she's a bit demanding, don't you think?"

"What happened to the milk-run?"

"My God, don't wemind me of that milk-wun. It started as a hygienic
model daiwy, and then the damn horse got some kind of a disease that
made its neck swell up in a big lump and then it died. All the cows had
their necks swelling up too and we couldn't deliver the milk. Sour milk!
Sour milk everywhere. So we turned the daiwy into a model cheese factory
but we couldn't sell the cheese and it went bad on us." Bleeby moaned
softly to himself. "God, it was awful! I can still smell it. The other chap
cleared out and I stuck to it as long as I could. Things were so tough I
thought I'd be sleeping in the Domain. If it hadn't been for dear old Bart
Jackson, I might have been. He'd taken a studio and fitted it out with
tapestwy and a gwand piano and I slept on his sofa. Now we've moved
another bed in and I share half the studio. I'm twying to get his brother
Ashton on the station."

People were forever trying to push their friends into the already tight-
packed pay-roll of 2RQ and whenever they managed to do so, someone
lost his balance and toppled off, so that the queue of persons waiting for
pay at the cashier's window always held a few new faces. To break into
those sacred studios, to see the little light wink on above the microphone
and the engineers behind their glass plate, inattentive and nonchalant as
fish in an aquarium, seemed to be the ambition of half the population.
The other half was determined to make the personal acquaintance of its

radio favourites. Adorers who wanted to meet Miss Lucy Rossingale or Bleeby Peverill, present them with a piece of birthday cake, ask them to put over a birthday call, or appeal to them for money, were met by the reception clerk on the office floor below and either thrown out with the utmost tact or passed on to Miss Hicks' courtesy, in her cubby-hole next to the washroom on the top floor.

Space at 2RQ was at such a premium that the staff ate its lunch sitting on the back stairs. The only quiet place was in the studios where there was peace but no air. The sound-proofing of the studios cut out all noises except an intermittent roar of traffic, but it allowed the odours of the incinerator in the court below the fullest possible opportunities. Announcers agreed that the caretaker kept a supply of old boots and rubber especially for their benefit. From time to time the waft of burning cabbage and manure showed that he had provided himself from other sources than the building, while there was always a lingering of old, damp rags. When the incinerator was not alight, the smell still nestled happily in the studios.

The big studio was at its best when a brass band packed into it, their instruments taking up all the available room and the performers red-faced, streaming with perspiration, making thirsty forays for beer. As they burst out of the felt-padded doors, a gusty essence of studio escaped with them strong enough to blow a delicate stranger backwards in a faint. The passage outside the studio steamed with fat men waiting for a drink. They sat on the stairs, wiped their moist brows and shouted to each other.

Often Miss Hicks, the lonely clicking of whose typewriter could be heard after all the office below was shrouded and silent, would press her way, polite, tired and pale, through the throng and pack into the lift with stout men and their instruments, or later still exchange a few friendly words with the control room yawning through the Night-Birds' session.

Shannon worked at night, not only on Lucy's mail, but on any number of odd jobs, from writing dialogue for "Fast and Furious," the comedians, to studying pronunciation and sentence construction for herself. Just as she had, little by little, taken on more work at the Abbey, so now she took on more at 2RQ. Those who are willing to work are seldom disappointed.

It was no use going back to the flat early, for Lucy never went to bed before one in the morning and liked company. Years of life as a theatrical star had given her the habit of setting very late and rising very late. By staying at the studio Shannon also avoided any gentleman who might be eager to conduct a tête-à-tête with Lucy. She also put in an hour at the studio before Lucy appeared to look over her letters and this hour went to the Birthday Calls. Lucy's method of sorting letters was to glance at the envelopes. She could tell by the handwriting whether there was likely to be anything interesting inside. She would toss the rejected pile to Shannon and slit the interesting envelopes herself. It was left to Shannon to send out the badges for the Smiles Club, sort the postal orders, post off photographs of Lucy, answer the telephone, dicker with advertisers about copy that was too long for the time allowed, go messages, confer with the advertising managers on the Saturday Snaps advertised.

"Now's here something that I know will bring you all rushing into the city on the next tram," Lucy's impulsive, gay voice would exclaim excitedly. "It's exclusive to this session. If you mention the name of 2RQ, you will be given a docket slip for their Saturday Snap, a pair of welted, black super-shoes with the new eyeletting, a pair of Wister's thirty-four and eleven-penny super-kid for twenty-nine shillings. And they're really marvellous value. Now you will go along early, won't you? And remember to mention 2RQ, because the shoes are exclusively for listeners of this session." Lucy would cast a lightning glance at the clock. "I think we have time for just one more record. This is one of my own very special favourites. 'Love in a Mist.' Pretty name, isn't it?" Her genial natural manner had always a little wistful accent, as if she said: "I do-so-want you to like me" with every word. And they did like her.

"If ever there was an angel walking this earth," one listener told the angel's secretary, "it's Lucy Rossingale. I've brought in a bottle of my own special homemade remedy for colds. I noticed, my dear, that Miss Rossingale had a little cough yesterday afternoon, and we can't afford to lose her, you know. You must tell her to take care of herself, and not wear herself out doing so much good."

Lucy was certainly indefatigable in good works. She would collect heaps of clothes or toys and blankets for every Christmas appeal, and pay for the taxi when she went distributing them in person. She liked nothing better than kissing curly headed tots in hospital. There were tears in her eyes when she put over an appeal for a particularly heart-rending case:

"Now I want all my Smiles Club to do their *very* best. I want a bed for the children and some blankets. Some of you must have an old bed you don't want, and if you could have seen those poor little children sleeping on the floor!"

For days after 2RQ was driven mad by delivery of beds. They came in every shape and size, double beds, single beds, three-quarter beds. Lucy ungrudgingly paid out of her own pocket storage for the fifty-three beds until she found an orphans' home in need of them.

Lucy was genuinely benevolent, giving time and energy to helping lame dogs, the orphaned, hungry, jobless, and moneyless, who repaid her, in most cases, with no more than a resentment that she should have it in her power to help them while they had nothing. Under Lucy's benevolence lay a deep strain of superstition.

"I've always had bad luck," she confided in Shannon. "Just when I'm on top, something smites me. Oh! I know what it's like to be broke and sick. That's why I'm worried about this job. So far it's all been too smooth." For three days she had not had a really good quarrel with anyone. "And I feel like crossing my fingers."

She was generous, not only with her own time and energy, but with other people's. She enlisted radio artists to sing free at concerts for charities, she persuaded advertisers to wrench themselves away from a percentage of their profits. She was always hurrying off to a prison or hospital or orphans' home because, as she said: "It gave her a real thrill to think she could help."

It also made a good deal of extra work for her secretary. Any recipes Lucy put over the air she tested herself in the kitchen of her flat, looking very cute and demure in a lace-frilled apron. Shannon and the maid did the washing-up, because, if the recipe did not turn out well, Lucy contracted a headache and had to lie down, and if it did turn out well, she remembered she still had her session to prepare for tomorrow. The current maid was always in a state of mutiny and so many left never to return that Lucy finally decided that it would be more convenient for Shannon to "just give the flat a whisk over before starting work in the morning." Also she found that Shannon, given a sewing machine, could perform miracles in remaking dresses, so she had her "run up a few little things" in her spare time. Lucy believed in bringing out people's hidden talents.

Lucy was really fond of Shannon, but she could not understand her, particularly her prudery. Shannon never slept with anyone, never fell in and out of love affairs as Lucy did. Shannon, Lucy considered, was just

F*

wasting her life staying home to read about the mutations of banana flies or the life of the eel, when she should be out and about doing some good for herself.

"You're ever so attractive," she argued. "It isn't as though you didn't know it."

"When I want to settle down and have children, I'll get married," Shannon reassured her.

"Who's talking of settling down and having children?" Lucy objected. "You're so frightfully old-fashioned, darling."

"Not at all. It's you that's old-fashioned. You've got this romance idea. Romance was invented in the Middle Ages by a group of noble dames who had lots of leisure and lovers. It's been fogging our ideas ever since. Now, biologically speaking . . ." Lucy groaned whenever Shannon began with the phrase "biologically speaking." Lucy knew she was going to talk like a professor. "Biologically speaking, mating is only a preliminary, a kind of bait that nature holds out to prospective parents. It's the young that are important, but the white races seem to have forgotten that. Child-bearing," Shannon carefully applied her lipstick, as she peered into the glass, "has been made indecent by the Protestant religious taboo on sex, and, economically, the limitation of families was inevitable."

She would go on for hours if Lucy didn't interrupt and Lucy rather liked being addressed as though she were a biology class. It made her feel intellectual. You could learn a lot from Shannon about bugs and 'wogs and the indecencies of snails and oysters.

"You're such a humbug," Lucy persisted. "Why not be human for once? Just let go. Give yourself a chance."

"It isn't in my line and I don't care for it."

"I wish I didn't care," Lucy said wistfully.

Visiting celebrities succumbed to Lucy's wooing in a way that later amazed their better judgment, when they found they had promised to talk or sing or play in her session for nothing. "Yes, I have luck that way," Lucy would admit modestly. "I can always find people to do things for me."

Living with Lucy, the dangerous exploiter of other people's time and energy, had its compensations. She loved fun and laughter and free theatre tickets and parties. If she had been bad-tempered or exacting, she was always so eager to make friends again; her craving to be liked was so strong that she would not rest until she had, with an impulsive good-nature, won her friend around. Truth to tell, Shannon took so little notice of Lucy in a rage that it was really effort wasted to try to make it up with her.

"I had so many rows at home," she explained frankly, "that now it just doesn't bother me."

Lucy expended her money even more lavishly than her emotions and it was gone almost before she saw it. She was reduced at times to borrowing Shannon's salary which had been increased twice. Shannon was becoming a valuable and important member of 2RQ staff these days, because she was always ready to do jobs other people refused as being outside the terms of their employment. So Lucy felt she was really justified in borrowing from Shannon and forgetting to return the loan. She loved taxis and she was not built for standing in trams.

"Why shouldn't I have what I like when I can afford it?" she argued. This principle held good for liqueurs, scent, flowers, little items of jewellery or "a duck of a hat." She always gave Shannon the clothes of which she had grown tired, so Shannon had nothing to complain about. Apart from the fact that she could not call her soul or her time her own, she was living well, and if it were not for her stupid habit of eating hardly anything at all and working on so many extra jobs, Lucy assured her, she would be looking splendid instead of pale and tired.

"It's so annoying for me," Lucy pointed out. "Just when I need a little relaxation and think of having a party, you want to go to bed." A kind idea occurred to her. "Suppose you ask Bleeby Peverill to drive us out to see your aunt on Saturday. The fresh air will do you good. Oh, yes, let's!" She clapped her hands girlishly; and Shannon remembered that Lucy had not yet landed that vibro-massage contract. "I'll ask Southy to come along too and that will make just a nice little party." Bleeby added to Aunt Edith and Vince Sladder would make the gathering a real reunion, but there was no reason why she should not bring someone with them more to her liking than Bleeby Peverill.

Bleeby would do as a companion for Shannon, and she could devote herself to Vaughan-Quilter. "We'll make it an all day picnic," Lucy planned. "Bleeby can bring the car and you and I can put together some lunch. I think we might cook a fowl. If you're staying away from the party on Friday night, you might just as well watch the fowl cook. Then on the way home from the picnic we can call in at the Home. Honestly, Shannon, of course your aunt is a fine old lady, but I can't stand too much of the place. Suppose we just drop in for an hour, and then we can get back here for tea?"

Shannon raised no objection. She did not really want to see her aunt or the Blessingford Home, or go driving in the fresh air, but if Lucy had one of her elaborate schemes, she might as well allow the Juggernaut wheels to roll.

"You'll have to ring Bleeby," Lucy decided. "Don't tell him I'm coming. Just let him think he's going out for a picnic with you."

Shannon and Bleeby Peverill had settled down into a working combination very nicely. Not only did Shannon handle his correspondence and prevent the guarded truce between Lucy and Bleeby from breaking into flames, but any time Bleeby wanted the voice of the Girl of his Dreams to murmur through his session, Shannon was handy as the voice. He agreed instantly that a picnic was just what he was needing, but he couldn't get away before eleven on Saturday. Southwell Vaughan-Quilter was pleased to come, because he wanted to see Shannon, but he couldn't get away before lunch.

"It looks as though we'll only be able to go out for the afternoon after all," Lucy grumbled.

Shannon was better pleased because she did not have to lose the much-needed sleep while she did the cooking for the picnic.

Saturday morning brought a roaring gale and squalls of grey rain which set into a steady downpour. Despite the fact that Bleeby Peverill's car was an open coupe, Lucy insisted on going.

The Abbot was rather silent and abstracted for he had important news which he wanted to communicate to Shannon, but Lucy gave him no chance. She would sit next to Bleeby in front, she decided, because she had a slight cold, and Shannon could sit in the dicky seat where she could get all the fresh air. So the Abbot squashed in beside his former secretary looking majestic and preoccupied. The Abbot in the dicky seat of a car in the rain could still manage to look majestic.

They started between the showers and whirled along the grey roads; Bleeby, who had not expected Lucy to join the party and had not intended going anywhere near Mr. Sladder, making the best of a bad job. For Shannon, the very sight of Southwell Vaughan-Quilter was a disturbance to her peace of mind which she tried to avoid. Not that there had been any break between them. She had just slipped from his employ into Lucy's, and whenever he appeared at Lucy's flat, ostensibly to see Lucy, she had kept in the background as much as possible. To sit beside him so close that it was impossible to pretend that they were not inseparable as two sardines was an experience which upset her equilibrium. She shivered violently and the Abbot looked at her with concern, thinking she must be cold.

"I came to see you at the studio last week," he remarked, breaking a mile-long silence. Shannon said nothing. She had seen him waiting in the hall and, with a beating heart, had slipped down the back stairs.

"I'm sorry we were both out," she murmured untruthfully.

The Abbot was going on to frame some sentence which would break his news without giving her the impression that he had been in any way influenced by her. He thought it over carefully. A more ordinary man might have said: "I was standing in the hallway and I had a sudden hunch. I said to myself: 'All those thousands of people listening to drivel; why not give them something worth listening to? Shannon was always insisting we could use radio.'"

On some such impulse Southwell Vaughan-Quilter had requested an interview with H. P. Holburry, and had been shown in immediately. H. P. Holburry knew of him but had never met him and was impressed. He was only too willing to welcome the Abbot, not only for the Abbot's sake, but for the sake of the Abbot's following. People drifted into the habit of leaving their radio tuned to one station. Why should not those "on the Middle Way" tune into 2RQ? Mr. Holburry agreed almost effusively with the Abbot's tentative outline for a session.

"Thinking for health! By all means, my dear sir. Tune into health. Give yourself half an hour a day to keep fit by thinking right. Splendid! Splendid!"

"It will link up with my psycho-therapeutic classes," the Abbot explained.

"Yes, of course," H. P. Holburry assented. "Train your mind and the body will take care of itself. It'll go over. I see it going over from the start. Suppose we call it the Consolation Hour?" H. P. Holburry pressed the buzzer for his secretary. "And, perhaps I can offer you a cup of tea, Mr. Quilter? No? Well, suppose I have a little discussion with my programme director and I can phone you in a few days' time when you have consulted your Bishop? I think you said it was your Bishop you must consult?" He knew there was no need to suggest anything as ignoble as a test. The Abbot's voice and manner made that quite unnecessary.

So the Abbot had gone off to see if Shannon were in her tiny office, but she was still out of the building.

"You remember I once said that I considered that radio had immense possibilities," the Abbot began slowly, now that he had an opportunity to tell her the news. "Well, it is almost settled that I should . . ."

Lucy turned round and cried at them: "Suppose we go straight out to see Shannon's gang and get it over, then we can make a little hay if the sun shines, go down to one of the beaches? Oh, let's do that, goody, goody!" She broke into a gay little song. "Sing, Shannon," she commanded. "We'll have the Smiles Club Song, thank you:

> 'Smile, smile, smile,
> That's what makes life worthwhile.
> Whatever your troubles, they will melt away like bubbles,
> If you smile, smile, smile.' "

Her gaiety was so infectious that by the time they swept into the Blessingford Home, Bleeby and Shannon were chanting "Smile, smile, smile" quite heartily. The Abbot looked sullen. If he had not been so dignified, it might have been said he sulked. He had, for some queer reason which he could not himself fathom, wanted to tell Shannon about this new venture before anyone else. He liked the thought that she might, in her spare time, be ready to help him with the session. She was very capable and she knew all the ways of the studio. Still there was plenty of time to talk it over later.

The Blessingford Home was so entirely surrounded by trees and high walls that it could not be seen from the road. They waited until a rusty looking old man unlocked the gate for the car.

"I never can quite feel so happy," Lucy complained, "when I see all those barred windows." She always came out with Shannon when Shannon visited her aunt, in pursuance of a policy of ingratiation. But even her high spirits were not proof against Mr. Sladder's private patients.

Not that the patients were obtrusive. On sunny days, a few might be seen wandering around the grounds like unquiet spirits. If one of them was sitting in the hall, staring vacantly at nothing, the attitude for the polite guest was not to notice. Indeed, the patients might have been so many ghosts. They were a set of footsteps, faint cries in the distance, perhaps a muffled clanking that showed Mrs. Soames, a quiet unhappy looking woman, was at work polishing door handles. She would polish away by the hour at the same door handle, and if she happened to pick on the door handle of Aunt Edith's drawing-room, as she did this afternoon, she was no more regarded than a quite harmless and eccentric spook.

Nevertheless conversation languished. A bright fire was burning; the room was well-furnished, even luxurious; but the air seemed damp and chilly, perhaps owing to the big camphor-laurel trees that dripped and threshed just outside the window, and blotted out most of the light.

The Abbot moved to the hearth-rug and installed himself on it by right of natural dignity. Aunt Edith, stiff and a little chilly, as though the cold had got into her voice and manner, was soon conversing with Vaughan-Quilter almost to the exclusion of the other three. Aunt Edith had altered considerably since the days when she presided over Clayton House. Her face had been lifted, and the tucks under her chin gave her a thin-lipped, careful air that she had not had before. Her hair was bleached and beautifully curled. She had abandoned the floury powder and the little neck railing, and wore an expensive grey coat and skirt. But she did not look happy. When the tea-things were brought in, Shannon noticed her watching the sugar bowl with a suspicious eye, and wondered if Aunt Edith thought it contained some invisible white powder to poison her.

The sight of afternoon tea after the cold, wet drive revived the guests.

"So depressing when it rains by the sea," Lucy ventured to their hostess, pleasantly. "I always think there's nothing worse than standing watching it rain into the water and knowing there's nothing you can do about it." She caught the sparkle in Shannon's eye and knew that Shannon for weeks would coo at her: "So depressing when it rains into the sea. Such a waste." Lucy almost choked and then controlled herself. "We were thinking of driving down to the beach later," she explained. "That's what made me think of it. So depressing."

"It is indeed depressing when it rains into the sea," Aunt Edith agreed cordially, and this time Bleeby Peverill nearly choked too. "Shannon, will you call your uncle from his study? He is talking to Dr. Knowles."

One of the reasons Shannon so seldom came to the Blessingford Home was her discovery that Dr. Knowles was installed there as a kind of assistant warder. He always looked at her with an expression half-cringing, half-blackmailing. "I ken you," it seemed to say. "You ken me. Dinna let us fall oot."

"Such an excellent man, Dr. Knowles is," Aunt Edith told the others. "He has the highest credentials. He's Scotch you know, and a little uncouth."

The conversation creaked on like an ungreased waggon wheel. It was a great relief that Dr. Knowles did not come in to afternoon tea. That would have been the last straw. Mr. Sladder, appearing in the doorway, broke into an atmosphere so thick with dreariness that he seemed a ray of sunshine by contrast.

"Well, well, Vince," Lucy cried gaily, oblivious to Aunt Edith's glare. "How goes everything? Merry and bright as usual?"

"My dear Lucy. Well, well, this is a pleasure." Mr. Sladder asked after Bleeby Peverill's welfare as though he were a lost son. He was introduced to Vaughan-Quilter and his pleasure at the introduction was genuine.

"But, my dear sir," he cried, "I have been so eager to meet you. Your classes in psycho-therapeutics are arousing immense interest. For years, my dear sir, literally for years I have been struggling on with the lonely pioneer work of scientific spiritual healing." He edged the Abbot a little off the hearth-rug and warmed his hands as though they too must glow with his own benign satisfaction. "Don't think for a minute that I am claiming the magnetic power I know you to possess, but in my own humble way I may say I have been following the same line of thought."

The party was becoming quite bright. Aunt Edith chatted of the trouble she had had with the plumbing, while Mr. Sladder monopolized his important guest.

"I don't want to bore you with my own efforts," Mr. Sladder was presently saying, "but as you don't drink tea and neither do I, ruinous stuff, I always tell my dear wife, suppose you allow me to show you the records of a few of my cases? My dear Edith, if you can spare us, I would just like to take his reverence to my study for a few minutes. I'm sure you'll excuse us just for a short time."

The frustrated expression on Lucy's face, as she saw her prey vanish, was worth seeing. She had come all this way out in the rain to talk to Vince Sladder about that advertising contract, and for the rest of the afternoon he would be discussing the laying on of hands with Vaughan-Quilter.

It was too bad! It was just too bad. Whenever the door was opened, the deep tones of the Abbot's voice and the more suave tones of Mr. Sladder could be heard above the rattle of Mrs. Soames busily polishing the study doorknob.

From that point the little party fought a losing fight against the silence which threatened to engulf it. Bleeby Peverill, forgetting his feud with Lucy, did his best to exchange merry back-chat. Shannon related all the news of Kerleuit received in a recent letter to which her aunt attended with the air of one listening because she must. She still seemed preoccupied by the sugar bowl, and kept turning over its contents with the sugar spoon, as though she were searching for something.

Just when the conversation had halted, exhausted, and showed signs of dying out completely, there was a sound of the front door slamming, and a high, cheerful voice yelled down the hall: "Ma! Yoo . . . hoo! Ma!"

"Goodness me!" Aunt Edith dropped the sugar spoon. "It isn't, it can't possibly be . . ." She sprang up and was across the room in an instant. "Beryl! Why, my dear Beryl!" Aunt Edith's voice trembled between astonishment and affection. She always liked Beryl better than anyone, Shannon thought. She's missed Beryl. It made her a little sad to see how animated her aunt had become of a sudden.

"The little, old returned prodigal," Beryl said, kissing her ex-employer soundly. "What-ho, all." If it was Beryl, it was a Beryl altered out of sight. She had been a thin, sandy blonde. She was no longer thin and her blondeness was a self-confident, bright, ringing blondeness. She had the glitter of a fun show, the laugh of a vaudeville comedian who knows his audience is with him. She was not dressed for the rain. Her small hat was a confection of flame coloured feathers. Under her fur coat she wore a flame coloured crêpe de chine dress on which Lucy fastened her eyes as soon as Beryl threw back that coat, which she did at once.

"Hell, it's hot in here!" she exclaimed. "Old home week, what?"

"Bewyl," Bleeby was dodging around Aunt Edith, waiting to take Beryl's coat, "my dear, you're looking magnificent. Where have you been and why didn't you ever get in touch with me?"

"Hello, Bleeby," Beryl said rather coldly. Her eyes had gone past him to Lucy. They exchanged a long look. The Beryl with whom Lucy was dealing now was a very different Beryl from the country lass of a few years before.

"But where have you been all this time?" Aunt Edith was insisting. "I worried about you and lay awake at night. There are such dreadful men about these days. I thought you might have been decoyed away."

Beryl shouted with laughter. "Decoyed!" she cried. "That's good. Ma, any man that thought of decoying me," she paused to hug Ma again, "I'd just show him my teeth and he'd know I was a big, bad wolf. What great big teeth, you have, Grandma. All the better to eat you with."

Mr. Sladder was disturbed in his conference. He had been expounding the benefits of vibro-massage and the added benefits of the Abbot sponsoring it over the air. They had almost reached an agreement when they were impelled to seek the cause of the uproar.

"Why, Beryl, Beryl." Mr. Sladder, taking in Beryl's prosperous appearance, decided like lightning to let bygones be bygones. "This is a royal surprise."

"How do, Pop?" Beryl slapped him heartily on the back, and winked at Shannon over his shoulder. "Got a couple of calves killed?"

"You know, I think," Lucy seized her opportunity, "that Shannon would simply hate to come back with us now, you've turned up again like this, Beryl. We ought to be going, Bleeby *darling,* if we want to get back *at all.* Shannon, you'll be down early on Monday, won't you? Bleeby and I have a simply frightfully important appointment." She took up her handbag and gloves. "Come along, Bleeby. Come along, South."

Mr. Sladder found time to draw the Abbot aside. "You'll think over that little matter I mentioned? Perhaps you could let me know. And I wouldn't say anything to Lucy, if you don't mind."

"I must consult Bishop Steele." When the Abbot decided to consult Bishop Steele, he had as good as accepted the offer. If he had said he would consult Herbert Bulfram, that always meant refusal. "I'll let you know, Mr. Sladder." His tone was very cold, not to say glum, for he was just realising that Shannon would not be with him on the journey back.

Bleeby lingered, reluctant. "Bewyl," he pleaded. "You won't go bolting off again, will you? Where can I wing you?"

"I'll let you know through Shannon." Beryl's eyes slid with ever such a slight glint at Lucy. "I'll be seeing you, Bleeby."

As soon as Vaughan-Quilter, Lucy and Bleeby had packed themselves into the little car, Beryl asked abruptly: "She still teamed up with him?"

"She is not," Shannon assured her. "They hardly say a polite word to each other."

"Trust her to let you think it was all the other way. How do you get on with her, Shanno?"

"Lucy has heroic virtues," Shannon replied thoughtfully. "There are times when I love her to death . . . but only for her virtues."

"Well, I don't want to hear about 'em. Look, Ma, I've been going to shoot out and see you time and again, but something's always cropped up to stop me. You'd get into town, meet the crowd off the road, swap stories, take a few drinks, and before you knew it, you were out on the road again driving like Hell. I didn't tell you—Bert's managing an amusement park of his own now. I quit him a devil of a long time ago and went on the road selling a line of lingerie. Wish I'd had you with me, Shanno. I had some dumb chucks of women wished on to me. Then I sold stuff for Forley's, good exclusive lines, imported knitwear and damn dear, but I sold 'em. Can I sell things!" Beryl patted herself on the chest exultantly. "Well, just to tell you how good I am, I'm managing Forley's city showrooms. It'll be a nice easy time after selling on the road. You'd get into a town, take a shop, skim the cream off the local ladies and be off again to repeat in the next town. Any tea, Ma? I suppose you can fit me in some place?"

"Oh, Beryl!" Aunt Edith forgot her uplifted face, and it dissolved into a lamentable mess of tears. "Oh, my dear, you've grown up, and you're so different, and I was hoping you'd come back for good, and I've been so lonely."

"My dear," Uncle Vincent said softly, "I wouldn't upset yourself."

"No, no." Aunt Edith tried to pull herself together. "I mustn't, must I, Vincent?"

"Pop," Beryl said firmly, "you bung off somewhere and Ma can come and sit on the side of my bed and upset herself all she likes." Beryl snatched up her suitcase. "C'mon, Ma. C'mon, Shannon. I've got something here I'm going to show you before I'm an hour older." Aunt Edith brightened up. Clothes had always been one of the greatest interests of her life. "Buzz off, Pop. You don't want to be pussying around. Little ole Beryl," Beryl chanted as she led the way upstairs, "is going to broadcast from right here. She's conducting the underwear session."

Mr. Sladder in his study doorway watched the procession pass upstairs. He made discontented tutting noises and chewed his ginger moustache. He smacked smartly at the hand of Mrs. Soames, eagerly outstretched to polish the doorknob as soon as he should have relinquished his hold on it.

Twelve

The studio by night, with the office floor shrouded and silent below, put on a very different face from its daytime one. It became, for that space of hours in which its occupants sang and played and acted, a warm gay little world, so pleasantly gay that Lucy would stay on and take small parts in plays, because it reminded her of the back-stage she had loved. Besides you met actors drifted in from all parts of the world, and exchanged gossip about the time you were playing in that terrible draughty old theatre in Manchester or Chicago or wherever it might be.

Shannon also found herself given small parts by producers with whom she had become friendly. "Why not let Shannon do it?" Lucy advised them. She was always generously ready to allow Shannon to take any of these little extra jobs, and Shannon enjoyed them, apart from the fact that she was paid for them. So much so that she found herself, to her surprise, landed with quite a large part in an important serial, the part of a very bad small boy, which she did remarkably well. She had a flexible voice, which was quite as suitable for an adventuress, so she was the adventuress with a fake Russian accent as well as the small boy.

She did not really need the money for she was now in charge of two typists as Head of the Mail Department, H. P. Holburry having created this important post after a conference and a general exchange of memos all round. It meant that Shannon no longer did four women's work but had two women to help her.

Perhaps her reasons for staying at the studio often when she might have gone back to the flat were not unconnected with her desire to hear Southwell Vaughan-Quilter's Consolation Hour on Thursday evenings. She could slip into the darkened studio and watch him, where the green-shaded lamp threw his face, as he bent forward, into a noble relief, and the aching of her thwarted feelings were intensified by these frequent encounters.

What did it matter if he was just another fake? Everybody was the same. As long as they could feel that they were dominating people, it didn't matter how they did it. Vibro-massage machines or laying on of hands in the Hall of All Souls, or Uncle Sladder's home for the semi-insane, it all came to the same thing in the end. Someone was getting money and a sense of power. Lucy had her sense of power glutted in her Women's Session. Bleeby Peverill always had the hall cluttered up with adoring little females and some of them were remarkably good-looking.

But these radio wonders couldn't break away. They were tied to this airless place, this round of unrealities, by their lust for power, their vanity. They loved it. At times she considered it good fun herself, at other times the thought of all the office staff so busily at work, supporting families, coming into the office day after day, being paid and worrying and planning, just to keep this set of inane entertainments going, was enough to make you wonder at humanity. So much money and time poured out and what was there to show for it? Some recorded programmes of symphony concerts; a good deal of jazz music; Bleeby Peverill; Lucy Rossingale; Southwell Vaughan-Quilter; and Jess Esmond crooning "My Baby Loves a Moon," while she was so worried about her divorce that she could hardly sing.

It was not only the incinerator that made the air of the studios unhealthy. The place was a hot-bed of emotion. The silent, deserted office floor was an excellent place to carry on a flirtation or those long, intimate conversations so likely to lead to one. But she could not cast any stones while she lingered on Thursdays to listen to Southwell Vaughan-Quilter. Her friends in the control-room chipped her about it slyly, for control-room men are the most irreverent of the human species, and a sacred passion is less to them than a soprano blasting the station off the air.

Lucy had been incensed at what she considered Southwell Vaughan-Quilter's underhand methods in snatching her vibro-massage contract. He had deliberately gone behind her back. It was in vain that Shannon reminded her that Vaughan-Quilter did not have any idea that Lucy was interested. At base, Lucy's animus was due to the knowledge that the Abbot's mail was already larger than her own. People listened in while he answered his letters so that they might sneer; before they knew it, they were writing him searing love problems, distressing tales of wrong and injustice and despair.

"My dear soul," the Abbot would reply over the air, in his grave sympathetic voice, "yours is one of those cases which arouse my deepest concern." He would give, without names, the gist of the particularly interesting human situation with which he was dealing, and then his judgment, the judgment of Solomon. "Do you not think that you could be a little more . . . shall we say, tolerant towards your sister's husband? After all, he has suffered for his early fault, just as he has made you suffer. I would like to see you. I would like to help you personally. Do you think you could come to me some afternoon so that we could talk the matter over?"

When he shuffled his papers together, he was aware of Shannon sitting in the dimness. He had come to look forward to her silent presence during his talks.

"Well?" he asked. "Did I do well?"

" 'The toil of all that be,' " Shannon quoted, " 'Help not the primal fault. It rains into the sea, And still the sea is salt.' Do you remember that dreadful afternoon when Lucy would go on and on about how she hated to see the sea when it was raining?"

"You mean you think I'm wasting my time?"

"Oh, no, no," she hastened to reassure him. "You're doing a lot of good." She said it mechanically, but the Abbot did not notice. He was always pleased by praise of his work on the air.

"Yet some of these poor people, their problems are such, that one wonders . . ." he waited for further assurances but they did not come.

"Why don't you chuck it?" she asked in a stifled voice. "Yes, I know all about doing good, and the poor people relying on you. But they're exhibitionists. They love to air their sores. They love to hear you reading their lacerating letters." The Abbot was frowning. "Oh, don't think I don't want to sit and listen to you. You really are good on the air. But it's just . . ."

"Shannon, you are never satisfied, are you? You're always looking for the flaw in things."

"Maybe that's it. I'm a grouch. Is there anything you want me to type for you?"

He was studying her closely. "You haven't been looking well. Are you sure this dejected mood isn't a sign that you're sick?"

She almost said: "Are you going to lay your hands on me and cure me?" but was very thankful that she had not. "It's just indigestion," she said lightly. "I get a pain in my chest." She shut her eyes. "Sometimes I think it's watching the rain fall into the sea. I go along the streets and watch the people and say to myself: 'I wonder what your kink is?' I know that if I started talking to them, they'd have some kind of kink. Sometimes

I think I'll end up in Uncle Sladder's menagerie looking out between the bars. Let me have any letters and I'll get them off for you. I've got to go and be Percy now."

Percy was the naughty small boy of the series "Ma and Her Little Darling." After Ma and her Little Darling had watched the little light flick out on top of the microphone, Shannon found herself being taken off to supper by a merry crowd of fellow actors, including one with whom she was conducting an amiable flirtation, a pleasant lad who complained bitterly about the new studio rule that all performers must wear a dress suit when giving their item.

"Why, when I take my guitar out of pawn, I have to put my dress suit in, and now I'm expected to have them both out at once. Uncle won't like it."

Their jollity was a pleasant tonic after the Abbot's soul-searching, and Shannon found herself as gay as any of them. They made dreadful jokes about Bleeby Peverill's lady admirers, and Shannon gave her well-worn imitation of a fourteen-stone damsel telling Bleeby that her husband didn't understand her. It was shocking, it was wicked, but for once Bleeby, who was of the party, did not seem to appreciate it. He had a hunted look.

The lad who objected to having his dress suit and guitar out of pawn at the same time, drew her aside when they were thronging out, after the proprietor had insisted on closing the cafe.

"Poor old Bleeby is in a spot of bother over one of his lady friends," he whispered. "Don't kid him about it."

Shannon's mind flew to Beryl. "Which one?" she insisted. "Tell me."

"The little one with the fluttering eyelashes who is always camped in the corridor. You know the girl who waits for him by the hour."

Shannon knew her. She had nearly tripped over her half a dozen times and wondered how anyone could have so little self-respect. "Serve him right," she said, relieved that it was not Beryl.

A few months later the studio rocked with laughter when Bleeby Peverill was ordered to appear in court on a maintenance charge. Nobody chaffed Bleeby because he was too sore, besides he had had a terrible interview with H. P. Holburry and nearly lost his job. But between the announcers it became a courteous greeting to ask if anyone had been playing any twelve-inch records.

A puzzled magistrate had addressed Bleeby in court in the grave way magistrates have when seeking information: "Mr. Peverill, you admit that this . . . this affair took place at the studio of the station?"

"Yes, your honour."

"But I understood," his honour polished his glasses, "that if the announcer at the time was not broadcasting—you were the announcer on duty, were you not?—that the announcer would be required to put on records and change records and so forth?"

"That's right, your honour." The disgraceful Bleeby was no whit abashed.

"Then how," his honour demanded, "how did this—er—occur?"

"It was a twelve-inch record, your honour," Bleeby Peverill explained.

"I see, I see." The magistrate hastily closed the discussion, but he went home still pondering.

As for Bleeby's work-mates, men who had suffered from Bleeby's popularity, their joy was pleasant to witness. Naturally the matter was hushed up. Apart from the personnel of the studio and twenty each of their friends, the magistrate's friends and the friends of everyone in the court, none of the public knew.

Lucy took the first opportunity to ring up Beryl and tell her all about it, a dastardly deed which only Lucy could have contemplated. A very tender budding little romance which had just reached the stage when Bleeby was looking at rings, came to an immediate halt.

"He's a human menace," Beryl raged at Shannon. "Imagine me being taken in a second time by a man like that! To think that he was talking about what a good husband he'd make, and how he liked to mow lawns. I'm through with him."

"He isn't such a bad sort."

"No?" Beryl asked grimly. "And what kind of a life would it be for me wondering where he was, when he said he was on the Night-Birds' Session, sitting up waiting for him to get in, having women gush all over him. That lad, take it from me, is too much in love with himself. He'd sooner sigh into the damn microphone than say 'I will.'"

At this point she burst into tears and demanded a drink. After several drinks she was still crying and had to be seen home. Shannon was very angry with Lucy who gurgled with pleased malice at scoring off Bleeby and Beryl with one fell stroke.

"You'll regret it," Shannon told her. "You just can't get away with a thing like that."

"Oh, can't I?" Lucy was unrepentant in her wicked mirth. "A twelve-inch record. Ho-ho!"

Three weeks later, Lucy, making for the lift, noticed one of the biggest bores in the Smiles Club waiting for her. She doubled neatly and made for the back stairs, which had always formed a convenient bolt hole, a narrow flight of concrete steps which she took at a reckless pace for a stout lady in little, stilt-heeled shoes. There was a crash and a loud scream as Lucy tripped and came tumbling down, moaning and white, with her leg doubled under her. A scared flock of typists gathered, people rushed up, there were calls for a doctor and an ambulance. Lucy had broken her leg. She insisted very bravely on going back to her flat.

"Shannon can look after me," she whispered. "You will, won't you, kid?"

"Why, of course," Shannon agreed loyally.

"And the session," Lucy was crying with pain, "I leave it in your hands. Don't let me down."

It was a busy time for Shannon, even with a trained nurse to wait on Lucy, and hosts of visitors to hold the invalid's hand. Lucy, listening-in to her own session, was divided between admiration and amusement. It was her own voice coming over the air to her, warm, eager, rather wistful, every tone and inflexion her intimate way of asking: "How did you like that? I think it's such a pathetic little song," when a record ended, or: "Here's another violin solo, 'Roses for Remembrance,' and talking of remembrance, you will remember, won't you, that Soggett's Sale will be opening on Monday with special reductions in all lines?"

"You know, kid," Lucy told Shannon thoughtfully, "I'm beginning to think you're a bit too good to stay typing all your days. The way you have of putting my stuff over makes me think that sooner or later you'll be running a session of your own." She regarded her companion with a hint of doubt. "Are they still asking after me?"

Shannon could see that she was just a little afraid that perhaps she had made a mistake in thinking the session could be best left in her comrade's hands. She did her best to reassure Lucy, told her that people were still ringing to ask after her, gave her the flowers that had been sent, all the little notes of regret and affection.

To her own dismay, these became fewer and fewer as the weeks went by. The mail was as large as ever, but little of it referred to Miss Rossingale. The public has a very short memory and Lucy began to fret.

"I think you might just mention," she snapped nastily, "that I'll be back on the air soon. Really, Shannon, I think it's rather hard that, in my own session, there seems to be a kind of conspiracy to ignore me. It isn't very much to ask that you should just let people *know* how I am. They're probably wondering if I've died, the way you never mention me."

Before she should have been on her feet, she was struggling into a taxi and bravely resuming work, reassured by the congratulations of all 2RQ. It was worth the pain to be back again in the midst of all the new bickerings and riots that had started while she was away.

"You put a hoodoo on me," she declared, half-playfully, half-threateningly, to Shannon. "Telling me I'd get paid out for ringing Beryl."

Shannon said nothing. Lucy was quite capable of believing that she had pushed her down the stairs simply for the sake of taking over the Women's Session.

They worked on together, but not with the same amiability that there had been between them before the accident. When a new series of adventures for "Ma and Her Little Darling" was planned, Lucy protested rancorously that Shannon put too much time into outside jobs and not enough into her own work.

"I know, of course, that as long as you can skim through my stuff, all you want to do is hang about and listen to Southy, but if you knew how *bad* it looks, Shannon, to be just throwing yourself at his head all the time . . ."

Shannon still said nothing. She was waiting for the real storm to break, when Lucy discovered that H. P. Holburry had offered her the Women's Session in Lucy's place, instancing Lucy's quarrels with all the rest of the station as one reason why he would be only too glad to see the last of her. Someone was sure to tell her sooner or later, for there were no secrets at 2RQ, and the chance to annoy Lucy was too good to be missed.

It would probably be Bleeby who was still smarting over Lucy's spiking of his romance with Beryl. Bleeby was so involved with his creditors that they waited in a hungry little pack on pay-days to garnishee his wages before he could spend them, and all Bleeby's attention was given to circumventing them. He had a neat scheme planned out which, with the help of Ashton Jackson, staved them off for a while. On pay-day, when the creditors assembled, Ashton was there in the midst, and it was the custom of these debt-collectors, while they waited, to tell each other in moving tones all they had suffered. Ashton was loudest in his grief. His wife was sick in hospital, his child was slowly wasting away, while he waited for the money from Bleeby that never came. He reduced all the debt-collectors to a sympathetic silence before he was through, and when Bleeby appeared, and they sprang forward with a great cry, Ashton was foremost of the throng, and, knowing his desperate situation, the others, with manly forbearance, gave way.

"Now, just a minute," Bleeby Peverill soothed them. "All in good time, you know, but first things first. Look, let me have a few minutes with Mr. Jackson, will you?"

He took Ashton by the arm and led him out. Around the corner, they had a few beers together and let the creditors tire themselves out waiting.

Lucy had a playful little trick of asking Bleeby whether Ashton's starving child had died yet, and Bleeby Peverill, annoyed beyond endurance, came back at her smartly one day with a hint that she was not half as indispensable as Ashton, that, in fact, though she thought she was so damn marvellous, she would be surprised how many didn't agree with her.

It was not long before Lucy had unearthed, from other sources, the deadly truth, and she was so angry with Shannon that she could have killed her. She found her associate selecting records in the record room, which was a quiet, retired place for a scene such as Lucy needed to relieve her feelings.

"Deliberately, deliberately, to go behind my back and try to steal my session! I've had a few dirty things put over me in my time, but this is about the worst thing I can remember. To think how I trusted you, how I absolutely delivered myself into your hands . . ."

"But I didn't try to take your session, Lucy."

"Oh, no! Of course not! Lying and scheming as though butter wouldn't melt in your mouth. Of course I'm a poor, simple fool, but I'm not as big a fool as that. I can stand a good deal, Shannon, but I can't stand cheating and lying and dishonesty, sheer mental dishonesty, that's your trouble. You go around sneering at everything. Oh, no, you're too pure-souled to behave like a human being. Shall I tell you what you are? You're a rotten, little snake, a crawling, dishonest, cheating, little bitch!"

"Oh, dear!" Shannon sighed. "I knew you were going to be upset about it."

"Upset!" Lucy flared at her. "Oh!" She was temporarily speechless.

Suddenly the realization chilled her that she was not really hurting Shannon. Shannon was no longer the little country girl who had arrived weary and travel-stained at her flat, with a crate of fowls; she was no longer Lucy's little secretary, nor was she only the head of the mail department, a trusted executive of the station and H. P. Holburry's pet. She had matured, grown bigger, like a tree ready to burst out of a pot too small for it, sending out roots into the open ground. Shannon, as herself, was bigger than Lucy.

From that moment Lucy hated Shannon and would never forgive her. All the things that were important to Lucy meant no more than the chittering of rats in the walls, to her former friend. The praise, the knowledge that people listened to her and admired her, the little press clippings, the swelling pride of being "a radio personality," meant nothing. While she could still feel that Shannon was her satellite, Lucy had loved Shannon; but now she hated her, with a hint of fear in her hatred. She could not really afford to quarrel with Shannon, whose position at the station was stronger than her own, but she could not restrain her blind rage. If she could not have her own way, she would create a howling storm about not having it.

"One thing, either you leave the station or I do. I tell you, I'm going to H. P. right away. If he wants you, he can have you, but I won't endure you a minute longer."

"Lucy," Shannon said gently, "don't be silly. I think you're a darling, and I wouldn't have your old session if they laid it on my coffin. If H. P. wants to give me a session, he can give me one on another station of the network."

Lucy stared at her with a distorted face. "We'll see," she retorted. "I'll show you if you can talk down to me. And you'd better find someone else to keep you. I'd like the flat to myself, thank you. You can go back to your precious Abbot, if he isn't sick of the way you throw yourself at him."

At that moment, one of the announcers entered the record room, and both its occupants smiled so sweetly and naturally that he had only his sound instincts to tell him that there had been a quarrel. 2RQ developed one's instincts in this respect. Just as animals, who depend on their sense of smell, become unnaturally acute, so announcers, who may be involved in the deepest intrigue before they know it, become very sensitive to atmosphere. This announcer was able to inform all and sundry that an awful storm was working up, which would involve H. P. Holburry, Bleeby Peverill, and anyone else Lucy could bring into it.

What Lucy had really wanted, when she accused Shannon, was denials, pleas for pardon, tears, and heart-rending forgiveness from her noble, magnanimous self, once Shannon had been forced to admit her perfidy. It had all gone astray, and Shannon had somehow forced her into the wrong. Lucy did not go to H. P. Holburry, as she had said she would. Her own position was too shaky. Instead she followed the traditional course of action at 2RQ. She waited and she intrigued, and she licked her hatred like salt.

Beryl, when she heard of the break, rejoiced openly. "I always knew you'd wake up to that woman sooner or later," she exulted. "Look, I can persuade Forley's, they practically eat out of my hand, to give you advertising, if H. P. Holburry gives you a session. You could make that cheap little bit of poison look like something left out in the wet. And there's tons of room for you to bunk in with me."

Beryl felt that, by receiving Shannon, she was once more scoring off Lucy. Besides Shannon was good fun, if she didn't get one of her philosophic fits. They could have a good time together.

"You're got to stand up for yourself," Beryl argued. "You make Holburry give you a session."

Station 2RQ was the biggest station on the Forsyth Network, but it would be easy enough for Holburry to have Shannon transferred to another station.

"When you're just beginning to get the breaks," Beryl urged, "you'd be a mug not to go your hardest." If Shannon wanted a change of work, she could come and sell frocks. "You'd be astounded, Shanno, at the money some women spend on dress. Why, one of our customers told me she spent two thousand pounds a year on clothes. She's got twenty evening frocks, and never buys a pair of stockings under twenty-five shillings a pair."

"And there're people in this city," Shannon said bitterly, "living in slums where the bathwater empties under the house, and they're thrown out of the place for five shillings' back rent. No, Beryl, thanks very much, but I'd hate your customers. I'd feel like spitting in their eye."

Shannon had no desire to conduct a war with Lucy. "I'd sooner get into something else," she argued. "I'm tired of the radio racket." While she was pleased to accept the hospitality of Beryl's lodgings for the time being, she considered the idea of beating Lucy at her own game ridiculous.

Bleeby Peverill naturally thought of his own session, when he heard that Shannon was discontented. "I've had you for the Voice of My Dweams so long, Shannon, that I'm damned if I'm going to let Lucy spoil my build-up. Let her twy."

With the producers of "Ma and Her Little Darling" she was also so much in demand that Lucy could do little harm there.

Southwell Vaughan-Quilter saw in this problem a chance for his very best brand of advice-to-listeners. "You let me see Lucy, Shannon. You know how she flies off the handle and regrets it later. I'll just have a little talk with her and show her how wrong she is."

Shannon shook her head. "I'm afraid not, South. No, I'm tired of this station. I'm tired of the life worse than I was tired of the Abbey. I'd just like to get out and leave it all behind me."

"Shannon," the Abbot told her magisterially, "you are a psychological problem, a classic example of the fugue complex. You always run away. You take to flight at the first sign of an emotional tangle. Why do you do it, my dear girl? Why don't you stay and face an issue, instead of rushing off blindly into the unknown? Why, where would I be," he tried the winning, personal touch, "without you? Now, don't do anything foolish. Your past life seems to be one long series of escapes. Try for once to take a grip of yourself and face your problems boldly. You let me talk to Lucy and make her see reason."

"I don't care if she never sees reason. She's just given me an excellent excuse for doing something I've wanted to do for a long time. I don't like working in radio, and I want to get out and do something worth while. I've only one life . . ."

"That I don't believe."

"Well, suppose we say I've only this life to play with at the moment. Why should I waste it doing things that seem meaningless? I want to go on until I find what I'm looking for."

"And what is that, Shannon?" Vaughan-Quilter's tone was accusing. "You don't know because you haven't any real aim. You're just going somewhere else. It's pure escapism, my child."

He did not know, Shannon thought, how sorely she had been tempted to do the very thing that he was advising. To stay on, to become better and better known, as one of those magical, wooing voices vibrating from ten thousand sets. A radio personality, someone with a place in public interest, someone that unknown people would talk about: "I can't stay now. I want to tune in to Shannon Hicks." To have a glossy varnish of approval licked over her, to have power. Yes, she had thought of all that. It had taken a struggle to set herself once and for all against the allurements of a little fame, a niche of her own. Surely it wouldn't be doing anyone any harm just to go along as she was going, getting better and better jobs? She was already liked by men who ought to know if she was good, and she could, oh, she could speak so well! It seemed a shame to deny her voice its chance. But, under all the reasonable arguments, something in her very blood urged her to go away—to go somewhere else. Always, at this time of the year, she thought; it's probably some ancestral, migratory instinct.

"I like a clean break," she at length answered the Abbot. "I can't see that there's anything pathological in that. If someone offered me a job cleaning roads, I'd take it with pleasure. Anything to get out of this. Everyone here knows they're not worth while. That's why they talk so loudly of all they're doing, how they're improving the public taste with real music, or putting over the best dance session in the world, or raising so much money for hospitals, or giving good service to the advertisers or the listeners. It isn't restlessness, South. I'll find something, you see." She smiled at him resolutely. "Maybe it won't be what I want, but I won't, no I won't, go on with a thing once I know it's a sham."

"We seem to have had this conversation before," the Abbot said wearily. "Would you come and have supper with me?"

"I'm sorry, South, I can't." Shannon looked disappointed. The Abbot had never asked her to have supper with him before. "I promised Clive that I would go with him to see Sasha."

"Clive?"

"You remember Clive who ran 'Foliage'? Sasha is in hospital with another baby. Clive insisted that I meet him tonight and go to see her.

'Foliage' has gone broke again and they're starting another paper called 'The Anti-War Monthly.'"

Vaughan-Quilter raised his eyebrows. The title did not appeal to him. "And does he expect you to write for it?"

"I suppose so, but I don't see myself doing it. We are supposed to go to some queer club or other afterwards. You wouldn't care to come?"

"No, I'm afraid not." The Abbot had a cold in the head. "I think I'll have a talk with Lucy, though, whether you like it or not."

He might at least patch up a truce. As he walked to the Quay, the Abbot, in his heart of hearts, could not help feeling that Shannon was right about Station 2RQ. For the moment, she had almost convinced him that she saw more clearly than he did. Then he shook the thought off. Why, one could do an immense amount of good, influence any number of people to nobler aims. He could quite easily carry on his own session without recommending Vincent Sladder's vibro-massage machine, although the recommendation probably did no harm.

He was feeling low-spirited at Shannon's resolution to leave the radio game at the first possible opportunity. His low spirits were also partly due to the cold in the head which this stuffy, germ-laden studio fostered. Half the staff was down with influenza, and, at the moment, an epidemic of it had struck the Abbey, but thanks to his excellent constitution and a firm determination not to give in, he was still able to carry on with his class in psycho-therapeutics. Even if his voice was husky, and he blew his nose until it was red, he was getting some amazing results in curing all kinds of complaints. The fact that he had a cold himself never seemed to interfere with his efficacy as a healer. He wished he could do something to exorcise the demon of restlessness from Shannon. She always made up her mind in this peculiar way and he knew, from past experience, that there was no stopping her once she did. It was just another vexation to a man who had Bishop Bulfram to deal with, two services on Sundays, the Consolation Hour, and two classes a week in spiritual healing, that the one woman he really trusted and admired should decide to cut herself off from everything in which he took an interest.

Thirteen

SASHA WAS IN HOSPITAL with her third baby, and of course Clive had made a mistake in assuring Shannon that they could go in to see her at any time. They were turned back at the entrance by a frigid attendant who received with a blank face all Clive's pleas that he had come in the daytime before and did not know the visiting hours at night. Obviously, the attendant thought a man who could not remember visiting hours had no right to have a wife and child in hospital, and Shannon felt like agreeing. Clive was so dreadfully irresponsible.

"This comes of only being able to afford a public ward," Clive complained. "Joseph was perfectly heartless. He gave us the money for a taxi for Sasha twice, and of course we spent it. Emmie Brewster was quite nasty about my borrowing her car without asking, but what was I to do? We hardly ever see you now, Shannon. Poor Sasha thought you might have come out and helped a bit when she needed someone. You must have plenty of spare time."

"Not so much spare time."

"Well now I have hold of you, I'm going to introduce you to a chap Sasha and I have been just *yearning* you should know. He paints the most astounding modern nudes . . . really modern. Jablitzsky. He's got a really new technique. Paints everything in long streaks, not cubes or triangles. See the idea? The Einstein theory in practice."

"Like a murder going somewhere to happen? Must I really meet this man? What about the club you were going to visit?"

"Afterwards, afterwards. We'll pick up Mischa Jablitzsky and we'll all go on there. You're so dreadfully impatient, Shannon."

They strolled in a light drizzle along the dark streets, stopping to watch the elephants eating hay behind Wirth's Circus, and then cut through a number of lanes and alleys to make a complete chord across the city. Clive always walked because he had no money, and Shannon because she was frugal. She had never conquered her original view that riding in taxis was a sinful luxury.

So they walked, Shannon enjoying the empty streets and the darkness as they tramped along. They crossed a little park that was a breath of mown clover wet by rain. The light glanced through the leaves of the few miserable trees and Shannon was suddenly homesick for Kerleuit, Kerleuit that she had not seen for so many years.

"How much further?" she asked Clive crossly.

"Oh, not far." Clive's ideas of far and near were those of a back country farmer. By the time they had tramped almost to Double Bay Shannon was exhausted. She began to say biting things to Clive, so that he was relieved when he could announce that this was Jablitzsky's lodgings.

The landlady told them coldly that Mr. Jablitzsky had gone a month before, leaving no address. Clive did his best to laugh off this mishap.

"It doesn't seem to be our lucky night," he pointed out gaily. "Well, I suppose we'd better go on to the Proletarian Club by ourselves, if dear old Mischa isn't here."

Shannon refused to go to the Proletarian Club. Her feet, she said, hurt her. They argued about it for some minutes while the drizzle increased to a steady rain.

"You won't need to walk, we can take a tram, and I've so much to tell you about the 'Anti-War Monthly.' Don't be a bad sport when you promised you'd come."

Finally Shannon allowed herself to be persuaded into a tram. "I suppose the Club will have closed down," she growled at Clive, as she gave him the money for their fares.

"Well, as a matter of fact, it isn't officially opened yet. It opens tomorrow night."

"Well, why are we going there now?"

"I half promised I'd look in," Clive admitted, "and give a hand cleaning the place up. It used to be the old Bolshevik Club, you know, but they've completely reformed, got new premises, a new executive, and I don't know what. Now they're going to uplift the workers by means of modern drama, art and literature. They're having a dance tomorrow night with an exhibition of black and white work. It will be a centre, don't you see? The outlet for all the stifled genius of the masses."

Shannon's bad temper grew. She had a bitter dislike of anything with culture or uplift attached to it. What a fool she had been to promise Clive she would come. Whenever she met Clive and Sasha, they led her into some kind of frantic dance like this.

The Proletarian Club was up a noisome alley near the docks. At the corner, sailors and painted girls laughed in dark doorways. There was a smell of beer-dregs and yesterday's prawns, where a hotel sheltered a fish stall in its beneficent shadow. Behind a high wooden fence was a stone courtyard and what had once been a flourishing stable. There were still a few horses stamping and stirring in their stalls. Above the stable, up a flight of wooden steps, the Proletarian Club was preparing for its gala opening the following night.

A large red curtain screened the doorway at the top of the wooden steps, and this Clive pushed to one side, posing theatrically against the excellent background it made.

"Only three of you?" he asked. "Where are the others? Olly, Mac, Bert, this is Shannon. Come on in, Shannon." He had thoughtlessly let the curtain drop, muffling his companion in its folds.

Three people were gathered drinking coffee and eating biscuits. They washed out two cups so that Shannon and Clive might join them in their refreshment. The girl, Olivia, was plain and tired-looking, but when she smiled, her face lit into the most vivacious and charming manner. Something about her simplicity, her careless gaiety, shone in the first greeting she gave the newcomer, so that Shannon found her irritation soothed away. It would be worth the miserable evening just to meet anyone so frank and friendly. Mac was a quiet, middle-aged man with hair thinning at the temples and a hesitating way of speaking. Bert was a six-footer, with a high voice and the beautiful flushed complexion of the consumptive.

They stood in a litter of wood shavings, dirt, brooms, dust pans and scrubbing brushes. Half the floor was scrubbed. Someone had been kalsomining the walls which badly needed such treatment, and the smell of kalsomine mingled with that of paint, sawn wood, dust and yellow soap.

"But you surely can't expect to have it clean and ready by tomorrow!" Shannon exclaimed.

"Oh yes," Olly replied. "We'll work all night."

"I'm afraid I'll have to get back to the children," Clive apologised. "I can put in an hour, but the kids sometimes wake up and become a nuisance. One night they set the place afire, silly little devils. Of course we've trained them to sleep while we're out, but you won't mind if I don't join you for long?"

Shannon began to suspect that he had meanly lured her into this as substitute for his own defaulting self, but the coffee and the company were pleasant. Also, the spirit of her mother, stirring within her, moved her towards the scrubbing brush. She rolled up her sleeves.

"But you needn't help," Olly protested. "You're a visitor. You just talk to us."

Shannon had already taken up the cake of yellow soap, so in lieu of further protests Olly handed her a tattered and grubby apron. Clive had not really meant Shannon should take part in the cleaning. He wanted also to talk to her about the "Anti-War Monthly" and make her promise to contribute to it. But he found himself addressing his remarks to the top of Shannon's head while he washed the cups.

"What we want are some smashing articles on rival imperialisms in the Pacific," he declared. "I don't see why you couldn't do Australian Imperialism. Of course we don't pay you anything, but it would be interesting, don't you think?"

"Any more soap, Olly?" Shannon shouted. "This cake's done."

"Coming." A large cake of yellow soap sailed past Clive.

"Well, if I can't be of any further use, I'll be getting along." Clive gave up the struggle. "Shannon, what about that article?"

"I'll think it over and let you know. Where did you say you were working, Olly?"

"Ever heard of the Pompadour Cafe? Talk about a sweat shop! You can't imagine what it's like."

"Can't I? Why I worked there myself."

"You didn't! But it couldn't have been as bad then."

"I bet it was worse. There were cockroaches as big as your middle finger, but they weren't the worst. There were rat holes under the cellar steps."

"They're still there. It's a wonder Litchin isn't brought to court. I've been to the union."

"We went to the union in my time. Is that little wizened bloke still secretary?"

They would have been friends without this common bond, but over the Pompadour Cafe they became almost sisters. Never, Shannon felt, had she met a girl she liked better, and Olly seemed to like her too. They hardly noticed that Clive had gone, but went on working heartily and talking. They scrubbed the floor of the huge, bare room that had once been a loft, they painted the skirting boards, cleaned the sink in the tiny alcove, painted it, cleaned the stove and windows.

"It's too late to go home now," Olly suggested, over a new brew of coffee. "How about getting some sleep here?" The floor was still wet, but there were a few hard wooden forms along the walls. "We could drag the forms together, and Mac lives near enough to bring us some blankets. Anyway, we can keep the stove alight."

Mac promised to return with blankets, but after waiting and wondering what had happened to him, they made do without. When he appeared at six next morning, he explained that he had been turned back by a policeman who found his account of his presence, with bedclothes, in the streets at three in the morning, not only insufficient but highly suspicious. Mac had been glad to beat a retreat to his own lodgings.

The three, stretched out on the hard benches, found the glow from the stove red and comforting in the dim, bare room. Shannon and Olly nestled together with their coats over them for warmth, while Bert lay crosswise at their feet. He refused to go home despite all Olly's insistence that he should.

"Couldn't leave you here," he objected.

"Why, Bert, you know your cough won't be any better for it. Now, please. We'll be perfectly all right, won't we, Shannon? Just to please *me?*"

But he remained, coughing restlessly, so that Olly dozed and started awake, and worried about him aloud at intervals.

As for Shannon, she was too tired to sleep. She lay wondering why she was so happy. Perhaps it was some quality in Olly that made her feel the cleaning of the Proletarian Club as a high adventure. Olly was so brimming with enthusiasm for this new club that it was impossible not to be infected by her. Shannon liked putting things in order and she lay happy and tranquil on the hard forms, in a damp space of floor. It was no use trying to sleep; they were all too exhausted, so they talked. Shannon told Olly and Bert all about herself, things she had not remembered for years. Some reminiscences of Mr. Litchin started her off, and she related how she and Beryl had run away from their first job in Sydney; how she had fallen sick in the Knowles' lodgings, Mr. Litchin's swooping down and carrying her off, all about the Balm Point colony, which the two hearers had visited and disliked. She even told them a little about the Abbey and her immediate troubles at 2RQ Station.

"Why don't you come and live with me?" Olly suggested. "Until you decide what you're doing next?"

"That's a good idea," Bert agreed. "Everybody stays at Olly's place. if they don't want to sleep on the floor at the club."

Olly chimed in again: "My family don't mind at all. They're used to it. And if you don't find another job, you can always help Momma. She has a stall in the markets."

"Oh, I couldn't."

"Why not?" Olly was genuinely surprised. "Everybody stays at our place." She seemed hurt. "You'd have a bed to yourself."

"But you don't know me at all."

Olly smiled happily. "Why, of course, I know you. Clive introduced us and you've been working here all night. There aren't many people roll up their sleeves and scrub the way you do."

"I'll say not," Bert agreed. "You do what Olly tells you."

Shannon changed the subject, but she was warmed by their simplicity and liking. The trio drowsed uneasily until a grey light aroused them to their uncompleted tasks.

"Have you ever had a banana milk shake?" Olly asked.

"Why no." Shannon was not addicted to milk.

"Well, I'm going to shout you one," Olly decided. "Just as soon as there's a shop open. Right round the corner there's a very early shop."

They had the banana milk shake together, solemnly, two tired young women with their overnight complexions caked to their faces.

"We do look such sights," Olly said, in her soft, cheerful voice, as though it was the most amusing thing in the world. "And I'll have to go straight off to work. You'll come to the opening tonight, won't you? After all, it's as much your opening as ours. It couldn't have happened if you hadn't thrown your weight about the way you did."

Shannon was pleased. "Yes, I'll come to the opening."

"Then you can look after the supper," Olly said happily. "I was wondering who'd do it. You don't mind if I put you down for the supper?"

"Not a bit."

Back at the Proletarian Club, Bert had been joined by the faithful Mac. There was also another man at the far end of the room. Shannon had never been so surprised to see anyone. It was the thin, stern-looking lodger who used to nod to her on the stairs of the Knowles' lodging house, the young man called Mervyn Leggatt. He did not wear gold pince-nez now, but horn-rimmed glasses, and they made his face more severe, his nose and chin sharper.

"You know one another?" Olly cried. "Why, Shannon, you're fitting in nicely, aren't you?" She gave the newcomer an account of Shannon's overnight exertions which he received silently and, it seemed, almost suspiciously. To him she was still the flighty comrade of the Jackson brothers, Mr. Poate's "little fuzzy."

"I don't suppose you'll be coming tonight, Comrade Leggatt?" Olly asked, as she and Shannon put on their hats. For some reason there seemed to be little love lost between the two.

"I think I may drop in for a while." He glanced obliquely at Shannon and she received the impression that this decision had been made because she would be there. But that was ridiculous! Mere vanity!

Olly, when they were in the street, gave her an account of Mervyn Leggatt which showed him as a very mysterious and important man in some way. "He's very high up on the D.C.," Olly remarked reverentially.

Shannon did not like to show her ignorance by asking what the D.C. was. She supposed that if she stayed round the Proletarian Club she would find out. He seemed a queer fish to be swimming there. She had expected long-haired radicals, throngs of them, but scarcely a Mervyn Leggatt.

II

The special series of pictures designed to uplift and cheer the opening of the Proletarian Club were black and white sketches; battle-fields with figures in the foreground, usually with a string of entrails proceeding from them, skulls in helmets, mutilated and blinded and unpleasantly distorted, corpses in all shapes and sizes.

The guests gave these decorations the admiration they deserved, and exclamations of: "Superb stuff, you know. What I like is their strength and vigour" were accompanied by a critical appraisal with the head on one side and the eyes half shut.

Besides these master works there were posters and banners by the members of the Bolshevik League, now the Proletarian Club, which represented the wicked capitalist gloating over bags labeled with a large pound sign, so that there could be no mistake about their containing money. Huge figures of the arisen worker, very angular and out of drawing, bestrode the world something like a large bun, or urged rank after rank of automatons with their fists and arms uplifted, the arms and hands much more like a spanner than a human arm and hand. Sometimes, a few factory chimneys in the background indicated that the spanner-like hands belonged to the proletariat.

For the evening, a band had taken possession of the homemade shallow stage, a capitalistic band, with drum and saxophone, to supplement the battered piano. The supporters of the proletariat had scarcely room to move their feet, the pack was so great.

"Of course, a lot of them won't pay anything," Olly confided to Shannon. "But it's a great success, isn't it?"

Certainly if noise and heat were any indication, the Proletarian Club was off to a flying start. There was no ventilation, a little matter that the committee had overlooked in its joy at the cheap rental, and there was some trouble ejecting a number of young gentlemen in dress suits who had brought their own liquor. An adventurous section of the gathering began to spread out on the neighbouring roof tops, like a set of cats, for a little stair led to a wooden platform above the Proletarian Club, whence it was easy to reconnoitre the surrounding stretches of corrugated iron. They even tramped thunderously overhead during the president's speech of welcome, and had to be recalled from their sally when they tramped even more thunderously back.

"We'll just have to make it a rule that no one is to go on the roof," Olly suggested to Shannon, for Olly was already taking it for granted that Shannon was a fixture.

Shannon had been out to buy milk from the milk bar where that same morning the two of them had absorbed their banana milk shakes, she had brought four pounds of coffee herself, the committee having overlooked the necessity of providing any liquid refreshment when advertising supper. Armed with dictatorial authority, she shooed out hungry helpers from the little alcove where the supper was prepared. It was a very busy evening for her, but she found time to dance gaily with a number of men she had never met before, and lost sight of the contingent she had brought from Station 2RQ, including Bleeby Peverill and Beryl who had not quite made up their difference as to Bleeby's character.

Shannon's friends were having a good time, although one of the lesser lights of the announcers' staff had his face slapped by a young lady whom he had led out on the roof. All in all, they agreed, it was a most successful night out. They would have been very surprised, however, had they known Shannon seriously entertained Olly's suggestion that she take the job of secretary to the Proletarian Club.

"I'm never very good as secretary," Olly persuaded earnestly. "The trouble is I'm too lax. Now you'd be just right, and then I could be assistant secretary." Olly was quite sure the committee would be only too glad of this new arrangement. "Merv Leggatt's on the committee," she urged. "You talk it over with him. I've asked him already. Do. Please do. Just to please *me.*"

Olly had this habit of wooing people. She could quite persuade herself that they, in taking something she had always wanted for herself, were doing her a favour. It had been her highest ambition to be secretary of the Proletarian Club, but this new arrival Olly liked and wanted to keep, apart from the fact that she had all sorts of connections with people who might help the Proletarian Club.

Shannon knew, when Mervyn Leggatt approached and asked her for a dance, that he intended a flank attack upon her refusal to accept even a position on the committee of the Proletarian Club. She danced with him and did not enjoy it. He moved as though he were performing some laborious task, and when he asked if she would like to look at the view from the roof, she agreed readily. Mervyn Leggatt, so correct and respectable, was in no way a dangerous companion in a wander on the roof tops.

"Are you still living at the Knowles's place?" she asked, when they had stepped carefully out on the iron roof and taken a seat on a low stone parapet belonging to a neighbouring warehouseman.

"Yes, I'm still there."

She asked a few questions about the Knowles family, but he did not know much about them nor about his fellow lodgers. Strange, Shannon thought, that a man could live in a place for years and know nothing of the people about him, but then he had always been a very reserved young man.

G*

"What are you doing here?" he asked, with a kind of blunt suspicion. His glasses glittered a little in the moonlight. She might have asked him the same question, but she replied simply:

"Just an accident."

"You've never been interested in the working-class movement?"

"I once tried to read a book by Lenin called 'Empirio-Criticism,' but I thought it was tripe. I'm afraid I don't know anything about the working-class movement. But I think the whole of society is out of joint, if that's any help."

"How do you explain society being out of joint?" he asked, like a teacher extracting the right answer from the pupil.

"It's like an animal with too many parasites. Anyone can see that without being thunderous about the working class." She spoke irritably for she was very tired.

"And how do you propose to remedy our diseased, parasitized society?"

"Well, I don't really see that I've any special mission that way. There are always plenty of messiahs about." Something in his superior tone irritated her. He seemed to sense this resentment and was quick to change the subject.

"Olly and Bert and Mac think it would be a good idea if you took on the secretaryship here."

"That's all very fine for Olly and Bert and Mac. I'm trying to hold down a job at the moment, and it's wriggling in my grasp. I really haven't the time. This place would be a full-time job for someone who was enthusiastic about it."

"And aren't you enthusiastic?"

"My enthusiasms have hardening of the arteries."

It was his turn to show disapproval, and from the impatient way he spoke, she knew he thought her flippant and slick. "The Proletarian Club may not seem very important to you, but it is, I can assure you, very important to some of us."

"I didn't notice you there when the floor needed scrubbing."

"I was at a union meeting. Besides I'm not very good at scrubbing floors." He smiled, doing his best to be ingratiating. "After all that's something you women are good at." He could not have made any remark which would more easily have earned him her dislike.

"Anything that is dirty or hard is women's work naturally. But I thought you reformers of the world were out for equal opportunities for all?"

"Of course. But that doesn't say I want to scrub floors."

"Oh, no. It's easy enough to plan a new society and leave the dirty jobs to other people." She was working herself into a temper that was partly weariness.

"Don't let's quarrel," he replied quietly. And she too was quiet, a little ashamed of herself. "Shall I tell you what I do for a living? I sort filthy bags all day long in a room filled with dust. We wear handkerchiefs over our faces to prevent it getting down our throats, but we cough, and we always have catarrh and colds, and we are always dirty and swearing." He spoke quite calmly. "The other men there . . . none of them ever want anything except more overtime money, or more beer, or a win at the races. I stand or sit all day with men who have nothing in common with me, whose idea of conversation is as filthy as the bags we sort, and always inside me I want a cleaner world."

His simplicity touched her a little but not enough to obscure her very shrewd realization of why he was persuading her to be secretary of the Proletarian Club. Someone was wanted with "good connections," in other words, someone who was not a bolshevik, so that all the good bolsheviks could say: "Oh, no, the Proletarian Club has nothing to do with us."

"We need good elements such as yourself." Mr. Leggatt had reverted to his dictatorial tone. He was apparently quite prepared to stay out on the roof all night, if necessary.

There was a clatter of feet up the wooden steps and Olly stepped over to them, leading a lean, dark youth by the arm.

"Shannon, I want you to meet my brother Joe. He's going to the University, but he never does any work." Olly's voice implied that surely Joe would be the clinching argument which might persuade Shannon that the Proletarian Club was interesting.

Joe glared at Leggatt. He was in a bad temper, because he had been lugged along to meet some middle-class woman that Leggatt, who had been sent to "clean up" the Club, wanted to foist on them as secretary. They had had some glorious times at the old Bolshevik Club, and if this place was going to be made a home for a lot of middle-class women, he would quit. Also he was only slightly sober.

"It is the system," Comrade Leggatt was explaining in his concise way to Shannon. "If we can change the system, we change people's lives, the way they think. It's a new . . ."

"It isn't," Joe broke in rudely. "It is the trout wanting oxygen." Joe's oxygen theory he had used before, either to shock the shockable or to display his own knowledge. "What happens to a trout that can't get into a running stream?" He addressed this query to Shannon, in a tone of denunciation. "It becomes sterile or it spawns later. Why does it want running water? Because there is more oxygen in running water. Our ancestors thrust themselves in search of more oxygen. Why does a girl paint her face? Because a pink and white skin indicates a better blood supply, better lungs, better reproductive system." He spat this out rapidly, provocatively. "A girl wants everyone to think she has a highly oxygenated, excitable blood supply."

"I love to hear you say oxygenated, Joe," Shannon encouraged. "I thought you weren't going to manage it."

"You let me tell you," Joe was not to be stopped, "what is the Proletarian Club? It is the result of reproductive anexoria." He brought this out very triumphantly. "A genesiac excitement encouraged by hormones produced in the sexual glands on the point of maturation. They're looking for fresh water, and they don't know why. Our society has too much mud, too much mud altogether. You think they're looking for some new social system? They're looking for it like a trout looks for a higher oxygen content in the water. So they can spawn. Why, look at the fall in the birth rate. All the trout going sterile. You see it in ancient Rome, all these old civilizations, just the same. Sodom and Gomorrah moving about uneasily looking for the way out of the mud pond."

Olly, in a perfect ecstasy of sisterly pride, glanced round to see that the young prophet's words were received with attention.

"Look," Joe said sternly and eloquently, "it is the trout. It feeds and gets fat, then suddenly it finds it has grown an abdominal tumour that takes up a fifth of its body. All its organs are squashed up and atrophy. It hates the sight of food. It's internally anxious like our present society. And why? The germs of the future are parasitic on it. It is eaten up by the new society, the collection of germs growing and growing on its fat."

"Go on," Shannon encouraged affably, "I'm listening if no one else is."

"Well, that's all," Joe said sullenly. She should have been shocked.

Olly turned on them a look which said: "Is he not wonderful?" and then snapped at her brother: "You go boring people, talking on and·on. You might try to stop because it's just a bad habit."

"I ·agree with Joe," Shannon said. "Just reproductive anexoria. Oh, look!"

The moon was falling slowly through the mauve morning sky. A faint light struck from the east. They stood watching the dawn break over the city, and, in the silence, it was as though the great cliffs of buildings sighed with all the burden of the lives they bore, with the strain of millions of stones pushing against each other and resting their weight on the resisting earth.

Shannon thought how good it was to be young. She had never felt so young before, so ready to laugh, so careless. All these dark, fiery young men, these girls, were accumulating a capital of happiness in fighting their mythical capitalistic society. When they grew old and were grave men of business, mothers of children, no longer ardent and restless and enthusiastic, they would look back on the Proletarian Club and chuckle. They would have a merry stock of memories to live on. It was a good world, a fighting glad world, and she was young. And Olly looked so funny when she pretended not to be proud of Joe.

"Yes," she said loudly, "of course I'm with you. Of course, I'll join, Mervyn. Anything you like, anything at all."

She could have hugged Leggatt with his hard, serious face, good-natured Olly, the dark tousled Joe. They were young, they wanted things she wanted, she loved them.

How strange, Leggatt thought, that Joe's biological mysticism has such a hold on fools. He had half thought Joe ought to be cleared out with the other rubbish from the old Bolshevik Club, but apparently he had his uses. Leggatt could not know that what had really made up Shannon's mind was a row of little cactus plants in pots. They belonged to Olly who believed there was nothing so satisfactory and homey as a piece of cactus. The sight of those cactus plants, spoiled by dust, used as a dump for cigarette butts, but still ranged bravely on the wooden platform of the old loft, had struck Shannon, in that early light, as so pathetic, so comical. They were a symbol of all the mistaken bravery and wistfulness at the heart of things; they were part of the mauve and pink and grey of dawn breaking, and the whine of trams in the street, the clanking of milk cans. To all the straining and groaning of the city was added the undertone of Olly and her cactus plants, living their own quaint lives, while the sunlight grew, and the city, dusty, pushing strands of streets from its brow, roared into its day's work.

Fourteen

Joe, Olly's brother, was a fair sample of the members of the Proletarian Club. Jewish, a smart boy on the make, with long dark hair and brooding eyes like a spaniel, he did his desperate best to keep from his friends the knowledge that his mother had a small stall in the markets to make the money on which he went to the University and loafed away his time. Later, he became a gigolo in London and was kept by a series of wealthy women who pampered him much as his mother had done.

There was also, in the Club, Mary Hatton who wrote weird poetry about old maids nursing poodles and repressions, and wore a hibiscus over her ear; merry little Josephine McCrea who kept a pet duck and fed it with spoonfuls of wine; and the producer of the drama group, John Charteris, which was, of course, a fake name he had picked out for himself. His real name was Harrigan. He had a white, tense face with nerves that stood trembling under his eyes. He knew literature backwards and, at times, took drugs, drank, and went raving mad. Seamen would shamble up to him and hold mysterious conversations with him in some dark doorway. When he got drunk, he would get wild, and decide to denounce everybody and have a splendid time doing it.

Many of the members were the dregs of the paper "Torrent," which had died out a short time before in the desert sands of bourgeois ignorance. The most competent journalist of them all was Clarry Stokes who was addicted to writing stories about a staid, suburban resident, who woke up in the night with a vague yearning and stole out on the front lawn to let the rain beat on his naked flesh. He was greatly prized as a find, and orders came through from those Higher Up which read: "Now that this great soul has been brought into the Movement, let your treatment of him be tender and soft."

With him, as the leading lights of the Proletarian Club, shone the poet, Chaverin Brome, also a fake name (these aliases became such a nuisance that the wall-paper of the Club sarcastically gave notice that "Everyone is forbidden to change his name more than once a day"). Chaverin Brome wrote poems about the black teeth of the factories grinding the workers into red meat. He wore a black velour hat and a small black moustache, and later married money and went to America with it where he interviewed Trotsky.

It was he who invented a new religion for a member who had to go into hospital and state his religion on a form. The religious sect was the Tarsinians who followed Paul of Tarsus and only worshipped one day a year which was the twenty-ninth of June, when they had to genuflect twenty-nine times with their backs to the sun. Brome had one devoted satellite, a little shabby chap called Nobby, a kindly friendly soul, who would buttonhole you and talk by the hour. His conversation was like some sort of soup; bits and pieces of all sorts of things floated to the top, and were usually so broken up that it was hard to say how they had come into his repertoire or from whence.

Chaverin Brome's cousin Harry, a tall bad-tempered lad, the son of a rich family, had a muddy, unscrupulous face and a voice like someone speaking through tinfoil, thin, nasal, and hard on the ear. Harry, who was in charge of the artists' group, went around quoting James Joyce. He had a collection of camera snaps of a very surrealist type, and he chanted poetry aloud, not always his own, and usually beginning: "You are a fawn, slant-eyed, remote." There were also more cynical pieces describing a garbage heap under a hot sun. He had an unscrupulous habit of lifting wisecracks, such as: "These women, they use communism as a cosmetic."

The majority of the members of the Proletarian Club were young men, but there was always a drifting crew of society girls who thought it would be fun to languish their looks on the intellectuals; and these last, regrettable to relate, were mercilessly exploited in the matter of small cash loans and donations to funds. There were other drifters who found the Proletarian Club a convenient address when they had no other. Of these was a mysterious member who would put his head in at the door and say: "If anyone asks for Norman Lindsay or Cashel Byron, tell them I'll be back later."

The caretaker, Wodgers, who lived in a little dark hole under the stairs, in a smell of horses, rats and the onion brew he was always cooking, was also a member of the Club, except on those occasions when the Club had paid no rent for a long time, and then he padlocked the door against them.

The members filed the padlock off and streamed in gaily as of yore. Wodgers had dirty, crinkled underpants hanging down below his upper garments. He chewed his false teeth. It was rather startling to hear this strange clicking noise from the very odorous darkness under the stairs. He had once been a gardener, had a manner at once cringing and domineering, and was always being hauled off to the lock-up for participating in unlicensed demonstrations and disturbances. If the police made a baton charge, he never failed to get his head in the way, and, with overweening vanity, wore dirty pieces of old bandage around it long after the bump had gone down.

The girls did not like him, because he was a sneaking tale-bearer against them and thought they ought to fall in love with him. One of the first rows in the Proletarian Club was over the long, abusive letters he wrote to Olly, who treated Wodgers kindly because she was sorry for him. He carried tales to the District Commissars about Shannon, asserting that she was a police spy, and he was given gracious permission to watch and report.

"Of course she may be a police spy," Comrade Leggatt agreed, when he was reproached with electing a spy as secretary of the Club. "There are men in this Movement who have been doing solid work for years and are still police spies. She's valuable as long as we can use her. What the Proletarian Club needs is not so many of these Bohemians and a lot more solid middle class. One thing about this Shannon Hicks, she is middle class to the core."

This was also the rancorous opinion of the wilder section of the Proletarian Club, who were unable to see why Shannon was secretary at all. The way she guarded the money that came in was most obnoxious. Instead of the old glad way in which every member had dipped for himself, the collection at the door for plays and lectures was strictly watched and listed. Dreary, trustworthy people like Mac were put in charge, and there were no more little suppers or private loans from the Club funds. There was a banking account, and those members who believed in the hatefulness of saving money were incensed. Comrade Leggatt who, everyone knew, had been sent to "clean up" the Club, backed Shannon vigorously and instructed the President to expel the opposition.

Then there was the matter of morals. Privately, they called Comrade Hicks "The Virgin," and took reckless bets on the chances of gentlemen members. Quite a number of otherwise feckless young men brisked up and worked assiduously, until they found that Shannon only smiled at them while they worked, and never when they tried to hold her hand. John Charteris brought off a brilliant coup when he insisted one night on seeing her home. Having been bidden good-bye at her door, he returned to the Club and gave such a wealth of circumstantial evidence that he collected all bets and was drunk for a week. After that, the members only grinned at Shannon's preaching, until John Charteris was made to admit that he had once more embezzled funds to which he had no right. There was no chance, however, of members getting their bets back.

Money came into the Proletarian Club from the weekly dance, from lectures, from meetings, and, most surprisingly, from the poster artists. Under Mac and Bert, who were hard workers, the poster department was paying its way. They even landed a contract, of course not as the Proletarian Club, but simply as themselves, to supply a series of posters for the National Assets Party which was running candidates for the elections. These posters showed bolsheviks in whiskers and fur caps stretching gorilla paws over Australia. They urged all right-thinking Australians to save their country by voting for a red-faced, choleric, old gentleman who was fond of roaring out that he and his party would not be: "Abused, spat upon, ground down, trampled upon, by those who abused our National Acids."

With the money from the posters of horrific bolsheviks, the Proletarian Club blossomed out in a bright, new set of red banners for itself, which were carried gaily in many a procession, either by the Proletarian Club or by borrowers from unions and leagues with like opinions.

The drama group was giving excellent shows, and actors of Shannon's acquaintance were only too pleased to work for nothing in plays that could never have been put over the air. John Charteris and Joe might be unreliable and emotional, but, as producers, they knew what they were about. All Shannon had to do was find the money for lighting, costumes, props, printing programmes, and the hire of theatres, when the crowds they drew were too big for their own hall. She had started in the Proletarian Club with a bank balance of her own, but so many calls were made on it that this soon became a thing of the past. None of the loans was ever repaid, because there never was a time when the money was not needed, and for a time the drama group was financially on the edge of extinction.

Then, luckily, a couple of the Club's plays were banned, and this allowed
them to hold protest meetings, collect funds for appeals, and give invitation performances to packed houses, so that there was enough in hand to
carry them on, when the ban was lifted and everyone rushed to see the
play. In a twelve-month, the Proletarian Club had one of the best teams
of amateurs in Sydney, had lost three of their best men to a film company,
and won two gold cups of which the actors were publicly derisive and
privately proud. The membership had grown to the point where it became necessary to move from the Club's tiny loft to more convenient
quarters.

"I'll be sorry to leave the old place," Shannon told Mervyn Leggatt. "It's
been such good fun here."

Shannon had grown so devoted to the drama activities of the Club that
for the magnificent sum of a pound a week she had become its full-time
secretary. She had been taking parts in radio plays and in anything Bleeby
Peverill wanted her for. She had even made extra money in a mannequin
show Beryl staged, and by writing script for advertising firms with whom
she had formed a connection at 2RQ. She meant to continue in these
money-bringing odd jobs, but more and more she found herself dropping
out until she was existing solely on the pound a week from her labours
at the Pro Club. All her energies were absorbed by it. She had struggled
for it, sacrificed her own funds that it might flourish, guarded its reputa-
tion, wooed into it good actors, thrown out people like Chaverin Brome
who were no use. The Proletarian Club was hers. Yes, with the devoted
Olly, Bert and Mac and Joe, she had built it up.

She was not very keen on the lectures, which were usually by some
palmer returned from the Holy Land of Russia. But one, at least, had
given her a sardonic enjoyment; when a returned lady novelist cried
enthusiastically: "And, oh comrades! Sexual intercourse in the Soviet
Union is so delightful!"

Shannon's view of the Working Class Movement was more than half
cynical, but she did not obtrude her view on the believers. There were
quite a few of the members who were more interested in the poster work
or the drama group than they were in the holy land, but night after
night the hall was jammed by people who listened without stirring to
the wonders of this other world.

They sat for hours in the foul air, solid with blue smoke; they put their hard-earned pennies in the china saucers passed down the close-packed rows of sweaty people. They sat with their faces upturned to the speaker on the little stage; hard, careworn faces; grim, dark faces; old faces; young faces; listening to the news of the Promised Land to which they too might enter in; and always Shannon's heart was stirred with pity. Even if it wasn't all so delightful, even if it was just another fake, why shouldn't they believe and hope? Surely it couldn't do any harm.

"I'm going to miss this place," she repeated sentimentally to Mervyn Leggatt.

There were the pigeons. They liked to strut and coo in the stone court-yard, but Wodgers, with a vindictiveness native to him, would never let them settle if he could help it. He threw buckets of water at them and drove them away whenever he could. They settled by night in two big trees which had maintained somehow their places behind a row of grim warehouses and a brewery. The golden evenings they spent in whirling about and about, the speed of their going making a whistling in the air, with an under-thud of rapid wing-beats. Grey-mauve, green-grey, they swayed, circled, slid uneasily, tirelessly above the streets, to come to rest in a whirr and flurry, sink to quiet, start up again and recommence their circling and flocking. Sometimes a bird left the close arrowy flight to hover alone, or two or three would soar up, then drop back to their fellows, when again they would whirl like water stirred in eddies.

"If you're not keen about the change," Comrade Leggatt suggested reasonably, "and I think the Club's standing firm enough for you to get out, how about coming with me in the U.C.D.L.?"

Shannon had long since grown accustomed to this habit of referring to every organization by its initials, and could even read the reports in the "Labour Call," which contained items unintelligible to those who were not of the Movement—such items as: "The monthly meeting of the Y.W.P.U. passed a resolution condemning the D.S.C. decision to follow the A.C.T.U. line in the matter of representation to the Annual Confer-ence of the A.L.P." As she thought over Leggatt's offer, she realized what a compliment he was paying her. She might be proud of the Proletarian Club, but he, in the United Council for Defence of Labour, had a much more important job.

"You don't think I'm a police spy?" she asked lightly. She had heard all about Wodger's tale-bearing.

"Oh, no. That's a long time past. Besides I might be a police spy myself. Just as long as you're useful."

"You'll get into trouble one of these days," she told him idly. "You're so careless, comrade." She called people comrade because it was an easy form of address, and they mostly liked it.

"I can get an order from the D.C. having you transferred to our team."

"No one has any authority over me and you know it. I don't belong to your party. I'm only a bourgeois sympathizer, an individualist, a left-social fascist with right deviationist tendencies," she quoted fondly from the opinions of Chaverin Brome, who had impeached her for her conduct of the Club. "I still think, and I've seen a lot of your party working here, that you all pick on each other too mercilessly. While I'm just a hoverer-on-the-outskirts, you'll treat me all right. If I were a party functionary, you'd be expelling me every time I opened my mouth."

"Well are you coming in the U.C.D.L.? We could use you." He was so ready to use people, she thought. He might have a genius for organizing, but after a twelve-month of his acquaintance Mervyn Leggatt inspired her with nothing besides respect and friendship. His mind was like a narrow steel rail built to carry traffic in the right direction. His logic was always sound, his reasoning correct, his work faultless. But, as a human being, he ranked below Olly who had such a generosity, such a kindliness, that no one could help loving her.

Olly would stay with the Proletarian Club, with Mac, with Bert and the rest. Why should Shannon leave what had been one of the best, the gayest groups she had ever found and go off into Leggatt's Union of Defence? She had done jobs for it before now, helped to get free legal aid in the fight for the arrested union representatives in the Mayer case, written up the imprisoned Indian Congress leader. The U.C.D.L. had a small dim room on the top floor of the Trades Hall, and if it might be nothing to look at, it had brought off some resounding strokes against the government. Give it a slight departmental bungle, and it would organize a protest meeting with representatives from hundreds of unions and every liberal club in Sydney. It would have protest meetings thousands strong in every capital city inside a month. Certainly, it would be interesting to work with the U.C.D.L.

"How am I supposed to live?" she demanded.

"You don't. Ours isn't the Proletarian Club. When we get funds, we spend them. When we don't, we starve." Leggatt was no longer working in the post office. He was a full time worker for the U.C.D.L. He might be shabbier and thinner than of old, but he looked happier. "We embezzle the funds for food, just the way the old Bolshevik Club used to do." He smiled. "You ought to come in and clean us up."

Mervyn Leggatt cracking a joke! It sounded incredible.

"What about the Pro?" That was what they always called the Proletarian Club.

"The team can carry on without you. But Charteris will have to go out. He drinks too hard to be reliable. Abe Andrews has twice his brains and patience."

They discussed the move to the new rooms, magnificent new rooms with a good stage, a water-tight lease, real seats instead of wooden forms, a supper room, dressing rooms, in fact, everything the heart could desire.

"You can come up and settle in the U.C.D.L. as soon as the new rooms are fixed up," Leggatt remarked, as they parted. "I'll have to steal a typewriter from somewhere." He gave her his hard tight smile and was gone.

No other year, Shannon thought, had flitted by so fast. It had been a whirl of a year, and she had enjoyed it, even living as she had done mainly on cigarettes and coffee. She had worked as hard for the Proletarian Club as she had for Lucy and 2RQ, but the difference was that she was building for herself in the way she wanted it. With unreliable, reckless helpers, with loyal, hard-working helpers, she had been Shannon of the Pro Club, someone in the scheme of things, among people who regarded Lucy Rossingale as a joke.

In fact, she had been in a new world and had made a whole set of new friends. She wrote for papers like the "Labour Call" that none of her former friends ever saw; she acted in plays that were so full of swear words that no nice radio station would ever be able to purge them clean enough for its air. She had enjoyed herself.

She counted over the few coppers in her purse and decided she had better walk home to Olly's where she was now living. She needed another pair of shoes badly, but perhaps she could make them last, or Beryl might have a pair she didn't need. All her life, Shannon reflected, she had been wearing cast-off clothes, sleeping in the spare beds of strange places, never being sure of tomorrow. Now once again she would be going on. But one thing; Mervyn Leggatt was a good, solid mate to have on any venture.

Fifteen

Beryl had been vexed by Shannon's decision to go and live with Olly. It was a possessive streak in her rather than a real desire to have Shannon's company. They had very little in common now, for Beryl was absorbed in her own affairs and her own friends. She clung to Shannon just as she had clung to Aunt Edith, tightening her grip on memories of their old life together. But they seemed to fade like ghosts from her grasp. Aunt Edith had lost so much of her old dominating personality and become a mere shadow of Vincent Sladder. Shannon had a harder, clearer insistence on her own way, and there was no longer any great bond between the three of them.

What really makes friends, Beryl thought gloomily, is working together. The oddest people become friends if they are every day faced with the same problems. Look at fat Miss Baxter in the fitting room; I couldn't stand her when I first went to Forley's and now we're as thick as thieves.

"I don't see why you want to rush away and bury yourself in a slum," Beryl grumbled. "I simply can't understand you going red to that extent."

"My board will help Olly's mother. Poor old Momma Asche, she's having a rough spin just now, what with Joe and one thing and another. She can do with the extra money."

Shannon was still working at 2RQ when she made the move; but even after she left, and her funds were proportionately straitened, she always saw that Mrs. Asche had the fifteen shillings a week for her board. Not that Momma would have minded. She was so used to Olly's friends staying in their tiny dim lodgings over Poppa's plumber shop, that she could no more have refused a friend of Olly's her last crust of bread than she could have refused Joe.

They had a little shop in the Glebe Road where Poppa kept plumber's fittings, and Momma stowed the miscellaneous collection of second-hand odds and ends she sold at the markets on Friday nights. Sometimes, Shannon or Olly would snatch an hour from the Club to help her, and they quarrelled fiercely with Joe about his snobbish refusal even to recognize the existence of that stall.

Shannon liked the markets and the crowds that drifted through the aisles; the piled fruits of the Chinamen's stalls; the cresses and green peppers; the pineapples and grapes and cucumbers; the wet-earthy smell of ferns in pots, and cyclamen with their tender pink hairy flowers; the huge bunches of marigolds and wallflowers and stocks scenting the air; the piles of old music and books; the cheap slop shops, where second-hand shoes lay in piles or hung dangling like pairs of dead rabbits from a rail; the storekeepers shouting their wares; the bacon and honey; the laughter and the anxious looks; the tea and pies and saveloys eaten on wooden forms ranged around a square of asphalt in which women washed glasses and dished up food as nonchalantly as they might have done in their own kitchens.

There were dispirited fowls huddled drowsing in pens and coops; motor trucks backed into odd corners; stall holders quarrelling or making friends with their next-door neighbours; the bacon vendor keeping up a feud with the seller of pickled cucumber and cheese; and the old woman with great combs of honey minding the baby for the tired couple selling cheap seconds of china and glass.

One night, in a burst of extravagance, Shannon and Olly came home in a fit of the giggles with two tiny turtles and a gold fish in a bowl, some grapefruit, and a cover for the dining-room table. The hard jokes, the noise, the hurry, the bursting paper bags; even the fact that everyone seemed shabby, even if they were only thrifty citizens who had left the car parked around the corner; all the smells, from onions to fertilizer, seemed friendly and interesting.

On other nights, the poverty of the people shopping in the markets was like a blow; their fixed, strained faces looked ghastly in the artificial light; the shopkeepers cursed in the savage snarl of men on the verge of starvation or desperation or both. Everything was hard and mean, harder than the asphalt underfoot or the lights overhead; and poor, old Momma Asche with her kind face, her little weak chin and spectacles, would have melted any heart; standing alone, striving to make a bargain, and nearly being beaten from her price, until she remembered Joe and the necessity for giving Joe his chance at the University. Then into her face would come that hard, desperate look, and she would shake her head firmly. "No, no," she would say to Shannon, almost with tears in her eyes, "I will not give the things away."

From Momma, Olly had inherited an impulse to give everything away. Momma gave food to neighbours who were unlucky or out of work. She gave the milk supply to the baby next door, because its parents couldn't afford milk. Poppa Asche berated her sometimes. He had his shop, which only just kept them from the dole, and with a roof over their heads. "Look at me," he would say. "Can I give things away? What a woman!"

For twenty years Poppa had been known as "the Red plumber of Glebe," and he was proud of the title. He attended all the plays of the Proletarian Club; he attended all the lectures, and his penny or threepence went into the china saucer sturdily to help the downtrodden toilers on strike, or the people's friends in gaol, or any of a hundred and one appeals. He was proud of Olly, proud of Joe, even proud of Shannon, Olly's friend, so distinguished and intelligent; and he would tell his customers all about them. He had to hear all the doings of the Club, and he and Momma would discuss between themselves any wrangles between members or committee arguments.

One of Olly's best jokes was about the time Poppa was so anxious to see the performance of "Dawn Shall Break," and had only sixpence in the house. None of them had any money, but Olly and Joe and Shannon were acting, so they got in free. They offered to get Poppa in free with just a word to Mac on the door.

"No," Poppa said. "Where I go, I pay." And he waited like a spider in the shop for a customer to come. By closing time, he had accumulated the one-and-six necessary for his ticket, and he was just about to close when Bluey, a big navvy who worked on the roads, rushed in still in his flannel vest and muddy trousers.

"For Crisake, Poppa!" he exclaimed. "Lend us a bob. I've got a thirst on me like a bloody desert."

Poppa sadly handed over his shilling. "What could I do?" he moaned. "Poor Bluey had to have his pot of beer."

When they left for the grand opening of "Dawn Must Break," Poppa was still hopefully keeping the shop open in case someone came in. It was a big show at the biggest theatre in the city, and when Shannon burst out on the stage in her part of the heart-broken wife, she peered into the dark for Poppa. There he was crammed into the cheap seats in the gallery.

Dear Poppa, with his grey head and his worry wrinkles all abeam with joy. A customer had come.

He was as serious over the new club rooms as though he were opening a new shop, and he saw to all the plumbing fixtures in person without any payment. He could afford it, he said. He liked to feel he was doing something for the movement, but he was sad to think that Shannon was going to take herself to the U.C.D.L. and only act in plays instead of running things.

"If you had been a daughter," he told her gravely, "I would not have felt better to see you so good a secretary." He liked her, not only as Olly's friend, but as Momma's helper, a girl, the only one of Olly's friends who had ever cleaned the kitchen or assisted in the shop. Most of Olly's friends, he said sadly, were no good at all. But look at Shannon!

Shannon was making jam, a proceeding that struck Momma as very comical. Jam came in tins from the grocer.

"Homemade jam, Momma, you can sell on the stall," Shannon argued. She was not willing to agree with Joe's theory that it was her middle-class upbringing coming out in her, but she admitted that her aunt made jam, good jam. She had borrowed bottles from all the neighbours, and there were several of Momma's friends cluttering up the kitchen, offering advice and enjoying themselves. It was tomato and ginger jam, and the next lot was to be orange conserve because oranges were cheap and Momma had been given a sackful by a fruit-vendor friend in the markets.

With a big wooden spoon and a saucer Shannon was ladling a little out of the pot to see if it would jell. All the neighbours agreed it was a magnificent jam. "You certainly have got a head on you," a stout matron admitted, as she tasted it; and Shannon, flushed from the cooking, flushed even deeper at their praise.

In this scene of domestic triumph, Olly seemed listless and depressed. She wandered in and out restlessly, and as soon as Shannon could detach herself from the jam making, Olly suggested that they go for a walk so that Shannon could cool down. Shannon agreed to go as soon as she had bottled her jam, and Olly helped paste on the labels. Poppa darted in and wrote the labels, anxious to help.

The exultant glow of the successful jam maker had not left her as Shannon stepped out into the streets down which a dusty, bitter wind was blowing, a wind that seemed full of sharp-cornered grits and bits of stuff and waste paper. It was an unpleasant change from the hot kitchen, and her high spirits fell. They fell even lower when Olly broke her news, which she did in a hurry, as soon as they had turned the corner, almost as though she had been screwing up her courage and was afraid it might fail.

"Shannon . . . now don't go being horrid about it, and you must promise not to tell Momma or Poppa . . . I'm sick. I think I'm going to have a baby." She laughed nervously and went ·on talking as though she would stave off comments. "Now I know what you think about it, so you needn't say it, and I only told you because I wanted to tell someone. You know Bert and I can't marry, and he's just had another haemorrhage, so for heaven's sake don't go telling him. Can you rake up five pounds from anywhere?"

Shannon felt in her pocket, not for the five pounds, for she knew she had at most a few shillings. She glanced down at her shabby shoes, so that her friend would not see her face.

"Let's go and have a banana milk shake," she suggested, and they walked in silence to a secluded little shop. "What are you going to do?" she asked, when they were thoughtfully drinking their banana milk shake.

"I think I can fix it for five pounds," Olly said carefully, casually. "If I can't get the five pounds, I'll just have to manage myself."

"Oh, Olly, don't!" Shannon burst out.

Olly gave her a hard, hostile glance. "If you're going to start preaching . . ." It was the nearest they had ever come to a quarrel.

"I wasn't preaching, Olly, truly I wasn't. But why won't you let me tell Momma? You know she and Pop would stick to you if you had any number of kids. Or why can't you marry Bert?"

"I knew you'd go on and on," Olly said, still in the hard, hostile tone she had adopted as a defence against her own thoughts that Shannon was voicing. "I tell you . . . no. Now don't be a damn fool. Just think about that five pounds."

Shannon thought. It was no use talking to Olly. She knew by sad experience that members of the Proletarian Club had before this met with mishaps. But not Olly, not kind-hearted, simple Olly. That was damnable. She thought hard.

"I'll go and see Beryl," she said finally.

Olly gave her the ghost of her old smile. "I don't mind Beryl knowing," she said. "Beryl's got some sense. She'll see how it is."

Shannon felt, as she went off to find Beryl, that Olly had lost confidence in her a little. But she would scarcely have been a good friend, if she had not tried to dissuade Olly from her set purpose. She felt a coward and a weakling. Surely in a situation like this she should do something to prevent Olly acting like a fool. But what could she do? To go to Momma would not mend things. Once Olly made up her mind, she was as stubborn as old Pop saying: "Where I go, I pay."

Beryl was at home, for it was Saturday afternoon and too unpleasant to go to golf. She was living in a fashionable boarding-house, with white-coated, under-paid waiters, oak-panelling, a billiard room, well kept grounds, and very poor food. The charge was exorbitant, but the place had the advantage, as Beryl explained to Shannon, that you could invite anyone there without being ashamed of it.

Beryl was in a lounge full of people mostly in golf or tennis clothes. She had just gone no trumps and Shannon's request that she come outside a minute made her sulky. She reluctantly stepped out on to one of the cold, windy verandahs where no one would be likely to overhear them. It was not a propitious setting for an attempt to borrow money. Shannon saw Beryl's face harden, and she plunged awkwardly into explanations.

"It's Olly, Beryl. You can guess why she needs it."

"It's not for yourself?" Beryl asked.

"Hell, no!"

"Well, I can't do it, that's all. You know I would have moved mountains if it had been you, but these kids you get around with," Beryl snapped virtuously, "they've no damn sense. Besides what's this Bert going to do about it? Why hasn't she told him? It's up to him, isn't it? Damn it all, if anyone's going around scouting for fivers, it ought to be him. I've got no time," Beryl said fretfully, "for a woman who gets in a jam and then goes whining . . ."

"She isn't whining," Shannon said hotly. "I've told you why she won't tell Bert. He hasn't a job . . . and oh, what's the use?"

"There! You see?" Beryl said triumphantly. "You're practically agreeing with me. No sense, that's the trouble with these girls. No damn *caution*."

"You can talk!" Shannon exclaimed angrily. "Beryl, I wouldn't ask you, if I knew anyone else likely to have any money."

"Well, I can't do it. Oh, Shannon, why did you ever get mixed up with such a crowd? I can get you a job tomorrow, if you'd only see sense. Look at you. Why don't you spend some money on yourself, think about yourself for a change?"

There was no arguing with Beryl. She refused point-blank to consider the idea of lending Shannon five pounds and that was an end of it. Shannon returned to Olly sick at heart, but secretly hoping that this refusal might make Olly change her mind.

But all Olly said was: "Well, that's that. Thanks, Shannon. I'll manage."

She had shut up like an oyster and evaded all Shannon's questions. If Shannon would not help and did not like the business, she could stay out. All Shannon's arguments Olly met with that same hard hostile glance, so that presently Shannon saw that it was no use arguing. Olly even avoided her at the Club, but she was deep in conference with Mary Hatton, whom Shannon had always disliked as the cheapest, most over-sexed little wretch who had ever come there. If Olly was going to do something foolish, Shannon decided, she should at least have the five pounds.

Nobody seemed to have any money. It was funny, Shannon thought, that when you wanted it, there was never any round. Finally she rang Vaughan-Quilter.

"I've got to have five pounds, South. Don't ask me what I need it for. Can you lend it to me? You'll get it back, I'll promise you that." Bleeby's new serial starts in three weeks, she thought, and I can get the girl's part in that; but it's three weeks before it starts, and three weeks make a lot of difference.

"Of course," Vaughan-Quilter agreed instantly. "Where can I see you to give it to you?" She felt a gush of grateful relief that she had one friend so dependable.

"Can you leave it in a sealed envelope at 2RQ Enquiries' Desk?" She did not want to see Vaughan-Quilter and have him screw the whole story out of her, perhaps try to argue with Olly. When she went to 2RQ to get the money, she shared the lift with Lucy who ignored her as though she were the smell of the incinerator.

Shannon felt very conscious of her old shoes. Well, she thought rather bitterly, if she thinks she's hounded me into the gutter and it gives her any satisfaction, let her go on thinking it. She had to hurry away and find Olly and give her the money. When it came to the point of giving it, she felt awkward and strange.

"Here's the five pounds, Olly," she said, holding out the envelope as though it burned her. "I borrowed it."

"It doesn't matter now," Olly said lightly. "I'm managing all right. You keep it."

"Oh no," Shannon exclaimed. "Olly, I borrowed it for you. You *must* take it." Somehow it seemed vitally important that Olly should have the money, even now, when she said it was no use.

"Thanks all the same, Shannon," Olly answered, in the dry polite way she had used lately for addressing Shannon. "As I told you before, I'm managing all right." She resented Shannon, that was very clear, resented Shannon's middle-class prudery.

Shannon would have done anything to cry: "Truly, Olly, my darling, I'm not condemning you." But it was so hard to explain away the horrible fact that she, Shannon, was not impulsive, open-hearted, gay and unheeding of consequence. They might almost have been enemies.

Olly went off to stay for the week-end with Mary Hatton. She returned on Monday and took to her bed. The same evening Shannon came home to find Momma in a fret awaiting her.

"Something's wrong with Olly, very, very wrong," she said, the minute Shannon came through the shop into the tiny living room. "She's so hot and feverish and in pain. Oh!" Momma wrung her hands. "She won't let me get a doctor. Not that I'd be able to pay him, but she won't let me."

Shannon ran up the dark, narrow stair.

"Olly!"

"I'm all right, I tell you." Olly's eyes were bright, but her teeth chattered. "Go away, Shannon. Do go away." Shannon was sitting on the bed hugging her, and Olly began to cry. "I tell you I'm fine," she repeated. "Please, Shannon, just to please *me*." It was the old, pleading, wooing Olly, but how pitiful that she should ask such a favour. "Don't say anything."

"I'm getting a doctor. I've still that five pounds."

"I'll never speak to you again," Olly moaned. "Oh, I'll never speak to you again if you do." The tears ran down her face. "Just when I've fixed everything so nicely, you want to spoil all."

Momma was waiting below for Shannon, and as soon as their eyes met, Shannon realized that Momma knew and had known all the time. "Yes, go for a doctor," she said brokenly. "Quick."

Shannon went with Olly in the ambulance to the hospital, but she was turned back at the entrance to the ward and told to come again tomorrow. There might be some hope. She was back again pestering the nurse for news; she waited about hopelessly, ambushed the doctor, got in the way of stray attendants, and was finally ordered out. She and Momma were there so early next day that orderlies were still polishing the floors. They were told that Olly had died at two o'clock in the morning.

"She never did speak to me again," Shannon thought, as she tried helplessly to comfort Momma's crying. "She was still angry. She never spoke to me again."

All her love for Olly settled in a cold, aching lump in her chest. Why did it have to be Olly, she asked herself dully. Why Olly, the generous, golden-hearted friend of the world? Olly would never again say with that wooing voice: "Oh, just to please *me*." Would never again tend those cactus plants in their pots. She remembered the time they had bought the two little tortoises in a brown paper bag and someone at the Club had absent-mindedly gone off with them. The time she had made the jam and Olly hated her; the fun they had had together; and how indignant Olly had been when Wodgers, at the Club, had deliberately pushed her cactus pots off the wooden platform of the loft; how she had gathered up the pieces of cactus from the cobbles and found new pots. I will have to borrow some more money, Shannon thought drearily, to help pay for her funeral. I will know other girls, but there will never be anyone so simple and generous again.

"I have no daughter," Momma kept on moaning. "I have no daughter. Olly, my daughter, is dead."

She seemed to be trying to remember that this was so, that Olly would never again come in laughing and tell her about the Club and the awfulness of the Pompadour Cafe. All her life, Momma had devoted herself to Joe and met his least wish, leaving Olly to look after herself, and now Olly was not there any longer to look after herself or to say: "Now don't do that, Momma. Just to please *me*."

I can't stay here now, Shannon thought. Her mind worked coldly and clearly. Perhaps I could get my old room at the Knowles's lodging house.

It's cheap. I could afford that. I can't stay here reminding Momma and Poppa of everything that happened.

"I did try to stop her, Mom," she said earnestly. She told Momma all about it; how she had tried to borrow the five pounds, the whole misery. She felt a little better when it was all told.

"That man," Momma said. "I could kill'um with my hands."

"Don't," Shannon begged. "Don't make it worse." Someone would have to break the news to Bert, but she was not going to do it.

She took down her coat. They were busy at the U.C.D.L. getting out an appeal for some hero in America who had been unjustly gaoled. Automatically she thought of the work waiting. She was tempted to see Southwell Vaughan-Quilter. It would be good to tell him about Olly, but how could she tell about a girl he never knew?

As she walked along the grey streets in the cold, she thought of all the women there were in the ward where they had taken Olly; they seemed to stretch in an infinite row of white beds; women who were the broken spears of a revolution against the future, who had said "Stop" to a Juggernaut. The street seemed to fade out into an endless ward of dying women about whom nothing was said, no statistics offered, no voices raised. They just died evilly and painfully. Everyone knew, even made jokes about it. But officially, there was no such thing as a woman like Olly who could not afford to go on living because the price was too high.

She reached the rather dirty front entrance of the Trades Hall and mounted the stairs to the office which the U.C.D.L. shared with the Grinders, Gasworkers and Mainbuilders Union. There was no one in the office except Comrade Leggatt talking on the telephone about a meeting of protest against something or other. Protest! Shannon thought, as she hung up her coat, there isn't any protest against death. And suddenly her grief overcame her, and she laid down her head on her little table beside the battered typewriter and sobbed. She had not cried so for years. She cried with the pain and grief, not only of Olly, her friend, but all the weight of loneliness and despair. Leggatt closed his telephone conversation abruptly and came to bend over her.

"What is it, Shannon?" he kept repeating. "What's the matter?"

"Go on," she almost howled at him. "Go on talking about protests. What the hell does it matter? Olly's dead."

He drew up a chair and patted her awkwardly on the head. He even put his arm around her heaving thin shoulders to comfort her. He transferred her hot forehead to his shoulder, devoutly hoping that none of his fellow workers would come clattering in at the door, and he let her cry and cry. There was some humanity after all in Mervyn Leggatt, even if it was deep down.

H

Sixteen

THE U.C.D.L., that thorn in the pant's seat of justice, was occupied between the hours of nine and five, and often late into the night, with legal fights which usually circled around the right of the arrested parties to speak, march, distribute leaflets, to collect money in public places or accept it when thrown by the audience. Most of their cases were fought free of charge by solicitors and barristers who were bored by nothing to do, were kind-hearted, or had ambitions to make a name for themselves in some big case; for no one ever knew when a U.C.D.L. case might not boom up suddenly and go to the High Court.

The U.C.D.L. raised large sums of money, but the five who were its working body, still lived on coffee, meat pies and charity. They huddled in shabby leather overcoats in a frozen room, because they could not afford a radiator, and planned to cut sub-section 5 (b) out of the Over-Riding Powers of County Councils Act. They paid over money for public dinners at which illustrious speakers would be welcomed by members of liberal organizations, and they ate themselves at a sleary little fish-shop whose proprietor was a supporter and gave them free meals. All that was needed to enjoy life on the committee of the U.C.D.L. was an elastic sense of humour, an iron constitution, and a complete absence of scruples.

Shannon had changed since she first came to the U.C.D.L. During the bitter winter, she sat huddled in a leather overcoat she had inherited from Beryl, and as she typed or telephoned, went in and out of lawyers' offices, argued whether it was worth while paying the fine for George or Morry Crowther or letting them take out their sentence, her knowledge of common law improved and the angle of her jaw grew more prominent. She could quote the Crimes Act clause by clause, and she began to know as much about the Debtors and Mortgage Act, the Cash Order Claimants Regulations, and all the decisions previously given by magistrates under the Public Disorders Control Regulations. She typed long précis to be submitted to counsel; she wrote articles for any paper that would publish them on the latest legal muddles; she mercilessly levied contributions from anyone she knew.

Day by day, through the office of the U.C.D.L. filtered the misery of the city, as greasy dishwater drains down a sink, and the misery left a deposit, a grey rim around Shannon's mind, so that even while she slept she was often revolving in her dreams the possibility of "taking up" the case of one or other of the men and women with work-hardened hands and anxious faces who sat patiently waiting for advice in the little outer office.

The U.C.D.L. were forced out of their room at the Trades Hall six months after she joined them. Pressure had been applied by the official and respectable labour party to make the Grinders, Gasworkers and Mainbuilders Union eject their undesirable sub-tenants. It was hard to find any other room so close to the Central Police Station, but the U.C.D.L. was presently established in a couple of bare rooms in a very respectable office building in George Street, where there was a lift and tiled corridors and frosted glass doors to the offices. They had no gas jet for their coffee, but they brewed it in the rooms of a friendly typist along the hall, and were naïvely pleased with the splendour about them.

In the outer office sat Comrade Hicks with a table, a typewriter, a cupboard, a wooden bench for visitors, and large files of papers. In the inner office, at a bigger table, sat Comrade Leggatt and his allies, George Benson and Will Siddons. Sometimes, Comrades Benson and Siddons were in the outer office picking one-fingered at Shannon's typewriter while she was out, or searching through old copies of the Sydney *Morning Herald*, but all day long there was someone coming or going, so that the door between the two offices was left open and they were practically one. Members of other organizations would drop in to the U.C.D.L. to discuss the meeting of the I.V.I., the M.S.U. or some other organization which had just passed a motion supporting the actions of the U.C.D.L. Some of the unions were so sympathetic that if the U.C.D.L. had asked them to pass a motion demanding four sets of eyes for humanity, they would probably have proposed it without question.

The strange turbulence of the city, its careless ferocity, was, perhaps, due to the large strain of Scot and Irish in the population; but it seemed that if anyone wanted to start a fight, there were always plenty of strangers ready and willing to join in. If the thing had a political flavour, the unions would take up the case, the labour leagues would take it up. Part of the duty of the U.C.D.L. staff was to be out addressing meetings of labour supporters night after night in little dusty halls all over the suburbs, "putting the case" for this or that protest. It was as though Sydney was encompassed with a network of separate spider webs. The spiders might be suspicious and ready to eat one another; they might be connected by a single thread, yet if you touched a strand of that network, a hundred spiders leapt and danced indignantly in their webs.

Sydney was their fat fly and its buzzings were music to their ears; not the Sydney of Venetian carnivals and amusement parks; the gala Sydney of little boats with paper lanterns, of rockets a-burst or of gold fire showering over waves that flamed back again; not the Sydney of the blue days and the race crowds; or of the electric signs, the lights of the theatres, the lamps of the streets glancing and glittering over the slapping water where the stone ring of Circular Quay holds all the churning of flotsam and oily sewerage, the great liners with a little proud plume of smoke over their funnels, the weeds and the water-rats in one impersonal embrace. Over that Sydney, the moon rises like a great bubble of light, above the dim walls smudging the water silver and grey and black; and the sign of the Grapes towering above the warehouses wrung amber and ruby drops into a great wine glass, the waters under the shadow of the wharves flaring in amber or sullen blood as the sign leaped and changed.

The Sydney of the U.C.D.L. was a network of lawyers' offices, of bare wooden meeting halls, committee meetings, annual conventions, labour conferences; their fireworks were words, more words, flaring up, sputtering down into the cold appraisal of yet one more weary magistrate. They wrung the ruby and amber out of the grapes of bitterness, and their exhilaration was no carnival but a really uproarious procession through forbidden streets with six separate arrests which could be fought with great sound and fury in a gloomy, quiet court room. The members knew the courts of justice as the good citizen knows the general store, and they were as keen on a point of procedure as he on the time of the morning bus. They knew where State laws conflicted with Federal laws, and just what loop-holes lay in the huge bungle of legislation.

Not all the cases of the U.C.D.L. had a political flavour. A middle-aged woman would come in to ask in a timid whisper if there was any way she could claim her furniture. She had bought it herself over years of hard work, but she had been living with a man not her husband, and he had turned her out of the house and taken another younger woman instead. Was there any way she could regain possession of her furniture? No, she had no documents to show it was hers. It was all in her man's name, because she had bought it on time-payments and for these the man must sign. A young woman, very pale and weak, with a tiny baby, came to ask if there was any way of helping her husband out of gaol. He had been a canvasser for a photographer's firm; things had been so hard; and she was going to hospital to have the baby. In a fit of desperation, he had collected commission on an order that was not to be filled until Christmas. Surely it wasn't dreadfully wrong? He had really taken the order. He had only collected £10 commission a little in advance and he was in gaol because he couldn't pay back the money. He had never been in gaol before. The shame of it was killing him. Oh, couldn't they please get him out of gaol?

George Benson told her briefly he would see her husband had a lawyer. He would probably get a month at the most and he'd better "take it out." The wife thanked them, in tears. She was sorry, she said, to cry, but she had come out of hospital only two days before.

"Damn fool," Benson growled, in an undertone, while the woman sat in the outer office. "Wanting us to pay the fine. Why, we've got six of our men in and they're not squealing. 'The shame of it is killing him!' Can you beat it?"

George Benson had seen the inside of English, Irish and Australian gaols. Hard-bitten and hot-headed, they had had no effect on him except to make him more a foe to all governments. But the woman's grief made him uneasy. He kept muttering and growling to himself while he rang up to find someone who would defend the woman's husband free. Presently he called Shannon: "Take her out and feed her," he ordered. "And here . . . give her this to go on with, poor devil." He abstracted a ten-shilling note from the stamp money. "I know I shouldn't do it, we're robbing ourselves. But, oh hell, who cares?"

Ten pounds, Shannon thought, a family broken up for ten pounds; and there are women who would pay that for a coat and think they were economizing. She was a little contemptuous of the young wife who was so neat and poor. Then she smiled as a comic idea struck her.

"You go along to Lucy Rossingale at 2RQ," she advised. "Don't say I sent you."

Lucy was getting a lot of pathetic cases from Shannon without knowing it. To Vaughan-Quilter she would not send people. She had never paid back that five pounds, and the recollection made her feel sore and miserable. She found herself avoiding all her old friends. Her clothes were not good enough for one thing. She lived free with George Benson's family and, as Leggatt had told her, when the U.C.D.L. had money, they ate; when there was none, they borrowed here and there and waited for better times.

George Benson, in what time he could spare from the U.C.D.L., was a cabinet maker and upholsterer. He had a quiet wife and three small sons, whose misdeeds he would relate with ill-disguised pride:

"There was I coming home the other afternoon from the Domain meeting, and I see three filthy little urchins sneakin' a ride on the tram. I was just wondering how people could let their kids run wild like that, when one of them yells: 'Hello, Dad!' and strike me, if it wasn't little George! I just went crimson, I can tell you, with all those women in the tram laughing. Oh, there's no mistake about it, I'll have to whale the hide off them one of these days."

He was indulgent to his family; he neither smoked nor drank; but his one vice was the U.C.D.L. for which he neglected wife, children and work. They shared their house with lodgers in order to pay the rent, but there were times when the Benson family was reduced to bread and dripping.

"Now it's coming summer," Bill Siddons observed with a grin, "we'll all have to get out of our leather coats and wear shirts again. It's going to be tough to wear a collar." Will had done very well enough with a muffler, a woollen jersey and a pair of trousers. "Maybe we could all pillage the press fund. Makes a better impression in court to be well dressed. The other day the new magistrate said to Morry Crowther: 'You are not one of these men, are you?' And Morry sort of preened himself in that grey, double-breasted suit of his, and gave the other chaps a sniffy look and said: 'Certainly not, your honor,' and the old bloke said, 'I thought not,' and acquitted him."

Shannon had taken to wearing her hair in a knob on the back of her neck because it saved the money for hair cuts; but taking stock of herself, she realised that she was disgracefully shabby. She had been so busy that she had not had time to worry, and everyone else she knew was just as shabby as she was. Living from hand to mouth, she had grown very thin. She had always had a good complexion, so her economies in cosmetics were not so noticeable as her shoes, which, with constant walking, were always wearing out. Perhaps, she thought, she had better go out and see Beryl.

After Olly's death Shannon had thought she could never speak to Beryl again. But was it just to saddle Beryl with the blame for something she could not have foreseen? She might have known it was no use asking Beryl for money. Beryl was generous with clothes, but she hated to part with money. After all, what had Beryl done that was so dreadful? Refuse a loan for a purpose of which no one could approve. Beryl was now among the just, the righteous. That was the whole trouble. And it was the just and righteous that Shannon was blaming so bitterly for Olly's death; the whole system of society which knew about people like Olly and told them they were fools. Still, there it was, Beryl had acted according to her nature which, while out for a good time, was always careful to see that the good times were not spoiled by any untoward incident, and Olly had acted according to her nature. Why blame either of them? Nature was just something so unalterable. If you wanted friends, you must take them in spite of their faults. She would not have discarded Olly because she was so soft. Why should she discard Beryl because she was so hard? Besides, she thought cynically, I need Beryl's old clothes, if I'm to look decent enough to go about.

She went out to see Beryl and it worked like a charm. The sight of her one-time mate clad in an old brown jersey and skirt in the warm weather gave Beryl a shudder of aesthetic horror.

"You should never wear brown," she exclaimed. "And so-help-me, look at your feet! You come here." She dragged her to a long mirror. "See that!"

Shannon blandly admitted that the effect was not pleasant. When she left, she was stocked out in a supply of Beryl's dresses, and as they took the same size in shoes, her worries were over for the time. Her appearance at the office on Monday was greeted with cries of mock astonishment, but there was no doubt the U.C.D.L. agreed that she paid for dressing. She sometimes ran into Bart Jackson around the police courts, and he too asked if she had come into money. But he seemed gloomy and preoccupied.

"Look here," he said, glancing uneasily about him. "You ought to get out of that crowd you're with, Shannon. I had a look at your dossier and it's as long as my arm."

"Really?" Shannon said gaily. She was rather pleased than otherwise that she had been paid this little attention. She was a good speaker, and her work on the latest disturbances had been particularly notable. She had been out every night flaming like a small firebrand. "They haven't got me mixed up with anyone else, have they?"

"Were you helping distribute leaflets last Sunday?"

"Yes, of course."

"Well, look out, that's all. I'm just giving you the tip. Another thing, the inspector was hauling me over the coals for knowing you. Warned me about bad company like a father." Poor, timorous, big Bart gave another uneasy glance around. "You ought to take a pull, Shannon."

Shannon's report of this conversation at the U.C.D.L. office was given earnest consideration.

"You want to be careful talking to coppers," George Benson remarked, with an uneasy scowl. "You know how easily you can get a name for a spy in the Movement."

"Anyway, you're too useful to do time," Mervyn Leggatt decided. "There are plenty of other people who haven't anything better to do, who can loaf in gaol."

But the matter did not end there. It went to the Great Ones, the Powers Unseen which moved behind the spiderwebs. Shannon and Leggatt and Benson appeared before three lean men in another small, dusty office elsewhere in the city, and were questioned, cross-questioned, reproved, threatened, and generally treated to a thorough overhaul. Shannon's connection with Bart Jackson was examined in great detail. She was warned against making friends with the police as a nicely brought up daughter is warned against strange young men. All of this left her a little bewildered.

"It means this," Leggatt said quietly, when they were back alone in the office. "There's a leak somewhere, and if it isn't you, who is it?"

A few weeks later Will Siddons vanished from the office and was seen no more.

"But Will's been working in the U.C.D.L. for years," Shannon protested. "You told me yourself that you'd been in gaol together."

"He was still a spy," Leggatt said, not looking up from his work. He took it quite for granted that happy-go lucky, careless Will, always ready for anything, useful, hard-working, should be a traitor. He would have taken it almost as casually if the leak had been through Shannon. Leggatt was never surprised, and this invincibility stood him in good stead in a job where anything was likely to happen.

When a knock came at the door and Shannon opened it to find two large plain-clothes men, she called Leggatt out of his office.

"Just having a look around," one of the men said easily.

"Got your warrant?" Leggatt asked. The two looked at each other; Leggatt stepped into the corridor.

"There's the office and there's the lift," he said, pointing. "You know the law, and I know the law maybe better than you do. Now you can step into that office if you like, but before you do, just remember the cases we've won."

The officers turned about and walked to the lift. Leggatt watched them with his hard, tight-lipped smile. Then he returned to his own table and went quietly on with his work.

The sight of those two had given Shannon a jolt. She thought they had come for her, and although she knew that the organization disliked a capable functionary wasted behind bars, there was always the chance. You could not kick the State on the ankles and expect it to love you like a little child. Her refusal to use different names as the others did annoyed her associates. George Benson had at least three different names. Leggatt took it quite as a matter of course that in some quarters he should be addressed as McCoy and in others as Bill Masters.

"Just a simple precaution," he had explained to Shannon.

"I've always been Shannon Hicks and I'm always going to be."

He had looked at her coldly. "You'll never make a revolutionary," he observed. "You're just a bourgeois liberal." That was where she was so useful. No one could imagine such a ladylike, well-spoken girl could be a dangerous red. Any time the U.C.D.L. wanted to look respectable, Shannon came in handy.

"As long as you can use me, Shannon flung this pet phrase back at Leggatt. He was always calculating if so-and-so could be used. It was a habit he had caught from the Movement's executive, who thought of little else than "using" people; and, when they were worn out, Shannon had observed, the "used" tools were discarded and new ones took their

H*

place. Of course nobody could blame the executive. Still, there it was: just a way of looking at human beings as though they were parts of a machine of which the powers behind the cobwebs held the master switch. She had grown so accustomed to this calculation as to whether Morry would be more useful in gaol or out, where he could best be "used," that the thought of "using" people who did not know they were being used had a less unpleasant flavour. You took so much for granted in the U.C.D.L.

Reading the morning paper with a blue pencil for any relevant paragraphs Leggatt said thoughtfully: "Here's something we can use. Four aboriginals have a death sentence for shoving a spear through a policeman."

Shannon reached over for the paper.

"We'll need some of the clergy," Leggatt observed, as he passed it. "We can always find a few writers and journalists. The anthropologists will come. You've only got to knock a fly off a native and they're up in arms. Shannon, from now on you're secretary of the 'Free Our Natives League.' Get right to that telephone and ring up 2RQ and ask for time on their air."

"We'll need some star performers," George suggested. He was eating his breakfast, a cheese roll, perched on the edge of Shannon's table. "An eminent legal light should say why they can't hang these Abos." The U.C.D.L. had several eminent legal lights who had no love of the mad tangle of legislation and were wickedly ready to shoot holes in it. "Shannon can go and interview that chap who's just landed from South Africa—the one who made such a stink about the way the natives were treated there."

All the morning Shannon was on the telephone using her sweetest tones. "Oh, Mr. Hereford, this is Miss Hicks. I don't know whether you remember me? I met you when we were speaking together at the Legal Rights Conference. Yes, that is correct, Mr. Hereford. I wonder if you could spare half an hour to see me? I have something very important to discuss. The matter of these four aboriginals to be hanged. Do you think . . . Oh, thank you so much. Twelve-thirty will do nicely."

"You'd better go straight home and change into your best dress," Leggatt advised. "If it's twelve-thirty, he'll take you out to lunch. Now, get Miss Hannah Longacre." Miss Longacre was an authority on aboriginal affairs, having once spent three months in the Northern Territory. She had been in hospital one month of the time, but that still left her two months to become an authority.

The number of distinguished persons who would be delighted to join the committee mounted until it was most impressive. Not that that would prevent certain disillusioned gentlemen in the Chief Secretary's department from deciding that this was just another U.C.D.L. façade. They knew from bitter experience that whenever there was a protest about something, the U.C.D.L. had a finger in the pie.

Shannon returned to the office late in the afternoon after a most successful day whipping up the Free Our Natives League. The visitor from South Africa had given her an interesting interview and she was settling down at her desk to type it out for the "Workers' Call" when a knock came at the door. Her first thought was that the two plain-clothes men were back with a warrant. But it was Southwell Vaughan-Quilter, his old majestic self. Shannon was pleased she had on her best dress. She felt better able to face him.

"Oh, South," she said hurriedly, "how did you know I was here?" She remembered that she had never repaid him the five pounds. The ache and the wretchedness of Olly's death had eased so that she forgot it sometimes for weeks. She had not wanted to remember.

"Your aunt rang me and asked me to come and see you, Shannon. She is very worried about you."

His glance wandered around the bare office, the piles of papers, the crumbs of someone's lunch and two dirty coffee cups that Shannon had not found time to clear away. Leggatt who had also, it seemed, expected another visit from his plain-clothes friends, came to the door of the inner office, so Shannon introduced them.

"South, I will have finished this article in a quarter of an hour. Could you wait for me?"

The Abbot agreed to wait and Mervyn Leggatt invited him into the inner office. Through the click of her typewriter Shannon could hear them talking about the Free Our Natives League.

"I don't suppose we could ask you to speak for us?" Leggatt enquired smoothly.

"Why, yes, I have always felt the treatment of the natives in this country is most unjust. If your meeting were on a Monday or a Friday . . ."

Shannon was so thunder-struck that she typed the same line twice. Southwell Vaughan-Quilter speaking on a Free Our Natives platform. No! She was not going to have the Abbot used; anyone else, if they liked, but not South.

"The Order of Human Brotherhood," Leggatt was saying, with a slight sneer. "Has it a political platform?"

He was not surprised to hear that the Order of Human Brotherhood was non-political. In his cold, incisive way, he set about at once a long argument which should have convinced Vaughan-Quilter that there could be no human brotherhood until the System was overthrown. Evidently, since Leggatt was taking so much trouble, he believed that here was a man they could use to great advantage. Shannon beat out the last line and ripped the paper out of her typewriter.

"I'm ready," she announced. "You won't mind walking down to the 'Workers' Call' with me? We can talk as we go."

Comrade Leggatt gave her his thin-lipped smile. "Don't hurry," he said. "Take your time." He might just as plainly have said: "Treat this man to everything. We need him."

Shannon was no sooner out of the building than she plunged into a frank description of the U.C.D.L. She placed their activities before Southwell Vaughan-Quilter in the most unfavourable light. She told him all the adroit tricks, all the "using" of people, the gay going to gaol of half the members. They turned into the dirty lane leading to the "Workers' Call" and mounted through the front entrance to wind their way between a series of little wooden offices, where Shannon twisted and turned as expertly as a rabbit in its burrow, until she deposited her interview and a note of explanation on the sub-editor's desk.

When they emerged again, the Abbot asked: "You have told me all the reasons why I shouldn't mix in this. Why are you mixed in it?"

"Oh, I suppose I've always had a kink against authority. Comes of disliking my father. It's just a form of blood sport."

"You're not still looking," he paused, "for something worthwhile?"

"I gave that up." Yes, she thought, that was true. In the world in which she found herself she did not believe that half a dozen changes of the social system would cleanse the sewers of human ignorance and stupidity.

"I thought perhaps this was the worthwhile thing you were looking for."

"Oh, no." She smiled up at him. "He who expects nothing is seldom disappointed. I used to be rather dreamy and metaphysical in those days at 2RQ."

She has changed, he thought, and grown harder. There was always something in Shannon that was hard; but it was rather a splendid something. She had clear outlines; so many people were blurred and indistinct.

"Why haven't you visited your aunt?" he asked, when, for the sake of a quiet place to talk, they had seated themselves in a small coffee shop. "She has not been well."

"I really will go, South, but it's so hard talking to her when she believes I'm an abandoned female." With so many important things to do, she had had no more time for dalliance than she had for visits to Aunt Edith. "I will go out and see her," she promised.

"You know I took my B.C.L. at Oxford," Southwell Vaughan-Quilter said quietly. "It might be a help if I were working with . . . with your League."

Shannon could hardly believe her ears. "I told you . . . I told you, South . . . that you'd be mad to have anything to do with the U.C.D.L."

"You don't want me?"

"It isn't that." She felt herself getting hot and embarrassed under his steady gaze. "But it will do you a lot of harm."

She tried to think harshly of him. He just sees himself on a platform, she thought, making a ringing speech, freeing the natives, straightening out legal muddles, right in the middle of all the excitement.

His next words confirmed her thoughts. "I am growing rather tired of the Abbey. I sometimes feel that there is not enough scope in the Abbey for a real effort to assist humanity. Bulfram has made himself very unpleasant over my divorce."

"Oh!" She could think of nothing to say. It was plain that this was his way of letting her know that his divorce had gone through. "Oh, I see." She sounded weak even to herself. "But I think you should keep away from the U.C.D.L."

As they parted, he remarked that he would be coming in to the U.C.D.L. next day. "To see Comrade Leggatt," he added, with a smile.

Shannon walked back alone to the office feeling slightly intoxicated. South Quilter hadn't really searched her out for Aunt Edith's sake. He wanted to see her, and he was going to see her again. He was tired of the

Abbey, ripe for some new adventure. What a scoundrel, she thought affectionately, that man was, what an unprincipled charlatan! He and she were really the counterpart of each other, born cynical, born restless, but whereas Southwell Vaughan-Quilter was human dynamite, she, Shannon, was very quiet and inoffensive.

She would not have thought so, if she could have heard herself a few evenings later harrowing an audience with the sufferings of the poor, helpless natives that she had hurriedly studied up half an hour before the meeting began. She had adopted Leggatt's cold, incisive manner, and she hammered at them until the gathering began to feel it was responsible for those sufferings. It unanimously passed a resolution demanding that the natives be freed and calling on all good unionists to support the decision of direct action if necessary. Speaker after speaker sprang up to advocate approaches to other leagues, a conference of freedom-lovers with delegates from all over Australia.

"It's booming along," Leggatt approved. "Keep it up."

Shannon borrowed sixpence from the collection for her tram fare home.

Seventeen

I

JUST AS THE Free Our Natives League was booming along nicely, with questions in Parliament and demands for the recall of officials, the International League of Peacelovers sent out a yell for help, and the U.C.D.L. was detailed to attend to the matter.

There had never been any love lost between the U.C.D.L. and the Peacelovers, who had elected as their president and chief battle-axe Shannon's old patron, Mrs. Emmie Brewster. With her on the committee was listed Mrs. Jane Bubbing, past president of the Women's Rights Club, a noted feminist, who wore little plush hats perched on the side of her untidy grey hair and was so fat that when she moved her corsets creaked. "How is Australianism to develop," Emmie Brewster demanded, "without peace?" We have peace, and we must keep this precious heritage for our children. Of course, we must have defence and adequate defence to ensure peace."

It made Shannon ill to see respectable revolutionary leaders muffling their wolfishness under the greasy sheepskin of affability, while they kow-towed to Emmie Brewster. They cherished her because she was a "Society" leader and her mere presence made the International Peacelovers acceptable to "nice" people. Janet Bubbing was there, because she had excellent connections with all the women's clubs. Janet Bubbing believed she was "using" all these people to get into parliament, where she might get women equal pay with men. She was also very loyal to her own opinion, which was that if all the governments controlled the making of armaments, they could turn them out more efficiently and cut out the middleman's profits which were a criminal waste.

The International Peacelovers were arranging a Congress Against War, and had invited delegates from near and far. One delegate was even coming from Europe, from the parent body of Peacelovers, and another delegate from New Zealand. It looked just another dreary conference

209

with resolutions calling on the government to do this and that; and it might have passed off without more notice than five lines of print among the Women's Interests and the market reports. Then came the news that the Minister for the Interior was being prodded by indignant conservatives and was not intending the delegates should land.

Various worthy men had pointed out to the Ministry that one of the numerous centenaries had drawn a visit from royalty and a train of celebrities. What a disgrace if they should find the country all littered up with peace conferences! What a bad impression it might make! Under this spur the Ministry of the Interior bestirred itself.

The delegate from New Zealand was not allowed to leave the boat and was carried straight back to New Zealand. The European delegate was not only not allowed to land in Perth, but he was refused permission to see his consul, his fellow peacelovers, even the banners and addresses of welcome. He was cooped aboard ship and taken on to Melbourne where police turned back the reception committee at the dock gates, and they had to filter in singly and in twos to see an ailing sweetheart or their grandmother. When several hundred persons had gone aboard to see their relations, there were still plenty left over to hire a launch and exchange insults with the complement of the Nazi warship in the harbour. They putted round and round the vessel on which their delegate was imprisoned, plastering it with stickers demanding the guest's release.

If only they could get him ashore, there might be some hope of keeping him, but the ship was ready to put to sea before they could bring their legal guns into close range. Just as the ship was putting out, the overseas delegate, rendered desperate, made a leap and crashed to the dock with a broken leg. The police on duty stolidly and illegally replaced him on the ship which had put back specially for him, and the mortified delegate was borne on to Sydney leaving behind him an uproar of protest meetings which quite dwarfed the original conference.

Meanwhile the New Zealand delegate returned anonymously, slipped ashore and "went into smoke" like some famous criminal. There were committees everywhere: committees of doctors, lawyers, journalists, state and federal members of parliament, union leaders. Everyone forgot about the royal visitor while they argued the rights and wrongs of the Ministry's action. More important than these were the anxious conferences in the

U.C.D.L. office, conferences in which the Peacelovers, the U.C.D.L., and all the left bodies of the city joined as one.

When the ship docked in Sydney, a High Court writ for habeas corpus was served on the captain; and the suffering delegate was free, for exactly seventy seconds. Then the Customs Department informed him that he was a prohibited immigrant, and since it was known that he spoke ten languages, the language test was given him in Gaelic. On his failing to translate the passage correctly, he was removed to a prison cell where, in the absence of a chair, he was expected to make his broken leg as comfortable as possible sitting on a board on the floor.

The delegate, who was internationally renowned for his sense of humour, his eye for a dramatic situation, and his flair for capitalizing it, found the whole situation a little too much. He had been in Nazi gaols, he roared at the warders, he had been in concentration camps, but never, never had he known such a mad country. He cursed it in the ten different languages he knew and some assorted dialects of which he had a smattering. He made as much noise within the gaol as his fellow peacelovers did outside. Finally, as his leg did not improve in the prison cell, he was removed to hospital with two policemen to sit by his bed. When he was released on a security of five hundred pounds, instead of policemen beside his bed, he had committeemen. To the horror of the hospital, they called for him pitilessly in cars and took him off to address protest meetings. He was constantly being returned to the hospital somewhat the worse for wear until he reached the stage when he could address meetings on crutches.

Meanwhile, the New Zealand delegate was electrifying peacelovers by appearing suddenly in cities six hundred miles apart, giving his speech and going away again. When the police force declared he was a myth, there was great indignation, and, on the U.C.D.L. recommendation, it was decided to have the New Zealander arrested so that he should be proved real. Just for the time being, however, their European delegate was giving them more publicity than they could cope with.

The plea of his counsel was that the test in Gaelic was not properly given, as Scottish Gaelic was not a language within the meaning of the Immigration Act. The officer who administered the test admitted he could not read a passage of that language (which turned out to be the Lord's Prayer) but protested that there was no need for him to know Gaelic.

The magistrate ruled that an officer administering a dictation test need not speak the language he was dictating. He found the test had been properly administered and gave the delegate six months' gaol.

The delegate, his sense of humour becoming more and more warped, was again removed to gaol, while the U.C.D.L. lodged an appeal to the High Court. All night, the U.C.D.L. sat up telephoning, trying to find the two hundred pounds' bail. They were waiting in the grey, early morning to have their man out. "I do not find this country amusing," the guest said dejectedly. "I think everyone here is a little mad." He had been searched, his finger-prints taken, his property removed from his pockets. He was not surprised to hear that U.C.D.L. members were always in and out of gaol.

The money was pouring in from collections, but it covered only printing, travelling, hire of halls and incidental expenses. The thought of the legal costs was to harass the executives. True, they were getting most of their legal talent free, but there were still all kinds of charges which must be met in the process of justice. The delegate from New Zealand dramatically allowed himself to be arrested at a peace meeting which developed into a riot. He was sentenced to six months' gaol and deportation because, on being tested, it was found that he could not read Dutch. This meant another High Court appeal, another £200 bail, and another all-night sitting before the £200 was raked together. Shannon borrowed five pounds from Aunt Edith after an immense amount of argument. Vaughan-Quilter raised a hundred himself.

Then the U.C.D.L. drove forward through the High Court of Australia and won a sweeping victory. Gaelic, it was decided, was not a language within the meaning of the Immigration Act. A new voice joined the baying of the pack, the voice of the Highland Society. Highlanders broke into print with a set of blistering comments on the judges of the High Court, the peacelovers, and all their ilk. It called down the curse of Macbeth and the three witches on all who would deprive a Highlander of his language. A libel case on behalf of the peacelovers was presently raging; and meanwhile the case of the New Zealander dragged on and on costing the government a mint of money. The Ministry for the Interior, with all the finesse of an elephant endeavouring to swat a mayfly, had set its heart on getting a conviction just on four o'clock, when it would be too late to lodge an appeal until next day, and the delegate might be taken straight to an outward bound boat. The counsel for the defence collapsed with the strain.

Finally, the New Zealander had to be acquitted, because he had been charged under section five of the Act (which carried no penalty) and had been sentenced under section seven (which carried six months' gaol). Even the Government's strongest supporters were beginning to wriggle with mortification. They brought in an amendment to the Immigration Act throwing the onus of proving he was not a prohibited immigrant on the accused. When this amendment was lost, a second one was proposed giving six months' gaol for section five as well as section seven.

This sop was granted and the Ministry retired from the fray to lick its wounds, while with banners, torchlight processions and gum-leaf bands playing the Internationale, the peacelovers broke into a new rash of meetings ere they farewelled their delegates. All the meetings loyally opened with the singing of "God Save the King." It was a little touch on which Mrs. Brewster insisted.

"The cause of peace," Mrs. Janet Bubbing exulted to Mrs. Brewster, "has never had such a splendid advertisement."

But under all the round of public dinners and meetings, the pleas for a cessation of wars between workers for ever and ever, a very competent little dog-fight was in progress between the U.C.D.L. and the united committee which set the U.C.D.L. to work. All collections at meetings had been taken up on behalf of the peace organization. None of it went to the U.C.D.L., and when it came to making the Peacelovers disgorge some of their gains, they were highly indignant. The U.C.D.L. had sat up nights and gone grey hunting for bail; well, that was the U.C.D.L.'s job. The International Peacelovers could use all the money they had, thank you. They did not need any help from a "set of most undesirable people." At least that was the view of Mrs. Brewster and Mrs. Bubbing.

"To think of it," groaned George Benson. "We don't get a red cent, not a flaming red cent."

II

Shannon had been elected assistant secretary of the Central Branch of the International Peacelovers. She had not wanted the job; it had just been assigned to her as the most able to talk to middle-class women in their own terms.

"But I don't want to talk to them," she complained. "One of the things I like best about the U.C.D.L., Merv, is that there are no respectable people in it."

"Don't be so extremist, Shannon. We must get into all the bourgeois liberal organizations, all the churches, the little progressive clubs, anywhere we can get a foothold. If we don't, the Fascists will."

Leggatt was not pleased to lose Shannon; but once a policy, like a set of steel rails, had been laid down for him by his superiors, his obedience ran along it unswerving.

Mrs. Brewster was shrewd enough to realize that Shannon's election as assistant secretary was no accident. She had done her best to see that Shannon was not elected, so she knew that the meeting had been carefully worded beforehand. Always these Reds, Mrs. Brewster thought bitterly, they work so much harder than anyone else and they come worming in. She greeted Shannon with a strangled displeasure.

"Dear me! Shannon Hicks, isn't it? You always seem to be popping up, don't you?"

But Emmie Brewster knew better than to provoke this unpleasant girl too far. She was secretly a little afraid of Shannon. After all, there had to be someone to arrange meetings, see that speakers did not take more than their allotted time, and send out notices of meetings. Shannon Hicks would do for that as well as anyone. Mrs. Bubbing specialized on emotional appeals for a unity of mothers all over the world to have no more children until war should cease; she was not very good at office work. Mrs. Brewster herself was deep in a pageant, Peace for All Nations, with groups of national costumes grouped prettily together. She was hoping that the Proletarian Club would cooperate to make the thing a success and stage their new play, "War! Wherefore?"; but the Proletarian Club last time had taken all the collection for itself.

Mrs. Brewster knew all about the "Left" policy of "using" obliging and gullible persons, be they bankers or biscuit manufacturers. But she was having a glorious time "using" the Left as audience for her pageants. Besides you met really interesting people in the peace organizations; for instance, she had just invited a most intellectual man, a Reverend Doctor Knowles, to speak. People were so impressed by all his degrees.

"He's a fake," Shannon said bluntly. "We can't possibly have him. It will discredit the movement."

Mrs. Brewster bristled. "I have had some experience," she said cuttingly. "Though perhaps to *you* his shy Scotch manner may appear rough, underneath the man is a scholar, and after all," this was the crushing retort, "he is a clergyman."

"He's not a clergyman and he has never taken a degree in his life; and my uncle recently threw him out for attempted blackmail."

Mrs. Brewster was inwardly a little disturbed, but she held tenaciously to her point, all through Shannon's account of how she came to know Dr. Knowles, claiming that there was no *proof* that he was an impostor. "Besides he was such a fervent speaker, and people liked to see a clergyman on a peace platform. They expected clergymen to be a little queer."

Shannon carried the matter to Leggatt, who agreed that Knowles would do the peace movement more harm than good. "They've got plenty of parsons anyway," he said sardonically. "I'll fix Knowles."

"You're not living at the Knowles' place any longer?" Shannon asked curiously.

He shook his head. She never found out anything about Comrade Leggatt's private life. Dear old George Benson had a home life and everyone knew it; but what happened to Leggatt when he was off duty? No one knew. She came to the conclusion that he was never off duty. For herself, she was so infernally sick of the International Peacelovers that she was brooding over a recurrent impulse to be quit of them. While she had been in the Proletarian Club, she had enjoyed herself. In the U.C.D.L. she had worked rather as a man takes drugs to drown the sickening feeling that there was nothing worth living beside the drug of work.

But she had liked Leggatt and Benson and the rest of the group. The International Peacelovers were sickening her of these bodies with a mission. All her life she seemed to have been arranging meetings, sitting in a stuffy draughty room with a typewriter and people talking all about her. She forgot the times she had enjoyed herself and remembered the wet shoes, the lack of sleep, the weary discussions of points of order. The U.C.D.L. was being practically disbanded with the wider spread of the new policy of uniting all liberals in one loving brotherhood. The order had gone out that there must be no more processions and fights, because they shocked liberal opinion and nice people did not like to be mixed up with organizations whose members might land in gaol.

"But it's so mad," Shannon argued with Leggatt and George Benson.

"Why call it a revolutionary party if it's going to spend its time being loving to labour parliamentarians who have been called everything from an illegitimate snake downwards?"

"That's the united front."

"But if you're going to have a front with any sort of dopes, what good is it?"

"We can dominate them and use them."

"I don't know about that. Who runs the Peacelovers? Me or Ma Brewster? Ma Brewster, of course."

A long explanation of the fallacy of her viewpoint did not convince her.

"Many of these people are very intelligent," George Benson assured her. "Take your Southwell Quilter. He's absolutely what we have been looking for."

"He's not my Southwell Quilter," Shannon said sullenly. She was very fond of South but the old magic of his voice and manner had worn somewhat thin for her.

If Vaughan-Quilter had wanted a wider audience, he was certainly getting it now. At protest and peace meetings he was rapidly becoming the star speaker, because his remarks on the necessity for human brotherhood, his genuine concern for the oppressed races, created the right atmosphere, put everybody in a pleasant frame of mind and did not commit the organizers to any political or religious panacea which might have jarred with their policy. There was a tacit and polite understanding between the clergy who ornamented the platforms of the peace movement, which suggested that it would be better not to mention God. The Christian religion, certainly; the need for a fuller and wider interpretation of the teachings of human brotherhood; but, on a platform uniting all, it was perhaps a little impolite to hint that human perfectibility had not yet been attained. On the other hand, the Peacelovers sincerely tried not to sneer too loudly at these preaching parsons and the dupes who still accepted the opium of the churches.

It intrigued Shannon to see Sasha vehemently making a ringing speech on the necessity of defending the Workers' Fatherland and advocating bigger and better armaments from a peace platform. These arms of course were to be controlled by the workers as a guarantee that they would not be wrongfully used. Sasha was widely regarded as an authority on Russia, because, although she had never been there, she spoke with such fire and certainty; also she had such a fascinating foreign accent.

Clive was still editing the "Anti-War Monthly"; but it had been considered expedient to change the name for the pacific one of "Indivisible Peace"; and the cover was now ornamented with smiling pictures of peasants in blossom-time, instead of the original death's head and the pile of corpses with dangling entrails. It might be said these days, when the Left was busily stamping on its firebrands and converting its wolves into doormats, that a spurious snobbery was the fashion. Any flamboyant opportunist, providing he did not drop his aitches, was welcomed; and people who were "known" as revolutionaries had to be muffled out of sight for fear they frightened the fashionable figureheads.

For Shannon, life seemed to be just one conference after another; with Janet Bubbing in the chair, calling: "Now, ladies, ladies, we have so much business, that I can allow only five minutes for discussion," and tinging a little bell.

At the latest of these conferences, the All Australia Conference of International Peacelovers, Shannon found herself sitting at the back of the hall scribbling amendments for trusted delegates to move when any dangerous motions arose; and, during a dreary speech, she fell into conversation with an elderly clergyman next to her, a man with a thin kindly face, who reminded her dimly of someone she had almost forgotten, John Terrill, the lover of books. She even asked him if he were in any way related to John Terrill, but he shook his head.

He was, she found, the president of a little peace group. He told her amusing tales of the anti-conscription fights of the last war. "Of course," he said, with a chuckle, "the Methodist Church fixed me. They took away my pulpit and I had to sell fruit and vegetables. Sometimes I think I might have been better if I had remained as a fruit vendor . . . more useful I mean." Shannon liked him instantly. At the end of the session she approached the committee and suggested that the old anti-conscriptionist be allowed to speak. What was his name? She hadn't asked him, but she pointed him out, the thin, elderly man just going out the door. Mrs. Bubbing and Mrs. Brewster uttered a simultaneous exclamation of horror.

"Do you know who he is?" Mrs. Brewster demanded. "He's a pacifist. Oh, no, we couldn't have *him!*"

"Never," Mrs. Bubbing echoed firmly. "There's a whole crew of them. Pacifists, Quakers, and the most awful people."

The International Peacelovers drew the line at pacifists and Quakers because they held so firmly to their ridiculous ideas. They must, to be affiliated with the International Peacelovers League, subscribe to all the nineteen points of the programme, and one of these points insisted on the grouping together of all states to fight any other state which seemed likely to, start a war. Somehow it was difficult to convince the Quakers and pacifists of the logic of this as a peace move.

III

One of the resolutions passed at the All Australia Conference of International Peacelovers demanded that the president, secretary, and anyone they liked to co-opt should proceed immediately to the national capital and there interview the Prime Minister, the Minister for Defence and any other assorted ministers. They were to convince these ministers that a wharf labourer who had tipped a truck load of pig iron into the harbour instead of loading it for Japan, should be immediately released. Mrs. Brewster and Mrs. Bubbing were uneasily conscious that this motion had never been on the agenda paper. They suspected the perverse Miss Hicks of slipping it in. Themselves, they had always avoided anything concrete and nasty.

It took several telephone messages from Mervyn Leggatt and enquiries from even higher sources before they reluctantly decided that someone was at work to see that the resolution was not shelved.

"I don't see that it has anything to do with us," Mrs. Brewster said peevishly.

"The money for expenses was voted," Shannon reminded them.

"That's very true." Her superiors brightened up. "After all, dear," Janet Bubbing addressed herself to Mrs. Brewster, "a little trip at this time of the year would not do us any harm. We can spare a day or so, and Shannon can stay and arrange things here."

"I'm coming too," Shannon said firmly.

"Oh, no." Both ladies were definite on that point. They were quite capable of handling the matter. In no circumstances would it be expedient for her to accompany them. When they started, Shannon was with them perched in the back seat of Mrs. Brewster's car.

There had been so much delay that it was late in the afternoon of the appointed day before they started. At the last moment there had been a furious round of phone calls from all the organizations who wanted a little lobbying done. Mrs. Bubbing was clutching a folder full of resolutions from the Domestic Women's Association which demanded reforms in everything from the price of butter to the introduction of a basic wage for housewives. Mrs. Brewster was full of the idea of staging a pageant of Australian democracy next time there was anything opened in Canberra. A new wing of the Commonwealth Archives Building would soon be ripe for a Royal visit, and why not a pageant to celebrate? The two ladies were so full of enthusiasm that they were even affable to the incubus in the back seat who had brought no papers and no luggage except a toothbrush and a pair of pyjamas. Mrs. Brewster and Mrs. Bubbing had enough luggage for a three months' voyage.

Just before they started, Janet Bubbing was struck by the battered appearance of Emmie's car. "I say, Emmie," she said, "are you sure, dear, that you can drive all that distance yourself?"

"Janet," Mrs. Brewster said magnificently, "if there is one thing I know, it is how to drive a car."

Before they had left the city, they had nearly run down a tram car, had been cursed by a lorry driver; and Mrs. Bubbing had been twice almost thrown through the wind screen when Emmie applied the brakes.

"It's not that I'm nervous," Janet Bubbing kept repeating. "I know you're perfectly capable, Emmie." She said this much as a believer in suggestion might repeat that every day in every way she was getting better and better, when she knew she was not.

They stopped for afternoon tea; they stopped for tea; and the winter darkness found them in the grim patch of forest between Moss Vale and Goulburn. It was here that Mrs. Brewster made the mistake, quite a pardonable one, as she explained later, of caroming off a telegraph post into the ditch. They were going at the time at the pace of an elderly tortoise, so there was not much harm except to their nerves.

"Now look what you've done," Mrs. Brewster said furiously, turning to Shannon who had been dozing placidly in the back seat. It was Shannon who had to walk the mile to the nearest telephone and call out a garage hand to tow them in. After a chilly wait, a couple of grimy looking lads in a little truck appeared and towed them out of the ditch.

They found there was not really much that could not be mended on the spot. They soldered a small leak in the radiator, adjusted the carburetor, which was leaking badly, tinkered about with the engine and pronounced the car as good as ever, except for the buckled mudguard. Mrs. Brewster indomitably declared that they should reach Canberra that night or perish in the attempt.

"If it hadn't been for Shannon sulking sarcastically in the back seat," she pointed out, "this would never have happened."

They did reach Canberra about eleven o'clock and made for the first hotel in sight where they were refused admittance on the grounds that it was full of members of parliament and their dependents who were sleeping three deep.

"Do you know who I am?" Mrs. Brewster stormed, when they were being turned away from the third hotel. "I demand, I tell you, I demand accommodation. I will report you to the Prime Minister."

Wrapped in furs, gloved and blanketed, she might have been anyone. The scared receptionist admitted that there was one room containing a single and a double bed. Two of the ladies would have to share the double bed. They were conducted along a network of passages to the extreme end of the building next to the bathrooms and installed in an apartment so large that the ceiling seemed lost in chilly gloom.

"Thank God we brought our hot water bottles," Mrs. Brewster exclaimed piously. She went out to demand a further supply of hot water bottles from the hotel. The water in the hot water taps was stone cold and the room itself like putting your face against a block of ice.

The two elder ladies had retired before they missed Shannon. "I hope she freezes," Mrs. Brewster said vindictively, from the single bed which she had claimed by right of her presidency.

Shannon was sitting in the lounge reflectively sipping hot rum. She felt she needed something to support her through the ordeal of sharing a bed with Janet Bubbing. When she crept into their chamber, there was no light, so she courteously refrained from switching it on. The snores guided her. Mrs. Brewster had a mezzo-soprano snore with a little whine to it. Janet Bubbing's snore was a deep contralto. It ran down the scale indicating that many brave hearts were asleep in the deep, so beware . . . beware.

I hope she doesn't overlay me in the night, Shannon giggled to herself, for the rum had made her feel very gay. Then came a muffled scream from the bed as she climbed in.

"What is it, Janet?" Mrs. Brewster started awake. "What is it?"

"A man's got into bed with me. Oh! Oh, dear! It's *you*. Smelling of drink. How can you expect me to sleep with someone smelling of drink?" Mrs. Bubbing heaved the bedclothes over her like a whale turning in a great wave, and presented her back to her bed-fellow. Then she gave another scream louder than the first. "She's put her feet on my back. Her ice-cold feet!"

"How can I sleep, Janet, when you keep yelling?" Mrs. Brewster exclaimed. "I'm wide awake and I know I won't drop off for hours."

It was indeed some time before the two ladies settled down. They lay and gave each other their opinions of Shannon until her gentle breathing informed them that there was not even the satisfaction of her hearing them.

Janet and Emmie had their revenge by hounding their junior out in the grey early light to pour hot water into the car radiator. All the garages were occupied and the car had been standing out overnight with a thin film of ice gathering on it. The kitchen boy, who helped with the task, told Shannon that it was only a slight frost. He was breaking the ice from the water trough as he said it. The radiator smoked like a little volcano as it melted.

"Now we don't need to stay more than today," Emmie Brewster told them over breakfast. "We'll just go and call on dear old Arthur Snelling and he'll tell us how to go about things. You needn't come unless you like." This was to Shannon.

"I thought I'd just stroll about and have a look at the place," Shannon said meekly. "I've never been here before."

The beauty of the Canberra landscape is that it has been carefully planned not for the convenience of human beings but of the trees. Everything a tree could possibly want is there; hordes of gardeners to tend them; fine, open spaces; and, dotted about, for a picturesque contrast, a few buildings. These cluster, almost cower, in a green scrub of arrogant trees. Between the patches of inhabited suburbs are long rows of trees, curved rows, straight rows, circles and squares, so that the stranger, if he keeps going long enough, will traverse the circumference of a circle and return to his starting point. Often he will do this without in any way desiring it, and he may go around and about several times before he discovers that the building he has been searching for is lurking in a patch of trees almost under his nose.

It is to be feared that in time Canberra, owing to this overweening regard for trees, will be submerged in the forest primeval. It was originally a waste of sheep paddocks considered unsuitable, by reason of its climate, for the thinner wool varieties. There is a legend that the commission which was sent to inspect this waste land, first passed across the floor of a vast lake, and then over a range of mountains. Is it always as cold as this, asked the members of the commission. "Why," said their guide, with considerable guile, "this is nothing. You wait till you get to . . ." And he named the opposition site for the National Capital. "I'll be damned first," the leader of the expedition swore. "If it's any colder than this, we're not going there. This'll do us, boys. Where I stand is where she's going to be." They piled in their car and went home.

Shannon sauntered on, her breath smoking on the air. All the trees were turning red and orange and crimson as advertised in the colourful tourist posters. Everything was as silent as the original sheep paddocks. Occasionally a motor car whizzed past. In those centres where houses were being dusted, children schooled, babies bathed, shops frequented, there was no undue haste or noise. All menials travelled daily from Queanbeyan eight miles away by bus, and were returned to their segregated quarters when they had served their purpose. The rents at Canberra were far too high for any unauthorized person to thrust in, even if they had been allowed to do so. All in one grade of income were isolated in a suburb far enough removed from the grade next below and above to hint that, perhaps, visiting so far out of their financial class might be inadvisable.

As she walked along, Shannon unknowingly traversed the seven-hundred-pound area to the five-hundred-pound incomes and was getting even lower down before enquiries among the shrubs led her to a yet more secluded residential district, where dwelt a parson friend of the lowly pacifist who had sat next to her at the Conference. When he had heard the resolution passed calling for a deputation to Canberra, her neighbour had whispered: "If you should be with this deputation, you might find my friend Hossell useful. He has a church down there and I'll give him a ring and tell him to do what he can." It was in search of the Reverend George

Hossell that she had now set out. Emmie and Janet would have felt that this hob-nobbing with pacifists showed a lack of taste. She felt a little doubtful about it herself.

She was cheered in her long trudge by the thought that at least she did not need to live in Canberra. She had been through some gruesome slums, had resided in dreary enough tenements; but she preferred the tiny, crowded grey streets to all this spacious and pretentious emptiness. It was a rich man's town and only a rich man could go there. A poor man would never be able to rake up the railway fare. She was contemptuous of these green beards of hedge around the chin of every house lot. She felt a gay hostility to all those big white buildings where the hot-air manufacturers of the Commonwealth were busily at work. It was good to be against such things, it gave her a feeling of virtuous self-approval.

The little garden of Mr. Hossell's home was full of bright flowers which did not seem to have suffered from the frost. He proved to be a tall, unassuming man who led her into his little study and turned the electric radiator her way. They were interested in each other, as two friendly creatures from different tribes might be, meeting in a trackless jungle. Shannon told him all about her bit of lobbying. She wanted the man who had tipped the scrap iron off the docks out of gaol. He had also been arrested for inflammatory speeches and acts liable to create a breach of the peace.

"Well, of course, I don't know if I agree with your friend," the Reverend Mr. Hossell said briskly. "But that's no reason why you shouldn't put his case. Now let me see how I can help. I know! Mr. Polvis, the Minister for Social and Industrial Affairs, is one of my congregation. Would he be any help?" He was as eager as a boy. "Then I'll ring him straight away."

Shannon spent the morning flirting earnestly with stout-waisted statesmen. She had never fluttered her eyelashes with more telling effect. She was shrinking, she was girlish, she was fiery and convincing and quick all at once. She was wearing one of Beryl's cheeky little hats and a coat that Beryl would never have given away had not her own clothes-sense told her that Shannon could wear it better than she could. It fitted like a lover's arm; it was debonair, dashing and very expensive; perhaps a little too tight, but all the better for that. She burst upon those bored ministers in the chill of winter like a breath of the warm spring; like an advertisement from a fashion magazine among notes on pest control. They loved her, they patted her hand, they clustered. From the time she first stepped into the private sanctum of the Honourable Henry Pulvis, M.P., she had no more trouble. He merely rang through to the secretaries of other busy ministers and Shannon could have been advocating a massacre instead of the release of a demonstrator, and they would still have been delighted to see her.

"I have always maintained," one important official said crisply, as he shook hands, "that there should be more pretty and fascinating deputations. Most of them are dreadful, you know. Stout and talkative, very."

Shannon thought bitterly that, for all her earnest arguments and her quoting of protests from various organizations, she had still not done any more good than she would have done talking down a manhole to someone who was not there. She returned to lunch with the friendly Mr. Hossell who had taken a fatherly interest in her progress and refused all thanks.

"After all, what are we here for?" he said cheerfully. "Only to help one another. But I didn't tell you a dreadful thing happened. I went out with you this morning in my old study coat. My wife pointed it out as soon as I came in. There's a frightful hole in the elbow. I hope I didn't disgrace you."

"I didn't notice," Shannon told him.

"Neither did I." They both laughed together, but Mrs. Hossell did not laugh.

"He's always doing things like that," she sighed. "And you've no idea what this place is like."

"I have an excellent idea of what this place is like." Shannon felt tired. The morning had been more of a strain than she had realized at the time. So many different men, and she had to be so quick varying her approach, so that it was the correct one for each. You had to tell by his face, his eyes, his clothes, even the way he parted his hair.

One of them had promised to bring the matter up in the House. The Minister most concerned had promised to give the matter his consideration. A few Members said it was a damn fool thing to do; everybody knew we would have to fight Japan sooner or later, but there was no need to be unpleasant about it, was there? They were all cheerfully unconcerned, and even if they were in a hurry, they were willing to talk with a charming stranger about almost anything except embarrassing and tactless persons who tipped already consigned pig iron into the harbour.

She returned to her lobbying after lunch and ambushed several members with varying success. Just as she was waiting to see if she could interview yet one more minister, a form she knew came stalking down the polished corridor.

"Why, Bleeby! Bleeby Peverill!"

"Well, well. What are you doing here?"

He listened to her hurried story with a mind that was obviously wandering and inattentive. Mechanically, he returned the greetings of acquaintances, as they hurried by on their way into the Chamber of Representatives. It was the opening of what looked like a long sitting. The Opposition had several dramatic questions and was hoping for a vote of no-confidence in the Government. Anything might happen, and an air of subdued excitement hung over the long, artificially warmed corridors, the shining spaces of entrance hall, the Members' Rooms themselves. Later, the Members might be all fagged and savage, but the sitting had only just begun.

"Seen Bewyl lately?" Bleeby asked.

"I borrowed this hat and coat just before I came away."

"Didn't say anything to you?"

"How d'you mean?"

"It might blow over." Bleeby sighed. "Never mind. Tell me again what you're after." Before she could do so, he broke in, "I'm doing a lot of special work down here. I'll be most likely managing the station if the network thinks it's worth while shoving one up here."

Shannon refrained from congratulating him. It might be a rise, but from Bleeby's grave-digger face, it might just as easily be banishment.

"You've been seeing all the wrong people," he told her. "You come along with me, and I'll lead you to the man who'll fix it."

He set off in a rapid pace along the corridors. Rounding a corner they almost came head first into Mrs. Brewster and Mrs. Bubbing, who were trotting along to hear dear old Arthur Snelling make his speech. Mrs. Brewster gave Bleeby Peverill a hard look and a slight inclination of the head.

"We'll be in the gallery," she called to Shannon, "Can't stop now."

Bleeby mounted to the first floor; he climbed to a second floor. He gained the third floor by a narrow flight of stone steps like a fire escape. "He may be in the House," he explained, as they knocked on a small door. "You there, Harry?"

The door opened. "Come on in." The occupant was a thick-set, dark man with a grim, staid air. "I was lying low in case it was the chief. Won't be anything doing in the House for another hour. I'm busy, though. I've got the economic conference stuff to do." He looked at them pathetically.

Bleeby introduced Shannon. The room was so small that the heating system took up most of the floor space. On top of the heater was a towel and a toothbrush which the occupant sedately removed. A table loaded with files and a couple of chairs completed the furnishings. The occupant drew up two chairs as the visitors showed no sign of taking his hint. "Cigarette?" he offered.

Shannon decided that this stocky, solemn man might respond best to facts and figures. She reeled them off like an economic expert proving that there will be either a rise or fall of consumption in the next five years. It was impressive but the hearer did not seem to worry.

"All the organizations in the world kicking up a row don't alter the fact that getting this guy out would take some doing," he interrupted bitterly. "Don't worry trying to tell us you're not a Red. We're all a bit that way here, aren't we, Bleeby? Only damn thing that stops us from going crazy. No! I'd like to do anything for a friend of Bleeby's, but it would mean I'd have to go to the chief and tell him all kinds of lies, and I'd have to make up the lies, things about his constituency and important interests. Sorry, of course." He brushed his hand over his thinning hair. "Come and have some afternoon tea with me. I haven't had lunch yet."

They followed him to the refectory overlooking a pleasant courtyard.

"And how do you like Canberra?" he asked the stock question, as he looked over the menu.

"I think it should see itself in the mirror."

Their host raised his eyebrow. "The place is much better now the trees have grown, you know."

"That wasn't what I meant. It's so divorced from reality, so sickeningly like a piece of left-over wedding cake full of weevils."

Shannon suddenly remembered that even if she had not done any good, it was hardly the fault of this rather tired-looking gentleman. Besides she should be polite in payment for the tea. She decided to amuse him, and she gave a description of Mrs. Brewster running the car into a telegraph post and yelling: "Now look what you've done!"

"Like the chief," he interrupted. "There isn't a tree or a milepost between here and Sydney that he hasn't hit."

He had lost his weary look, but perhaps that was just the improving influence of food. For Bleeby's benefit as much as his, she gave him an imitation of Lucy Rossingale putting over an advertisement and a rehearsal night at the Proletarian Club. It was a long time since she had done any clowning, so that her repertoire was a little out of date. But her new acquaintance laughed. He laughed until Shannon wondered if he were not a little overstrained.

"Oh, excuse me," he said, wiping his eyes. "But this place gets you down, you know. Bit of a relief to find someone refreshing. Tell me that again. She didn't really say: 'Sexual intercourse in the Soviet Union is so delightful!' She couldn't have said it. Impossible!"

The gathering was beginning to brighten up. Fortunately the House was in session, and the eating apartments empty. If it had not been for Bleeby's feelings, Shannon would probably have given the court scene of the twelve-inch record.

"I say, I'm giving a bit of a party tonight," her new friend confided, after three more stories. "Just a whisky and sandwiches party. I don't suppose you could come? We'd drive you back to your hotel, wouldn't we, Bleeby?"

"Wather," the preoccupied Bleeby sighed. "It'd be just like old times."

"How about our man? Does he get out?"

"I'll tell you what I'll do." Their host was serious again. "You be at my party and cheer the gang up the way you cheered me up, and I'll fix it. Now that's a promise. I'll fix it."

In the visitors' gallery, Emmie Brewster and Janet Bubbing were still waiting for dear old Arthur Snelling to make his speech. When anyone finished speaking he would leap to his feet with the others and cry "Mr. Speaker!", but the Speaker had not so far nodded in his direction. It was rather like a class of school boys trying to get their recitation heard by the teacher.

"Not one woman Member," Janet Bubbing hissed. "Disgraceful!"

Shannon thought it showed the good sense of the female sex; perhaps

I

it might not be good sense, but lack of interest. No one could fail to be struck by the puerility and fretfulness of the whole proceeding. It was a club of men who were on the inside, who were there to govern the country. And who really did govern the country? The under-secretaries and hangers-on, one of whom had just given her a highly important political concession in return for half an hour's entertainment.

"We have had a most exciting and interesting day." When they got outside, Mrs. Brewster importantly bustled Shannon towards the car. "We didn't bother the Prime Minister. Poor man! He looked so tired and distraught that I had not the heart to do it. Dear Mr. Snelling said he would see what could be done about the pageant and bringing down the price of butter. He took us out to lunch and introduced us to some most interesting people. Of course, Shannon, it was impossible to say anything about . . . you know . . . that man. It would have been in the worst of taste to introduce it."

That evening, Mrs. Brewster decided that she would keep Shannon firmly under her eye until bedtime. But Shannon just slipped out. "And we don't know," Mrs. Brewster said in a severe tone, "just what mischief she may be up to. She is very wild and erratic." Except for a message at the reception desk that she would not be back until late, Shannon seemed to have vanished into thin air.

It was half-past two in the morning when poor Janet Bubbing uttered the piercing scream that indicated that her bedfellow was joining her. "Her cold feet!" she cried. "She's put her cold feet on my back! And you've been drinking again! Oh, really! really! We can't have it! Emmie," Janet Bubbing was thoroughly aroused, "I demand, I *demand,* I tell you, that you sleep with me. I will not stand it any longer."

Shannon lay in the dark and laughed to herself. It was half-excitement, for it had been a good party, a tough and very reckless party; and it was partly cynicism. There is nothing so likely to strip away the illusions as the talk of confidential secretaries when they foregather and relax.

What chance have we? Shannon thought. What chance, when their environment corrupts them. These men started out with ideals. They get into this hot-house and it saps them. Look at Hennery! They were talking about him tonight. He used to come to the U.C.D.L. rooms and he was sincere. A crawler, that's what they call him now, and they are right.

Ready to do anything as long as he's a good fellow, just the right tone of the other good fellows.

She turned over and listened to the mezzo-soprano and contralto snores. They seemed to be rendering "Oh, that we two—were a-maying," and it kept her awake waiting for the next notes. She was determined that never, never again was she going to have anything to do with organizations, good or bad. When she reached Sydney, she would be quit, clean quit of the Peacelovers and find herself a job. She even contemplated tossing a pillow at the double bed. This might be a little too much for the overstrained ladies it contained, so she turned over.

I'm through, she thought, through, finished and done. Never again a conference, never again a resolution, or even a speech in favour of the motion. Hang the Peacelovers. This trip with Emmie and Janet would cure anyone of the Peacelovers if those two are all that stand between this country and war.

Her immediate prospect of a job was one demonstrating a patent bean stringer in a big department store. It might still be open. Anyway it would be better than Canberra, better than the Peacelovers, better to be free.

The change of the year, she thought. I always want to flit at the change of the year.

Eighteen

By the time Mrs. Bubbing and Mrs. Brewster had finished with the story of Shannon's midnight exploits, it sounded as though they had shared the double bed for mutual protection. Mrs. Brewster's tales of her drunken and disorderly conduct Shannon countered by telling Leggatt the truth. She had not expected him to laugh, but he made a little grunting noise, as though some unused muscle was creaking. His interest in her doings was, she saw, only concerned with results.

"You think he'll be let out?" Leggatt did not care about the prisoner but the effect on the Movement that his release would have. It would be a political triumph. "They must have thought of something," Leggatt reflected aloud. "Something that made them see it would be a good move to let him go. Yes, that's it. Now I wonder what it is?"

He would fit in so well down at Canberra, Shannon thought. That's the way the political men think. Now your move, then mine. I wonder what you're going to do. Ah, now I see. It was a game they played: a game which was all the more interesting, because other issues than their mere triumph hung on it. They had power. They had the secret music of self-acclaim in their ears; they had the loud brass band of public notice. Oh, it was a great life, if you liked that sort of life.

"You're looking rather pale," Leggatt said thoughtfully. "You need a holiday."

"I need more than a holiday. I'm resigning."

He looked at her sharply. "You can't resign in a movement like ours. You are either expelled or you become inactive and are expelled." He changed the subject. "There's someone been ringing you up here while you were away. I gave them the Peacelovers' number."

"Someone's been ringing for you," Mrs. Bubbing greeted her on her return. "Where have you been?" Her words indicated that, even if the help had been given notice, she had no right to take half the morning off.

The number on the phone pad was Beryl's and Shannon rang it at once. "That you, Shannon?" Beryl's voice had a triumphant tone. "Have I got news?" Shannon suggested that she communicate the news. "You won't guess," Beryl shouted into the telephone. "I can't wait to tell you. You're going to be a bridesmaid. I'm going to be married."

"Good Lord!" Shannon said nastily. "Who is it this time?"

"I could beat you over the head," Beryl threatened. "Try and be human. Guess!"

"Bleeby Peverill?" Even as she said it, Shannon remembered Bleeby's gloomy looks. "No, wait a minute. The sandy chap who takes you to golf."

Beryl rang off indignantly in her ear. Shannon had to go to all the trouble of ringing Beryl again and soothing her, while Mrs. Bubbing, who wanted to use the phone, stood by making clicking noises to express exasperation.

"Well, I can't go into it now." Beryl was sulky. "Come over tonight. I suppose even if you don't want to be bridesmaid, you can come and see me for an hour?"

"I'll be bridesmaid," Shannon protested, chuckling. Beryl could have found a bridesmaid or half a dozen bridesmaids among her friends, but the streak of sentimentality in her had evidently come to the top. How like Beryl to want her old friend and enemy to be present at the triumph. Shannon rang Aunt Edith while Mrs. Bubbing grew more and more annoyed.

"Who's Beryl marrying, Aunt Edith?"

"A very rich man, a very respectable man." Aunt Edith was only too delighted to give all the information she possessed. "He's one of the wealthiest men."

"He would be," Shannon interrupted cynically.

"Well I must say, Shannon, that your tone isn't very nice. After all she's one of your oldest friends, a very loyal dear girl. I am most pleased and happy to think Beryl has done so well for herself."

"But who is he? Who is he? Come on, Aunt Edith, I can't wait all day."

"You remember a Mr. Litchin who looked after you so kindly when you were sick? You were working in one of his teashops. He has always had the highest regard for Beryl. It's quite a romance. And what are you going to wear, dear? I know Beryl would like me to help with the dresses."

"Let you know later," Shannon said hollowly. " 'Bye."

Joseph Litchin of all people! How had Beryl ever come into contact with him again, and what was more astonishing, how had she managed to marry him? What a fearful fate for Beryl! Or was it?

Shannon let Mrs. Bubbing have the telephone and sat pondering on the curious, the utterly irrational set of circumstances which would make Beryl marry Joseph Litchin. Of course he was rich; but he was as mean as dirt, and Beryl was making good money where she was. He was eccentric to the point of lunacy, and he loved emotional scenes. It was extraordinary, simply extraordinary. So that was why Beryl had thought it might be fitting and proper for Shannon to be bridesmaid.

"I always thought, old pal," Beryl said sentimentally, when Shannon congratulated her that night, "that I'd have him in the end. I'm not getting any younger you know. Thirty-or-so is a mean age. It gets you down. You're not getting any younger yourself, kid. You want to watch it. All very well having a gay time, but you've got to settle sooner or later. We've all got to settle down. No sense in not facing it. One thing, with Joe I'll always have plenty."

"You never even told me you had seen him again. But marrying him! You always slanged him so."

"Now you shut up about Joe. I like him, and he's mad about me. And if the dear old scout," Beryl went on sentimentally, "is just a bit dotty, well, what with Ma and her loonies, and living with *you*, I've had plenty of practice. I guess I'll handle him all right. You trust little Beryl for that. The first thing we do is buy a big house, near a good golf club with a crowd of nice people. Then I cease work. I cease work for keeps. Hear me? No more running after fat women and telling them it will suit them down to the ground. No more rows with the fitting room. No more getting up in the morning."

"Where are you getting married?" Shannon asked. "Registry office? Or is he a Greek?"

"He's a naturalized Australian citizen," Beryl replied indignantly. "And we're having a wedding in the biggest Presbyterian church I can pick out. Joe doesn't mind. All the family are coming over to see the McLaughlin daughter do it in style. As for the wedding breakfast, I said to Joe that it wouldn't cost much because he can do all the catering himself."

Shannon held her head. "Suit yourself," she said. "But why, why did you pick on him? You've always had plenty of men hanging about."

"But *not*, not with so much of what I want, and that's dough. Might as well be honest about it. I wouldn't give you that," she flipped her fingers, "for a man who couldn't keep me the way I think I ought to be kept. Now, lay-off, Shannon. Don't sit there goggling as though you thought I'd knocked him on the head and dragged him in. Forget about Joe, and think of my dress. I never did look good in satin, too like a wet fish. I got our designer to run out a few snappy suggestions. I'll stand you your dress, so you can go the limit. Anyway I'll get the material cost price and the firm ought to stand me something decent for a present. How about white crepe charmante for me—with diamanté?"

"Too loud. Cut out the diamanté."

They plunged into the details of what they would wear. It was like old times, Beryl reminded her, sitting on the side of the bed arguing about clothes. They might have been back in Headstown.

"Joseph Litchin wasn't in the picture then."

"He's been in my life," Beryl said romantically, "hanging about like a bad smell almost ever since. Just think of it. He finds out through his sister who knows you who knows me that I'm living here, and he's been sitting on the mat like a lost dog, poor old Joe. Faithful, that's him. Why, when I said: 'How about marrying?' he just jumped at it. Might have been the biggest deal in his life the way he put it through. What I like about Joe is his zest."

There was not so much zest about Joseph Litchin, when he faced the final clause of the contract and walked up the aisle talking fiercely to Clive, who was best man, about Clive's bad manners in not wearing the correct clothes. "You shame me," he stormed, "in front of the assembled McLaughlins. You come in a sports coat and sweater to show I am poor and shame me." Clive had been given the money to buy himself a wedding garment. Why, why, Mr. Litchin demanded frenziedly, did he not wear it then. Because he had spent the money. Never more would he look upon Clive as a brother-in-law.

In the vestry, Mr. Litchin was quite as fierce to the minister. "He has done nothing for his money. That a marriage! I do not believe it." At the wedding breakfast which was held at the Pompadour, he acted like an ogre to the assembled McLaughlins asking them what they did for a living. "Now your daughter is a wife, now that I marry her, I am master. Do not think I am rich. I am poor, very poor. My own sister does not come to my wedding. She disowns me and says that I am mad to marry. I will throw her in the gutter. She has lived on me all my life and sucked my blood."

He had a splendid time telling a young lady from the fitting room of Forleys that he already thought he had made a mistake. He should have married, yes, but to one lovely and fat, fat as the young lady whose hand he was holding. Perhaps he might fatten his wife. Yes, when she had children, she would fatten. The young lady retreated in consternation and Mr. Litchin turned with a demoniac grin to Shannon.

"She is worth it," he whispered. "You think I spend all this money for nothing, huh? You think old Yosif is gone mad at last. You will see. It is her head. She has the brains." He tapped his forehead significantly. "Let her but wait."

"You know," Shannon replied thoughtfully, "I withdraw all my objections. I think you're going to hit it off splendidly, Yosif." She had been watching Beryl who, with great complacency, devoted herself to her own circle of friends.

"Time we were getting a move on," was all Beryl said to her bridegroom. "Snap into it, Joe."

"I am coming," Mr. Litchin cried, leaping up and kissing her with great relish and exactitude. "We will have the most beautiful children and they will take after me." Then he reverted from his rendering of the amorous bridegroom and became a business man shouting orders to the staff of the Pompadour. "You may turn them out now," he could be heard saying from the kitchen. "Do not let them eat all night. And you idle! You take my money and stand there. To work!"

"Yosif seems to have ambitions," Shannon said thoughtfully to Beryl. "I'll love to see you with your tribe of children."

"Don't be disgusting," Beryl replied haughtily. Then she giggled. "I sent Lucy Rossingale an invite but she didn't come. Half a minute," she called to the driver who was waiting by the door with a curious crowd. She darted off into the kitchen and returned dragging the bridegroom.

"Dear me," Aunt Edith gave a motherly sniff as she came over to Shannon. "Dear girl. So sweet. And look at the success she has made of her life. I only wish, Shannon, you could do as well . . ."

Mr. Sladder had been reviewing a grim-faced contingent of McLaughlins and cheering them with the assurance that the bridegroom was not as eccentric as he sounded and was twice as wealthy. He came beaming up.

"Well, this is a notable occasion," he claimed. "Edith, I think we should have insisted on Beryl being married from our home."

"It would have been grand," Shannon agreed unpleasantly. "Only they would have thought Yosif was escaping."

"Now, now, Shannon," Uncle Vincent patted her shoulder in his old way, "don't be sarcastic, my dear. Don't let people think you're jealous." There was something very feminine in the way he brought this out. "After all, Beryl knows what she is doing. She always has been able to take care of herself. Envy is a very unpleasant quality on an occasion like this. You should try to understand your own motives."

He gave her an unfriendly glare. Uncle Vincent did not easily forget past wrongs, and today he had been reminded of all his niece's petty and unkind behaviour, how she had nearly wrecked his marriage by running away from her good home and the profession he had planned for her, all her recalcitrant and sulky tempers. He had endured quite enough, that look seemed to say, without Shannon trying him too far when he was cheering Beryl, a far pleasanter girl, on her new way of life.

Mr. Litchin climbed into the car which was to take them on the first stage of the honeymoon. He was loudly complaining that his boots hurt him and his first move was to take off the offending boots and shake them out the window. He enjoyed showing his contempt for weddings, but at the same time he was beaming with pleasure that he had had a nice wedding and now had a nice wife. Deep under Joseph's eccentricities was a strain of wistfulness. Other men had homes to show off, wives to manage their homes. Why shouldn't he?

He was quite pleased that he should have a residence with servants and a gardener in a high-toned suburb, and he brought to it a queer assortment of visitors with whom he stormed and rejoiced. Beryl also filled the place with the members of the golf-and-bridge club, and held little cocktail parties, and was happy quelling Joseph and complaining about him when she lost a battle. One of the biggest fights was over Beryl insisting that Joseph no longer subsidize Clive and Sasha. They could work, couldn't they?

Then, as the newness of her lounge suite and her cocktail cabinet wore off, she began to show signs of restlessness.

I*

"I've been thinking," she said to Shannon, "about starting that piece-goods business I was telling you about. Joe will put up the money." She prowled out into the hall and switched off a light. "These girls," she complained, "they leave lights switched on all over the place. The bill's simply enormous. As I was saying, the real profit these days is in cheap goods, cheap and shoddy. Forleys were finding that out. Now, I can get me a factory, nothing more than a big room with the machines, and work it up. I know people who are simply coining money, raking it in hand over fist."

"But you don't need to do it."

"That's not the point. The way I look at things," Beryl said severely, as she poured herself another drink, "is that in this world you've got to *work*, got to have an aim in life, see? All very well these women frittering their time away at golf and bridge, but they haven't had any training . . . they wouldn't know how to run a business if they tried. No, I'm going in for cheap, shoddy lines, and, oh my! can I sell them? I just think I can."

"It is her head," Mr. Litchin beamed. "I tell you she has the business head. I know it. Always I have known it."

"You keep your face out of it," Beryl said. "I'm going to run this business, not you." She kissed him loudly to soften the blow.

Six months after her marriage, Beryl was catching the business boat to the city on her way to work. She sat all day long in the office of her little factory keeping a sharp eye on the forewoman and seeing that none of the girls went off to the washroom to snatch a smoke.

"You've got to watch them," she complained, "every minute of the day."

Nineteen

I

Shannon found her job as demonstrator of a patent bean slicer quite restful and pleasant. She had insisted on a high stool; she refused to stand all day, and if, as she told the floor manager, they had never provided a demonstrator with a stool before, now was the time to begin.

All she had to do was to sit on her stool in a crisp white uniform and look industrious fiddling with her beans. She only began to string a bean if a likely looking customer came along. The floor manager hated to see her heartily cutting into beans just for the fun of the thing, as she had done on the first day. The huge pile of beans was always put away carefully in the refrigerator every night, for beans were dear and the store stingy with them.

"You've got to look nice now," Mrs. Benson remarked. She took more interest in Shannon's position as a professional bean stringer than she ever had in the U.C.D.L. Nor was it Shannon's board money that aroused the interest, for, with the U.C.D.L. practically dissolved, George Benson was working regularly and earning good money. "You ought to look after your nails and do something about your hair."

All the other young ladies in the departments on the ground floor had their hair done elaborately in curls and whisks, but Shannon's stood straight out from her head as of old. If she smoothed it down, it only stood up again the next minute. She did agree, however, to have it cut short so that it would go into small curls and not a fierce fuzz. Day after day, she sat on her stool, fiddled with her bean stringer and gave her mind a rest.

She sold more bean stringers to susceptible male shoppers than she did to housewives. Men would stop to look at the gadget from curiosity; then they would glance at the demonstrator, and decided that the wife must have a bean slicer. Because she did not care if she held down this job or lost it, she did very well. There was something striking about her looks that cut her off from the pretty, curled and painted lasses behind the

237

counters. She drew attention to the bean slicer simply by the way she slashed it about.

As she was chopping industriously at a particularly tough bean one afternoon, she heard a cough behind her and found a well-dressed, dark young man regarding her with a look of such sentimental pity that it startled her.

"Comrade," the young man said earnestly, "don't think I'm intruding, Comrade Hicks, but really . . . how do you . . . that is . . ." he floundered. "It's a dreadful thing to see you wasting your talents in a place like this."

Shannon racked her brains to recollect where she had seen his face before. "Oh, I don't know," she replied, wilfully misunderstanding him, "I've sold four bean stringers this morning and two more since lunch."

"Of course, you wouldn't remember me, Comrade, that is, Miss Hicks. I was on the Free Our Natives Committee."

"Well, well, Mr. Quinlan," Shannon greeted him cordially. He had done nothing at all on the Free Our Natives Committee, except to lay down at intervals what he considered Lenin would have done, if he had been sitting in Mr. Quinlan's place. She had thought him a harmless and amiable crank, but he had been planted on the committee because he had money and was very generous with it. "Wait a moment," she exclaimed. "Didn't we meet before that, years ago out at the Showground? You were talking about Lolita."

It all came back to her, the wet night when Uncle Sladder had washed his hands of Beryl and his troublesome niece by marriage, the little office, the tea in paper mugs, Bert smirking possessively at Beryl, and this young man handing round snapshots of a fat, solemn, girl-baby.

"Oh, yes, Lolita." He seemed rather disappointed. It was in his character as a committee man that he preferred to be remembered. "It's my teeth," he explained, "that makes all the difference. I've had them out."

"And how is Lolita these days?" Shannon decided to be friendly.

"Oh, I don't see much of her. You know the committee absolutely went to pieces after you left. Her mother took her when we separated but she goes to school. You knew they gave those chaps penal servitude for life, didn't you? I thought some protest should have been made, but as I said before, Comrade, that is . . . Shannon . . . you don't mind me calling you Shannon, do you? The committee wasn't ever very efficient after you left. Really, I suppose you carried the thing. No wonder you didn't remember me. What are you doing with yourself these days?"

"I'm demonstrating a bean slicer," Shannon reminded him patiently.

The floor manager was hovering in the distance ready to admonish her. He did not like flirtations in business hours. But Mr. Quinlan continued to stand there absent-mindedly snapping beans in half with one hand.

"I don't suppose you could come out some night?" he asked suddenly. "Don't think I've got a terrible hide, Shannon, but I want to talk over a business proposition, and I can't very well discuss it here, can I?" He had become aware of a shadow hovering behind a table of imported *hors d'oeuvres* and eyeing him very suspiciously. He supposed it was the shop detective. "Do you think you could meet me tomorrow night and we'd go and have a bite to eat somewhere?" he asked, hurriedly, replacing the bean he had been about to break in halves. "Say you meet me outside the Metropole at half-past six? That do?"

Shannon signified that she was quite agreeable. After all, it was not every member of the Free Our Natives Committee who had enough money to invite people to eat at the Metropole. She would wear her very dashing hat and coat to work, just to show him that even if she sold bean stringers, she could still, in borrowed plumes, look reasonably pleasing.

"Good," he said, moving away. Then he circled back again. "I really do want to talk business," he assured her. "You don't think I'm just trying to . . . that its hide on my part?"

"Not at all."

"Good." He was off again, and then once more returned. "You might give me one of those things." As she wrapped him up a bean slicer, he scowled back belligerently at the floor manager. "Don't suppose I'll ever use it, seeing I'm living at my club. Half-past six. Don't forget."

This time he really did go away, and Shannon drew a relieved breath. He was a nice fellow, but he talked in such a confused way. How he ran his father's seed and plant business was beyond imagination. He might be an efficient vendor of bulbs and annuals, but he was not very bright. How funny, how very funny, that he should pity her. He had looked like a calf whose mother had disowned it. The poor beggar was probably lonely if he was separated from his wife. Anyway, if he thought he was going to hold hands and tell her his troubles, he was mistaken.

Mr. Quinlan did not disguise his pleasure at her fashionable appearance when they met at the appointed time and place. He conducted her carefully to a reserved table talking all the time.

"It's like this," he said, as soon as they were seated. "I've always in a sort of way wanted to start a bookshop. Not an ordinary sort of bookshop, but one selling really modern literature. All the best left writers, the ones you can't get. I have some fine times, I can tell you, getting the Dad's bulbs through the Customs, and I could get the books through at the same time, which would save expense, and if I put up the money . . ." He drew a deep breath, clutched the menu from the waitress and handed it to Shannon.

The menu came like a life-belt. She had grasped from Eddie Quinlan's discourse that he was opening a bookshop, but there was a further implication that he was going to ask her to work in it. She looked at the menu without really seeing it. The vision of that bookshop drifted before her eyes; handling books; living among books; reading all the books she had ever wanted to read; even, perhaps, buying books. It was a dream and she would wake up. In the meantime, she concentrated such a look of admiration on her escort that he quivered.

"Go on," she whispered. "Go on telling me about the bookshop."

Mr. Quinlan was immersed in the wine list. It was evident that he was going to do this well. He countermanded Shannon's order and planned the dinner himself.

Then he sat back while the waiter poured the hock.

"And here's to the Leninist Bookshop," he proposed. Shannon drank the toast recklessly.

"Eddie," she said affably, "tell me more about it."

"Well, I was going to ask you . . . that is . . . do you think you would be interested to manage it?"

"Me?" Shannon looked tremendously surprised. "Oh, that's splendid of you, but I couldn't undertake it until I had consulted Mervyn Leggatt."

"Comrade Leggatt?" Quinlan looked respectful. "Why, of course. I would have mentioned it to him myself, but . . ." He took a gulp of hock to hide the naked truth which was that, although he had been talking about this scheme for a long time, Shannon had crystallized the idea into something practical. "But it's all off," he said, frowning, "if *you* don't handle it. You tell Leggatt that." All his business man's training rose to the surface. He wasn't going to start a bookshop if the left functionaries insisted on some snuffling and superannuated comrade taking it over.

Shannon felt very expansive. There was an orchestra playing somewhere, waiters moving about, the noise of voices, the smell of appetizing food. It was a glorious world, and she was sitting with a charming man who wanted to buy her a bookshop. She gazed upon Eddie fondly. She had never seen anyone, even South Quilter, she liked better. A bookshop!

"Would I be paid for it?" she asked.

"Whatever the rates are. I think it's about six pounds a week. Would that do?"

Of course, she thought, the correct reply would be: "Do not think you can buy me, dastardly villain." It tickled her sense of humor that this pleasant soul should be innocent enough to think she was at all deceived by his little scheme. Such a pretty compliment, she thought: offering her a bookshop. Perhaps she had better put up her value a little.

"I can make it pay," she said earnestly. "I think I could almost guarantee your capital back inside a year. How much would you need to start with?"

Eddie Quinlan was pleased. He knew she was efficient. If she had been only a fluffy little thing, he would never have entrusted his bookshop to her care, for he firmly intended to make it pay, even if he also intended to derive some pleasure from Shannon's society in the process. He went off into a long string of financial calculations which she wrote down on a slip of paper she had taken from her handbag. Merv Leggatt would be interested.

"Perhaps I could help raise some money to finance it?" she suggested; but Eddie Quinlan frowned down the idea. It was his bookshop and he wanted sole control.

As the dinner progressed, he spoke of his ideals, his ambitions, his understanding of political theory, his wide reading of the better-thought-of books, his disastrous marriage to a woman who had never been his mental equal.

"You know, Shannon, the thing that matters most in a woman is brains. You can't get away from that. Brains and looks, if you like, but anyway brains. Now Clare, that's Lolita's mother, hadn't an ounce of brains. Of course, we're good friends, but we realized that we just didn't hit it. You can quite see how it was, can't you? You can't expect two people who haven't a thing in common to keep on all their lives . . ." He had another drink.

Shannon was not drinking. "It's getting rather late," she suggested, and he helped her into her coat.

"I'm afraid it's too late for a show," he complained. "Would you like to go anywhere special, or could I see you home?"

He took a taxi and held her hand in the taxi. Evidently he was out to see that this business partnership started off on the right footing. He even tried to kiss her. Shannon pushed him away gently.

"Comrade," she asked, "would Lenin have done a thing like that?"

"No," said Mr. Quinlan in a tone of remorse. He sat up very straight and stiff. "He wouldn't, would he? Sorry." Shannon was also determined to see the business deal remained a business deal.

II

Mervyn Leggatt was, for him, enthusiastic over the bookshop proposition. He had been relegated by the refining influences at work to the secretaryship of the Grinders, Gasworkers and Mainbuilders Union, and was back again in the grey, dim little room on the top floor of the Trades Hall, where he could spin the rather spiderish politics of the Labour Movement, reckoning up support for certain of his projects, planning to dislodge hostile officials.

It affected him very little that the U.C.D.L. was for the time being muffled out of existence. Wherever Mervyn Leggatt went, he carried his own atmosphere of calculation and policy, just as he carried his neat clothes or his glasses. In his own mind, he was the perfect functionary, so relentlessly devoid of human feelings that he fell into all kinds of mistakes which ordinary humanity would have prevented. At the same time, unconsciously, he made many little pleas for sympathy and recognition. As far as the world was concerned, his world of committee meetings and interlocking webs of radical unions, he got nothing but kicks; the Central Committee continually expected more from him than was humanly possible. He never had any thanks from the people he had helped in the U.C.D.L., because it is the nature of human beings to resist the idea that their own powers have ever been so low that they could not help themselves. He comforted himself with the delusion that thanks or kindness meant nothing to him.

Shannon (who had always admired her own qualities) saw him working hard, unrecognized and uncared for, and slowly developed an affection for him. It took the form of a desire to mother him; but Merv Leggatt never cared if his office were clean or his tea made. He seldom even noticed.

However, news such as Shannon now brought him aroused in him an intense interest. "Fine," he said. "I always felt Quinlan wasn't such a dub as he looks. He'll be able to start this bookshop for us, and we'll put in someone who knows just what we want."

"*I* am to run this bookshop," Shannon pointed out. "After all," she added angrily, "it's Quinlan's money, and if he wants me to run it, I suppose he can pick whoever he wants, can't he?"

"Ho-ho," Leggatt said thoughtfully. He tapped his front teeth with his pencil, an irritating habit he had when thinking. "Do you think you're up to the job?"

His disparagement annoyed her; not only annoyed her but cut her to the quick. "Suit yourself," she said, trying to sound flippant. "It's me or no one, no bookshop, in fact." The tactless beast, she thought, he might have let me think I was valuable and useful. But no, not he. He has to tread all over me. "It's like this, Merv. This Quinlan lad, and don't think I'm flattering myself, thinks he's rescuing me from a fate worse than death demonstrating that bean slicer."

Mervyn Leggatt did not smile; he frowned. "I don't like it," he said, shaking his head. "A man who has a good scheme like this and the money to back it, should have only the Movement in his mind. Otherwise he's undependable."

She could have battered him with her fists she was so angry. The silly prig sitting there sententiously laying down the law!

"Very well," she exclaimed. "If you want to look a gift horse in the mouth, I'll tell him that you don't want to be associated with it, shall I?"

"Don't be unreasonable, Shannon. I can't get the Movement mixed up in anything that might just fizzle out. I can't go rushing at this like a bull at a gate." He tapped his teeth again. "Of course," there was a glint of humour behind his words, "if this were just an arrangement between you and Quinlan . . ."

Shannon looked very noble. "I thought at once . . . at once . . . what this would mean to the Movement," she said, in an excellent imitation of his own tone, and then she began to laugh wickedly. "Oh, Merv, I didn't do anything of the sort. I just thought how I'd like to be handling books all day. And he tried to hold my hand in the taxi, and when he wanted to kiss me, I said: 'Comrade, would Lenin have done a thing like that?'" Her peals of laughter were so loud that Merv Leggatt looked at the door uneasily. "Oh-ho, I'm being seduced! Goody-goody!"

Mervyn Leggatt was forced to smile; he was also a little embarrassed at her bad taste. Such a pity, he thought, that she couldn't control these sudden bursts of merriment. He said: "Shannon, really, the way you talk anyone would think you were still in the Proletarian Club."

"I wish I was," Shannon sighed. "I still miss it."

"That's just the trouble. No discipline."

"Now, don't nag, don't nag." Shannon got up and walked over to the window which refused to open. "Ooh! look at the dust and dirt." I'm sure this will be known as the Age of the Great Naggers. You never let people alone, do you? Can't bear to see anyone different from you? Let me tell you I don't want to be disciplined."

"But you must be."

"Who says so?"

"I say so. The Movement must have disciplined comrades or how can we function at all?"

"I don't see that it matters two hoots in Hell if you don't function. You *do* think you're running the universe, don't you? *We* demand two more sets of hands. *We* protest against being born and dying. Why, you'd nag God, if you got the chance." She was only pretending to be angry, for arguing with Merv Leggatt was like hitting a wall.

"To return to the bookshop." Mervyn Leggatt, his countenance unmoved, would not give her the satisfaction of seeing he thought her unreliable and silly. "I think you'd be well-advised to accept it."

"A fate worse than death," Shannon moaned unctuously.

"I wish you'd leave off harping on your own personality," Mervyn Leggatt suddenly snapped at her. Evidently something she said had got him on the raw. He had gone one shade paler in his anger.

"I'm sorry." Shannon tried to be penitent, but she was still full of vanity and amusement. "Oh, Merv, you remember Mr. Poate and the two Jackson boys?" She insisted on telling him the whole unsavoury story. "Think of poor Eddie. Suppose he snatches back the bookshop if I won't play?"

"You're being very egotistic this evening, aren't you?" Leggatt passed his hand wearily over his brow. Shannon was behaving like a bad, small child. She was punishing him because he had talked about putting someone reliable in her bookshop. Many another girl would have hated him forever for that blunder. She went on annoying him. He had a streak of old-maidish nicety in his composition and it disturbed him to see Shannon strolling around his office inventing and acting disgraceful scenes between herself and Eddie Quinlan. She refused to be treated as a pawn, to be "used" like some mean tool; she was a human woman and she would make Mervyn Leggatt accept her as such.

He watched her sardonically, then sighed. "Oh, shut up!" he muttered wearily. Then, as she continued to tease him, he sprang up, seized her by the shoulders and kissed her soundly. "Now," he said desperately, "now will you stop?"

Shannon, triumphant in her wicked plan to make him treat her as a human being, was still astonished. "Would Lenin . . ." she began reprovingly.

"Blast you! Blast Lenin! Now get out of here."

He conducted her to the door and pushed her out. He had a lot of work to do and Shannon disturbed his peace of mind. He went back to his table and sat with his feet up on it frowning at the dim electric light globe. She was a devil of a girl, he thought ruefully; she had deliberately provoked him to behave in a way of which he should be ashamed. How could he think her reliable when she acted like a spoilt child? Yet, in a way, she was reliable, even admirable.

The best thing he could do, he decided, was to avoid her. In the U.C.D.L. they had neither of them time for flirtations, but more and more he had felt that Shannon was leaving her old self of the U.C.D.L. behind. There she had been resourceful, quick, capable. But what was the use of these qualities if they were to be accompanied by a constant, ironic merriment? She wouldn't take anything seriously, that was the trouble. She wasn't taking this bookshop seriously. It was something new to play with. The desolating truth about Shannon was that she did not care. She simply did not care for anything on earth.

With an impatient shrug, Mervyn Leggatt drove from himself the contemplation of his former work-mate to the more immediate question of whether it would be better to put up old Sunny Frankson for the job of president of the annual conference of wheat-lumpers, or back O'Kellaher, who couldn't be trusted, but who knew the job backwards, and was so sore with the way he had been treated by his own team that he would be ready to fall in with any suggestions the militant section might make.

He found it difficult to concentrate on the problem.

III

Shannon had now been in Sydney so long that she could have told her way blindfolded anywhere between the Quay and the University. She no longer noticed the shop windows, the smells of milk bars, cheap chocolate shops, hotels, chemists, the glare of neon signs, because these had become part of sub-conscious scenery in herself; and she had stood on a street corner and had been greatly surprised when someone pointed out that a big theatre had been pulled down. She had not noticed it was gone, because she had made it part of that internal landscape, and so was able to ignore it completely day after day, while it was being demolished. In the same way, she nodded to a news-vendor in a wheel chair, and he always raised his hat to her, because they had become part of each other's internal scenery. She would probably have nodded automatically, as she turned the corner, after the paper-seller had vanished from his pitch.

The city was no longer a collection of unfamiliar units. It was an aggregate, an organism through whose bowels she wriggled as unconcernedly as any microscopic bacillus through the roaring darkness of living veins. The fretwork of roofs against a peacock sky, the street corners where noises met together like boisterous acquaintances celebrating a reunion, the sparrows splashing in the Archibald Fountain, all were part of her and she was part of these things. The city spoke with the voice of Southwell Vaughan-Quilter and Lucy Rossingale; its face was the accustomed face of Mervyn Leggatt; it was the sum total of her friends and acquaintances; and she had so many of them that she could not walk down a street without meeting someone she knew, someone who treated her with the casual acceptance, a phenomenon as much to be expected as the next tram.

Eddie Quinlan's bookshop might never have become a reality had not Shannon found a little, shabby place full of dusty volumes, one of the innumerable bookshops which lurk in odd corners of arcades or are sandwiched between bigger, brighter shops. This little old place, full of the smell of ancient paper, its decrepit owner was only too glad to sell out. She swung Eddie Quinlan away from his grandiose schemes of a great bookshop to the state of mind when he was ready to buy up all the useless stock in order to possess the little dingy shop.

Eddie pointed out that it was a bad location for chance buyers, a depressing dreary little hole. That, Shannon argued, did not matter. They were not dependent on chance buyers. There was living space attached to the shop, and it was the thought of having a retreat of her own that enchanted her. All her life, she said piteously, she had been sleeping in lumpy, spare beds, dragging her few books from one lodging to the next. With the bookshop went the old man's few sticks of furniture, for he was going to live with his daughter, and these Shannon determined to repaint and refurbish for herself.

"Think," Shannon urged, "when you're tired of your club, you could drop in, Eddie, and have a cup of tea, and I'd cook you spaghetti." She refrained from mentioning that he would find himself out on the cold pavement, if he tried anything more than just drinking tea.

Eddie Quinlan brightened at the prospect. Yes, he said, they could start in a small way and build the bookshop up together.

Actually the shop was in a very strategic position; down a quiet lane between two wide roaring streets, a lane that was used as a short-cut. Shannon could hardly wait for the old man to move out before she moved in. Long before he was ready to go, she was heartlessly cleaning the shelves. The old man doddered about blinking pitifully at the havoc she made of all his settled arrangements.

"Now that's a shelf," he would pipe, "that I haven't touched for seven years."

As soon as he had gone, she had a sale. No one noticed the sale besides a few bibliomaniacs, so Shannon shifted out the oldest books and stacked them in what had been the living-room of the dwelling, now converted to extra shop space, and the new books went up on the newly painted shelves.

No sooner had the news passed around that Shannon was installed in a bookshop than all the radical organizations, the Forward Theatre Guild (latest alias for the Proletarian Club), the Movement for Cultural

Progress, the International Peacelovers, the editorial staff of "Peace Indivisible," "Public Interest," and "The Weekly Banner," moved in and started to make the place their own. They posted up notices on the windows, they left bundles of "literature" for sale or return; they held meetings in Comrade Hicks's sitting-room.

Poor Eddie Quinlan appearing for the promised tea and spaghetti found his bookshop occupied by busy groups who were turning out leaflets, arguing with each other, using the shop's typewriter for their own purposes, and brewing tea on the gas stove.

People like Sasha, who lived a long way out of town, found it handy to change their clothes or take a bath or sleep overnight. Little groups with nothing to do would say: "Let's not have coffee. I've just had coffee. Let's go over to Shannon's and talk there." They sat about in the room at the rear of the shop, sometimes making themselves useful, more often just exchanging the news, arguing or reading the new books free. It seldom occurred to them that this was a place for selling books. Clive, who had been left in charge for half an hour, was found, on Shannon's return, arguing a customer out of his resolution to buy a volume Clive was anxious to read.

"What do you want it for?" Clive was demanding indignantly. "Don't you know this is the only copy in Australia, and we're not likely to get another?"

In self-defence, Shannon added a library for the incessant swarm of borrowers and charged them for keeping out books overtime.

"You never seem to be alone," Eddie complained somewhat sulkily. "Doesn't this mob ever go home?"

"Never mind," Shannon consoled him. "Let's leave the shop and go for a breath of fresh air."

Eddie's car was one of the things that Shannon liked about him. She never had a suitor with a car before. She made him drive her out to the Blessingford Home so that Aunt Edith should have the happiness of speculating about him. She introduced Eddie to Beryl again. She even sat in the car with him and looked at the moonlit sea and let him kiss her occasionally. Her conscience was clear. She was making money from the bookshop. It was not a loss to Eddie, so she did not really need to let him kiss her. She just liked being kissed.

Who would care, she thought, if I did let Eddie stay the night? No one, except me. But she just did not want him, and that was all there was about it. She could manage Eddie with one hand tied behind her back, and she rather pitied him for being so simple.

Southwell Vaughan-Quilter quite approved of her managing a bookshop. He often came in, settled down in one of her office chairs and helped her in the cataloguing of the books. He called round on Saturday afternoons, when Eddie might be expected, and would out-sit him. The two of them would play chess together, a dogged, tense game which Quilter usually won, or they would go out together in Quinlan's car. Eddie came to be resigned to Quilter's guardianship. He had gathered the impression that South Quilter had some claim on Shannon and he deferred to him, just as he deferred to Leggatt, when that worthy functionary made one of his quiet tours of inspection. These were big men, and he knew better than to resent their presence. Only the fact that he owned the bookshop gave him any claim, a claim he did not push too far on their acquaintance. He was very proud that they should call him Eddie and treat him rather patronizingly.

Shannon also patronized Eddie. She ordered him about, scolded him, advised him, and sometimes mothered him a little. Southwell Vaughan-Quilter she never mothered. He could take care of himself. He would sit serenely in the midst of a circle of revolutionaries of all shades of colour and out-argue them in their own terms, with Eddie piping up "But Marx says . . ." at intervals in the background. The Leninist Bookshop became the favoured meeting place of the Left, and many a stirring and wordy combat took place in the rear room of the shop.

Vaughan-Quilter maintained that it was essential to get into parliament men pledged to a change of the social system. "People are always writing heart-breaking letters to me, and when I analyze them, fully half these heart-breaks are due to criminal poverty, poverty that should no longer exist with the spread of knowledge." Eddie, the complete armchair Marxist, still clung to the conception of direct action. Only direct action, he maintained vaguely, was any use. Mervyn Leggatt confounded those who were prepared to scoff at the Abbot as a soft humanitarian, by asserting the need to combat Fascism by the "use" of parliament.

Shannon did not join in these arguments, but attended to the customers. Talking no longer seemed to her to matter much. It surprised her how tolerant she had become of what once seemed to her abhorrent insanities.

Even when Dr. Maurice Knowles sidled one day into the shop, with a prosperous look, a clerical collar that seemed to have widened by at least an inch, and a suggestion that she should display some advertisements for a tuberculosis cure he and a few of his friends were promoting, she felt only amusement.

This underground amusement was like a stream which nourished the roots of her new liking for everything and everybody. Sometimes, she felt restless and dissatisfied, but only when her visitors went on endlessly talking. She was so tired of politics, so tired of the working class as a subject of discussion, so tired of the solemnity with which everyone brought out opinions that she had heard over and over again.

"Tell me, Dr. Knowles," she asked curiously, "did you ever study for any of those degrees of yours?" She gave him the same wide, serene gaze that she turned on most problems.

Dr. Knowles started, eyed her doubtfully, then said in a whisper: "I read all the buiks." His voice was at once fierce and wistful. "They gie ye a lang list of buiks and Ah read them a'. If I may noo hae gane to the University, I read all the buiks." He edged up to her defiantly. "Dinna ye think I hae a right to ma letters?"

Shannon was sorry for him. Poor monster, to have thirsted for the far-off mirage of formal learning! In the same way, when old Colonel Brewster took to dropping in and boring her with his anecdotes, she had not the heart to deny him. Had poor Eddie Quinlan only been a little more pressing in his attentions, she might have become his mistress from sheer good-will, and good-will in her was a new thing. But Eddie was always a little in awe of her. She gave him the feeling that she was secretly laughing at something, an uncomfortable feeling for a man who might be the object of that laughter.

It was the new feeling of security that made Shannon laugh. She had so much less need to be hard and tense when the bookshop was doing well. She could relax and forget what it was like to have an aching tooth and no money for the dentist, a hungry feeling and no lunch. At the U.C.D.L. she had felt that she was covered with the grey mud of human misery; even now the faces of the men and women who had wanted help, sometimes rose before her in the night, but no longer with the same hopelessness. Even Southwell Vaughan-Quilter, with his session, his Consolation

Hour, was in closer touch with all this seethe and stir of anguish than she was herself.

There was a little radio set which Eddie had deposited with her to mind for him, and she sometimes listened to South's session, chuckling a little at his sonorous sympathy, his paternal advice. She was in this complacent, pleasant mood, when Vaughan-Quilter appeared one evening, as she was shutting the shop, and accepted her invitation to stay to tea. He seemed disturbed and uneasy, and when they had settled to their meal, with the kettle singing pleasantly, she asked him what the trouble was. Without comment, he handed her a letter from the leather despatch case in which he always carried his Consolation Hour mail. She glanced over it unconcernedly. Only when she came to the signature did she raise her eyebrows.

It was a long, wordy letter, in a sprawling female hand, the kind of letter South Quilter was always answering in his session. She was so unhappy, the writer said, that she had felt forced to confide in someone. She had been separated from her husband and was living with her mother, but she had always hoped that her husband would come back to her. "He was always going out with his own friends, Mr. Quilter, he left me at home night after night, and I might have stayed for the sake of my little girl, but he said we could never be happy together, so I agreed to live apart from him, but now I find he is living with a woman in the city and has bought a shop for her, where he is always to be seen and my friends say I should get a divorce. Do you think I should, Mr. Quilter? I have no one to ask and you sound so good and kind and I am sure you will advise me. If you only knew what I have been through . . ." There was a great deal more, but it was signed "Amory Quinlan."

"Eddie's wife," Shannon commented. "She sounds beautiful but dumb." She handed the letter back. Southwell Quilter replaced it among his correspondence. "Poor brat!" Shannon said, with a sigh. "I wish I could do something."

"Do you really, Shannon?" Southwell Quilter seemed relieved. "Of course, I know she's mistaken about Eddie."

He had not known until the very minute when Shannon handed the letter back. It had given him a sleepless night wondering whether Shannon and Eddie were really justifying Amory Quinlan's suspicions. But now he felt relieved and pleased. Of course, it was Shannon's business what she did with her life, but an affair like this had not seemed like her. If she had been in love with Eddie, he thought, he would have known it. He had known Shannon so long; he knew every change of her face, every ripple and shade of expression.

"Look, South," Shannon had been thinking hard in the silence that had fallen between them. "Suppose you ask her to see you. Then you could bring her in here and we could talk it over. After all, Eddie is such a mutt that any woman who loves him ought to be given a medal. But he's a decent scout and she seems a decent little idiot. We ought to be able to fix up something." She removed the kettle which had just begun to boil, and made the tea thoughtfully.

Southwell Vaughan-Quilter decided that he had never loved her so well as he did then. He could have gathered her in his arms. "You're a darling," he said softly.

Shannon met his eyes. "I'm not sorry about the shop," she told him. "I'm afraid I'd have snatched at the shop even with Eddie definitely on the mat. I was so fed up with everything, South. But there's no reason why Amory shouldn't have Eddie back."

"You are a darling, Shannon," he said again softly.

"Well, think of something," she urged to hide her confusion. "You're supposed to be the grand advice giver."

The atmosphere of her little kitchen was so full of emotional tension that she was glad when a rap on her side door gave her the excuse to leave him. Strange, how whenever she had reached the stage when South Quilter was just ready to bring their relationship to some kind of finality, she always sheered away from him. The situation had been indefinite so long that she had come to prefer it. She did not quite know how she would react to a change from the very intimate friendship to something nearer.

The knock at the door was Sasha bursting with a dreadful grievance against Clive. She had waited for him for three-quarters of an hour, and he had not appeared to meet her; she was laden with parcels, tired and furious. She knew instinctively that Clive was somewhere flirting with a young, beautiful woman. South Quilter and Shannon exchanged glances of amusement over the jealous Sasha's head. There was no more occasion to discuss Amory Quinlan's letter, but when Quilter rose to go, he said casually by way of farewell: "I'll bring her in the day after tomorrow."

"Who is he going to bring in?" Sasha demanded. That was the trouble with women friends, Shannon reflected. They always wanted to know everything and considered it an offence if you withheld the slightest confidence. They lived emotional lives and were absorbed in their own and their friends' emotions to a degree of intensity which a man would consider unhealthy.

"Just a friend of his," Shannon lied casually. "He wants me to meet her."

Amory Quinlan was beautiful but dumb, as Shannon had suspected. She was small, rather plump, with a baby doll face and big, rather stupid blue eyes. In advance, she had decided to be resentful and haughty to the woman who had stolen her husband, but this attitude gave way to self-pity almost immediately. She sat very straight on a chair in the office and called Shannon "Miss Hicks" with frigid politeness.

"Of course, I know it doesn't matter to you, Miss Hicks, perhaps you can't see it my way . . ."

"Have a cigarette?" Shannon offered.

"Thanks, I will." She would have refused, but Shannon had already pressed the cigarette upon her. "You can't see it my way, I know that." With the cigarette, she felt a little less hostile. "It isn't that I haven't other chances. Don't think I'm spineless or that I tried to see you. If I'd known Mr. Quilter was a friend of yours . . ." She wandered on rather confusedly and Shannon let her talk.

"And now," she said briskly, when Amory Quinlan seemed to have talked herself out, "we'll think of some way to bring old Eddie back home, huh?" She took another cigarette herself and her eyes twinkled. "With your looks, Amory, you must have been pretty dumb," she repeated it judicially, "yes, pretty dumb to have him wander away."

"He never would learn to dance," Amory Quinlan said querulously, "and I liked dancing. I suppose just because I went dancing and he went to awful meetings, that's my fault?"

"Well, do you want him back?" Shannon asked frankly. She knew she had no right to patronize Amory Quinlan, but it was very hard not to stroke her as though she were a kitten.

"He's my husband," Amory said primly. "You can't get over that."

Even Southwell Quilter could have shaken her. She was more stupid than they had expected.

"I think," Shannon said, with that twinkle in her eye that had so disconcerted Eddie, "that you ought to take an interest in this bookshop. Suppose you came in sometimes and gave me a little help?"

Amory looked uncomfortable. "I might meet him."

Shannon nodded. "I thought of that. And if you did, would you just smile brightly and say 'Hello, Eddie,' and not nag him?" Amory Quinlan was about to begin again on a long recital of her grievances, but Shannon stopped her. "Say 'Yes,'" she demanded. "Go on, say it, silly."

"Well, yes." Amory was startled. She thought Miss Hicks was strange and intimidating. She could not see what in the world Eddie saw in her. And she was such a bully.

"That's a good girl," Shannon said gently. "We'll get on very nicely together. You can start now and I'll show you the shop."

She nodded to Southwell Quilter that he could leave the kitten with her. The kitten looked a little frightened but presently it was frisking. Shannon learned all about what a nice chap Eddie had been, and how strange it was that he had changed and taken up with dreadful politics and things that Amory's mother thought were not at all nice.

"But you'd sooner live with Eddie than with your mother?"

Oh yes, Amory was dreadfully tired of her mother. Mother bullied her, almost, she thought, the way Miss Hicks did, but not so nicely. She was beginning to like her. She could be very nice. "May I call you Shannon?" she asked, as she put on her hat.

Shannon petted her. "Now don't worry," she advised. "And don't tell Mother, if you can possibly keep it to yourself. Mother wouldn't like it."

"She says I've no pride," Amory agreed ruefully.

On Amory's fourth visit to the bookshop, she was sitting on a high stool chattering away trustfully while Shannon took very little notice. Neither of them was aware for some minutes that Eddie was standing in the shop, a picture of resentment and startled displeasure.

"I hope you don't mind, Eddie?" Shannon called. "Your wife's been a great help."

"Hello, Eddie," Amory piped up from her stool and dutifully smiled as she had been told. Eddie gave her an unfriendly glare. He drew Shannon into the rear room.

"That's a nice kind of trick to play," he flared. "You know, you know as well as I do that you got this up yourself. Well, I'm not falling for it. I think it's mean, it's rotten, it's unsporting, it's . . ."

"Don't be so uncivilized." Shannon's voice was icy. "All this ridiculous, spoilt-child fussing because your wife is acting like a woman of the world. She doesn't care what you do. I think it's very sweet of her. Now understand, Eddie," she became very sharp and peremptory, "you may have bought this bookshop, but I'm running it. I've a right a protect myself from scandal-mongers. I've my good name to consider." It was a phrase of Aunt Edith's, and it came in very handy. "Your wife's presence here squashes all the things people have been saying. I'm not even asking you to be nice to her. I'm just asking you, for my sake, to behave in a civilized manner."

Eddie was quelled, but he still nursed a sense of rankling injustice. Shannon and her good name! That was a little too much. However, he went back into the shop and said grudgingly: "Hello, Amory."

"Oh, Eddie," Amory trilled, "we've been cleaning and cleaning. These books do get so dusty."

Eddie ignored her and addressed himself to Shannon. "I thought you might like to hear the news. South Quilter's going to stand for Parliament as a Socialist Labour candidate."

"What!" Shannon exclaimed. "I don't believe it." She had gone quite pale. Why, the fool! He who had been the calm, majestic Abbot of the Order of Human Brotherhood, who had played at being God for so long, to descend to compete for a job! Deep down there still lurked in her the old admiration for him as the priestly and sanctified Abbot. Could he shed all that like a skin? He might engage in his radio Consolation Hour, but he had still something of detachment. This meant that he was coming down, down from the clouds, and she had always liked him best in the clouds, even if she had called him a dreamer, a charlatan, who only half believed what he preached. "It can't be true," she repeated. "He would have told me."

"Merv Leggatt was talking to him over the phone in my office just now." Eddie expanded with importance that he should be at the core of such great affairs. Shannon suspected that Mervyn Leggatt had gone round to see if Eddie would put up some money for the election campaign. "It's the by-election for Wilmot. Old Storey died a couple of days ago, and

Merv reckons that a Socialist Labour candidate would have a fair chance."
He really felt that he was paying Shannon out for wishing his wife on
to him. She was not looking secretly amused now.

"South Quilter accepted at once," Eddie told her. "Merv Leggatt told
him he'd run the canvassing and organizing side of things. Leggatt said
to tell you he'll be coming round to see you later."

He would, Shannon thought. She knew what this meant. She had had
to do with elections before and had hoped never to go through another
one.

"Oh, isn't it grand," Amory exclaimed, in her character of enthusiastic
convert to Eddie's interests. "Mr. Quilter is so marvellous! I suppose he
will have to work very hard to be elected."

Shannon groaned. If it had been anyone but Southwell Quilter or
Mervyn Leggatt, she would have told them firmly that the shop took up
all her time.

"I got the impression," Eddie said carelessly, "that Merv Leggatt wanted
you to go out and supervise things rather."

Shannon had suspected as much.

Twenty

I

THE ELEVATION of Southwell Vaughan-Quilter to the Federal seat of Wilmot was a shrewd tactical stroke on the part of the militant Left. For some time they had argued that if they could only break through the reactionary ring of the official Labour Party, if they could push into Parliament a small group of determined Labour Independents, who were not chained to the party machine, but who were ready to work for the Party's avowed aims of socialization of industry, there was already in Parliament a discontented body of Labour men who might swing over and throw their weight behind the rebels.

The electorate of Wilmot was the first testing ground for this theory, the providential by-election permitting the Left to swing all its forces into the battle at one critical time. Leggatt's demand that Shannon be sent out in command of the flying squad of helpers met at first with much opposition.

"She's too flamboyant," one of the functionaries argued gloomily. "We must have someone with a sense of responsibility."

However, Leggatt had his way. Just that touch of flamboyancy, he argued, was what they wanted. If it were not so, why put up Vaughan-Quilter instead of some steady-going, hard-working activist who had proved himself through years of loyal self-sacrifice?

Wilmot electorate covered an area of residential waterside suburbs inhabited less by Reds than by Pinks of all shades and hues. It had been a fashionable rich man's locality in the days of mansions and aristocratic families. Now, the houses covered with Virginia creeper, shaded by deep verandahs, were mostly boarding-houses, or split into quaint, self-contained dwellings for several families. Big new blocks of modern flats were rapidly replacing many of the old homes. The steep, precipitous streets winding up from the ferry wharves, and the waterside parks and boatsheds, were lined with pink and cream stucco palaces with Mexican names, their own tennis courts and hot water services. Middle-class people

257

with jobs in city offices could look over the water, watch for their morning boat, while enjoying a last slice of toast, and think how pleasant and peaceful it was to inhabit Wilmot, pitying distantly the crowded, dirty suburbs, where there were no balconies, no blue water, green trees or modern flats.

The hard-bitten Shannon, taking up her quarters in an empty shop soon to be plastered with huge posters "Vote for Vaughan-Quilter," reflected that the cash which went to pay for the Labour Independent's headquarters, for the loud-speakers, the big posters, the hire of halls, all the equipment for capturing this bastion of the bourgeoisie, came not from the residents of Wilmot but from the dirty industrial suburbs, from the pockets of people who would be mercilessly fleeced by leaders such as Leggatt. The middle-class Lefts and Pinks of Wilmot did not put up any money. They would think they were doing a favour by voting for Vaughan-Quilter.

They did not realize that in the working-class suburbs loyal followers of the Movement were paying extra dues on top of already heavy dues for this by-election. On the other hand, it did not seem at all curious or inconsistent to the working men who put up the money that they should be doing this to assist into Parliament a man they would have despised as their own representative.

Shannon put such thoughts firmly from her. It would not do now to give way to her weakness for discovering inconsistencies. Instead she began to draw up lists, to divide the electorate into streets for the can-vassers. "Flamboyant," she thought, for the remark had been duly reported back to her. Leggatt knew it would annoy her. "I'll give them flamboyant." If it took every ounce she had, Vaughan-Quilter would go to Parliament.

She began to draw up another list of the important men of the electorate, men whose opinions carried weight. She would see those men herself, and if guile, personal magnetism and argument could win them, they were in danger.

At first, the electorate viewed with a natural suspicion the posters: "Vote Southwell Vaughan-Quilter, Labour Independent," this new luminary shining in their midst. They did not know whether his advent heralded disaster and tumult or a new era. Vaughan-Quilter's University degrees, his scholastic careers, his English origin, were carefully advertised, and his connection with the Abbey of Human Brotherhood not over-stressed. The impression on the casual voter was that Vaughan-Quilter was an immensely cultured churchman, a scholarly recluse, who had been roused from his peaceful Abbey, urged to descend into the bitter hurly-burly of politics by his burning conviction that reform, sweeping reform, was a duty which the most disinterested of scholars and gentlemen must take upon themselves.

His burning sincerity impressed even the jeering. He was handsome and dominating. He was a magnificent platform speaker and, in this respect at least, a welcome change from the average politician. His portrait looked well on the posters. His opponent of the official Labour Party was a local publican who had won the right of nomination less by ability than by years of membership in the local branch. He was fat and stolid and with no more glamour than a ham. The United Australia Party candidate was a professional Tory politician, uncannily able, but who had unfortunately been involved in some charge of promoting companies whose foundations would not bear the weight of investigation. He himself had emerged without spot or stain, but he was annoyed by the questions about those companies cropping up at every meeting.

The flamboyancy of Vaughan-Quilter also annoyed him. He had never seen such a fantastic election, "a play-actor's turn-out," as he complained to his supporters. Certainly, the Proletarian Club, or rather the Forward Theatre Guild, added a colour of its own by presenting plays staged on lorries, in halls, in the ten minutes' interval between speeches. All these plays emphasized the urgent need for those reforms advocated by Vaughan-Quilter. Wheat farmers in despair and in dusty garments groaned of their needs; little children appealed for kindergartens and better schools; all united in the plea for Vaughan-Quilter to save them.

These little dramas kept the crowds entertained and set them in a good humour. A sudden uproar along the street; the blare of a loud-speaker; large posters adorned with "Australianism and Vaughan-Quilter," "Quilter for Peace and Prosperity"; lorries with symbolic figures of Australia and the Spirit of Eureka appealing to the elector—announced with surprising frequency that Mrs. Brewster was conveying her pageant in procession.

Part of Shannon's job lay in interviewing the inspector of police who was grimly convinced that these processions and pageants constituted

K

a breach of the peace. He pointed out that the other candidates did not resort to such measures; but he was arguing with someone who knew every statute and by-law regarding street demonstrations. The mayor had been interviewed; half the Council was of the opinion that the interest this by-election was exciting had put "Wilmot on the map." So the inspector could look for little support in that quarter and Shannon let him know it. Had Leggatt or any of his men tried half the flauntings that Shannon planned, they might not have got away with it; but Shannon was out for free shows.

"This is a mean age," she sighed to Leggatt. "Not enough bread or circuses." And her experience with the Proletarian Club stood her in good stead. Publicity, publicity, and then more publicity was what she asked. It did not matter if the papers attacked Vaughan-Quilter as a charlatan and an opportunist. That only gave him the chance of a ringing reply, and she saw to it that papers likely to print bitter things had at least a striking photograph to accompany their articles.

Vaughan-Quilter was discussed over dinner tables; families split on the question whether a man who forthrightly advocated socialism could make a good member of Parliament. In the buses bouncing downhill to the wharves, morning newspaper readers were faced with Vaughan-Quilter full-face or profile. As a topic of conversation on the ferries, he left even the critical state of Europe in the shade. Little groups of men who had travelled together, occupying the same seats for years, every morning reviewed the latest news of the candidates, and one clinching argument was advanced in every discussion. Someone was sure to say as the group rose to make its customary dash for the gangway: "Well, he must be *sincere* in what he says. He's got no need to go into politics. He's not like most of these fellows just out for a fat job. He's got a comfortable position and he's got no need to come out and sweat." The people who put up this argument had never had to deal with Bishop Bulfram.

The first large meeting in the town hall had been a triumph of underground organization. People who drifted in listlessly, expecting an evening of dreary speeches, were almost lifted out of their seats by the ringing enthusiasm of a sizeable section of the audience whose faces were unfamiliar to older residents. All the right questions were asked. There was a comic drunk, and a rousing fight between orthodox labour supporters and a small ferocious group of Quilterites.

The inhabitants of Wilmot learned that it was worth attending Quilter's election meetings, if only for the excitement. The canvassers had worked furiously, and, from their reports, the support promised exceeded expectations. Janet Bubbing's women's organizations had been busy, for many of the voters were young women with jobs, and the promise of equal pay for equal work attracted them almost as much as Vaughan-Quilter's magnetic personality.

Balm and oil had to be poured on Mrs. Brewster's wounds before she would consent to recognize Shannon even as a fellow-worker in the cause. Mrs. Brewster felt she had suffered so greatly from Shannon's inconsiderate and riotous behaviour on the trip to Canberra that only the most profound apologies could restore the *status quo*. The apologies were forthcoming, fluent apologies. Shannon almost stroked Mrs. Brewster's fur. The good work she could do for Australianism and the cause of peace by championing Vaughan-Quilter moved Mrs. Brewster to throw her not inconsiderable weight behind the election forces. "Such a brilliant man," Mrs. Brewster told her friends, and there were many of them in the Wilmot electorate. "He has become so imbued with the Spirit of Australianism."

It really did seem that Southwell Vaughan-Quilter knew exactly the right note to strike on every occasion. He was frank, dignified, thoroughly at home with his hearers, full of profound earnestness, yet ready with a jolly laugh, an appropriate reference. He knew his facts, his programme was clear cut. Moderate, unassuming, yet sure of himself, he moved as easily through Wilmot as a ferry boat through the accustomed waters of the harbour, a ferry boat so punctual, so steady that it struck the same set of waves each trip.

"At least we won't be forfeiting our deposit," Shannon assured Merv Leggatt. "Even if he doesn't get in, we're giving the gang a good run for their money."

Mervyn Leggatt could not be in Wilmot the whole time, but he managed to appear frequently in the election rooms, usually with a shrewd idea, some sharp advice or a little encouragement. He had enough to do to keep the money coming in. He raised money doggedly from all kinds of odd corners. Money was flowing out like water, and it was impossible to keep down expenses. Sometimes the pile of bills made him look a little paler and sharper than usual, but that was all.

"It will be worth it," he said, "if he gets in. We're staking a lot, Shannon." The peculiar character of the electorate, he thought, the mixture of snobbishness, aroused by Vaughan-Quilter's M.A., B.C.L. (Oxon), with the vague emotional sympathies of a large section of voters fretting for Parliamentary reform and a change of governments, should form a winning combination. Leggatt had stacked his personal prestige on the result of this election. He had convinced hard-headed functionaries that Vaughan-Quilter was their best chance, and his stake in the game was their respect and reliance. To forfeit that would be a more bitter blow than even he cared to contemplate. He liked to think that he was insensible to personal opinions, but the good will of his colleagues, the sense of power which he enjoyed, his knowledge that, from a distance, he moved a winning pawn in the game, these were things that mattered to him.

"You ought to be contesting this election," Shannon remarked fretfully. "Why aren't you? You know that you'd be twice as good as South if you got into Parliament."

"Someone has to manage the campaign," he replied. "Besides I'd never do here."

If Mervyn Leggatt ever put up for Parliament, it would be in some grim, grey industrial suburb, not in a neat, sunny electorate where even the water seemed to have been spruced and tidied, and the council took pride in its improvements and gardens. Far better appeal to the muddled emotionalism of such a place, the love of sensation, the queer streak of craziness that lay in the Sydney dweller who could afford such luxuries as electing Vaughan-Quilter.

However, Leggatt was thawed a little by Shannon's recognition of what he secretly admitted to himself, and that he was a far better organizer, a clearer thinker, than Vaughan-Quilter. Night after night, with ringing sincerity, Southwell Quilter gave his speeches, the notes of which Leggatt had planned for him; he explained the policy that Leggatt had outlined, he twisted into long, flowing sentences the strands of Leggatt's common sense.

Shannon knew it was Leggatt's work, that Southwell Quilter, as a political figure, was his moulding. Leggatt had taken a mystic, an emotional prophet, a writer and preacher of another world, and turned him into a first-rate politician. He was proud of his work, grimly amused, under his mask, that this secret jest at the expense of Wilmot was succeeding. Shannon almost hated him. She hated him for what he had done to Southwell Vaughan-Quilter. It seemed to her that these days there was hardly anything of the Abbot left, hardly a trace of the man whose remembered voice and face had kept her heart aching so long, so secretly.

While her acquaintances wondered what was wrong with Shannon Hicks, why in a flippant, cold way she discouraged the men who had wanted to marry her, she had been content to live in a secret world worshipping the image of Southwell Quilter. She had not even sought his company, because whenever she did so some of the lustre of that image seemed dimmed, its pedestal trembled ever so slightly. Now, listening to Vaughan-Quilter night after night, while she admitted the old charm, acknowledged the little leap of heart certain old tricks of voice still brought her, she knew certainly and sadly that Vaughan-Quilter was no longer the man she had dreamt him, a man so big that he could take the world for his hearth-rug. He was just the makings of a first-rate politician. Illogically, she blamed Leggatt for this metamorphosis. He would have argued that he had merely taken advantage of something already present, something that everyone could see, namely, that Southwell Quilter could be made to feel with conviction almost any opinion that was presented to him as advantageous, if it was presented so subtly that he could seize it as his own idea.

Shannon found herself comparing Leggatt and South Quilter, and more and more admitting that of the two she respected Mervyn Leggatt more than she did his magnificent tool. She was almost afraid at times of that detachment which Leggatt cultivated. Just as she was ready to admire him wholeheartedly, he would show her a side of himself so coldly unscrupulous that even she, mocking and city-tough, could not but feel repelled.

The Jesuits in the great age of European politics had left the same impression of treachery for the same reason. They were loyal and self-sacrificing beyond the limits of sense. They believed, like Leggatt, in an all-good, all-authoritarian system. But, at least, they believed they were conspiring that men might be delivered to the bliss of an eternal Heaven; they did not lie and forswear so that men might have better-filled bellies and self-respect and an easier life in this world. Not that Shannon, with her own experiences of economic necessity, was at all contemptuous of the cravings of ill-filled bellies. It was like being choked with grey mud;

and, in the streets, in the trams and trains every day, there were hundreds of people whose faces, their weary looks, their broken strength, told that they were struggling in the ugly ooze of private misery. They would struggle more and more feebly until it gulped them down to their graves. Mud people, with dull eyes and cheap clothes, and earthy, drubbing, deadened and worn looks. From the bog in which they pressed down one another's bodies, treading the fallen, scrambling, sweating, clutching, dreading, it was Leggatt's aim to haul them, whether they liked it or not.

Merv's millennium, Shannon thought, had its advantages over the poor Jesuits' life-to-come. Men like Leggatt believed so firmly that the revolution would dawn in their time from sheer necessity. *They* were to bring about that great age when the Worker, as mythical a figure as the Son of Man, would appear in his glory. The Revolution would be won, the godlike Worker would be supreme over those heretics who profited by capitalism, whose bodies would pass through the fire that their souls might be saved from the sin of private ownership of the means of production.

This was a mean way of stating Mervyn Leggatt's private convictions. He could have proved, with the soundest logic, that it was a travesty of his philosophy. He would have argued that he despised Shannon, not, as she had often reproached him, from class-conscious snobbishness, but because her thoughts and actions were irresponsible and emotional. Reason, logic, sound common sense; these were his gods. But why, Shannon argued, did he think he had a monopoly of these good qualities? Leggatt would have replied with humility that he simply followed the leadership of men wiser than himself, the revolutionary tacticians who said "Go," and he went, "Come," and he came.

Shannon carried on arguments with herself over Leggatt, because it did not need any sixth sense to divine that, since that night he had kissed her so deliberately in the dusty little office of the Grinders, Gasworkers and Mainbuilders, his attitude towards her had altered. He carped and nagged and baited her until she flared up, and then he would be secretly pleased, while he explained that she had no right to lose her temper at a little comradely criticism.

At other times, he would come in and sit down answering only yes or no to her remarks, often staying there silently for an hour before he went out abruptly as he had come. The Leggatt who had worked with her in such a companionable indifference in the U.C.D.L., belonged as much to the past as the Abbot of the Order of Human Brotherhood. They were just two men, and both of them, she knew, interested in herself, Shannon Hicks. They were fretful, if one found the other with her, petulant over trifles that before they would not have noticed. It was a complication to an election already complicated by more practical issues such as the annoyance of Mrs. Brewster and Mrs. Bubbing at being, they considered, unduly passed over in favour of other speakers, and confined to the giving of afternoon tea parties to ladies favourably inclined to helping the candidate.

All the comrades, all the old familiar forms of Shannon's radical friends, reappeared in Wilmot clothed in the white raiment of respectability. The members of the Forward Theatre Guild canvassed for Quilter as members of a newly formed branch of the Socialist Labour Younger Set. Sturdy old battlers of the U.C.D.L. appeared as the Socialist Labour Club (Wilmot Branch) and distributed leaflets and pasted up posters. They went out by night and defaced whole streets whitewashing Quilter's name on the sidewalk. Clive and Sasha shared his platform on alternate nights with an Anglican bishop and an already-elected Member of Parliament. Several Methodist ministers, the President of the Business Men's Reform League, Bleeby Peverill and all kinds of resounding and influential persons spoke for him. It was certainly a superb example of good organizing to combine these human ingredients into one homogeneous group.

"All sections of the community," their publicity announced, "have an equal place, an equal right to representation. Southwell Vaughan-Quilter is the choice of the intelligent elector."

Leggatt's dry, short speeches were among those to which least attention was paid. He was ready with his statistics; he was useful for squelching questioners; but he had no colour, and colour was what the electors were enjoying in good measure.

"You're looking washed up," Leggatt snapped at Shannon, the night before polling day. The helpers had all gone and it was nearly midnight. "Couldn't you get a holiday after this?" He bent towards her across the table and surveyed her as though he were regarding some office fixture he was thinking of replacing. But behind his glasses, his eyes were wistful and hungry. Often she caught him watching her covertly and it made her vaguely uneasy.

"I don't know." She felt flat and dispirited. "I'd better go back and gather up what remains of the bookshop."

The bookshop had been left nominally in the charge of Amory Quinlan, but Amory had found it much more exciting to commandeer Eddie's car and drive about sharing the toils and triumphs of the election. Eddie's car had been a godsend, and Amory no less as chauffeuse, but the shop had suffered sadly from a succession of negligent volunteers, who were supposed to mind the place, but did little except sit in the back room and discuss international politics, no matter how loudly a customer knocked on the counter.

Eddie did not worry because he had ceased to take any interest in the bookshop. He was enthusiastic over the election at Wilmot, but whenever he appeared to assist Shannon, he seemed to find himself fobbed off on a job which partnered him with his wife. He had become resigned to this; in the end, he came to expect it. Amory, he admitted, was not as silly as she used to be. He did not like to hear Shannon order her about, and he thought Amory was wrong to be so slavish to Shannon. After all, who was Shannon Hicks to order his wife about? Sometimes he felt like speaking about it pretty severely, just reminding her that it was his car and his wife she was commandeering. Shannon never listened to him, and at least Amory, even if she didn't understand what he was talking about, did listen. He had been mistaken in his feelings for Shannon. "These strong-minded, brainy women," he complained to Amory, "they all get snappy."

"Haven't you a family you could go to?" Leggatt pursued his subject tenaciously. "You said something about your father working at a butter-factory?"

"That was because you kept on saying I was middle-class. There's nothing middle-class about a father who works in a butter-factory."

"Well, couldn't you go there?"

Shannon stared at him, amazed. Kerleuit! The idea of going back to Kerleuit had never occurred to her. "You don't know Kerleuit, Merv. The people there are all good church goers who tear up one another's reputations all the week. Haven't you read any books about country towns?" She flung out her hands dramatically. "Haven't you ever been in one or heard of one?"

"Don't be silly. It would be cheap and you'd get a rest."

"It would cost a fortune in fares." She found herself considering the proposal from a practical point of view. "Of course, I suppose I could." She sighed doubtfully. "But why should I? Why this sudden solicitude?"

"I just mentioned it." Leggatt hated Shannon when she laughed at him. "You can't do good work if you're worn out."

"Funny I never thought of going *home* for a holiday." Perhaps she had never thought of it because her mother's letters were always so full of complaints.

"Poor dear Doris," her mother had written in her last letter, "has had an abscess on her knee. She has been in hospital a week with a tube draining it and she has to go every day for another week to have the dressings put on. Your father is as usual. They were all put off for three weeks and he has been working out a place along the Burning Road. A new man has just come here and I must say he has some funny ideas. I got up the other morning at five o'clock and tripped over the back step I've been asking your father to mend it but you know what he is a really nasty gash. What with the expense of Doris and your father being off things have been pretty bad but you have always the best of everything and don't know what it is to have to worry the soulcase out of you. Now you have this shop Shannon I wonder if you can do anything, if it was only to help with Doris's hospital money."

Shannon had sent money home whenever she had it; when she had written home in need of help herself, her mother had answered advising her to trust in God, pointing out that this was what came of deserting her family for an aunt who never did anything for her.

"Shannon!" She was so sunk in thought that she had almost forgotten Mervyn Leggatt. "Shannon, did it ever occur to you that together . . . you and I . . . we make an unbeatable combination?"

"My beauty and your brains?"

"Be serious for a minute, just for a minute. I've never known a woman who could work the way you can, but it isn't only that . . . look at it clearly and logically. We suit each other . . . we've the same interests and aims . . . We . . ."

"Don't tell me this is a proposal? Beat, beat, my heart!"

"You can take it that way if you like. Yes, even if you wanted to be married in a church, although I hope you wouldn't . . . if you wanted me

K*

to take some kind of regular job and support you. Anything you like, but there it is. I've reached the stage where you've simply got to tell me where I stand. It's hellish. I can't work. I can't even think straight."

Shannon was about to reply that she had not noticed any difference, but the humbled tone of Mervyn Leggatt would have aroused pity in a rock.

"You do feel some sort of affection for me," he stumbled on, awkwardly. "If it were only a little at first, in time you might come to feel more the way I do. I know I'm not setting the thing out in the best light." He was watching her wistfully. "But I'm not good at saying things like this. If we could go on working together, living together on a different footing, I'd give almost anything in the world for the chance . . ." He drummed on the table with his finger tips. "You wouldn't think it over?"

"Poor old Merv," she said gently. "I'm so sorry." It was almost a misfortune that this sudden disorder should have seized his cold nerves. He was as ashamed as a boy; he made her feel embarrassed to be the cause of his suffering. She knew, how well she knew, the sharpness of such pain. "Please don't ask me now because I am . . . very tired. We've tomorrow to think of . . . I'm worried." She looked up at him sadly.

He drew his chair round beside her and rested his head against her neck. "You don't know how often I wanted to do this," he murmured. "Just let me sit here for a while. It won't hurt you, even if you won't . . . think about it."

"When I come back from this holiday." She put off the idea of hurting him. "Let's not talk about it now."

"There's one thing." He did not seem to care that it was long past the time when they should have shut up the room and gone, that it was so late that only the hollow click of a late footstep occasionally startled the darkened streets. "If Quilter had asked you what I asked you, what would you say?" His face was haggard, as he raised his head from her shoulder. "What would you say?" he repeated huskily.

"I just don't know. That's the honest truth. I don't know." Shannon rose and went to the door. "We must really go. It's dreadfully late."

Outside, the cold wind met them and braced them. Shannon said abstractedly: "It should be fine tomorrow." They had missed the last boat long ago, and would need to go around by the Harbour Bridge, a long, wearying trip at that time of night. There was not even a tram in sight, so they walked together in silence until they were overtaken by a bus. "I don't think I'll see you home," Mervyn said unsteadily, when they parted at Wynyard Station. Shannon was not used, in any case, to being escorted. She had learned to find her own way about the city at odd hours. When they parted with a formal "Good night," she turned to watch him going resolutely away, without a glance behind him. Even with her deadly weariness she could not sleep for thinking of him.

Twenty-one

THE SATURDAY of the election was blessed with such bright, clear-washed sunshine; such fresh, challenging air; such merry blue sky and water; that it seemed as though the very ripplets and splashes of the tide broke against the little bays, expectant and joyful. Shannon Hicks, early on the scene, to see that everything was ready from the tables outside the polling booths to the pencils of the scrutineers, was so influenced by the glorious morning that the night before seemed a fantastic dream too shadowy and strange ever to have happened.

She forgot her emotional evening, and busied herself with a last-minute survey of all her arrangements and helpers; but she did it without any real concern. Why worry? the day suggested; elections were not so important after all. People were going about their own affairs and nothing mattered very much. Everything that could be done had been done, and now she could loiter, chatting with friends; taking an occasional shift at one of the tables; give out voting cards and numbers; or just wait on the street corner for the next voter or any reports.

The sun was pouring down its five-million horse-power of energy per square mile and there did not seem anything more to do than just to enjoy life. All the happiness she had enjoyed in the years she had spent in this city seemed to flash before her; blue days on the beaches; good picnics in the bush; rowing parties coming home blistered and singing at sunset; camps and tramps and happy-go-lucky people. From these pleasant reflections, she was awakened by the apparition of Mervyn Leggatt.

"I've been looking for you," he snapped. "There's nobody at the big wooden gate round at the back entrance of the Town Hall."

"But there must be. Clive and Sasha should.be there."

"I've just been round and there's nobody. Not a table, not a How-to-Vote card."

Shannon set off for the scene of the crime, Mervyn Leggatt at her side bitterly and accusingly silent. He was right. There was nobody there.

Shannon set about remedying the state of affairs by taking over the neglected position herself. Not that any voters were likely, she considered, to come by what was almost a back street. It was just like Mervyn Leggatt to go picking on the one place she had overlooked.

Opposite the Town Hall, Mrs. Brewster had rented an upstairs room from which hung an enormous blue flag with the Southern Cross in white —the flag of Eureka. It had hung across the back of Vaughan-Quilter's platforms ever since the campaign began, and there it was nobly and foolishly flapping until the last.

"While we have Southwell Vaughan-Quilter," Mrs. Brewster had declaimed, "the Spirit of Eureka Stockade is still alive."

The enormous blue rosettes with streamers sported by the helpers were Mrs. Brewster's pride. There were young men who had never worn any but a red tie appearing in beautiful royal blue neckwear. Red, for this day, was carefully banned.

Feeding the helpers, particularly those important people, the scrutineers, was one of the laborious tasks of the day. Grizzled stalwarts, who had contributed all they could afford, and more, towards the election; cheerfully travelled long distances; and paid train and tram fares to be present and stand all day on a hard pavement, would have been outraged had they not been fed. There was a solemn ceremony of relieving the guard at morning-tea time, when, from the houses of local supporters, the morning tea was carefully carried out in great jugs and buckets and drunk from large pannikins.

The lady helpers, lively and cheerful, were very much in evidence. The distribution of nourishment was their forte, and they took pains to impress those they succored with the uncomplaining and loyal service the Ladies' Auxiliary was rendering. Their efforts met with no lack of appreciation. One would have thought that the free lunch, which was all the reward of the helpers, was what made the day so important. They talked about the free lunch and anticipated it. When at last they were seated in the best front room of some sympathetic householder and the little banquet spread, the air of festive enjoyment was out of all proportion to the boiled vegetables, cold meat, and a pudding of such unmentionable horror that the mind turned from it instinctively. Yet the helpers attacked even the pudding and devoured the bitter chunks of rhubarb embedded in its depths.

It was policy on the part of the candidate to appear at these separate households, while the feeding was in progress, and submit to the jollity and hospitality and cries that he must at least sit down and have a cup of tea. After all, he would need this gang again at the next election, and must impress the sense of his personal obligation on each and every one of them. By tea-time, a few of the helpers had sorted themselves into little groups of old friends who preferred to eat and exchange impressions over a friendly meat pie at some tiny cafe; but there was still a large number who appeared hungrily to clean up the remains of the rhubarb pudding.

Leggatt, as campaign director, was too busy to bother about this side of the election, and it fell to Shannon to see that the shifts were changed, the helpers appeared at their right houses to be fed. She spent a day of sweetness and light, being tactful and appreciative of the Ladies' Auxiliary, seeing that no one was left without due meed of praise, tending those tender buds, the scrutineers, whose important functions gave them something of the interest of nursing mothers.

Clive strolled into the Socialist Labour rooms in good time for lunch. He had been put off a train by a callous ticket-inspector for travelling on an expired ticket, and his nerves had been so rasped by this encounter that he had gone home to recuperate and collect the money for his fare from the neighbours.

"It's all very well for you, Shannon, getting a lift over in Amory Quinlan's car, but now we're not living at Balm Point, and I've such a long way to come . . . Oh! by the way, Sasha won't be here. She said she knew instinctively that everything would go off all right."

"Well, now that you are here, how about doing a little work?"

Clive looked injured. "I think I'd better get something to eat first," he suggested. "Then I can go on with the afternoon lot."

He stood about the Socialist Labour headquarters exchanging speculations on the possible outcome of the election with other drifting and bungling incompetents who refused to be driven out. Everyone had to give a long, detailed description of his experiences and sum up his opinion of the intelligence of the electors.

"Why, one old lady asked me if Vaughan-Quilter was a good-living man. She said she wouldn't like to vote for him if he wasn't. I told her he was the best living man she would ever meet and that he went to church twice on Sundays. She said: 'God bless him, then I shall vote for him.' Can you beat it?"

The dusk came down with a bitter wind blowing like a personal insult around the chilly corners, where little tables still bravely offered their services to the voters. The water of the bay turned to a cold, steely grey, but the clatter of the election, the hurry of news-bringers still continued.

At eight o'clock, when the returning officer turned out the last voter and shut the door, outside which the policeman solemnly took up his position, the time came for counting the bundles of votes. This was Leggatt's great moment. As the personal representative of the Socialist Labour candidate, it was his business to challenge any doubtful count. The scrutineers, who all day had maintained an attitude of polite hostility towards one another, grew colder and more hostile. Leggatt, knowing that inexperienced scrutineers were often too polite to find fault with the official returning officer, went to every table and glanced over the bundles himself. He challenged sharply. If there was any hesitation over some doubtful vote, which might go for his man, he pounced at once on the chief officer and made him give his verdict. Nothing escaped his exhaustive care. And he had the triumph of seeing his candidate in the lead with a big majority.

The voters of Wilmot were notoriously fickle, but that they should have swung over to such an extent was almost incredible. The truth was that the electors were disgusted with their sitting government and took this way of showing their disgust. This by-election and the series of by-elections which followed it, were only a prelude to the general election which later placed Labour in power.

Vaughan-Quilter had come down to the party rooms to hear the result, having perhaps some little delicacy about harrowing Bishop Bulfram's feelings by receiving the news at the Abbey. He was still in residence there, although his duties as Abbot no longer occupied him. He found the company of his helpers and supporters more congenial than the disapproving growls of Bulfram, the wistful spirituality of old Bishop Steele, and the bewilderment of his fellow workers in the Order of Human Brotherhood, who could see only carnality and materialism in anything as sordid as an election. Outside the Abbey, he breathed more freely; he could call his soul, his astral body, his physical body, and any other planetary appurtenance, his own. He was a free man at last, free to make his impact on the life of this material plane, as he had never been free since he set foot in the Abbey; and he knew the first use he was going to make of his freedom. He drew Amory Quinlan aside and pressed her hand.

"Amory, my darling," he said exultantly, "I want you to do me a favour. I want you to let me borrow Eddie's car just for tonight."

"Why, you could have just anything," Amory carolled. "Why, of course." She had so lost her heart to South Quilter that she never cared if Eddie returned to her or not. "Eddie won't mind a bit."

Not that it mattered if Eddie did mind. He was busy explaining to a group of serious thinkers that this by-election was a proof of what Marx had always said, and he would be there for hours yet.

Through all the self-congratulatory helpers Southwell Vaughan-Quilter threaded his way, stopping to chat, returning handshakes, giving thanks, but edging ever closer to Shannon.

"Meet me outside," he said, low in her ear, "in five minutes."

As she collected her hat and coat and slipped out the door, she had one last glimpse of Mervyn Leggatt. He was staring after her with an expression that ill-accorded with the triumphant part he had played. There was no flush of success and pleasure, only a hungry, despairing appeal. That manoeuvre executed by the new Member for Wilmot had not escaped Merv Leggatt's all-seeing eye.

"Poor Merv," Shannon thought; but she really did not care that she was deserting him. She stepped into the Quinlan car unquestioningly, and the ex-Abbot of the Order of Human Brotherhood drove off far too fast for safety. They whirled along the grey roads, the headlights cutting a path through the dim huddle of houses and trees and fences, as though, with this great sickle of light, he was reaping the suburbs of Wilmot into a harvest heap.

South Quilter seemed to know his way. He turned off the broad concrete highway through a bare stretch of headland and brought the car to rest on the crest of a cliff. By day, this was a well-advertised scenic drive through a suburban park, but now by night it was a peak overlooking a great blaze of lights and waterways, the well-loved, inter-woven waterways of the Mad City. A dim, throbbing roar; a string of lights across the skyline; denoted the harbour bridge. Below, in the dark shadowed water of the bay, lay the decayed hulk of a famous sailing ship; under the shadow of a further hill the ferry boats clustered for the night in their dormitory, amid the coal heaps and grey wooden wharves.

All was quiet darkness, the hushed rustle of the night wind through the low bushes. The lights of the city seemed as far away as some distant galaxy. Beyond the lit waters, the dark wharves, it roared and trembled and shone, the pulse beat of its enormous fever throbbing through the silver arteries of the rails, clamouring from the chiming clock towers, pealing with bells and horns and gongs, the drumming of wheels, and the whine and scream of trams, the hooting of ferries. But the quiet and the whisper of the wind in the dark brought only a faint, hushed murmur to their ears.

The Abbot slipped his arm comfortably about her waist. He was in no hurry. He liked to sit quiet, not because he was tired, but because darkness and the grey, cold dimness of water were as pleasant to his sensitive tastes as good music.

"Whenever I think of the city," he said in a low voice, as though he did not wish to disturb the quiet whisper of the water and trees, "I think of it as a strange girl sitting alone in a poor room. All over the city there are lonely women leading their own queer lives, starving quietly and decently, or timorously clinging to some job or other. At night, I can almost imagine that the sky over the city shivers a little at the thoughts of women lying awake, questioning the order of things, flinging out a challenge to whatever lies behind it, searching up beyond space for the ultimate cold darkness where there is peace, and coming back full circle through infinity, down to the windy streets and the corner lamppost and the milk-jug left on the doorstep and the cat slinking by along the gutter." He drew her closer. "And I'll always think of it as one particular woman who was never satisfied, who went on asking and searching and plucking at her nerves, as though they were harp wires on which she made troublesome music. You're such a pest, Shannon, such an irritating, maddening, honest, lovely annoyance."

She rested her head against his shoulder and wondered at the enormous vitality of the man. He had come through the election without turning a hair, as though it were a brisk run before breakfast. He could sit and talk abstract nonsense when most men would be in a gush of exultant details, going over the election inch by inch like a boy with a toy railway. But South Quilter was taking out his jubilance in kisses.

"How soon will you marry me?" he asked, pausing for breath.

"I haven't said I would marry you."

"Of course, you'll marry me. Members of Parliament have to have wives. Who would you marry beside me? Leggatt? Anyway, why are you kissing me if you're not going to marry me?"

"I like it," she sighed. "Don't spoil all this by talking about Parliaments and marriages. Let's forget all about it." She did not want to spoil this moment which should be sheer unalloyed happiness, but her mind would not leave her alone. It called up pictures of Canberra, the horrible prospect of life as South Quilter's wife chained to the political career he had opened up for himself. It made her cold and sick to think of it.

"No, I want an answer." He was disappointed that this night of his triumph should not see him doubly safe, safe in his electorate, safe in Shannon's promise. "I've waited so long, Shannon. Sometimes, I think the real reason why I decided to stand for Parliament, the final hair in the balance, was that I thought: 'I could marry Shannon.'"

"Don't say that, South." The idea that she might have had anything to do with such a decision dismayed her.

"You should be pleased. You're a good influence, a guiding star." He spoke light-heartedly. "Think how you can use all your wise ways forwarding your husband's career. I tell you," his tone was suddenly fierce, "I can look over the city tonight and think 'Ah, now you will see what I can do, now I have a real chance.'"

"I hate to think what Canberra will do to you." He was too susceptible to impressions not to fall a victim to the trees and their stately attendants; the conservatory atmosphere; the clubman's jollity; the right people who knew "all the boys" and called one another by their Christian names. Oh! he would be easy. His manner would take him easily into the right circles where the air was too rare for outsiders to breathe and the insider lost all touch with the ordinary men and women who sent him to the National Capital to represent them. He would have his enthusiasm toned down, he would be "shown the ropes," let into the workings of the machine.

She thought of Leggatt and his plea of the previous night; Leggatt who should, by rights, have been where South Quilter was. "I'm going away for a month," she answered him, when he demanded again that she say how soon she could marry him. "And when I come back, I'll tell you yes or no." I owe Mervyn Leggatt that, at least, she thought.

"A month's a long time, Shannon."

She set it before him clearly and reasonably. She needed a rest and he would be very busy taking his seat in Parliament. However useful she might be to him later, honeymooning and beginning a parliamentary career did not mix very well together.

"I'm not promising to marry you, South. Just leave it for a month."

"But why? Why won't you?"

She made no answer.

"Very well," he said quietly. "But whatever you say I don't believe you could ever marry anyone but me. If you did . . ."

"Let's forget about it," she said hastily. "Tonight's too good to waste."

And looking out over the water and the flare on the far side of the harbour they forgot everything except the long, aching loneliness for each other, the fevered hunger for the withheld caresses. No single night could efface the long years, heal the cruel twisting of the knife of longing.

"We've grown so used to doing without each other," Shannon said, with a shaky laugh. "Perhaps, South, it doesn't matter."

"Be quiet, Shannon, be quiet."

They held each other close, looking out over the dark water, the flare of the city shining as it would shine all night, a challenge to the lights of the sky.

Twenty-two

I

THE SENSE OF RELIEF and escape with which Shannon left Sydney lasted all over her journey, even the last, irritating, jolting stretch covered by the late afternoon train for Kerleuit, which dawdled its way from one small station to the next, pausing for the tumbling-out of empty milk-cans and leisurely gossip between the guard and divers gentlemen with nothing to do. Behind her lay the complications, the upsurging changes that threatened to drive her into yet another life, but ahead lay Kerleuit which, if it had altered at all, had only turned over in its sleep.

She had forgotten how clean were the colours of Kerleuit, the deep, dull blue of the sea, colder and fresher than the warm kindly seas north, a blue that rolled and shuddered and shone all the way from the ice of the Antarctic. Above the violent green of the hills, big purple thunderclouds were rolling and crackling with a dazzle of pink lightning in the hollows of their great, smoky-white curves. Rain had fallen earlier in the afternoon and through the hot, steamy atmosphere a waft of wet hawthorn flower reminded her of the little, old, white hotel where the bees buzzed in the golden-drowsy sunlight, shaking the creamy, quivering mass of hawthorn.

As the train drew into the station and flashed past the ranked silver row of milk-cans, she had a sudden, vivid picture of a lost child, a child who had set out in a hot, candy-pink dress and Aunt Maisie's cut-down coat, who had started on her travels so nervous, so dogged, so full of stormy possibilities. The station had not changed; there was her mother on the platform, older, grey, and so shabby, poor darling; the stout station-master; the same little group of farmers waiting for parcels and papers.

"Why, Shannon, how you have altered, not a bit like the photographs." Her mother came forward to kiss her. "Is this all the luggage you brought? Doris wasn't feeling very well and Mary's getting the children's tea. I told you we had Mary with us, that she'd left Harry? Yes, she's home with the three children."

As her mother, from shyness, chattered thus much more than her habit,

278

they made their way through the few passengers and their welcoming friends to the gravel-covered approach where stood several battered cars.

"You won't mind walking, seeing you haven't much luggage?" her mother suggested eyeing the town's one taxi. "How's your leg? It doesn't worry you now?"

"I haven't noticed it for years," Shannon said, with stiff lips. A bitter dart shot through her. Her mother would, of course, plump down on her one weak spot. No one of her friends dreamed that Shannon was a little lame, because she walked with a long stride that made it quite unnoticeable. Her friends complained that they could not keep up with her and asked her not to walk so fast. No one knew about her leg. It was a shapely leg; she danced well; she walked well; and she had forgotten, almost, that it was a little shorter than its fellow. Trust her mother to bring her pride down at once. Kerleuit, she thought, reduced her to a harmless cripple, a defective ne'er-do-well. A hot self-consciousness flooded her and she felt she was limping, that everyone noticed it. Her mother, unconscious of the small sharp hole she had pierced in her daughter's armour, went on hurriedly giving all the news.

Behind them, a man had emerged from the station entrance and stood hesitant. He started towards one of the battered cars, then turned and came towards them.

"I don't suppose you remember me?" he said, smiling.

"Why, John Terrill!" They shook hands joyfully. "What in the world are you doing here?"

"Where have you been all these years, Shannon? Your father told me you were coming home."

"You never wrote to me, not once. And where have *you* been all this time?"

"How long are you staying?"

Mrs. Hicks waited in surprised impatience. This duet of unanswered questions struck her as perfectly ridiculous. To her, John Terrill was just the man who had bought the old Williams' place out on the Burning Road. She could not understand the fuss Shannon was making. The man had mentioned that he knew her and had once stayed at Edith's place, but you would think he was some long-lost brother.

"I've got the old bus here," he suggested. "Let me take your luggage."

He seized the two suitcases which Shannon considered quite sufficient for a month's stay, and dumped them in the back of a battered old ruin with flapping patches on its hood. He had not changed, Shannon thought exultantly. How wonderful to see John Terrill again, the same, kind, sensitive, impulsive failure! If he scraped a living out of his farm, it would be all he did. He must have been waiting at the station especially to see her and then he had been almost too shy to speak.

"You've changed so enormously." He had looked forward to the old, untidy Shannon with her glowing energy and wild hair. That bad-tempered girl had given way to a woman with a calm face, wide, well-shaped mouth and big, dark eyes whose expression puzzled him. She was so much at ease, and she had not lost her old gift for making people feel they were welcome, but she was a different Shannon. They talked and laughed together, as he drove her and her mother up the neat little main street.

"Did you bring your swimming costume?" he asked. "We'll be able to run down to Denthaven for a swim. I must show you one of the most beautiful views you've ever seen. You go up to the top of one of these old craters . . ."

"I was born here. I know this place better than you ever will," she objected, laughing.

"We'll see." As he helped them out at the Hicks' front gate, he did not make any arrangement to call for her, but she knew he was already planning their next meeting. They had so much that could not be voiced before Doris and Mary and Mary's three children, several interested neighbours on the footpath, and more behind their window blinds.

"You won't mind sharing a room with Doris," her mother whispered to her in the kitchen. "I was at my wit's end to think where to put you. Mary's getting very tired of not speaking to Harry, and I guess she'll be going home again soon. Not that I'm pushing her. He hasn't been a good husband, but he *is* her husband for better or worse and she's just got to put up with it. That's what I tell her."

"I could go to the hotel," Shannon suggested.

"You could not!" her mother replied hotly. "A child of mine staying at the hotel! What would everyone think? No, I've put you in with Doris and you can share her bed. You did it often enough when you were little."

Vincent Sladder could have made a mint of money out of Doris, the perfect invalid. She always had something gruesomely wrong with her, but she was cheerful, religious and uncomplaining to a painful degree. She had made invalidism her career, and as she kissed Shannon she murmured: "I may disturb you in the night but I know you won't mind, will you?" What she meant was that she would be very much disturbed by Shannon but that she would bear it without a word.

By teatime, it was plain to Shannon that Mary resented her; her mother was uncertain how to take her; Doris felt overshadowed and correspondingly saintly; and Mary's children only stared open-mouthed, not answering when she spoke to them. Strangely enough it was her father with whom she found most in common. Shannon asked about the butter factory and he went off into a long detailed series of grievances against the management.

"Oh, eat your tea!" his wife said impatiently. "You're never done grumbling."

"How about your union?" Shannon asked with real interest.

"Ah! now that's where you've got it," her father responded. "It's like this." He gave her a long analysis of the reasons why the union was ineffectual, and she listened keenly.

"Well, can't you get him out?" Her first impulse was always to displace an inefficient secretary. "Merv Leggatt had the same thing in the Grinders, Gasworkers and Mainbuilders and they had that secretary out in no time. If you started a minority movement and got into touch with the other men in the district . . ." She realized that the female members of the family were regarding her with scornful amazement, but she went on explaining to her father how the whole union could be reorganized.

He shook his head doubtfully. "Ah! you couldn't get them to stick," he answered disgustedly. "Not but that I can see the point if they did."

"I must say," Mary said coolly, "that you seem to know a lot about it, but I can't stand these union things. When Harry talks about them, I shut him up good and proper."

"There's nothing about it in the Bible." Mrs. Hicks folded her lips as though this settled the matter.

"Oh! isn't there?" Shannon retorted. "Look at the ten commandments. Six days shalt thou labour. The first trade-union regulation's right there."

"That's blasphemous," her mother returned quickly.

"How about the parable of the men who came at the eleventh hour and got the same pay as the men who had been working all day?"

Mrs. Hicks retired into a disapproving silence, but Shannon's father smote his hand delightedly on the table.

"That's it," he seconded. "By Christ! for years I been telling her one of these days she'd come a cropper on that Bible!" He mischievously was egging Shannon on. "You tell her some more about them trade-union regulations."

Shannon decided she did not want to antagonize her mother. She turned the conversation to Mary's children to give Mary a chance. Sooner or later Mary must be allowed to show her superiority and then she would feel more kind. Shannon had no children, and Mary, expanding about her own, her troubles with her husband, was able to look on the stranger with less hostility. After all, poor Shannon had never been married. She didn't know what a mother's feelings were. Doris had her aches and pains and her spiritual consolation; Mary had her children; Shannon had nothing.

"And what have you been doing all these years?" Mary asked amiably, when the children as a subject of conversation had been almost exhausted.

Shannon racked her brains. What had she done? All her whirl of activities seemed to vanish like one of those willy-nillys that go whirling over a hot, waterless plain, just a separate vortex of dust dancing in emptiness.

"Oh, I had a job in radio, then a job running a club, and then I was typing for some men I knew." She noticed her mother's clouded face. This was just another clue to what Mrs. Hicks had suspected all along. Shannon was ruined. "Then I was selling bean-stringers and now I've got a job in the bookshop."

"Well, it doesn't sound much the way you tell it, but there," Mary was a kindly soul, "I guess when the aunts come in tonight, you'll loosen up a bit."

Shannon suppressed a start of alarm. She had forgotten that there was sure to be some ceremonial ordeal of inspection and criticism, inseparable from this homecoming.

"What a pity poor Grannie isn't with us," Mrs. Hicks sighed. "I think you might have come when we wrote that she was sinking, Shannon."

"I didn't have the money." She found herself speaking more impatiently and abruptly than usual. She had a long evening before her of self-effacing courtesy and charm, and it would take all her guile and forbearance, if she was not to be flung back into the position of a rebellious adolescent.

Her mother must, of course, be allowed to display the daughter who had gone away, who had been "given her chance" and taken it. Trust mother not to confide her secret conviction that Shannon was ruined, that her smart clothes and general affluence were due to her being a "kept woman" like the betrayed young things in the confession magazines. It would be hard enough to keep the aunts from her affairs ("What! no young man of your own, Shannon?") when they would be revolving in their minds the logical corollaries of Shannon's single state. If she was not married at her age, she was either a bad woman, or an old maid, which was worse. Shannon caught her father's eye and he winked at her. He knew what she was feeling at the prospect of a family gathering in the best room with the faded wallpaper.

"How's Edith?" he asked, when the two of them were left in lonely state after tea, Shannon having been released from washing-up on the grounds that it was "her first night at home."

"Uncle Vincent is making more money," Shannon replied with a complete absence of expression, "than any three doctors in Sydney." That would give her mother something to tell the aunts.

"Edith always had a set on me," her father reflected, pulling at his pipe. "Before I met your mother I'd sort of thought Edith was the one, but as soon as I seen your mother I knew I'd made a mistake. Yes, Edith got a real, vindictive set on me for that. Went off and married fat old Joe Wallis just to show she didn't want for a chap."

"You hold your noise," his wife called from the kitchen. "Anyone 'ud think to hear you talk that you were some kind of marvel. Edith didn't do so badly for herself." There was a complacent note in Mrs. Hicks's voice that belied the sharpness of her words. "She's never had to worry and scrape the way I have."

"Yeah, but look what she missed," Darcey Hicks responded with a slow grin. "Me, that's what she missed."

Shannon's father and mother seemed friendlier than of old. There was none of the rancorous antagonism that marked their attitude to each other when she was a child. Her mother came back into the sitting-room carefully removing her apron from her best dress and wiping her hands on it. She regarded her daughter and husband with a look that mingled fondness and scorn. She might talk about worrying and scraping, but the family seemed easier, happier than Shannon remembered it. The ceaseless anxieties of child-bearing and child-rearing lay in the past and the friction it had bred between her father and mother was gone. Now they could afford to be fond of each other and comfortably at ease. Habit had worn off the sharp edge of their personalities. Shannon was glad for her mother's sake. A man could always find refuge outside his home but a woman was, in most cases, like poor Mary, a waif and stray away from her own roof, particularly if she had children to drag about with her.

She regarded her family with after-dinner indulgence. Her mother's insistence that she should eat an enormous meal had been something of a strain after a diet which consisted chiefly of coffee and cigarettes. She had never quite overcome her inheritance of the "Hicks stomach" and found large meals a trial. Her mother's determination to "fatten her up" must sooner or later be vanquished, but if she was going to have a fit of indigestion, it might as well be later when the relatives were at their worst. Whatever else had mellowed in Kerleuit, it was too much to expect that time had made any change for the better in Aunt Elsie.

"That Terrill feller," her father reflected aloud, "he's got a real nice little dairy herd, but he don't look after it right. Mucking about with flax." He sighed wistfully, remembering his own ambitions. "What ruined him, I guess, was being in one of these experimental farms. Can't say it don't affect 'em. Never the same after."

He liked talking to Shannon. With her close-cut hair, her determined face, and neat insolent chin, she looked like a boy, much more like a boy than his sons who had drifted away to jobs on farms in the district. Shannon's younger brothers had grown up rather stolid, unimaginative young men. They took after the Hicks family and were ruminant young animals, slow of speech and action. Shannon, her father thought, had inherited his brains if none of the others had.

II

Shannon's holiday resolved itself more and more into a day long picnic with John Terrill. They drove, they swam, they talked, most of all they talked. She listened to all his ideas, his experiments with soil fertility, his plans for more intensive farming.

"The most fertile soil in the world, Shannon, and what do they do with it? Marvellous volcanic soil given over to cows! And the land that could be improved out of sight left undrained, undernourished. All they do is cut down the trees."

He inhabited a large, roomy, weatherboard dwelling on the top of a hill, but it was in a sad state of neglect. Mrs. Sandleberry, wife of the faithful George Sandleberry, who worked on the farm on a profit-sharing basis, came in and cleaned it whenever the owner was absent, but it had an unkempt appearance. Books and discarded articles of clothing and unwashed pots lay about the kitchen which was also the living room, and the other rooms of the house were never lived in.

The sunny blue afternoons they spent in pursuit of John's hobby which was the collection of tombstones. He had, he claimed, the finest collection of tombstone epitaphs in Australia, all of them collected by himself, and he would spend hours on small, pleasant water-colours of some tombstone which had taken his fancy. The finest tombstones were, in his opinion, the work of a by-gone craftsman by name of Cobby (or so he signed himself) who had flourished in the eighteen-forties or fifties. Cobby specialized in a pleasant, hand-worked sandstone of mellowed cream-brown, and they scouted together through overgrown, abandoned, little graveyards in pursuit of the Master's works. A Cobby tombstone was distinguishable by its line, its perfect combination of hand-carved ornament and clean simplicity.

They found a beautiful specimen on a little, quiet hilltop at the back of Denthaven one Sunday afternoon towards the close of Shannon's stay and settled down contentedly; John to reproduce in water-colour the drooping willow, the golden lichen, and the creamy tints of Cobby's masterpiece; Shannon to lie on her back chewing grass contentedly and discoursing of the world at large.

"What I hate about going back to Sydney," she declared, addressing an old brown horse which was cropping among the graves, as much as John Terrill, "is that it seems so hopeless. Of course, Johnny, you're mad about soil and morbidly interested in tombstones, but you're not mad the way people are in the city. You haven't a closed mind. The people I seem to fall in with have all closed minds. They live in their own neat little systems where everything is simple and logical and sound, *until* you come to test it against someone else's system. It's like a lunatic asylum with every-one in sight thinking they're going to save the world. This wouldn't be so bad if they didn't try to convert you to their way of thinking. They're always insulted because you don't follow it earnestly, whole-heartedly. I don't believe you're listening. Damn you! Speak up!"

"Uh-hurm," her companion replied agreeably.

"Now if I go back and marry South Quilter, I'm committed for life to thinking whatever South thinks. He's like that. It pains him to see anyone unconvinced because he has the missionary spirit. Always busy like Merv Leggatt. And I'd be rushing around, organizing, organizing, sitting on committees for getting things done or abolishing this and that, when, dammit, I don't care a hoot in Hell. *I* don't mind if everyone is different from everyone else. What annoys me is this ceaseless gnawing and nagging and converting and proselytising. Of course, I don't mean the mass of the population is like that, but the people who come bubbling to the surface are. They're mad because civilization is mad and getting madder every day. I wish I could find a flaming mountain top and sit on it."

"Well, why don't you?"

"Because I've got to live, I suppose. Oh! I don't know. Just better give up thinking, and drift along. But it's mad all the same. I'm practically committed to marrying South Quilter."

John Terrill removed the spare brush from his mouth where he had been holding it for safety.

"I don't like the sound of this Quilter enthusiast," he remarked. "Look here, how about staying and marrying me?"

Shannon sat up on the grass. "I didn't think of that," she exclaimed truthfully. "That's nice of you, Johnny, but how would you keep me?"

"Well, you know," John said modestly, "it's no great snap. Matter-of-fact I hadn't thought of it till this minute. But we could manage, that's if you'd take it on."

"Let me think!" Shannon cried excitedly. "Oh! John, it would be grand!" She lay back in the grass with her hands behind her head. "But what about poor South? Think of Merv Leggatt, think of the bookshop going to rack and ruin."

"You're just as mad as anyone, Shannon. You have this idea you're indispensable. People always manage somehow. Another thing," he had the spare brush between his teeth and his articulation was somewhat muffled, "life isn't real and earnest in a city. Life is pretty futile and meaningless when you're jammed up against a million other people, but out in the open you can see things clearer. In a city you can't see the place for the people. I bet you'd like it," he added reasonably, "if you married me."

"I know I would. But, John darling, can I call you darling? . . I was just trying to be sensible."

"Why bother?" He held his head on one side and surveyed his water-colour, then added a tiny dab of bright yellow to the lichen on the stone. "You could keep chickens and bees, and slave around the place like a good little housewife and add to my income and feel hellish useful." He gave her his shy smile. "Don't think I'm trying to persuade you or anything like that."

She laughed at him. "I believe I will," she murmured. "I believe I'll just run away from all of them. Oh, John, it's a dreadfully bad habit this running away. You know I'm a coward, don't you? I ran away from Aunt Edith and Uncle Sladder. I ran away from one job after another. I don't suppose I'll ever cure myself now."

"Escape is different from running away. Say escape, it sounds nicer. If you'd come over here, I could kiss you."

"If you'd come over here, it would show you wanted to. If you do any more to that, you'll spoil it. Oh, John, I like you tremendously. You're so sane! Almost the only sane person I know. You're sure you won't regret it?"

"Not if you don't."

"This," Shannon said happily, "is what is known as a whirlwind court-ship."

III

To have a quiet wedding in Kerleuit was as difficult as having a quiet war. Although only Shannon's relatives and Mr. and Mrs. Sandleberry had been invited, those neighbours, acquaintances and onlookers who could not squeeze into the church, had to content themselves with standing around the doors and windows to see the fourth Hicks girl and Jack Terrill and comment on the probable motives of their marriage.

There was no honeymoon, for work at the farm had piled up, and it would need their united efforts to catch up; there was no buying of lounge suites or cut-glass dressing-table sets, because the cream-cheque was needed for urgent repairs; but Shannon had a glorious time with Mrs. Sandleberry cleaning the house and garden, the orchard and fowl run, and learning the neglected art of milking.

This was the last drop in Mrs. Hicks's cup of bitterness. She had welcomed Shannon's marriage, because she hated the idea of her going away again and had come to depend on her; but that she should be brought to the lowly status of a milker, breaking her back and hardening her hands, working herself to death for a man who hadn't even bought her decent furniture . . . no, it was wrong, it was dreadfully unfair.

"I didn't bring you up to it," Mrs. Hicks proclaimed. "All my life I fought against my girls milking. I wouldn't let your father have cows because I didn't want you brought to this. Why did I ever send you away or give you a chance? You might as well have stayed at home."

She had an additional grievance in that Shannon's father spent all his spare time lovingly tending John's cows. He felt that at last he had a part share in a nice little herd of Jerseys. It took Shannon some time to realize that cows have different characters, but even if the stooping hurt her back and arms and hands, she had a monetary interest in milking which repaid the toil. She co-opted Minnie Sandleberry as assistant dairy superintendent, and with Minnie, a stout, hearty, thunderous woman, she was soon on terms of the most intimate friendship. Their mutual admiration was founded on the same capacity for work, the same enjoyment of a joke; and they had much in common, planning bee-hives, a fowl-run, jam-making and pickling and all the small and, sometimes, profitable sidelines which the farmer's wife manages.

At Denthaven, when summer came again, there would be visitors staying at the hotels and boarding-houses, and Shannon was already planning the sale of vegetables direct to such places. She took over the accounts, the writing of business letters; and when the old, battered typewriter arrived, which she had inherited from the break-up of the U.C.D.L., she flung herself furiously on all John's neglected correspondence.

"I never knew such a woman," he declared, when, one fine Sunday afternoon, she refused to come out because she had too much to do. "You gather work round you like a hen scratching a nest. Now drop it. There's a grand little graveyard you haven't seen yet, way out along the coast road. I don't want you growing into an avaricious, stony-faced, grasping hag."

But it was for him that she worked hard, to free him and give him time for his real work, which was the chemistry of the soil. Little samples of soil occupied a shed to themselves, and, in time, Shannon came to understand what he was talking about, mainly through the process of reading his notes. Phosphoric acid, potash and sodium, became more than mere names, and nitrates took on an importance they had never had before.

John's discovery of little graveyards had originated in his plotting a soil map of Kerleuit and its environs for many miles. He had fallen into the habit of classifying the farmers of his acquaintance by their land. "He's got a patch of calcium-deficient acid soil that ought to be improved right away." Or, "Nice piece of ground Joe showed me, colloidal with a high magnesium concentration." But whenever Shannon suggested cunningly that he let her put his notes into a thesis, he evaded her. He was not, he said, going to have her shoving in her buttery snook and turning him into a tin-pot professor. His job was to find out all he could about soil. Someone else could go mucking about publishing articles in scientific journals.

But if he refused to dispute in print with the few other men in his line whom he respected, he was only too willing to dictate long, private letters to friends called "Mac" or "Bill" telling them what he was doing.

"Now you let me alone, young puss," he commanded, when she tried to alter his verbless sentences. "You take it down the way I say it and shut up, or you won't take it down at all. Running revolutions may be an art, but so's this. Just because you can deal with live people doesn't mean you know anything about live soil, and soil *is* alive, every particle of it. A revolution of whole populations in the dirt, that's what I'm after. Most of these chaps take dirt as though it was just an abstract mass, it isn't. Now don't stick in your oar."

"Right you are, John," his meek amanuensis would reply. They had a happy life, a busy life. In six months it seemed impossible that they had ever managed to exist without each other.

"You know what?" Minnie Sandleberry exclaimed to Shannon. "You're getting to look more like John and he's getting to look like you. It's a thing I've noticed when you get a couple suits each other. They don't talk, they just know what the other one's thinking about. Now me and George can be sitting by the fire with the kids in bed, not doing anything in particular, and I'll say: 'About little Sam's teeth . . .' and George'll finish the sentence: 'I was just thinking you ought to take him to the dentist.' You sort of blend in."

The blending-in process was perhaps accelerated by tremendous quarrels which broke out at less and less frequent intervals. Shannon and John quarrelled over some chance remark, some hasty judgment, and then fought it to exhaustion. "Just settling down," Minnie Sandleberry philosophically declared, when Shannon swore she was going back to Sydney, that she could not stand John's bad temper any longer. Sure enough the storm would blow over and, as for going back to Sydney, that was a vain boast. She had been spoiled for city life.

Amory Quinlan had sent down her books and her few belongings, and wrote that the shop was doing nicely, so Shannon did not feel quite such a guilty deserter. She had written the difficult letters to South Quilter and Merv Leggatt; she had broken the threads that bound her. She had escaped yet once again. The bursting into war of Europe, which had been brewing war for many years past, seemed far-off, like the howling of a gale to one sitting snug.

"The blister's burst," John commented, when the news came over the air. He seemed a little abstracted. "Everyone knew it was coming anyway."

"It's madness. It could have been stopped. Perhaps it won't reach this far."

"I don't know so much. This country is going to be in the same spot that Britain was when the Roman legions sailed away."

There was no sense in worrying. They could only wait for the radio news and the newspapers, while the terrible tide of suffering rolled and thundered around the other side of the world. The cows had to be milked; the ploughing done; Shannon sold her vegetables and eggs to the Denthaven hotels and boarding-houses, driving the old car down the bumpy road until she met the smooth coastal highway that swept past, ignoring their little obscure corner of the earth.

"How glad I'm not in the city," she exclaimed, after listening to a broadcast. "Women's auxiliaries, funds for this and that. I know I'm selfish, but I couldn't stand it." She felt sometimes uneasy and guilty, a deserter who had left the battle. At others, her vision of the madness and confusion of civilization stood by her. "Why don't you go on with your classifying, John? Surely that's more important than waiting for the news."

"Can't settle down to it," John muttered. The war was like a great, smoky cloud over all the bright fields, the clear skies. He seemed increasingly restless and troubled.

When a telegram came, he snatched it and slit it open before noticing that it was addressed to Shannon. "Sorry," he said unhappily. "Thought it might be for me."

It was from Beryl and announced: "Sladder copped at last. Ten years and lucky to get that. Better come and get Ma." This laconic message they deciphered together as meaning that Mr. Vincent Sladder, after many years of assorted illegality, had met the due reward of his professional activities.

"You'd better bring the old lady down here for a while," John suggested.

Shannon was reluctant to go back to Sydney, even for Aunt Edith, but John was eager that she should go. "Be a nice little holiday for you," he hinted. "I can manage."

"I suspect you of some evil design," Shannon responded. "Come on, what is it?"

"I simply think you owe it to the poor old lady to go up there now she's in a jam."

"Oh, very well," Shannon exclaimed. "If you won't tell me, you won't. You're a secretive, double-faced beast—I love you."

He drove her in to Kerleuit and saw her off on the morning train promising to carry the awful tidings to her mother. "She'll have a fit. Can't I just hear her?" John had a chuckle at his mother-in-law's expense, for she had impressed Kerleuit with the riches and respectability of her sister Edith for so long. "If it doesn't get in the local papers she'll be able to muffle it. Nobody ever reads the Sydney papers."

A sickening sense of loneliness overcame the departing passenger, as that casual, smiling figure, with the station platform, whirled backward from view. They had been so happy, so righteously happy; and now she was once more off on her journeyings. Well enough to say it was only a visit, only a flying rescue of poor old Aunt Edith; but nothing would ever be the same again. The halcyon time was broken.

"It doesn't matter," she thought defiantly. "We *have* been happy."

L

Twenty-three

I

BERYL WAS SO VOLUBLE concerning her own generosity that it was hard to get out of her the full story of Mr. Sladder's downfall.

"There's one thing you can't say of me," Beryl declared, as she drove Shannon from the station, "and that is that I ever went back on a pal. If you knew what I've gone through with Ma—Joseph tearing out handfuls of his hair—bailing out Pop Sladder and mucking about with lawyers. The old goat didn't have a leg to stand on, and what beats me is that he only got ten years. He ought to be doing a life sentence."

"What did they get him on?"

"Carrying out an illegal operation to procure a certain event," Beryl repeated sonorously. "Not manslaughter."

"Why did he want to go in for that game?" Shannon asked impatiently. "I thought that blessed home for neurotics and halfwits was minting money."

"I don't believe it. Besides Pop Sladder must have been lowering the population figures for years, and he'd built up a nice little clientele. The trouble with him was," Beryl said severely, "that he simply couldn't let a chance go by of making money. If there was a rich, ripe opportunity of raking in the shekels, he just had to have his claws around it. He wasn't the only one lowering the birth-statistics of this fair city, not by a long chalk. Seems pretty hard when you think of the number of doctors and chemists and philanthropists in the same line of business—practically one of our major industries. Someone was needed for an example to frighten the others, so they picked out Pop."

"How about Aunt Edith?" Shannon asked.

"Well, that's where you come in. Don't think I'm wishing her onto you, but you know what Joe is. I can't have the two of them on my hands, especially now when I'm changing over to war production. Just got the contract the other day. Nice little line of officers' shirts. I'd take Ma in with me, because she certainly knows all there is about getting the most

292

work out of a girl, but she doesn't seem to take an interest. A nice little holiday in your neck of the woods might buck her up. I've told her she can come in with me any time. Matter of fact she could buy a half-interest and we could expand the factory out of sight with her capital." Beryl paused and considered. "I think she's got a soft spot for old Pop and she's going round saying I've got dictaphones in the walls and she's shadowed by strange men. Honestly, I think she's going right off her rocker at last."

"The home was in her name, I take it?"

"It was. Nothing will induce her to go back to it. You'll have to see about storing the furniture and getting a lawyer." Beryl heaved a sigh of relief. "I'm glad you've come, Shanno. I can tell you I've been having a hell of a time."

"Well, if you'd told me before I would have been here before," Shannon snapped.

"Thought you'd see it in the papers. Pop got a page in *Truth,* and the judge's remarks," Beryl added judicially, "were hot stuff. How about a drink before we eat? Hey, Ma!" With three servants Beryl had never cured herself of the habit of yelling down the hall. "I s'pose she's in her room."

Aunt Edith was in her room. She was huddled in a chair looking lost and forlorn. She kissed Shannon without warmth.

"Hello, Auntie," Shannon greeted her. "I came as soon as I could."

"That was very good of you." Aunt Edith said no more until Beryl had flung out to see why the telephone was not answered. Then she turned with an extraordinary intensity and gripped her niece's hand. "I can't stay here," she said rapidly. "They're all spying on me, particularly Beryl. I hear their voices in the night whispering outside my door."

"That will be all right," Shannon said gently. "You come and stay with me, darling, until things settle down a bit."

"I don't want to be with that chemist Terrill," Aunt Edith said, in the same rapid, dry voice. "You remember he tried to poison me. I wouldn't trust him." She looked at Shannon suspiciously. "You're all in league. All plotting."

This was an unexpected development. "We won't talk about it now," Shannon suggested. "Have you seen . . . Uncle Vincent lately?"

"Beryl took me out to see him." Aunt Edith shivered slightly. "A dreadful place."

"Well, let's not talk about that either. If I were to go out and ask him and he thought you ought to come with me, would you come?"

"I don't know." Aunt Edith shook her head uneasily. "He was never a good man. I should have known he would come to a bad end. All those years when my poor husband was dying," she wandered on strangely, "Vincent was staying at our place . . . at the Clayton. My own husband dying and he deliberately mesmerised me into sin. I should have known then that his guilt would find him out." Shannon was amazed. Aunt Edith's idea that Uncle Sladder's ten years was the punishment not of his professional activities, but of some old-time trifling with his boarding-house landlady seemed to her the height of egotism. "Oh! it's my fault as much as his," Aunt Edith went on fiercely. "You can't escape just punishment. I thought when I married him that I would atone." She shook her head again with a virtuous severity. "He laughed at me. He never felt his own wickedness. But I *knew*, I knew his sins would find him out."

Beryl kicked at the door, and was admitted carrying a tray. "If there is one thing I can do," she declared vigorously, "it's mix a drink. Get this inside you, Shannon, and then we'll eat."

"Won't you wait for Joe?" Shannon asked. It was Saturday, and on Saturday Mr. Litchin was usually at home.

"Oh, he's out annoying Sasha with his troubles."

Shannon did not need to be told that the presence of Aunt Edith in his home was enough to upset a more stable gentleman than Joseph Litchin. Aunt Edith, during the meal, tested the food suspiciously, and Shannon racked her brains for subjects of conversation which would not lead around to the absent Mr. Sladder. She was going to have trouble with Aunt Edith and must write at once to John for his advice. Perhaps she could ask him to ring her long-distance.

The three women sat in silence; Aunt Edith gloomy and preoccupied; Shannon already homesick; and Beryl restless and fidgety.

"I'm not sure we weren't better off," she burst out at last, "back in the old days when we had to sweat with a lot of boarders." Sourly she eyed her grand cut-glass, her splendid dinner-service. "Where's it got us, that's what I want to know? Shannon milking cows, Ma up a gum-tree, and me still working."

"You're only working because you don't know what to do with yourself if you stop."

"I could go loping round to afternoon teas and charity bazaars like
a lot of goops I know. But where does it get you? Beryl poured herself
another drink. She drank a good deal too much, Shannon thought, and
her new hair-dye did not suit her. "I can't see much sense in things."

The only realities, Shannon suggested, were hunger and love; when you
were not hungry or in love, you just filled in your time, scrambling for
power. The malady of power was what people suffered from most.

"Don't you believe it," Beryl replied. "Work, that's what everyone
needs, lots of work."

"Yes, but what's the use of work if, as you say, it isn't getting you anywhere? You're only trying to fill out a sense of your own importance.
Every human being wants to be important. We even read books to
increase our sense of power. Everything we do is a clutching at power
over other lives, trying to expand into them. We aren't content with our
own life. Nobody carps at the things civilization can give us, cars and
radio sets and fine clothes and houses; but it's the way we get those
things that puts a curse on them, the curse of slavery. So that men can
live free, easy lives, other men are turned into white ants without air
or sunlight. What we're doing in the cities is breeding white ants, not
men. We drain away the lives of men into machines and factories, then
wonder why we have half-men, half-women, monstrosities."

Beryl rang for dessert. She made no answer to this outburst which, she
felt, was only old Shanno blowing off steam after a weary, irritating trip.
"Back to your soap box," she said briefly. "Ever see anything of that pal
of yours, Whoosit-Quilter?"

"No."

Aunt Edith broke her gloomy silence. "Shannon's trouble," she observed,
"has always been this unladylike shouting. I'm sure, Beryl, that that girl
has her ear against the door."

"What's the use of your money to you, Beryl?" Shannon asked sullenly.
"If you had any children to leave it to . . ."

Beryl was about to point out that Shannon was in no position to bring up
that subject, but she restrained herself. "I get a kick out of running my factory," she replied with commendable good-humour. "I don't see what good

people who have children are doing with themselves with this war on."

"For behold the days are coming," Aunt Edith quoted gloomily, "in which they shall say, Blessed are the barren."

The conversation was veering around unconsciously to Mr. Sladder's profession. It was like a sore toe, mercilessly in danger of being trodden on. Despite Beryl's warning shake of the head, Shannon refused to give up the last word.

"It's like my old friends, the banana-flies," she said with forced lightness. "When times are good and there's plenty of bananas, they breed out of sight. When there's no food, and they're crowded in the test jar, they stop breeding. If you crowd people in cities and don't give them enough food or too many anxieties and complications, they stop breeding."

Aunt Edith rose from the table. "You are a terrible girl," she exclaimed. "I am going to lie down. I have a headache."

"Now, there you go!" Beryl remonstrated, as Aunt Edith swept from the room. "Nagging and nagging. You might have known you'd upset her."

"We were just discussing an abstract problem," Shannon insisted.

"You can't discuss an abstract problem. It always boils down to a personal problem. Have some of this liquor? Shut up about children and let's talk about winning the war."

"No one will win the war." Shannon had been rendered all the fiercer and more dogmatic by Beryl's excellent cellarage. "Except the machines. What this war will do is to bring the age of machines closer. The day will come," she pointed a prophetic finger at Beryl, "when every city will be a great, living, humming machine, and the humans in it will be bacteria crawling about its entrails, tinkering with it and keeping it in good health. They won't be able to get out because they will have lost the power; they will be frightened and uneasy, unless they are in with a crowd of fellow-bacteria. They will breed and mate and move in the machine-cities. Why, I shouldn't be surprised if you haven't a couple of million of bacteria in you at this moment thinking they run *you*. I have a revolution going on at the moment in my stomach."

"Well, let's not talk about the war," Beryl cut in impatiently. "Trouble is you and I haven't much to talk about, have we? We don't know the same people, we don't work in the same place. I can't ask about your farm, you can't ask about my factory."

"Tell me more about Uncle Sladder," Shannon responded. "Our common acquaintance."

Beryl shook her head. "If ever I was sick of any subject!"

"Aunt Edith believes that Sladder was brought to his doom by the hand of fate because years and years ago he was fool enough to sleep with her illicitly. Such colossal egotism!"

"Cripes!" Beryl breathed. "Imagine poor old Ma being led astray. However, I don't suppose I should laugh. Poor old girl's had a rotten time. What it is to have a conscience! Now Vince Sladder never had any more conscience than a snake. This'll give you an idea. One time he discovers that one of his lady patients is about to bleed to death on him and, on the principle of always disposing of the body, before it becomes a corpse, he calls in his dear friend Dr. Knowles, and they dump this poor woman in the tram waiting-room and leave her there. Sooner or later some passing Samaritan sees she's a goner and calls the ambulance. That woman was dying in hospital with two detectives camped beside her bed hammering questions at her whenever she regained consciousness, and all she said was: 'I done a big wash,' and died. She left four children and a husband dependent on her. Huh! wonder they didn't get Uncle Sladder years ago, the women he's killed."

"Why didn't she give him away?"

"Just feminine loyalty," Beryl said cynically. "Just the heart of gold."

They sat for some little time in silence contemplating the problem.

II

Sunday, with the September leafage glowing against a blue sky, tempted Shannon to stroll through her old haunts to the Domain. She had avoided the people and places of pre-marriage days from a sense that she was once more a stranger. She had lost touch with the thrumming, throbbing world of business and pleasure, of plans and activities which had once submerged her, as it still submerged them. Certain relationships embodied in the perceived universe are essentially interconnected, so that they only exist in the interconnection. If all the people who took for granted the necessity of living in a certain way in this city were to suddenly lose that conviction, that will to live together, would they see that this city existed only as a phenomenon whose existence vanished with that interconnection?

Shannon had vanished and was lost, because she was no longer part of the woven mesh of so many other lives, the huge unmanageable mesh in which hundreds struggled and fought like stranded fish. She was homesick for the empty green of the paddocks, the enormous light skies of Kerleuit. But for Aunt Edith and her furniture and belongings, her tenacious hallucinations, such a warm, summery afternoon might be better spent lying in the grass of some abandoned graveyard, while John painted his small, clear water-colours of Cobby's sandstone.

Towards the Domain trickled the intermittent, dark streams of people, strolling up past the brown bulk of the Cathedral, across Hyde Park, past the vendors of peanuts and oranges and newspapers. She knew the Domain, from the small evangelistic crowds with a harmonium, the health experts proving that a cold bath and a meal of raw carrots every morning would save your life, to the huge mass meetings with banners and bellowings. On one side of it, through the trees, reared the bulk of the huge hospital and the library; on the other, screened by more trees, the Art Gallery, while the Gardens sloped in a green tracery of tree-tops to the water. A definition of Sydney, Shannon thought, was that it was confusion surrounded on three sides by water and on the fourth by the hospital.

This great, green forum was the voice of the city, but the siren screech of speakers sounded faint and thin and meaningless under the wide sky, across the stretch of grass. People wandered into the Domain and were lost in it; strolling from one group to another; listening to advocates of medicine, religion, policy, with the same, detached, slightly weary air; a multitude of strangers solidifying here into a large clot, there into a smaller clot, with little particles detaching themselves or joining or drifting away again; all fluid, free-swimming, active, all with different motives and lives and anxieties; all searching and restless.

They were puzzled by the war; they had come to hear the different views of it with a judicious nicety, views that would never find expression in their morning paper.

On one large platform stood George Benson, his full-throated, brass-lunged roar hardly audible at the edge of the crowd. Above him hung a red flag and a large placard announcing: "Not a Man, Not a Ship, Not a Gun for Imperialist War." Far over the other side of the green slope,

Comrade Leggatt was doggedly and logically preparing to follow Sasha, who had just left her place under a flag of the hammer-and-sickle hanging in peaceable companionship with a Union Jack and a banner: "This is a Just War."

Sasha had been giving an impassioned and eager speech on the necessity of all good comrades joining the army. "Comrades," she cried, "we must trust the Workers' Fatherland. Whatever the Soviets say must be right."

Leggatt taking her place had a well-reasoned analysis of the events leading up to the war. He was not, in his own mind, satisfied, but the C.C. had spoken, and his not to reason why, his but to see that the policy was carried through. In a week or so time, with the signing of a pact between Russia and Germany, the war would be anathema, but in the meantime it was right and just. He looked across at George Benson, the traitor and recreant, with a real glow of anger.

George, honest George, brought up in the old school, which accepted as an article of faith that all wars arose out of the contradictions of capitalism and were noxious to the workers, had been too slow and heavy-footed for such lightning changes as a well-oiled Marxist mind must make in following the tricky little twists of a changing situation. George doggedly clung to the idea that no war was a good war, and he had been promptly expelled and spewed forth. Wherefore, feeling lonely with no party to keep him from the bewildering nakedness of making up his own mind, he had joined with the next best of the unorthodox groups, trying to keep from himself the awful realization that he had become that lowest of abominations, a Trotskyite.

He, too, could see his old comrade, Mervyn Leggatt, across the Domain advocating the direct opposite to his own policy. The sight urged him to greater efforts; he shook his fist at the upturned faces; he roared at them; he flung up his hands to heaven and called them fools.

"Letting yourselves be led by the nose!" he yelled. "No brains, no brains!"

Intrigued by his anguished roars, the language that they loved, the outer rim of Mervyn Leggatt's clot began to melt and dwindle, to drift over to the opposition platform. Mervyn, truth be told, was not an inspiring speaker. He depended upon minute analysis rather than im-

L*

passioned proclamation; but, as he saw this exodus, his light eyes glittered with a zealot's fire. He began to denounce George with a cold and bitter bale; he traced George's career as a snake from its earliest wrigglings.

"Traitors!" he spat at them. "Dividing the workers, paid by the hireling murderers who sabotaged the great reconstruction of the Soviets, paid to sabotage, wreck, divide and leave us powerless. There is only one good turn you can do a traitor and that is to put him against a wall and shoot him."

He was lashing himself into a lather of hate. For years he had worked with George; he had gone to gaol and shared his last meat-pie with George; and the remembrance goaded him to greater heights of invective. He, Mervyn Leggatt, the pitiless and cool, had felt a human emotion for this man. It was a judgment on him. His trained eye had caught sight of yet another traitor, standing, looking up at him with that cool, judging glance which he knew of old, a glance with a little glint of amusement in it. At her, as well as George, he flung that dreadful diatribe on traitors, his face set, his voice rising harsh and cold.

"Down with them!" he shouted. "Fascist traitors and murderers. Tear down their lies."

The more earnest of his followers, with a roar of enthusiastic discipleship, set out at a quick trot for the banner flaring out "Not a Man, Not a Ship, Not a Gun for Imperialist War." Leggatt hesitated, then with the quick dialectic resolve to seize the situation and use it, he sprang from his platform and set off, placing his small, wiry frame well in the forefront of the attackers. George Benson beheld the approaching squad of indignant believers, and as they came, he roared defiance.

"Do we," he shouted, "stop other people from speaking their minds? No, we believe in freedom, in the democratic right of all peoples to determine their own way of living and thinking. We . . ." But his voice was drowned in the battle that raged briefly below his platform.

The banner "Not a Man, Not a Ship, Not a Gun" was wrenched down and torn up; its supports broken into so many staves which defenders and attackers tore from one another's grasp and used as weapons.

The contest was brief, for the police arrived from their brick stronghold, strategically situated under a large tree on the top of a rise, and marched off all engaged in combat, among the fighters Leggatt still full of ferocity, bile and martyrdom. George Benson, gripping the remains of his banner, had the unspeakable anguish of seeing himself ignored, and those same police form a polite cordon around his platform, so that he might unmolested continue his attacks on the Government and the Imperialist warmongers.

It was enough to break any man's spirit, but this was not the worst blow in store for George and his party. A week or so later Russia signed the pact with Germany, and Leggatt and his companions decided that the war was an Imperialist war; and the Federal Government declared Merv Leggatt and his friends illegal; seized their printing plant; smashed up their bookshops; raided their homes and created havoc generally in their ranks. George Benson and his friends, the true enemies of the capitalist class, were yet once again dishonourably ignored. They wrote indignantly to the papers pointing out this slight and injustice, and the Attorney-General, when these protests were brought to his notice, belatedly but with gratifying liberality agreed to their request and declared them illegal also.

It was with a thoughtful face that Shannon strolled towards the gates with the thinning crowd, as the darkness turned the sky a deeper blue, and the lights of the serried houses, thick as barnacles on the hill, put out little tentacles of light. At the gate, like that ancient sentry of Pompeii, who had stood at guard while the flame and soot fell from Heaven, was her old friend of the U.C.D.L., the tough, nobbly Morry Crowther, still surreptitiously offering papers and magazines to the unheeding passers-by.

"Well, if it isn't Shannon!" he beamed. "Where you been, comrade."

"I'm out of things now, Morry," Shannon told him rather wearily, as she fished in her purse for money, not because she wanted his "literature," but because it would gladden Morry's heart to sell them.

"There's times I wisht I was," Morry murmured wistfully. "If I could get a job."

"Morry," Shannon asked abstractedly, "what do you really think of the revolutionary movement? Come on, now. Honest."

"Well, seeing you're out of it, Shannon," Morry said in a hoarse whisper, "I'll tell you. My old dad used to say it in his day, and I guess it still holds good. He used to say: 'If God was to issue white wings to every genuine working-class leader, the whole damn lot of them would be footsore.'"

Twenty-four

Aunt Edith was in a pitiful state of hesitation. She could not stay where she was; she hated the thought of getting herself in the power of her sister; her brother-in-law and the "chemist Terrill," but for all her doubtings, she had a real dependence on Shannon. There was something about Shannon, some core of hard rock on which poor, bewildered Aunt Edith rested the sole of her foot. Beryl, whom she had always liked best, seemed to have changed, and besides Beryl could not have her staying permanently, for there was Beryl's terrible husband to consider, a man Aunt Edith could not endure at any price. Without Shannon, she saw herself condemned to loneliness among strangers, for she had no friends, and she clung to Shannon.

The first hint her niece had of Aunt Edith's resolve to follow her into the wilderness was when the old lady began to talk of the benefits which might accrue to those who pleased her. She had sole control of the ill-gotten gains of the Psycho-Coordinator. The sale of the Blessingford Home, while it hung fire, would bring her in a useful sum, and she had certain shares in that Vibro-Massage firm which the unlucky Mr. Sladder had helped to found. She mentioned these investments, as though by chance, and Shannon smiled secretly. She did not mind Aunt Edith convincing herself that her shadow cast a blessing, that Shannon would never lose by her hospitality. If it comforted Aunt Edith to think that her niece had a wholesome respect for money, there was no harm in it. Aunt Edith began to look forward to the trip.

"I have just a few things I want to do myself," Shannon told her, "and then we'll start."

"The few things" resolved into one definite errand. In the old days of the Pro Club and the U.C.D.L. she had been on good terms with a quick-eyed, fiery little doctor, a lady with a tremendous vocabulary and a truculent set of spikes concealing her sensitiveness.

"Well, come on up then," growled Dr. Worthington into the telephone.

"Three fifteen," but when Shannon appeared, she greeted her much more softly. "Where have you been, darling? I heard you'd gone to live in some unheard-of place. And you're married? Now, isn't that nice!" Her tone was sardonic, but half-affectionate. "How about coming out to dinner tonight? Bring your husband if you've got him with you. It isn't a big dinner." Dr. Maida Worthington loved giving dinners. She had an almost oriental opulence where food and drink were concerned. "You're still too thin," she observed critically. She herself was far from thin. Then, taking on her sharpest professional manner, "What's the trouble?"

"I want to know why I don't have any children."

Dr. Worthington rolled her eyes at the ceiling. "Am I God?" she asked, and then incredulously, "You don't mean you *want* to have children?"

"Certainly."

"What an odd idea!" Dr. Worthington commented sardonically. "Now almost everyone in my waiting room has quite the opposite aim. We must really see what can be done to gratify your original ambition. Let's have a look at you."

Shannon bore the deep-sea soundings patiently.

"I should say it was chronic underfeeding," Dr. Worthington said thoughtfully. "You do expect a lot, you know, darling. Nature intended you to marry at the age of about eighteen, before your bones or your prejudices were set. What do you do? You live on coffee and cigarettes, you don't eat, you work too hard for years. You're a case of chronic malnutrition, not enough to kill you, not even enough to bring you up with a jolt. But if you work too hard and don't eat, something's got to starve. Now, I'd say," she scratched her chin reflectively, "that if you lived a nice open-air life with plenty of milk and eggs and green vegetables . . ."

"But, Maida, I'm wallowing in them. I milk seven cows myself."

"Well, milk less and drink more." Dr. Worthington snapped. "Even then I can't promise anything. Say a couple of years to recuperate and you might build up."

"There's nothing you can do about it?"

Maida Worthington rolled her expressive eyes upward once more. "Am I God?" She scribbled a prescription in a careless, illegible hand. "You get this made up and take it. Only iron, darling."

"It's strange," Shannon said, twisting the paper reflectively. "My grandmother had fourteen children, my mother had six, and I have none."

"Are you coming out to dinner tonight?" Dr. Worthington asked.

"I have to wait in for a long-distance call from my husband."

"Tell him I said you're not to work hard and you're to eat a lot." As she let Shannon out, Dr. Worthington called with ribald gusto: "And keep trying!"

Once more in the wide street Shannon tore the prescription into little pieces and shrugged her shoulder as the pieces fell in the gutter. Perhaps, if she were patient and lazy, as Maida said, she might retrieve her lost opportunities, but it was hard to expect a woman to change now. She went off to book the tickets for herself and Aunt Edith, and then returned to prowl impatiently around the telephone. John had said in his letter that he would ring her at seven o'clock that night and it seemed a century until seven struck. A quarter of an hour later the call came through, and then she lost all pleasure in his voice; it sounded faint and distant.

"John, darling, I'm so glad you rang. I've booked our tickets and we're coming the day after tomorrow."

"Speak slower, Shannon, I can't hear you . . ."

"I said we've booked our tickets." She lowered her voice.

"Good." John always had this maddening habit of being perfectly audible over a telephone and reproving anyone else who was not. "Shannon there's something I must tell you, something that may make you alter your plans. I've enlisted."

Shannon said dully: "You needn't have done it behind my back."

"It wasn't behind your back, Shannon. I'd thought it all out. I thought perhaps you might want to stay in Sydney with your aunt."

"You're wrong. We'll be in Kerleuit in a couple of days."

"Shannon, I don't want you to be stewing and grinding over this all the way. I just thought I should tell you. Shannon, don't be angry."

"I'm not angry, John."

"Say you love me."

"I love you."

A new metallic voice cut in on the conversation. "Three mins'up," it croaked. "Want-nextension?"

"Yes . . ." John's voice was drowned by Shannon's. "No, we don't want an extension." The line went dead.

Aunt Edith, who had been hovering in the lounge-room politely out of earshot, came questioningly into the hall."

"Is everything all right, Shannon?"

"Everything's all right, Aunt Edith. You can start packing."

"Well, I'm sure that's very kind of Mr. Terrill, John, I should say. You know, Shannon, I appreciate the loyal, kind way you have behaved, dear. After all, I can't live forever, and if you and John should have any children . . ."

"Don't talk about it, Aunt Edith," Shannon said gently. "Let's just think about going home."

She had adjusted her mind rapidly enough to the Machiavellian workings of John Terrill's mind. He was so used to her as the dependent of her aunt that he had taken it for granted that she would resume her old place by that lady's side. If she did, he had reasoned, she would not be left to the miserable pittance of a soldier's wife, for she could sell the farm. Knowing John so well she should have been suspicious of his restlessness, his inability to work. She gave the same little pitiful shrug she had given that afternoon when she tore the prescription in pieces.

"It was nice while it lasted," she said aloud.

She stood for a minute staring attentively at the telephone table and wondering why she had never noticed before that it had a highly polished surface of green glass. As she looked down, she could see her head and shoulders dimly shadowed as in water. Down her eyes plunged into that stony green, as though they sought to read the future. Her mind was completely empty, empty and hard as the glass slab. An impulse to escape from Beryl's bright, well-furnished, rather hideous house sent her wandering through the lounge to a glassed-in verandah where, by opening the door, she could step out on the wet glass.

A light rain was falling, and to her bare arms it felt like the tickling of tiny insects' feet. As she stood motionless in the light that fell from the lounge-room window, letting the tiny particles of moisture settle on her, she wondered what she was going to do, but not caring particularly. She felt she had lost the capacity for suffering. Or had she ever had any? Olly's death had affected her more perhaps than any other single event in her life. She had been tortured by the troubles of others, pressed and suffocated by the weight of misery which from time to time she had encountered, a diffused misery penetrating everything like this fine rain; but now, when her life was torn up by the roots, when the man she had come to regard as part of herself, was about to leave her, she felt hardly anything.

She lifted her bare arm and noticed in the light that the rain had given it a fine, silver fur. She brushed her fingers down the wet hairs and the cold damp of it helped her, brought her back to reality. She remembered that member of the Proletarian Club (Who was it? She could not remember his name) who used to write stories about householders going out into their front gardens and letting the rain "beat on their naked flesh." The recollection made her smile a little. Aimlessly, she wandered down towards Beryl's ostentatious wrought-iron gates and then back again. A queer feeling came over her that she was only a ghost with no real existence of its own. Somewhere, in a hot, brightly lit room, her real self in some other body was living a tempestuous, anxious life, about which she knew nothing. Perhaps all the people in this city were part of herself, different scraps of her life, going their own way with their own cares and fears, while she experienced this dim anaesthetic of non-being.

John would be killed. There was something about the man that invited death. Joining the army was an expression of a secret vice in him, a peculiar will-to-die that she had sometimes sensed. He was drawing on his fate, writing in the sum of that blank cheque each man is issued when he is born. She regarded him, not as self-sacrificing, but as purely selfish. There were men in whom the impulse to live throbbed only faintly. She did not much want to live herself. Quite often she found herself thinking "When I am dead," with a little secret sigh of relief, but she had not written in the sum of years on that blank cheque.

John was the bourgeois gentleman of the long-forgotten story who, with so many others, was pushed by vague impulses out of the brightly lit room into the darkness. This will to live, she thought with a clear brain, perhaps the lack of it in us, was what drew John and me together. South Quilter, Merv Leggatt, Sasha, Beryl, have all that feeling of their own identity, their own vital principle. They believe living and the small things that make up living count enormously. If I do not believe the death is any great evil, why was it that Olly . . . Perhaps I felt so sore over Olly because she had that will to live more than anyone and it betrayed her.

Brushing the silver fur from her arms mechanically, she walked back to the gate and looked through the wrought-iron bars like a child. Tear off a crab's claw, and it lives and renews the claw; let a bird tear out the entrails of a locust, and it lives and sings as though nothing had happened. To live! To live! The desperate will to go on existing, however tortured and mangled the life! Just to go on crawling and suffering. This was the principle that upheld them all from the worms to the angels. Perhaps this war was a sign that the will to live was breaking down. There was a desperate gap in the minds of men through which the darkness had pushed its way. The madness she had noticed, the avoidance of children, were both signs of a contest between the will to live and the circumstances which made that living intolerable. She struck the iron gate lightly and it rattled a little. The noise had the same effect on her nerves that such a noise might have had if she were under a real anaesthetic.

"Wake up," it said. "Wake up. Go on!"

Simultaneously the head of Aunt Edith appeared cautiously poked from the doorway of that glassed-in verandah.

"Shannon," she called, "are you out here in the rain?"

Shannon drew a deep breath and unconsciously straightened her shoulders. The realization that John had enlisted became a terrible pain in the middle of her chest, a suffocating feeling of indignation, despair, hate and loss.

"Yes, Aunt Edith," she called lightly. "Just an attack of indigestion."

She went quickly up the path to the bright light of the lounge-room and the grey bony face of Aunt Edith perplexed but affectionate.

II

The bustle of their return; the responsibility of Aunt Edith; the luggage; the long journey; and, when she arrived, the preoccupations of the house; even the flood of news from Minnie Sandleberry, helped to set a surface over the grave indignation which seethed like lava through Shannon's thoughts. Aunt Edith approved of the farm. She was more interested and cheerful than Shannon had known her since the old boarding-house days.

"I wonder if you would mind," she asked at tea-time, glancing around the bare room, "if I asked them to send some of my furniture down here? It is no use whatever stored away."

This furniture of Aunt Edith's, particularly a mahogany sideboard, had been a bone of contention when she was selling the Clayton House. Where Aunt Edith went, there she was followed by a trail of huge crates containing her household gods. Shannon's lack of such impedimenta seemed to Aunt Edith as shocking as nakedness.

John cast an uneasy glance at his wife's set face. "Shannon told you I'd enlisted, Aunt Edith?"

"Why yes, John." Aunt Edith called him John quite naturally. "But she will be keeping the farm?"

Shannon nodded. "I'll be keeping on this place, John, if that suits you?" Her voice was mild, almost expressionless. She might have been asking if she would give him another cup of tea. "We might even take in a few boarders over the holidays."

It was not until Aunt Edith had retired to the stretcher-bed which John had borrowed that he felt free to open up the very sore subject of his enlistment. He had got leave to settle his affairs, but if she persisted in her determination to remain on the place, it would complicate all his plans.

"What I thought," he suggested, almost humbly, "was that you might go back to Sydney or Melbourne."

"I could always get some kind of a job, couldn't I?" Shannon agreed, still in that dangerously mild voice. "I'm so capable?"

"Yes, I'd thought of that."

"But you weren't willing to talk it over with me first?"

He was silent.

"You just disposed of me quite easily with your other chattels?"

"Now, Shannon, what's the use of being savage?"

"You don't expect me to sing: 'We don't want to lose you but we think you ought to go'? That's a little too much." She cupped her chin in her hand and watched him intently.

"Shannon, I never wanted you to become a drudge, a farmer's wife. I hate seeing you worked to death, milking and cleaning and washing, always eternally busy about something, a sort of domestic Martha. Don't hate me so, darling."

"I don't hate you, John. You were always so sane and honest, the only sane person I'd ever known, I thought. And now the insane streak is coming out. Why of all people do you need to fling yourself into this? Your work is so important. There are thousands of men who aren't doing anything half as important."

"Shannon, no man is more important than another. You can't weigh and judge and measure men. I just felt I had to do it. And I was afraid," he admitted, "of what you'd say. Yes, I was cowardly enough to wait until you were out of the road."

"And it wasn't just an impulse?" she asked, her voice still mild and reasonable. "You had it planned all the time?"

"You see I knew your views. You'd told me so often that this war was just another kind of madness. But, damn it!" he burst out, "if the rest of the human race is mad, then I'm mad too, and I'd sooner share with other people than sit aside and judge." He began to wander about the room, fingering a book on a shelf, dropping it, taking up one small article after another. "You're an anarchist, Shannon. You simply refuse to accept people as they are, things as they are. But you can't alter them."

"Then why did you join the army if you don't think you can alter things as they are?"

He would have been happier if she had stormed at him, wept, done anything except preserve that steely self-control. "I joined up because it was the only thing anyone could do."

"You joined it to escape, to escape life. Half the world is committing suicide and you join that half. It isn't I who's running away now, John. It's you."

"Have it your own way," he said sullenly. "You might try to understand me, Shannon, instead of judging."

"Weren't you happy with me?"

"You know I was happy. Damnably happy."

"And you had to leave me, leave this place . . . Oh! I know there's no sense in talking, but do sit down and stop prowling around like a trapped cat. Tell me this," her voice was suddenly fierce, "if we had had any children . . . would that have made a difference?"

"Yes, no, I don't think so. I felt I just had to go." He was profoundly miserable and indignant that she should make him feel guilty. "You turn everything upside down. I'm not deserting you or skulking away. I'm just doing what any man would do."

"Yes," she sighed. "That's what I'm complaining about." Then, with a swift, impulsive movement, she caught at his hand. "Let's not waste time arguing. There's so little time left. Let's not say any more. Just kiss and forget it."

"But, Shannon, we've got to settle what you're going to do."

"I've told you. I'm staying here. Aunt Edith will look after the house.

I'll have to do what I can with the Jerseys. Why, if it comes to that, Dad would sooner give up his job at the butter-factory than see a neat, little herd of milkers go out of the family."

"But I tell you I didn't want you to drudge," he argued wearily.

"Well, if I must drudge at something," she said more cheerfully, "I prefer drudging at what I like. This is my place. I'm sticking to it. And if you come back with a few arms and legs blown off," her eyes filled with tears, but she brushed them hurriedly away, "there'll be somewhere for you to come. See?"

He was moved by her attempt to stifle those tears. "I haven't treated you well, Shannon. I'm sorry I . . ." She came over and curled up beside him, her arms about his neck.

"When do you have to go into camp?"

"In a few days." His face was averted.

"Well, let's make the most of them. Let's go and look at the sea and neglect the place and be late with the milking and use up all the petrol we can, and then when you get leave and come home, Auntie will have the house all civilized and full of silver forks and cake plates. She's really a grand old stick." When he looked lost and miserable like a little boy, Shannon could do nothing but console. "And I'll have Minnie Sandleberry and George, and George's two boys are big enough to help. You'll see. We'll manage somehow."

He began to be soothed, but the lost look was still about him. "You always were a demon for responsibility, Shannon."

"Then when you come back, it will all still be here. You can go on sorting soil and testing it for amino-acids and you'll be surprised at all the new chicken-runs and the pigs . . . I think I'll have some pigs and turkeys. And, by Golly!" she was talking on and on just to smooth over the hurt, "I'll have Auntie write to old Briscoe, you remember, Briscoe and the Wyandottes, prize show-birds, every one. Briscoe is living on the old-age pension and he'd love to come and bring his hens."

"Don't complicate things too much," he warned her. "I know you, Shannon. One of these days you'll want to up and quit. You'll just walk out and leave the lot."

She laughed. "But, darling, how could I? I'll be waiting here, you see, a good, faithful wife . . ."

"You make me feel a skunk."

"Well, stop feeling a skunk." She kissed him soundly. "There! Now, let's go out for a walk to clear our heads, and you can tell me all about the sergeant and the camp. Think of the beautiful parcels I'll be sending you."

She went on talking brightly, carefully, while her hungry eyes watched him, storing up the way his hair fell over his forehead, the clean profile, the little wrinkles around his mouth, the few grey hairs above his ears. In a few days' time she would not have anything of him except letters and the waiting for him to get leave. She would have to fill in the days, work very hard, so that at night sne might be able to sleep instead of lying awake thinking of him. There were so many women lying awake all over the world. Into her head came the words that South Quilter had uttered on that night, when they had looked over the dark water towards the glow of the city. "I think of women lying awake at night."

Twenty-five

The rising sun was as yet only a pale, upward shining from the sea's rim, but above the place where the sun would presently appear, glowed a great star that drew an added lustre from the light below. To the west, in a sky of a deep, clear blue, the old moon was sinking, as in the other scale of a balance; yet another magnificent star poised immediately above it, a star that fronted its brother, the sun's friend, with an antagonistic radiance.

"You may be rising now," the setting star seemed to say, as it flamed across the deep spaces. "You may be rising triumphant, the sun's friend, and I be sinking with the old moon, but we are thus, brother, for only a moment in many years. The skies change, brother, and we, the sweet bubbles of the sun, are spun on the stream of darkness in uncertain eddies. Who knows when you and I will front each other thus again drawing around us the ripples of chance?"

From the dim cow-shed came a heavy breathing and munching, a clank of milk-cans, and a querulous "Get over, blast you" from Briscoe who hated milking, and felt that his rheumatism should exempt him from early rising. There was a faint succession of low groaning murmuring from the cows, as they waited their turn religiously, for they knew as well as their milkers that Matchless came into the end bail after Sooky left it. Their mild impatience to be done with the ceremonious beginning of their day was tempered by a half-erotic anticipation of human hands relieving that uncomfortable, strained pressure on the udders. This, their mild stampings and mooings seemed to say, was what human beings were for. They had been put into the world to see that cows had food, to milk, and set out hay; and they should be treated kindly for their usefulness to the bovine world.

The sun had now lifted itself above the sea; the great star dwindled, shone and vanished, to become an invisible attendant on that great daystar. The cock-crows mounted in thin spirals of noise above the clucking and chattering of the aroused hen roost, and Briscoe set off, grumbling, for the tins of mash. The fowl-houses were little more than heaps of old sagging timber and wire held together by a thick, green cover of passion vines; and Shannon, emerging from her milking, promised herself, as she did at least once a week, that all that old rusty wire and board must be cleared away and new pens put up. John, while he lived, had never bothered about fowls or ducks or those geese who had set up for themselves a semi-independent state at the foot of the slope in a grove of great Moreton Bay figs surrounding a big, black, mucky pond.

The turkeys were also running wild in the paddock of white, ring-barked trees, which they had taken for their own domain. Briscoe caught the drift of Shannon's thoughts.

"If we get a strong young feller in," he grumbled, "to clean up and do some work, not that lazy loafer of a Sandleberry . . ." He always had some private petty feud with George Sandleberry who worked stubbornly at ploughing or sowing or harvesting, but had no time, he contended, "to be mucking about" with such things as vegetables or hens.

Shannon's insistence that they grow peas was to him dangerous and heretical thinking. He admitted, when the peas were bagged, that they had brought in more than he expected, but he still stubbornly maintained that it wasn't the right soil for peas "nor potatoes neither." He had followed John Terrill's commands with a dogged respect for "a feller who knew what he was doing"; but he was always on the point of telling "the woman" that, if she thought she could run the place without him, he could always make more money in the city.

How could a woman, with only an old thing like Mrs. Sladder, and a cripple like rheumaticky Briscoe, boss him? But boss him she did, and he resented it. He grumbled to his wife; but Minnie was always hand in glove with the woman on the hill; and he chewed his discontent and worked on, dimly conscious that he could no more desert those steep, green slopes than he could starve his horses. He always ended by saying he "couldn't see the poor thing left" and congratulating himself on his own benevolence.

Emerging from the milking shed, George stretched his cramped frame and shot at "that woman," in her old dirty slacks and shirt, a look at once hostile and loyal. Even the clothes she wore affronted him, as though they were a sign in her of something different from skirted women like his his wife, an assumption of masculinity that aroused all that was masculine in him to wordless protest, that made her as unapproachable, as un-womanly as a rock. She was not even pretty, with her cropped hair and thin face, but she dominated him.

"After breakfast," he reminded her, "we got that fence to see to. Bloody horses just walking through it."

"Right you are." Shannon knew George took pleasure in any job which would give him the chance of ordering her about. ("Hold that post straight, Shannon. Hand me that wire and run her out.") She did not grudge him such small enjoyments, for she knew she was lucky to have such a solid worker now that almost every able-bodied man had left Kerleuit.

Her mind was more occupied with the problem of some young cherry trees which should be waiting for her in the goods shed at Kerleuit. The new station-master had a habit of leaving consignments of goods to look after themselves, and she was framing a few crisp remarks to be delivered by telephone which would jolt him into noticing those cherry trees. There was the cream to be taken to the fence where a truck from the butter factory would collect it. The scalding of the separator was one job she could never leave to George or Briscoe but must always do herself; and, after breakfast, she looked forward to a morning of post-holes and sweat.

As she moved towards the kitchen, she was thankful for Aunt Edith. Without Aunt Edith and cantankerous old Briscoe the eternal work would have beaten her long ago. Aunt Edith was so happy rubbing and scouring and polishing her furniture and the house. She had insisted on putting up a brass plate on the sagging wooden gate, which caused terrible mirth among the truck drivers. "Grey-Stanes," the brass plate announced ele-gantly to all who had for so long called this "the Terrill Place." Aunt Edith even took down a little tin of metal polish and anointed the rain-stained countenance of her name-plate. "It makes the house look civilized," she explained.

Minnie Sandleberry appeared after breakfast, stout and smiling, with George, her eldest son, toddling by her. She was armed with a kerosene tin and a sharp knife.

"Them mushrooms," she announced, "is real big in the far paddock, and I thought I could take 'em into Denthaven to sell when you went on Monday, Shannon." She beamed upon George's "boss" with the fond protectiveness which the stout and motherly so often extend to the smaller, harder types of womankind. To be with Shannon, to feel the little spark of liking which Shannon's quick looks and words stirred up in her, was as much her motive as the mushrooms. Sometimes, she thought, George was so jealous of this liking that he "took it out of Shannon" all because Minnie was so dotingly fond of her.

"I'll come too," Aunt Edith said quickly. "It will be quite a little outing." She glanced timidly towards George who she always suspected would one night murder them in their beds.

"Anyone 'ud think it was a bloody picnic," George grumbled, as he shouldered the spud and the post-hole digger, and prepared to stride ahead. Women, he thought gloomily, nothing but women sticking together, getting in the road.

Briscoe was out among the fowls, pottering about with a setting of turkeys' eggs, and Minnie loitered to comment favourably on his work.

"You'll have a lot to send away at Christmas, Shannon," she remarked. "I'll come up and help you with the cleaning." She glanced mischievously at the retreating back of her husband. "Did I ever tell you about the time I came home from hospital with too much milk? I had ever so much more'n Georgy needed and it was a terrible nuisance. Well, we was rearing up a coupla hundred little chickens and d'you know what I did? I mixed that milk with their mash. Real nourishing it is. And them little chickens was that fond of me! When I went out in the yard they was all over me . . . just as if they *knew*."

Shannon laughed so loud that the distant figure of George swung round suspiciously to see if "that woman" was laughing at him. "You'd better see about getting another spell in hospital, Minnie. You certainly don't want to waste a gift like that when you could fatten up some more chickens."

"Go on with you, Shannon. You've got a hide!"

They were still laughing as they climbed through the orchard fence, kerosene tins banging, Minnie's skirt catching on the wire, little Georgy wriggling under the lowest strand.

Shannon, with a coil of wire over her shoulder, set off after George, although she would have preferred to stay picking those mushrooms poised on tender stalks like little dancers, pink frilled ballet-skirts under their white flounces; but she was the responsible head of a household and must set herself to jobs she hated, like repairing fences.

The morning, which had broken in such tranquil gold, like a daffodil from its sheath, grew chilly and dull; a hard scud of frozen cloud, the grey froth of some stormy sea-soup washing up across the sky. The green slopes which, for the mushroom gatherers, had had a crisp chilly dew, a bright tender green, seemed to shrink under that dull sky and grow ugly and hard, as though the bones of rock jutted through the skin of grass. Long after the mushroom gatherers had gone home to prepare the midday meal the two dogged figures worked on.

"Going to rain again," George muttered. "All that damn corn we put in to get the benefit of the shower," he mimicked Shannon sarcastically, " 'ull be washed clean out of the ground."

Shannon lifted the coil of wire he had left in the grass. "I'd better take this in," she replied. "No use letting it lie here rusting." This was a thrust at George's careless habit of leaving tools about.

"Gimme." George took the coil from her and they trudged together over the chilly paddocks. The rain was beginning to spit down in cold, scattered drops.

"I could always sack you, George," Shannon suggested lightly, "and get some of these land army girls."

George's answer was unprintable. "Only one damn thing them girls is good for," he added to his analysis of this proposal.

Shannon chuckled to herself. George's indignant outbursts when she got a dig home, were not important. Under their quarrelling, they were friends, as only two people who work together can be friends. She could no more sack George than he could leave "Grey-Stanes."

Her father was sitting in the shelter of Briscoe's small, independent abode at the end of the yard, a shanty held together by vines in the same way as the fowl-houses. He had brought out Shannon's mother on one of her Saturday afternoon visits, also Aunt Elsie and Aunt Maisie. Shannon groaned at the news, but brightened when he told her he had remembered to fetch her cherry trees. She sat down beside him on an upturned box, resolved to let the aunt-ridden kitchen settle down for a little.

Aunt Edith would have an afternoon of stately hospitality, with her tea-set, her silver cake basket, silver cake-forks and appliquéd linen tablecloth. The cherry trees provided an excellent excuse for avoiding aunts, and she would plant them that afternoon. Her father, as usual, was full of small legal problems. He was always bringing her important letters to type for his friends, engineering her into unwanted secretaryships of the

School of Arts committee, the First Aid group, the Prisoners' Comforts Fund. To see his daughter respected, an independent ruler of her own farm, a woman noted for miles round as "having a head on her" gave him enormous pleasure. Her fame as a doctor of minor ailments, legal adviser and letter writer was of her father's spreading. He wanted to know what she thought Harry Adams should do about those two grandchildren his daughter had left him when she died. Their father wanted them back now he had a job, but he'd never paid a penny since they were born.

"Now, *has* he got any claim on 'em, Shannon? That's what I said I'd ask you. Can he take them kids away?"

Shannon's advice on this perplexing problem was interrupted by Aunt Edith in the kitchen doorway. "Shannon! I've been keeping your dinner this last hour not knowing you were there!"

"Good-bye," her father muttered. "I'm off." He headed down the hill to pick up George Sandleberry who always on a Saturday afternoon went into Kerleuit to fill himself up with beer.

The kitchen, under the pressure of four elderly ladies, had absorbed an essence from them which was as pervasive as the smell of the onions Aunt Edith had cooked, an essence made up of soft, bolstered female flesh, the impalpably different flesh of old ladies, which resembles the flesh of a young girl as much as a stuffy, close-shut room resembles a rose garden.

The formidable atmosphere of these ladies was enhanced by their wearing of their best clothes which, in the case of Aunt Maisie, consisted of a crimson knitted jumper over a brown skirt and a pink blouse with a cluster of bilious green artificial flowers pinned in the bosom. Aunt Elsie, on the other hand, wore a dress of navy silk patterned with large orange and yellow flowers. Shannon's mother was neat and snappy in black. Aunt Edith, expecting visitors on Saturday afternoon, had arrayed herself in a dull, dark blue piped with grey, which gave her something of a regal air. Into this massive company, the muddy and disreputable Shannon plunged recklessly with the excuse that she must plant cherry trees that afternoon.

"You oughtn't to work so hard," her mother snapped. "It isn't right for a woman to work like you do. You'll ruin your insides."

Aunt Elsie added her word. "Maybe it don't matter about Shannon. Not having no children she's got no insides to ruin."

"I don't see that," her mother snapped back. "Stands to reason she's doing herself no good. I didn't bring my girls up to make slaves of themselves."

"You ought to get married again, Shannon," Aunt Maisie put in kindly. "Can't say there isn't chaps would have you knowing what a one you are for work."

From this conversation Shannon escaped gladly into the rain and mud of the orchard, determined to make the cherry trees last her until dark set in; but, at afternoon tea-time, Aunt Edith appeared at the orchard fence with a sack held over her head and such a woe-begone look that Shannon was reluctantly persuaded to face the party of lady relatives.

She sat in the warm kitchen, pleasantly tired, listening to the rain drumming against the windows and watching the swift, steely needles flick briskly as socks were knitted. Those grey heads bent over their wool brought to her mind the legend of the Grey Sisters who had only one eye between them. Mother and the aunts had only one view of life. They saw it through the somewhat distorted lens of an all-procreative impulse. Their small neat world extending from Kerleuit to the coast around Denthaven was an open book from which they read the news of death and birth, success and disaster. The thunderous voices of the outside world were only important as they affected Kerleuit.

"How'd you like it," Aunt Maisie asked, "if the Japanese come and take your farm?"

"I guess I'd manage," Shannon replied; and there was a little movement among them which was a tacit acknowledgment of the truth of her words. Shannon would manage, would stand cool-headed and rocky, if the skies flamed. She had the old, hard mockery of the lóng, green slopes, the evasiveness of the sea. And because of this in her, the hard metal she had beaten out of loss and change, they depended on her more than they would admit. Without a roof over her, or food, or money, Shannon would stay herself, as independent as a song.

Aunt Maisie gave a little cough and glanced at Shannon's mother deprecatingly. Something important, Shannon guessed, was in all their minds. They were far too polite.

"What we really came out to see you about . . ." Aunt Maisie began mildly, "was the Hennessy girl. You remember the little fair one?"

"What's up with her?"

There was another exchange of glances between the feminine diplomats.

"She's always been a good girl," Aunt Maisie went on quickly, her needles flashing in time with her words. "But her family are real nasty to her. She got into trouble and they want to send her away."

"Why doesn't she marry the child's father?"

Aunt Elsie coughed virtuously and snatched this more appetising portion of the story from Aunt Maisie, as one of the Grey Sisters might have snatched the eye. "It's my belief she doesn't know him from a bar of soap. If you count back, Maisie, you'll remember it was just about the time them soldiers from the camp came down to the Church of England ball . . ."

"And you all thought it would be a good idea," Shannon asked sarcastically, "if I took her in?"

Aunt Maisie's eyes wandered to a framed photograph of Edith's first husband which hung above the mantelpiece, a photograph of a fat man with frog's eyes and a walrus moustache. "Well, we did say we might just ask you," she admitted.

"I said it wasn't fair to Shannon," her mother snapped. "Someone's always loading her up with their troubles."

"Well," Aunt Elsie put in, "not having any children of your own, and Edith here saying it would be good company . . ."

Trust Aunt Elsie to rub in the salt! Shannon planted her small, wiry frame on the hearth and stubbornly fronted that meddlesome bevy of ladies.

"I'll tell you something," she said heatedly. "I'm not a charity home. I've had lame horses dumped on me and stray dogs. If anyone's cow's dying, it's: 'See if Mrs. Terrill can do anything.' If anybody wants to borrow, they try to borrow from me. Do I look *soft*?"

"You always were one to *manage* things," Aunt Maisie flattered her cunningly. "She'd work, Shannon, and her family are that mean and beastly . . . She hasn't anywhere to go."

"I know just what would happen," Shannon asserted, with flinty hostility. "I'd have to look after her, and she wouldn't be able to work. I'd provide the baby clothes, pay the damn hospital bills, look after the brat . . . or Aunt Edith would. Then it would be: 'Oh, Mrs. Terrill, if you could just look after the baby until I get work,' and off the Hennessy goes to a munitions factory, leaving me literally to hold the baby. You can all go to Hell!"

At the sight of their crestfallen faces, she felt a rush of affection for them, the meddlesome, tiresome, old wretches! She could have hugged them all.

"No," she exclaimed, with that astonishing smile which had made up so much of her charm when she had worked at being charming. "I don't really mean it, darlings. Just you tell little Hennessy I'll think it over."

They stayed to help with the milking, and when they had gone back on the cream truck, Shannon drew a guilty sigh of relief to have only quiet old Aunt Edith with her. She felt like fanning the air to dissipate the warm atmosphere of cooking and motherliness and bring back the old, clean, lonely chill that rested her nerves. Aunt Edith she could endure, but the Hennessy girl, plump, giggling, exuding that dreadful femininity, would set her nerves on edge.

Or was she merely jealous, she asked herself honestly, when, with Aunt Edith in bed, and her feet in their ungainly boots planted on the stove, she settled down to the one hour of the day she counted as her own. She sat alone, hugged to herself, in the lonely house, her only company the light of Briscoe's fiercely independent abode still shining at the end of the yard. She did not like women, and the thought of a strange woman sharing her kitchen, making little leagues against her, trading on her, was too much. She knew that Hennessy girl, a little, plump, giggling thing, and she was angry at this imposition. Perhaps, she thought, I am merely jealous. Anyway, as she stretched out her feet to the stove, she was glad to be alone.

She switched on the radio, but the static crackled and roared like a miniature thunderstorm in the dial, and she switched it off again. Southwell Quilter, M.H.R., loyal supporter of the Labour Government, was to have spoken on the "war effort," and she had promised herself a sardonic smile as she listened to that ex-pacifist. Here she sat, on her mountain, self-contained, while the world rolled and thundered, its discordant voices mingled in an unholy screech. Hers was the generation between two wars, a generation which was being wiped out, whose voice had been drowned between the voices of older people and the rising of a new world's birth screams, a generation which had had confusion for its godmother and sucked the milk of unwholesome knowledge. Outside, the rain splashed down, as though it would wash away the whole human race, even the hard, rock-like Shannons of the world.

Under that pelting downpour, a solitary stray cat was making its way in a series of starts and scurries; its belly-fur brushing the mud, its sides palpitating with terror. It was a tame cat whose owners were far too kind to drown kittens, so instead they had sent the cat out in a sack to be released in the most lonely of the patches of scrub near Denthaven. There the cat would starve to death without disturbing its owners.

For two days the cat had had nothing to eat except one silver-eye, which was just a mouthful of feathers. If she did not have food and shelter to-night, her kittens would share her fate. She was frightened of this storm, as she slunk towards the house on the hill. All the air poured in one direction, inland, carrying with it the crumbling roar of the sea, the thrashing of leaves, the high whine that might have been the complaint of the tortured sky itself.

At a more intense roar, the cat turned, hypnotized by a booming shadow with huge eyes, then, just in time, she shot across the road.

"Missed 'er," the driver muttered, disappointed, as the truck lumbered on.

The cat lay for a little while before she struggled forward again. Her ribs had been bruised yesterday when a boy flung a stone at her; her paws ached; every muscle in her body was a living pain; and the wet that soaked her was the worst of all. Big, dim faces should bend down, big creatures bring milk. She had never been away from them before, but she knew they were treacherous. To be kicked was terrible, but it was worse to be out in vast desolations, with violet flares of light bursting overhead and exploding in sound.

Just ahead on the rise was the house, and she slunk up to place her soft mouth-fur by the door and sniff. There was a little hole broken from the side of the door, and to this she placed her eye. Sitting alone before the stove was an ambiguous figure, and the cat sniffed again. A nose is not to be deceived, and suddenly confident, she lifted up her voice and wailed.

The door was flung open. "Get out," Shannon called sternly. "Get back where you came from."

The cat retreated until its eyes were gleaming points in the darkness. It wailed again.

"I am wet," the wail said. "I am alone and hungry, and my kittens will be born in the rain. I shall die!"

"Damn it!" Shannon turned in the doorway and fetched a saucer. "Here," she called. "Puss! Puss!"

The eyes advanced bringing with them a shrinking body, very heavy, very soft and bulging. It stopped a foot from the saucer in the doorway and miaowed faintly.

"Come on then," Shannon encouraged. "Come right on in." She opened the door wide for the cat to enter. It settled itself by the fire with little purrs and lickings while she found some cold meat. "There," she said gloomily, setting the food on the floor. "Make a hog of yourself."

The cat advanced and then looked up at her. "It's all right," Shannon told her. "I'll keep you. Let 'em all come. Mothers and kids, cats and old women and old men. Damn it! What am I for?"

She began to laugh softly. The cat looked up, then, reassured, went on eating.

www.ingramcontent.com/pod-product-compliance
Lightning Source LLC
Chambersburg PA
CBHW032047050726
47590CB00001B/157